N.H. Anchor   18.00

P9-CKT-928

CHAMPION

By L. Christian Balling

CHAMPION

A novel by
L. CHRISTIAN BALLING

THE ATLANTIC MONTHLY PRESS
NEW YORK

Copyright © 1988 by L. Christian Balling

All rights reserved. No part of this book may be reproduced in any form or by any electronic or mechanical means including information storage and retrieval systems without permission in writing from the publisher, except by a reviewer, who may quote brief passages in a review.

Published simultaneously in Canada
Printed in the United States of America
FIRST EDITION

Library of Congress Cataloging-in-Publication Data

Balling, L. Christian
Champion: a novel / by L. Christian Balling.—1st ed.
ISBN 0-87113-198-6
1. Pembroke. William Marshal, Earl of, 1144?–1219—Fiction.
I. Title.
PS3552.A468C48   1988   813'.54—dc19   87-33476

The Atlantic Monthly Press
19 Union Square West
New York, NY 10003

FIRST PRINTING

For Natalie Greenberg

CHAMPION

PROLOGUE

◈

Berkshire, England—a.d. 1153

The child should have been hanged at noon, but hour after hour, King Stephen had extended the deadline he had set, hoping the boy's father would relent. When at last the twelve knights assigned to witness the hanging led the boy to execution, sundown was not far off. Slowly the grim-faced knights rode up the hill nearest Newbury Castle and solemnly drew into a semicircle beneath the oak tree that would serve as gallows. The boy was to hang in full view of the besieged castle's garrison.

The setting sun was at their backs, and the light cast the shadow of the noose dangling behind the boy's head onto the ground before them, the shadow swinging slowly in response to a soft summer breeze. The boy, whose spindly legs were too short to reach the stirrups on the horse on which he'd been placed, tore his gaze from the terrible shadow and looked up at the Earl of Arundel with wide, frightened eyes.

"Courage, son," the old earl said hoarsely. "I won't let you suffer."

The boy's chin was quivering, and the saddle beneath him creaked in time to the trembling in his slight body; but he said nothing and did not cry. The earl felt tears start in his own eyes and had to look away. This was a dirty business, but it had to be done. An example had to be set.

The earl cleared his throat and addressed the assembled knights.

"We are here to witness the execution of the death sentence imposed by His Majesty, King Stephen of England, as just and necessary punishment for the treachery of John Marshal. It is a bitter thing to take the life of a child, but it is the traitor—not the King—who has condemned his own son.

"John Marshal has rebelled against the King and joined forces with Empress Matilda and her son, Henry of Anjou, who would usurp the

Throne of England. But it is treachery, not rebellion, which we punish here today.

"When we laid siege to Newbury Castle, we found it undermanned and unable to long withstand our siege. At John Marshal's request, and in accordance with civilized custom, the King granted him time to secure Empress Matilda's permission to surrender Newbury with honor. The traitor's youngest son was given as hostage to guarantee that the time not be used to reinforce the castle garrison."

The earl paused and gestured angrily at the castle before them, its square tower keep bathed in the orange light of the setting sun.

"We have seen how John Marshal has kept his word! Two nights ago, under cover of darkness, he sent one hundred men-at-arms into the castle. Now, how many of our own good men must die to take Newbury—men betrayed, as was our King, by the faithless word of a traitor?"

"John Marshal has refused our repeated demands to surrender. He has forfeited all honor. Now he must forfeit the life of his son."

In the heavy silence that followed, the trembling boy turned his pale face toward each of the assembled knights in turn, but only the earl was willing to meet his eyes.

"Sire," the boy croaked, his voice so low that only the earl could hear him, "what did my father say when he refused?"

The earl shook his head, not wanting to answer; but the boy's wide eyes bored into him, insistent and unrelenting. The earl could have lied, and to his dying day he never knew why he did not.

"Your father sent this message to His Majesty," the earl said softly. " 'Hang the boy if you will. I have the hammer and tongs to forge more sons.' "

The boy winced, swallowed convulsively, and turned to look up at the castle walls, as if seeking an answer to the betrayal he could not fathom. The earl nodded to the black-robed executioner and tightened his grip on the cudgel he held concealed behind his back. He would stun the boy as soon as the executioner had adjusted the noose.

But as the executioner reached for the rope, a drawn-out cry from the direction of the King's encampment stayed his hand. The knights turned and saw King Stephen galloping toward the hill, bent forward in the saddle, his cloak billowing out behind him.

"Hold!" the King yelled wildly, spurring his stallion up the slope. "I order you to hold!"

The King hauled on the reins as he crested the hill, and his stallion, hooves churning, skidded to a halt beside the condemned boy's horse. Stephen reached out and swept the boy into his arms.

"I'll not kill a child," he gasped in an anguished voice, his tired face haggard from the accumulated strain of years of civil war. "Not for the sake of my crown—not for any reason!"

Defiantly Stephen looked around at his knights, thinking that some might rebuke him for his weakness; but no one challenged the reprieve, and few of the battle-hardened knights could hide their relief. In silence they watched their King turn his horse and ride back down the hill with the child clinging to him.

"Our King may lose his crown," a knight mounted on the earl's left said quietly, "but I'll warrant his soul is safe."

The earl nodded absently. He was as relieved as any of them, but he was also disturbed that the traitor had won his gamble. It was a small victory, perhaps, but one of a growing number that threatened to overwhelm Stephen. The King was losing his will to fight; he was no longer a match for the implacable Matilda and her son, the young, vigorous Duke of Normandy. It would not be long, the earl now admitted to himself, before Henry of Anjou became Henry II of England.

"I wonder if the boy really grasped what was happening," said the knight. "He can't be more than six or seven."

"He knew," the earl grated, wishing the boy had not.

What sort of man would he become? the old earl wondered. The boy had been through the fire, and the earl had no doubt that a hard man had been forged this day. But had the King's humanity tempered the steel, or would it be brittle and corroded, forever flawed by the father's brutality?

"What's the boy's name?" the knight asked, possibly thinking along the same lines.

"William," the earl replied. "William Marshal."

PILGRIM

I

Palestine—May 1, 1187

Marshal sighted the enemy as he crested a hill overlooking the high, sun-baked plateau extending eastward toward the Sea of Galilee, and despite the merciless desert heat, his hands grew cold. The Saracens were still too far away to see, but their dust was visible—a great, yellow cloud hovering above the desolate plain. The dust cloud showed clearly against the brown, mountainous ridge on the horizon, and pinpoints of light flashed on the cloud's periphery where the enemy's steel lance tips caught the sun.

From the amount of dust being raised, Marshal knew the horsemen would number in the thousands. It would be madness for the sixty Templars of the Kakun garrison to attack the army advancing across the plain, but Gerard de Ridefort, Grand Master of the Templars, had brought them out to fight. Surprised in Nazareth by news of the Saracen invasion, Ridefort had ridden in a fury to Kakun to call out the garrison.

Marshal shivered slightly in response to the icy brush of unaccustomed fear, a momentary chill that quickly suffocated in the bakeoven heat. Summer had struck Palestine early this year, and sweat soaked the thick padding Marshal wore beneath his hauberk, a forty-pound tunic of interlaced steel rings covering his torso and thighs. His legs and feet were also encased in chain mail, and laced to the collar of the hauberk was a mail coif. Because of the heat, he had pushed back the coif to allow his scalp to breathe, and it lay in folds at the back of his neck.

Marshal's squire, with their packhorse and two battle chargers in tow, was coming up the hill behind him. The buzzing of flies about the horses and the scrape of hooves on rock only emphasized the stillness of the arid land. Scrub bush clung to the lower slopes of the limestone hills bordering the plain, and spring wildflowers splashed the hillsides with patches of yellow and red, but the gray, eroded crests remained barren, the vegetation finding no sustenance in the rocky, crumbling soil.

As Marshal's squire drew rein beside him, the boy's eyes widened as he registered the size of the enemy force.

"Water," Marshal said, and the squire quickly untied a goatskin water bag from his saddle pommel and handed it to him. Marshal drank briefly, swallowing only enough of the stale, warm water to relieve the dryness in his throat. His thirst demanded more, but he resisted the urge to slake it. Thirst, like fear, was something a man had to endure if he was to survive.

He turned and looked back at the distant Templar column for which he was acting as scout. Templar discipline was strict; there were no songs or jesting on the march, and the column raised no telltale dust as it silently wound toward him through the hills.

The knights' snow-white mantles, embroidered with the scarlet cross of their order, shone in the blaze of the midday sun. Knights and squires alike wore full chain-mail armor, and the men rode two by two, each pair of knights followed by their black-robed squires. The alternate rows of black- and white-robed riders matched the black-and-white motif of the Templar standard, flying beside the Grand Master's banner at the head of the column.

Unlike the knights in Europe, the Templars' weapons and trappings were devoid of adornment. No jewels studded their saddles and bridles, and their shields and lances were unpainted. The caparisons that protected the Templar chargers' necks, chests, and hindquarters were of plain, padded canvas.

Marshal was a pilgrim knight who had ridden with the Templars for three years, wearing the white Templar robe without the insignia of the Cross, and as he watched the approaching riders he felt a brief surge of pride in the comrades he had chosen. These were tough, dedicated warriors whose battle discipline had no equal.

But as his gaze settled on the distant figure of the Grand Master, riding beside Marshal's friend, James de Maille, commander of the Kakun garrison, his expression turned bleak. If the Grand Master insisted on battle, few, if any, of them, would survive. Perhaps de Maille could make the Grand Master listen to reason, but Marshal knew it was a frail hope.

"Drink some water, yourself," Marshal said to his squire as he handed back the water bag.

The boy shook his head. "Thank you, sire, but I've already had more than my share."

"Drink, Eustace," Marshal commanded in a tone that brooked no argument.

Eustace was a pale, slim youth who barely met the Templars' standards, and the hauberk Marshal had given him was too wide in the shoulders and hung down well below the knees. The boy was too young and too weak to last long without extra water, and he needed it more than his master. Age and experience had hardened Marshal, inured him to thirst, exhaustion, and pain.

Eustace drank only enough to satisfy Marshal and then secured the water bag. Looking out at the enemy, he said, "Sire, why didn't the Count of Tripolis challenge the Saracens as soon as they crossed the Jordan? Why is he allowing them to march unopposed through his territory?"

"To save his strength for the real battle when it comes," Marshal answered. "Saladin has declared a holy war against the Kingdom, and he'll fight us to the bitter end. What you see out there is nothing but a demonstration—a show of force—and Tripolis knows it. This is simply the Sultan's way of throwing down the gauntlet."

Eustace blinked and swallowed hard. "Then no one else has been called out? The garrison will be riding against them alone?"

"If the Grand Master orders it," Marshal said without inflection.

It was some comfort to Marshal that the Templar Rule forbade squires to ride into battle beside their masters. At least he wouldn't have Eustace on his conscience. Providence might yet spare a few of the knights, even in a suicide charge, but the boy wouldn't have a chance. He wasn't ready, and perhaps he never would be.

Marshal knew he never should have taken Eustace on as his squire, for the boy lacked the necessary stamina and coordination. Courage Eustace possessed in full measure; but without strength and a talent for combat, courage was not enough. Yet Marshal had been moved by the boy's desperate determination to become a knight, and he had finally yielded to Eustace's pleas for the chance to prove himself.

He had come to regret his decision. It was painful to watch the boy's dogged, day-by-day struggle against his physical limitations. It might have been easier if Marshal had liked Eustace less, if he had not appreciated the boy's wit and imagination.

Marshal could see from his squire's expression that the boy didn't realize what was coming. It wasn't simply faith in God's protection that blinded Eustace; the boy believed that the Templars—and his master in particular—were indestructible. In Europe, Marshal was a legend, and his reputation had followed him to the Holy Land.

In the twenty years Marshal had been a knight he had never met his match in tournament or on the battlefield. As his reputation in tournaments had grown, his purse had swelled with prize money, and the royal courts of Europe had opened to him. Lesser knights had flocked to his banner to share his fortune.

It had been heady wine for a young, landless son of a minor English baron; but with the years, the flattery and social rituals of court life had palled, and Marshal had wearied of the empty bravado and ostentation of the endless rounds of tournaments. Even his pride in his own accomplishments had waned as he had realized that his skill with sword and lance was inborn. He was simply stronger than most knights, his reflexes faster, his balance and timing surer.

Somewhere along the aimless road of the knight-errant, Marshal had lost his taste for glory; and now, on this desert hilltop, watching death move inexorably toward him across the plain, he was filled with a bitter sense of futility. What had he to show for his forty-one years of life? He had accomplished nothing, and if he died today, he would leave nothing behind—no wife, no sons, no legacy of any kind.

He had reached the peak of his tournament career as captain of the household knights of young Henry, eldest son of Henry II. Prince Henry had gloried in the pageantry and drama of the tournament, and Marshal had served him well, leading the Prince and his followers to victory after victory. But for Marshal the joy and excitement of battle for its own sake was no longer there; he had come to crave a purpose, a direction for his life.

When without warning Prince Henry had been struck down by fever and lay dying, he had begged Marshal to fulfill by proxy the vow of pilgrimage he had made so lightly only months before. Marshal had agreed at once, hoping to find in the Holy Land the sense of purpose that had eluded him.

For a time, with the Templars, he had thought he'd found what he sought. To keep the hostile Turks and Saracens at bay, the Crusader barons of the one-hundred-year-old Kingdom of Jerusalem maintained their own feudal armies, reinforced by European knights on pilgrimage;

but the mainstay of the kingdom's defense were the two great military-religious orders of knights; the Templars and the Hospitalers.

The knights who entered these orders swore oaths of chastity and strict obedience to the order's Rule. They lived a monastic existence with but one purpose—to defend Palestine against the Moslems. In battle they gave no quarter and received none from the enemy.

Marshal had been drawn to the Templars' austere existence and dedication, and they had welcomed him into their midst. But the undercurrent of fanaticism he had found in the order had held him back from taking the Templars' vows.

As the months had slipped into years and Marshal had come to understand the political realities of the Crusader kingdom, he had been increasingly dismayed by the intrigue and jealousy that divided the kingdom's leadership. Yet he had stayed on in Palestine, unwilling to return to his jaded existence in Europe. Now, he realized, he had stayed too long. . . .

Abruptly Marshal tugged on the reins, wheeling his horse about to face the way he had come. If his life was to end in a cul-de-sac, there was nothing he could do about it, and self-pity disgusted him. The Templar column was now within hailing range, and Marshal had no wish to delay the inevitable. He cupped his hands to his mouth and called out in a clear, powerful baritone that echoed through the hills: "Tem-mplars!"

Marshal saw the Grand Master react immediately, spurring his mount forward and moving out ahead of the column, followed an instant later by de Maille, whose mane of white-blond hair gleamed in the sun. They covered the half mile to the hill at the gallop and spurred their horses up the hillside, scattering an abandoned flock of sheep that had been grazing on clumps of grass hidden under the thornbushes.

As the riders approached the crest Marshal turned his horse back toward the plain and gestured for Eustace to move out of earshot. The Grand Master and de Maille reined in beside Marshal, and for a moment, as they looked out at the Saracen army, no one spoke.

James de Maille was the first to break the silence. "Jesus," he breathed, exchanging a look with Marshal. "There are thousands out there."

Marshal nodded. "Too many," he said tonelessly, his eyes on the Grand Master.

Gerard de Ridefort said nothing as he gazed fixedly at the cloud of dust, which was already perceptibly nearer. The Grand Master was in his fifties and too heavy; in a few more years he would be unfit for combat. His dark face was flushed and slimy with sweat, and his breathing was labored, but it was not the Grand Master's physical condition that concerned Marshal; it was the look in his eyes. They glittered with the feverish intensity of a fanatic.

Ridefort's fanaticism was not rooted in faith but in his own overweening ego. Ridefort was his surname, but to Marshal he was a Lusignan, inheriting from his mother a full measure of that clan's willful, mindless arrogance.

"They're moving fast," Marshal said tightly, his words directed at the Grand Master. "No infantry and no heavy baggage. Tripolis was right; this raid is nothing more than a show."

But the Grand Master did not respond; he continued to stare out at the Saracens' dust. De Maille twisted around in his saddle and signaled to the riders coming up the hill behind them to fan out across the slope, below the crest, and out of sight of enemy scouts. He looked again at Marshal, and his expression was grim.

"What do you intend, Master Gerard?" de Maille asked, suppressed tension bringing out his latent German accent. He had a hard, sharply chiseled face—a Viking's face—and although he had put himself under the strict dictates of the Templar Rule, there was nothing slavish in his obedience.

With visible effort the Grand Master tore his gaze from the Saracens, whose banners were now discernible—tiny patches of green, scarlet, blue, and gold, shimmering in the heat waves rising from the sunbaked ground. "Intend?" he rasped, looking up at de Maille in surprise. "We'll await them here and charge when they come within range. What else?"

Marshal's jaw muscles knotted as anger bubbled up inside him like vitriol. Ridefort could lead them straight into hell and they were bound to follow—de Maille and his knights by their oaths of obedience, and Marshal no less by honor. Men like the Grand Master were destroyers who made a mockery of the ideals of the knights they led.

De Maille shot Marshal a warning glance. He knew of Marshal's lifelong hatred of the Lusignan family, and he knew that in Palestine, Ridefort and Marshal had come to know each other too well. Marshal's intervention now would only inflame the Grand Master.

"There are four, maybe five, thousand horsemen out there," de Maille said, trying to keep his tone respectful. "If we charge, they'll wipe us out. We'd be playing right into Saladin's hands—throwing away men who will be needed for the army Jerusalem is raising."

A fly settled on the Grand Master's nose, and he casually waved it away in a manner that dismissed de Maille's objection as well. "You have too little faith, de Maille. We'll cut right through the heathen bastards."

"But we'll never be able to sustain a charge," de Maille protested, his voice rising sharply as he rebelled against Ridefort's mindless confidence. "Surely you can see that!"

The Grand Master's eyes narrowed, and he gave de Maille a withering look. "And what do *you* suggest?" he said with a sneer. "That we turn tail and hide from them—like that traitor, Tripolis? We're God's own warriors, man!"

"God gave us brains as well as sword arms, Master Gerard," de Maille snapped, stung by the Grand Master's contemptuous tone. "Tripolis has used his head, and I suggest we use ours!"

At that the Grand Master bridled. "And I tell you that we'll scatter the dogs," he growled. "We'll—"

"There are too damn many!" Marshal cut in harshly, unable to curb himself any longer. His pulse was pounding at his temples, and he could feel the hot flush on his cheeks. The man's blind arrogance would kill them all—and to no purpose, no purpose at all.

"Who asked you?" the Grand Master snarled, turning on Marshal. Sweat ran down over Ridefort's face in rivulets, and he was panting, filling the air with the sickly smell of his rotting teeth. "We all know your reputation, Marshal, you can be sure of that. But it means nothing to me—nothing!"

"Then you're even dumber than I thought," Marshal said, his pent-up contempt for Ridefort spilling out. De Maille made no attempt to restrain him, for they both knew it was hopeless. They were lost.

The Grand Master's face contorted with fury, and though his mouth worked, for a split second no sound emerged. "How *dare* you speak to me like that!" he hissed, spitting out the words. "I knew you could be insolent, Marshal, but I didn't know you were gutless as well."

"You go too far!" de Maille gasped. "There is not a man here who would not follow Marshal's banner into battle."

Marshal saw Gerard de Ridefort's eyes suddenly turn wary, and he realized that the Grand Master was afraid de Maille might actually desert him. For a moment Ridefort lost his arrogant self-assurance—but only for a moment.

Although the Grand Master misjudged de Maille's loyalty, he knew how to enforce his will. As yet only the nearest of the Templars had heard what their leaders were saying, but now the Grand Master raised his voice so that every knight and squire on the hill could hear him.

"I know why you have no stomach for a fight, Sir James," he shouted. "You've grown too fond of that pretty blond head of yours, and now you're desperately afraid of losing it."

De Maille's face paled, and with evident satisfaction the Grand Master watched the shudder of rage that passed through de Maille's body as he absorbed the insult. De Maille had no choice now, and the Grand Master knew it. Slowly de Maille's features solidified into a mask, and his eyes went dead. "So be it," he said icily. "We'll follow you, Master Gerard, but mark my words: It will be you, not I, who turns and runs when they break our charge."

For an instant Marshal was aware of nothing but the blind urge to drive his fist into the Grand Master's face, to wipe away Ridefort's ugly grimace of triumph; but it would accomplish nothing. They were trapped, and had been from the moment the Grand Master had called them out— trapped by their own code of honor.

The enemy's forward squadrons could be seen clearly now, the masses of horsemen flowing amorphously over the plain. The Saracens would break the Templars' charge with sheer numbers, surround them, and hack them to pieces.

"Give your orders," the Grand Master said impatiently to de Maille.

De Maille's eyes locked with the Grand Master's. "First I want your assurance that we leave the squires behind."

"Of course," the Grand Master snapped, turning away. "I don't need you to remind me of the Rule."

White-faced, de Maille wheeled his horse about and rode back to address his men. Marshal waited a moment to fully regain his self-control and then turned and rode up beside his friend.

"Do you think we have any chance at all?" de Maille said woodenly.

Marshal shook his head.

De Maille sighed inaudibly. "Neither do I," he said, straightening up in the saddle, "but we can at least carry on with style."

De Maille had no need to call his men to attention; every eye was on him, and as he faced them, head erect and shoulders back, he was a gallant, commanding figure.

14

"You see the enemy," he called out in a firm voice. "When the Saracens come within range, we will charge them in three echelons, drive to their center, and kill the commanders. Master Gerard will lead the first echelon, I will lead the second, and Sir William will lead the third. In accordance with the Rule, squires will remain with the horses. Prepare yourselves, brothers, and may God be with us."

And that was all. No call to glory, no appeal for discipline or bravery. With these knights it was not necessary. God, what a waste, Marshal thought bitterly. What an obscene waste. And yet the thought of ignoring the Grand Master's insane order simply did not occur to him, nor to any of the knights on the hill.

As the knights and their squires dispersed to prepare for battle, de Maille turned to Marshal. "Keep your eye on Ridefort," he said grimly. "If that bastard turns and runs, it will be every man for himself. Try to cut your way out, Will; you'll have a better chance than any of us." Then he reached out and gripped Marshal's arm. "I wish you had taken our vows."

Marshal knew what de Maille meant. He was the only one who would die without the Templar mantle to shelter his soul. Marshal shrugged tiredly. "Knight of the Temple or pilgrim—I doubt it will make much difference to God."

De Maille glanced back at Ridefort, and he shook his head bitterly. "You should have gone home, Will, as soon as you saw the rot setting in."

Marshal looked out over the parched, rocky plains and barren hills they were fighting for. It was a wasteland as harsh and unforgiving as their enemies. Whatever Marshal had been looking for, he hadn't found it. A fatalistic half smile flickered briefly on his cracked lips. It was too late for regrets. "Now you tell me," he said.

The Templars had deployed in three ranks across the brow of the hill. Marhsal, in the third rank, swung up onto his big gray, the stronger of his two chargers. The stallion was seventeen hands high, with a deep chest and massive quarters, and Eustace had had difficulty with the horse; Marshal was among the last to mount.

The gray was skittish, tossing its head and unwilling to stand still; but once Marshal was in the saddle, he quickly brought the stallion under control. All the chargers were restless. A hot desert wind had sprung up, carrying with it the sound of the Saracens' coming and the scent of their mares.

The Saracens were now less than two miles away. The rippling of their great silk banners streaming in the wind and the snapping of thousands of pennants together with the hoofbeats of five thousand horses produced a rumble that rose from the plain like distant rolling thunder, punctuated by the deep, insistent beat of marching drums.

The squires had hobbled the spare horses on the rear slope, and now they stood beside their masters as the knights made final preparations. Marshal twisted his head to be sure he had not laced the mail coif too tightly. Beneath the mail, his padded felt undercap was already soaked with sweat. He stood up in his stirrups and rocked the saddle, testing the girth.

He knew Eustace had done the job properly, but going through the routine helped him for a few moments to ignore the tightness in his gut. Only once before in his life had he been sure he was going to die, but then there had been little time to think. Now there was too *much* time.

The halter was secure, and the padded canvas caparisons protecting the gray's chest and hindquarters were hung correctly. Eustace had lashed a spare sword to the pommel, and Marshal checked to be sure it would pull free easily in a cross-hand draw. "Shield, Eustace," he said, and his squire handed up the heavy, kite-shaped shield of seasoned, iron-hard wood.

"I gave your colors a fresh coat of paint, sire. I hope it brings you luck."

"Thanks," Marshal said, managing a smile, and once again he found comfort in the knowledge that the squires, at least, would be spared. He passed the shield's security strap over his head, allowing the shield to hang at his side. Despite the Templars' scorn for decoration, he had retained the blue-and-white colors on his shield—for luck, he had told Eustace. But he had no confidence in luck today.

Impulsively he reached down and gripped his squire's shoulder. "You're a good lad, Eustace, and you'll make a fine knight one day." This last encouragement was all that he could give the boy now.

Marshal regretted his words at once, for Eustace picked up the unintended note of finality in Marshal's tone. The boy looked anxiously out at the plain, as if really seeing the enemy for the first time.

"There *are* too many of them, aren't there, sire," he said, his voice cracking, and Marshal realized with surprise that Eustace was actually fond of him. In his attempts to toughen the boy, Marshal had worked him almost to the breaking point, and he had always assumed that Eustace thought him a tyrant.

"Don't count us out just yet, lad," called a burly, red-haired Templar on Marshal's right. "We'll give the bloody Turks a run for their money."

He, too, was an English knight, and like Marshal, he spoke French with an Anglo-Norman drawl. Although the English-born descendants of the Norman conquerors were usually conversant with at least one English dialect, Anglo-Norman French was their principal language.

Without warning, the English knight's squire, a sturdy, rawboned youth of twenty, grasped his master's hand and cried, "Sir Peter, I demand knighthood!"

The squire's cry transfixed the men on the hill, and knights and squires alike turned to see what would happen. The English knight was caught by surprise, and Marshal saw the conflicting emotions play across his face as he looked toward de Maille for help.

To demand knighthood in order to join a battle was a time-honored custom; but this was not Europe, and this battle could have only one outcome. The knight did not want to humiliate his squire by refusing, yet he didn't want him to share their fate.

"No!" de Maille thundered. "My order stands; squires remain with the horses. And we will grant no knighthood this day!"

Marshal looked toward the sudden confusion in the front rank as the Grand Master wheeled his horse about. "I countermand that order!" Ridefort cried, his expression exultant. "That squire does Our Lord honor, and his request shall *not* be denied!"

"You bloody bastard!" Marshal yelled in rage, knowing what would happen now. "You goddamned stupid bastard!"

But it was already too late, and Marshal's shouts, along with de Maille's, were drowned out in the chorus of demands that immediately rippled through the Templar ranks.

"Sir Bertrand, I demand knighthood!"

"Sir John, I demand . . ."

"Sir Gawain!"

"Sir Richard!"

Marshal looked quickly at Eustace, who was staring up at him, his eyes wide with excitement mixed with fear. Marshal shook his head vehemently. "No, Eustace. Use your head, son. For God's sake, use your head."

But everywhere squires were kneeling to receive adubment from their masters, who were reluctantly leaning over in their saddles to deliver the ceremonial blow. Slowly Eustace bent his knee, his eyes still on Marshal, silently pleading with Marshal to ignore the fear he could not hide.

"Sir William," Eustace cried hoarsely, "I demand knighthood."

Marshal glanced about desperately, but there was not a squire on the hill who had not accepted the Grand Master's challenge. The bonds of tradition and honor were sweeping them all into the maelstrom of Ridefort's mania. Still Marshal hesitated, hoping for a way out. Eustace was not ready; he wouldn't have a chance. . . .

"Please, Sir William!"

Marshal saw the tears in Eustace's eyes, and he knew that he had no choice; he couldn't humiliate the boy—even to save him.

"I will grant it," Marshal heard himself say, and Eustace bowed his head, waiting.

Slowly Marshal balled his fist. Then he leaned over and struck Eustace hard on the side of his head. As tradition demanded, it was a stinging blow that momentarily stunned the boy, and Marshal waited for Eustace's eyes to clear.

"Arise, Sir Eustace," Marshal said formally, masking his bitterness. He wouldn't rob the boy of his moment in the sun. He reached down and pulled him to his feet. "Be brave and upright, that God may love thee."

"So I shall, with God's help," Eustace responded with equal formality, and then suddenly he grinned, bursting with pride, the fear gone from his eyes. Marshal had seen it countless times—this transformation from boy to man, wrought by a few ceremonial words—yet it still awed him.

Only today the ceremony was a death warrant.

"Take my roan," Marshal said brusquely. "He's yours now. Remember to use a light rein; he has a tender mouth."

"Yes, sire," Eustace replied, handing Marshal his helmet and lance.

"I'm your sire no longer," Marshal said. "You're the equal of any knight, Eustace. Remember that."

"Yes, si—yes, William. I won't forget, and I won't betray your confidence in me."

Marshal quickly looked away so the boy wouldn't see what he was feeling. The enemy's center would soon be directly in front of them, passing at a distance of half a mile. The Saracens had strengthened the flank nearest the hill, but they clearly did not expect an attack. Why should they? It was madness.

"Get moving," Marshal said. "There's not much time."

Eustace ran back to join the other squires, who were hastily arming themselves and mounting their former masters' spare chargers. Marshal looked bitterly toward the Grand Master and his mouth set in a grim line. If Ridefort did turn and run, Marshal was determined to see to it that he didn't make it out alive.

2

"Lace helmets!" de Maille cried, and the waiting knights, their number now doubled to one hundred and twenty, donned their helmets and laced them to the collars of their hauberks.

The squires and a few of the veterans wore the old conical Norman helmet, which covered the ears and the back of the neck and had a thick steel strip extending down over the nose to give some protection to the face; but most of the seasoned knights wore flat-topped steel cylinders completely enclosing the head, with only slits for the eyes and mouth. Because of this helmet's weight and the difficulty in breathing once it was in place, the helmet order was only given moments before a charge.

The thunder from the plain was abruptly muted as Marshal lowered the massive steel helmet over his head, and the world, seen through the eye slit, seemed suddenly remote. He felt cut off from the past and the future; there was only the present, rushing at him moment by moment, crowding out his thoughts, his bitterness, and the last residues of fear. It had happened to him many times before, in tournament and in battle, and the part of him that remained introspective was grateful that today would be no different.

Deftly he tied the helmet down, put on his mailed gauntlets, slipped his left arm through the leather loops on the inside of his shield, and lifted his lance to the rest position, its steel-capped butt resting on his right stirrup. Nailed to the lance below the tip was his banner, a rectangle of heavy silk divided into blue and white squares, matching the colors on his shield. Like the triangular pennants of the ordinary knights, Marshal's banner was not simply for decoration; it prevented his lance from penetrating too deeply into an enemy's body.

He turned toward the Englishman on his right. "Good luck, Peter," Marshal said, his voice unnaturally loud inside the helmet.

The English knight's helmet, with a fringe of red beard poking out beneath it, inclined briefly in Marshal's direction, and Marshal turned to Eustace, whom he'd positioned on his left.

The youth's narrow face was pale, but his eyes were clear and his jaw was firm. Marshal edged the gray sideways, closing the gap between them; he wanted Eustace to see his eyes. "We'll be going any second."

Eustace swallowed. "I'm ready."

"I know you are, son. Now listen, and listen well. You're to stick to my side and a little behind me—and I mean stick! Keep that in your head and nothing else. When my lance finally breaks, you shift to my right. If I turn, you follow. Have you got that?"

"Yes," Eustace said, swallowing hard. "And thank you, Sir William," he added quickly, "for giving me this moment. Please believe me, I never hoped for more."

In the front rank, the Grand Master raised his arm, and Marshal tensed. It was time.

"Templars—forward!"

The Grand Master's arm swept down, and the three Templar lines advanced in unison, thirty yards apart. The knights held the pace to a walk, but their stallions, nostrils flaring and necks arched, strained at the bit.

On the plain below, the Moslems' response was immediate, the horsemen on the enemy's near flank swirling into a new battle order to meet the unexpected challenge. Black-turbaned Turkish horse archers and Saracen lancers with white turbans and round, brightly painted shields clustered around their units' streaming banners and turned to meet the Templar charge. At the army's center, toward which the Grand Master would drive, the Moslem heavy cavalry massed, the sun glinting on gilded helmets and chain mail.

"Couch your lances!" cried the Grand Master as the front rank reached the break in the incline at the base of the hill, where a final, gentle slope led down to the plain. The Templar lances swung down into attack position, and the chargers broke into a trot.

Marshal shifted his grip on his lance, lowering the steel-tipped, eight-foot shaft across the left side of the gray's neck, and clamped the lance butt under his right arm. He blinked to clear away the stinging sweat running down into his eyes.

"Stay back, Eustace!" he yelled harshly as he saw the boy's lance tip moving forward. "Behind me, damn it!"

Marshal's gray was prancing and shifting restlessly from side to side despite a tight rein, and Marshal could feel the same visceral, unreasoning excitement building within him. Both man and beast had been bred and trained for the charge.

Now there was no holding the stallions back, and the Grand Master's charger surged into a gallop. The attack was on. As the three Templar lines swept down off the hill onto the plain, their battle cry burst from one hundred and twenty throats.

"Do—the—right!"

Marshal shouted as loudly as the rest, swept away as adrenaline flooded into his bloodstream. The Templar shout was answered by Moslem war cries that merged into a single, inarticulate roar, like that of a gigantic, enraged beast, drowning out the throbbing drums and blaring battle trumpets. As the Templars pounded across the plain, waves of horse archers and light cavalry thundered to meet them: seven hundred—a thousand—too many to count.

Marshal's lips drew back from his teeth in a grimace of animal ferocity as instinct displaced thought and he became what he was born to be: a fighting machine.

The gap between the charging Templars and the onrushing enemy horsemen closed with incredible speed. Five hundred yards . . . three hundred . . . one hundred.

Turkish horse archers were in the lead, with no body armor to weigh down their swift, desert-hardened mounts, and as the gap narrowed to sixty yards, the Templars rode into a swarm of arrows that rattled off their helmets and shields like hail. Arrows by the dozen lodged in their saddles and chain mail, and caught in the chargers' caparisons.

A random arrow found the eye of a stallion in the first echelon, and Marshal saw the horse's forelegs crumple, catapulting its rider forward. The Templar sailed through the air and struck the rock-strewn desert floor headfirst, snapping his neck. The body lay inert as the knights behind rode over it.

There was no time for a second fusillade, and the archers' ranks parted before the onrushing Templar lances. The Turks peeled off to the sides as the Templars hurtled through them to close with the Saracen lancers racing up behind the archers.

Rising above the enemy's roar, Marshal heard the furious, transported bellow of the Grand Master as the first echelon crashed into the Saracen line and the slaughter commenced.

The Saracens carried light spears designed for thrusting and hurling, and their low saddles gave them little support. A Saracen lancer was no match for a charging knight. Each Templar was firmly seated in a high-backed, molded saddle, with his heavy lance of seasoned ash rigidly clamped against his side. The lance was but an extension of horse and rider welded together as one, and when it struck its target, the lance carried the momentum of fourteen hundred pounds surging forward at full gallop.

As the two sides met, the enemy spears glanced harmlessly off the Templars' superior shields, and the air was filled with the splintering crack of Saracen shields bursting asunder and the screams of the riders as they were skewered or thrown from their horses. The Templar stallions were as fierce as their masters, and when they collided with enemy horses, they knocked them aside or drove straight over them with unstoppable fury.

The first Templar echelon scythed through the leading Saracen ranks, and the knights in the second echelon cut down the riders who slipped through the gaps. For the moment the Templars in the third rank had no targets for their lances, and Marshal concentrated on controlling his stallion as they raced over ground littered with Saracen bodies and downed, thrashing enemy horses. With knee pressure and a light neck rein, he guided the gray to the left or right past obstacles he could avoid, spurring the stallion into a jump over those he could not, hoping Eustace could stay in position behind him.

Already Marshal's throat burned from the hot, dry air he sucked in through clenched teeth, which were coated with dust. The dust swirling in the air was rapidly obscuring his field of vision. The Grand Master's standard was only barely visible through the yellow haze. But he did not need to see to know what lay ahead.

The Templars were cutting through the thinnest of the enemy ranks—the first of the Turks and Saracens to meet their charge—and they couldn't hope to maintain their momentum. Hundreds of dead lay in the Templars' wake, but thousands were massed in front of them, too densely packed to penetrate.

A horse writhing on the ground appeared directly in front of Marshal, too close to avoid, and the gray leapt over the dying beast. Marshal's helmet slammed down on his head with the shock of landing, but he barely registered the jolt as he swung his lance tip toward his first target, a Saracen who had slipped through the first two Templar lines and was charging straight at Marshal, his right arm cocked to hurl his spear.

The man's nut-brown face was contorted with fury, but though his mouth was open wide, his yell was lost in the tumult. As the Saracen hurled his spear he lowered his shield slightly, and Marshal instantly raised his lance tip. The Saracen's spear caromed off Marshal's helmet as Marshal's lance slipped over the top of the Saracen's shield and drove straight into the man's face. A shriek and he was gone.

Another Saracen appeared out of the dust with a second lancer charging up behind him. The first man swerved left, and Marshal passed him by to strike the second rider's shield squarely in the middle, his lance shivering at the impact. The Saracen's shield splintered as Marshal's lance drove through it, and his lance caught the rider's left shoulder, throwing him from the saddle.

The enemy's numbers were multiplying second by second, and the third echelon was now fully engaged. The Templars continued to drive forward at a gallop, but Marshal knew the charge would break soon. He heard, rather than saw, the leading Templar lines ahead of him telescope together as they hit the enemy's own massed, heavy cavalry in a crescendo of bellows and shrieks amid the crack of shattering shields and breaking lances.

An instant later he and his men broke through the dust cloud raised by the countercharging Moslems and saw that the Templar line had broken against a solid wall of armored men and horses less than fifty yards ahead. The Templars had drawn their swords and were hacking their way into a sea of heavy cavalry.

Yelling wildly, the final Templar wave, with Marshal in the lead, hurtled into the swirling melee.

Marshal saw a gap open in the disintegrating Templar front, and he flicked his reins. The gray responded instantly, shifting to the right and charging into the gap. Marshal's lance skewered a Saracen poised to strike a nearby Templar, and despite the banner affixed to Marshal's lance, the lance tip emerged from the man's back. There was no chance to pull the lance free, and with brute strength Marshal maintained his grip long enough to bury the lance, on which the dying man still writhed, into the chest of another Saracen's mount.

Marshal's lance snapped in two as the gray barreled foward another twenty yards into the packed Moslem ranks. Sword blades crashed against Marshal's shield, and a Moslem on his right raised his sword to strike at Marshal's unprotected side. Marshal caught the sword blow on the splintered haft of his lance and, in a single fluid motion, reversed his grip on the haft and drove the iron-shod butt into the Saracen's face, knocking him senseless.

A sword blade rang off Marshal's helmet with a deafening clang, and another blade struck his armored shoulder with agonizing force. He pulled his own sword free and swept it around in a blind strike at the assailant behind him. He felt the blade strike home and recovered with an overhand blow at the head of a Saracen in front of him, cleaving the man's gilded helmet and splitting his skull.

Marshal was no longer thinking as he scythed left and right with his sword, cutting down every man unlucky enough to come within range of the four-foot blade, which he wielded with uncommon strength and deadly precision. The frenzied yells of the combatants merged into a continuous, mind-numbing roar punctuated by the ringing of steel on steel as blades crashed against blades, helmets, and shield bindings, like the ringing of hundreds of hammers on anvils.

Marshal was barely aware of the battle noise, or of the furnacelike heat inside his helmet, and he ignored the countless bruising blows to his back and shoulders as the Saracens clustering about him hammered in vain on his armored body. There was only the desperate need to keep moving forward through the press of enemy horses, to cut his way ever deeper into the endless sea of flashing swords, knowing that if he were stopped, he was lost.

It was hopeless, but Marshal no longer knew that—or perhaps he knew but no longer cared. He was no longer a rational man; he was a killer blindly fighting to survive from one second to the next.

Such was the strength of his wrist and forearm, that his short, quick sword strokes sliced through the Saracen chain mail as if it were cloth, and he struck with a speed his opponents could not match. His sword was red with blood and gore. As he continued to press forward he littered the ground with Saracen bodies, which fell to earth with severed arms, split skulls, and gashed shoulders. But for every man who fell, there was another to take his place.

There was no longer a Templar line; individuals and pairs of knights hacked their way forward, the strong forcing the way for their weaker, tiring comrades. The Saracens, unable to penetrate the Christian armor, shifted their attack to the Templars' horses, thrusting and slashing at the animals' legs and bellies.

The gray's caparisons were stained crimson with blood, and al-

25

though Marshal killed every man who came near, it was only a matter of time before a chance thrust brought down his horse.

The Templar standards still flew, and they continued to inch forward. As Marshal twisted around to deliver a backhand blow, he saw Eustace fighting close behind him, sheltered to some extent by the swath Marshal continued to cut in the enemy ranks. But time was running out; one by one knights slipped beneath the Saracen sea as their horses foundered.

Dimly Marshal sensed the flagging strength of the Templars fighting near him, but the knowledge had no significance. There was nothing but to fight on and on, striking left and right, oblivious to the shrieks of the men he felled, heedless of the ache in his shoulders and back from the unremitting rain of sword blows and of the fatigue seeping into his sword arm.

His bloody sword was blunted along both edges now, and he dropped it and pulled his spare sword free just in time to catch a blade descending on him in a long arc. As the attacker raised his arm for a second strike, Marshal's short, chopping counterstroke sliced three inches into the man's armpit. The Saracen's black eyes went wide with shock, and he toppled from the saddle.

In that instant Marshal saw the English knight who had ridden into battle beside him go down, his horse crippled or killed. Marshal wheeled the gray about and spurred the stallion toward the swirl of Saracens striking down at the fallen Englishman, whom Marshal could no longer see. But before Marshal could cut his way through, he was struck hard in the back by the lance of a Saracen charging up behind him.

The lance caught him below the shoulder blades, doubling him over, and before he could recover, a second Saracen lance found the belly of his horse. The gray shrieked and started to rear up, and Marshal kicked free of the stirrups just before the stallion fell sideways, throwing him from the saddle.

Marshal struck the ground on his back, his head slamming against the inside of his helmet. The fall knocked the wind out of him, and despite the padded lining inside his helmet, he was momentarily stunned. As he had fallen, he had instinctively covered his body with his shield, and it was the shield that saved him from being trampled to death.

His vision cleared and he sucked in air in a ragged gasp, but before he could move, the sky was blotted out as a Saracen rode over him, crushing the air from his lungs. Again he gasped for breath, and again it was crushed out of him. He was suffocating, and the heat inside his armor was suddenly unendurable. A red mist filmed his vision, and the earth spun. The tumult above him faded as he fell away into darkness. . . .

Marshal's blackout lasted only seconds, and when he recovered, the press of horses around him had miraculously loosened. He could breathe again. He rolled off his back and rose groggily to his knees, driven by the blind instinct to survive. His shield still hung at his side, but he had lost his sword. He didn't try to find it; he had to get to his feet. Somehow he had to get to his feet.

Swaying like a drunk from dizziness and exhaustion, he heaved himself up, staggered, and nearly fell again as he was knocked sideways by a riderless horse. All the horses around him were riderless, he realized dazedly, and then, as his head cleared and his eyes snapped back into focus, he saw why.

Above him was Eustace on the roan, shielding him from the Saracens pressing in on them, hacking and slashing with his sword with the strength of a madman. The boy's eyes were wild and his face was the color of chalk. He held his reins clenched in his teeth, for his left arm, nearly severed at the shoulder, dangled uselessly at his blood-drenched side.

"Eustace!" Marshal cried.

His voice was lost in the tumult, but it was already too late for the boy to hear him. Eustace's eyes rolled upward, and he toppled from the saddle, still clutching his sword. He was dead before his body crashed to the ground in a crumpled heap of lifeless steel.

Marshal seized the boy's sword, and then the reins of the roan. The stallion's lips were flecked with foam and his chest and neck were gashed, but none of the wounds was crippling. Seeing Eustace fall and missing Marshal in the confusion of riderless horses, the Saracens had turned away in search of fresh prey, giving Marshal a chance to mount.

The roan shied away as Marshal started to mount, and he didn't waste time trying to get his foot in the stirrup. Drawing on his last reserves of strength, he took hold of the pommel and swung himself bodily up into the saddle. Instantly Saracens turned toward him to attack, and he lifted his shield and tightened his grip on Eustace's sword.

The Templar standards had fallen, and only a scattered handful of knights still fought on. Marshal's own endurance was nearly at an end, but now, for the first time, he thought of escape. The main body of the Moslem army had already regrouped and was moving off toward Nazareth, leaving only a contingent behind to finish off the last of the Templars. Marshal was surrounded by a force of less than one hundred men.

He cut down the first Saracens to reach him, grunting with the effort of each sword stroke, his ragged gasps whistling in his throat, and he wheeled his horse about, seeking an avenue of escape. Had he been fresh, he surely could have cut his way out into the open; but his sword arm was numb to the shoulder from exhaustion, and dizziness threatened to overwhelm him.

As if in answer to a prayer, a Moslem captain, frustrated at finding himself on the fringe of the final, swirling battle, caught sight of Marshal.

Mounted on a proud Arabian draped in scarlet silks, he charged Marshal, bellowing to the men in his path to clear the way. Far more afraid of their own officers than of the enemy, the Saracens opened a lane in their midst, giving way to the captain in his gilded armor.

Marshal saw his last, desperate chance and spurred the roan toward the glory-seeking captain, who charged him right hand to right hand, disdaining the protection of a shield, his long, curving sword blade raised high.

Less than fifty yards separated them as the roan surged into a gallop, and the Saracen leader had time for only one shout of *"Allah akbar!"* before the gap closed. Perhaps he was too confident or too anxious to bring a full measure of strength to his sword stroke, but he swung the blade in too wide an arc and he was a heartbeat too late.

As the Saracen's blade flashed down, Marshal lunged forward in his saddle, and his short, wrist-whipped stroke sliced off the captain's head. The Arabian charged on, still carrying the blood-spurting trunk, but Marshal did not see the gruesome spectacle. Bent low over the saddle, he raced through the gap the captain had left in his wake, sweeping his sword from left to right with the last of his strength, scattering those who tried to close it.

The roan galloped into the open, carrying Marshal out of the death trap, but Marshal was too exhausted to feel relief or to wonder at the lack of pursuit. Had the Saracens realized that his strength was gone, they might have given chase, but they had seen their captain's head fly from his shoulders, and they were willing to let this Christian knight flee.

Clinging to the saddle pommel, Marshal raised his head to get his bearings. As he turned his mount toward the hills bordering the plain, he saw that another knight had broken out earlier and was fleeing toward the safety of the hills. The distant rider was too far ahead to see clearly, but Marshal recognized him.

It was the Grand Master.

Marshal slowed his horse as soon as he was out of range and continued on at a walk. He was certain the enemy outriders had seized the Templars' spare horses and pack animals, so there would be neither water nor fresh mounts to find. He dared not push the exhausted roan too hard.

Gerard de Ridefort was not as cautious, and five miles farther on, Marshal came upon the carcass of the Grand Master's horse. Facing a desert trek on foot, Ridefort had discarded his shield and armor, which now lay in a heap beside the carcass. Flies from the swarm covering the dead horse buzzed up around Marshal as he reined in.

He waved the flies out of his face and shaded his eyes. Far ahead he could just make out the figure of a man on foot, the blurred image wavering in the heat waves rising from the ground. Ridefort was heading for Kakun.

Marshal extracted some cloves from a pouch hanging on his belt and popped them into his mouth. His thirst was not yet critical, and chewing the cloves seemed to relieve some of the dryness in his throat. If thirst was not yet a problem for the Grand Master, it would be soon. Marshal's lip curled, and he prodded the roan forward, following in Ridefort's tracks.

The Grand Master, trudging along the southern base of the range of hills, didn't hear Marshal coming up behind him until the distance between them closed to fifty yards. As Marshal's horse clattered over some shale at the bottom of a gully, Ridefort swung around, swaying drunkenly, his mouth agape.

"Marshal!" he croaked. "Thank God! Have you got water?"

His dark face was contorted with exhaustion and thirst, and his left arm hung limply at his side. The sleeve of his linen undershirt was torn and bloodstained where a sword blade had managed to slice through his chain mail.

Marshal didn't answer, and the Grand Master came stumbling toward him.

"Marshal! What's the matter with you? Have you got water or not?"

Slowly Marshal drew Eustace's sword from his scabbard and

deliberately raised the blood-encrusted blade. They were alone, and there was nothing to prevent him from killing the Grand Master, as he'd vowed to do. It would be no more a crime than scotching a viper; Ridefort deserved to die.

The Grand Master's eyes went wide as he saw the look on Marshal's face, and he stumbled backward in alarm, reaching for his own sword. They both knew it would do him no good. "No, Marshal! Are you crazy? Stop looking at me like that!"

"What's the matter?" Marshal said hoarsely. "Are you afraid of losing that ugly black head of yours?"

The Grand Master heard the hatred in Marshal's voice and his nerve broke. As Marshal advanced on him he gave an inarticulate cry, turned, and began to scramble madly up the hillside.

Through slitted eyes Marshal watched him run, feeling his hatred dissolving in disgust; there would be no satisfaction in killing the man. But he owed it to Eustace, to de Maille, and to all the others. . . .

Marshal flicked his reins and dug in his spurs, guiding his mount up the slope to cut off Ridefort's escape. As Marshal rode him down, Ridefort gasped in terror and turned to slash desperately at the horse looming above him. Stumbling backward, the Grand Master tripped on a rock and fell onto his back, his sword clattering from his hand.

"No!" he cried as Marshal's shadow fell over him. "Please, no!"

Marshal was poised to strike; but as he looked down on the helpless, panic-stricken man, disgust overwhelmed him again, and he knew he couldn't do it.

Seconds ticked by as Marshal stared down in silence at Ridefort, his eyes locked with the Grand Master's. Slowly, deliberately, Marshal gathered what little saliva he had left in his mouth, leaned over, and spit directly in Ridefort's upturned face.

Then he turned his horse and rode away, mentally putting the disintegrating Kingdom of Jerusalem behind him. He had fought his last battle in the Holy Land; it was time to go home.

But if Marshal had seen Ridefort's expression as the Grand Master struggled to his feet and stared after him, he would have reconsidered leaving Gerard de Ridefort alive.

CHAMPION

3

Pembroke, South Wales—April 1188

"I could have you whipped!" hissed Prince John, glaring malevolently at the girl standing before him. "Flayed until you beg for mercy."

Inwardly the girl flinched, but she pressed her lips together to keep them from trembling and forced herself to meet John's black, liquid eyes. He was drunk, and even his rage could not overcome the laxity of his wine-soaked body; but there was nothing comical or pathetic about this besotted youth who sprawled in the high, canopied chair that had been her father's. John, Count of Mortain and youngest son of Henry II, was as dangerous as a snake.

"I cannot do as you ask, sire," the girl said huskily, her voice barely above a whisper. "I cannot surrender my rights."

"Rights!" John snarled, spittle flying from his lips. "You are my ward; you have no rights that I do not grant you!"

John lurched forward in the chair and shook the fist in which he clutched a half-empty wine cup, spraying wine over the rushes on the floor. "I'll have your signature on the order tonight, or by God's legs, I'll have you whipped."

The aged servant hovering at John's side, an old man who had served in Pembroke Castle since her father's time, moved hastily to refill the cup. Horrified by what was happening, he glanced furtively at the girl, silently imploring her to yield. His hands shook as he poured the wine, spilling several drops on the sleeve of John's flowing silk surcoat.

"Begone, damn you!" John barked, shoving the old man away.

The servant scurried backward, and as he left, closing the heavy oak door behind him, an ominous silence descended on the bedchamber, broken only by the hiss of the fire in the hearth. Now the girl was alone with John. Years ago this had been her father's room, every inch of it as familiar to her as the back of her hand, but John's alien presence seemed even more threatening in these surroundings.

The prince stared coldly at the girl over the rim of his wine cup as he tilted back his head and drank, the wine gurgling in his throat in time to the bobbing of his prominent Adam's apple. At twenty-one, John still had the look of an adolescent. He was thin and angular with black eyes, black hair, and a black, carefully trimmed beard. He might have been a handsome youth had it not been for his soft, almost feminine lips, which curved in a suggestion of sensuous cruelty.

John drained the cup and let it fall to the floor. He continued to stare at her, the light from the candle stand beside his chair glinting in his eyes. The girl wondered suddenly if he'd intentionally waited for nightfall to confront her.

"Well?" John demanded.

He had intended his tone to be threatening, but his demand coincided with an involuntary belch that sent alcohol fumes drifting across to the girl. Her nostrils twitched with disgust, and her disgust rekindled the pride and anger that had driven her to challenge his authority in the first place. This drunken prince who sat so arrogantly in her father's place deserved contempt, not obedience. Her father never would have endured such treatment from any lord.

The girl's spine stiffened, and she drew herself up to her full height, drawing on her memory of her father's strength and on her own reserves of courage. Her parents were dead and she was their only child; on her shoulders alone rested the burden of the family honor.

As she faced John now, she was no longer simply a frightened nineteen-year-old girl; she was Lady Isabelle de Clare, granddaughter of an Irish king, daughter of the Earl of Pembroke, and heiress to the richest lands in the empire of Henry II.

"I will *not* sign the letter, sire," Isabelle said hoarsely. "Sir Ranulf de Barre received Kilkenny Castle from the King's hand to hold for me until my marriage. I cannot order him to surrender it, nor will I request him to do so." She lifted her head higher and thrust out her chin. "I know full well that you have been parceling out my Irish lands as if they were fiefs of your own to give—lands that were entrusted to you as my guardian. If you wish Sir Ranulf to surrender Kilkenny to your man, Meiler fitz Henry, it is the King to whom you must turn. Then we will see, sire, how His Majesty responds to a prince who would steal a ward's inheritance."

Isabelle's voice had risen in defiance as she spoke, and now her fists were clenched at her sides as she braced herself for John's reaction. Her mind shied away from the thought of a lash tearing at her back, but she stood her ground.

John said nothing. Slumped in his chair, head lolling, he stared at her in silence. Then, quite suddenly, he smiled, and Isabelle felt goose-flesh rise on her arms. It was the smile of a boy who amused himself by tossing cats into an open fire.

Languidly John lifted his arm and wagged his finger at her. "I know something you don't know," he said in a singsong voice, and the drunken slurring of his words did nothing to soften the sly cruelty in his voice. "I know that your treacherous little priest never left this castle."

John's smile broadened into an evil grin as he heard Isabelle's startled intake of breath.

"What—what have you done with him?" she said, unable to suppress the tremor in her voice.

"Done with him?" John grinned. "Why, nothing. It's a crime to lay hands on a priest. Becket taught my father that lesson, didn't he? No, when we caught him trying to sneak out last night, we simply persuaded him to stay. Then we *persuaded* him to tell us where he was going—and why."

John wagged his finger at her again. "You shouldn't have done it, you know. Imagine how it hurt me to learn that you tried to send a petition of complaint to the King, accusing me of—what was the word?— ah, *malfeasance*, that's what it was. Now *that* word, I'll warrant, the priest put in your mouth."

"Where is Father Bertrand?" Isabelle said, and once again her voice was barely above a whisper.

John spread his hands in a gesture of innocence. "I really don't know. He seems to have disappeared, and no one has been able to find him."

Isabelle shuddered involuntarily, and tears flooded her eyes. Father Bertrand had been more than a confessor to her; he'd been a friend—a friend who had agreed without hesitation to carry her petition to the Bishop of Llandaff for presentation to the King. But they had both thought a priest would be safe, even from John. . . .

"I am the guardian of your person *and* your lands," John said with renewed harshness, "and I'll tolerate no interference—from *anyone*. I trust, Lady, that you understand that now!"

John glared at her and took another swallow of wine. "It was Ranulf de Barre's misguided defiance that put wild thoughts in your head, and if you countersign my order to surrender Kilkenny, I may find it in my heart to forgive your impudence. But you must sign *now.*"

The girl swallowed convulsively, tears spilling down her cheeks, crying not for herself but for Father Bertrand. She was sure he was dead. Fear, anger, and now helpless grief had battered her in turn, and she had to fight for control. But fight she did. John was counting on her weakness—a woman's weakness—to give him what he demanded.

Now, more than ever before, Isabelle wished she had been born a man, able to defend her honor and rights with a sword—a sword to avenge Father Bertrand, a sword to strike at John! But her only weapon now was defiance. It was pitiful—almost nothing—but it was all she had.

She was sure John would not willingly go to the King. He wanted to steal Kilkenny as he had her other lands—quietly, like a thief in the night. And Ranulf de Barre, the bravest and most faithful of her father's old knights, would never yield without her consent. The girl had never liked John, nor trusted him, but now she hated him with a fierceness that overcame the icy fear of what he might do to her.

"I will not sign," she spat out, and with a contemptuous toss of her head she spun away from him and started for the door.

Behind her, she heard John's angry snarl become a grunt as he lurched to his feet, the sound followed by the crash of the candle stand as his reeling body knocked it to the floor, plunging the chamber into semidarkness. Isabelle instinctively bolted for the door, but she was not quick enough. Snarling, John lunged across the room and caught her from behind.

Isabelle cried out in fright as his hand clawed her shoulder and spun her around. His face, faintly lit by the flickering orange glow of the fire, glistened with sweat, his features distorted by anger and sudden lust. Before she could pull free of him, he clamped his hand over her mouth and pressed hard against her, bending her backward.

"You little minx," he breathed, tightening his grip. "I'll have your signature and my pleasure, too, this night. By God's blood, I will."

Wrenching his hand from her mouth, he groped wildly for her breast, and her shock was smothered in disgust. As she sucked in air, her senses reeled from the smell of him—alcohol, sour sweat, and the cloying scent of rose water, and she thrashed desperately in his grip. Her left arm was pinned to her side, but she freed her right arm and drove her fist into John's stomach.

John grunted but did not release her, and in her effort to pull away she lost her balance and fell backward, with John still clutching her. Her cry of pain as her back hit the floor was cut off as John fell on top of her, crushing the air from her lungs. The shadows dancing across the ceiling were blotted out as John covered her mouth with his.

Isabelle fought like a wild animal but strangely without fear; she felt only disgust and white-hot rage. Twisting her face away from him and groping for the dagger on his belt, she gasped, "I'll kill you!"

Panting with exertion and lust, John seized her arms and pinned them to the floor. He rose on his knees for greater leverage, and for an instant Isabelle's legs were free. With all her strength she drove her knee up into his groin.

John's mouth flew open in a gasp of paralyzing agony, and he toppled sideways and rolled onto his back, clutching his groin. Isabelle was on him like a cat. Seizing his head by the hair, she lifted it high, and before he could resist, she slammed it viciously down onto the floor.

The rushes covering the floor tiles cushioned the blow enough to save John's life, but the force of the blow knocked him senseless. Her chest heaving, Isabelle looked down at him for several seconds, her face twisted with loathing, and her eyes strayed to the knife at his belt. It would be so easy to kill him. . . .

Gradually her breathing slowed, and she got unsteadily to her feet. Killing John was not worth dying on a gallows. The prince's legs twitched spasmodically, and he groaned; but then his breathing deepened and he began to snore. The blow to the head had only speeded what the wine would have accomplished in time. John would not stir till morning.

Isabelle's face was flushed, and her arms and legs trembled from exertion. She wiped the sweat from her forehead and took a deep, measured breath, astonished that her mind was working coldly and clearly. She knew what she had to do now.

There were barons to whom she could flee for protection, but not without putting them in jeopardy; and she could not hope to reach the King, who had not yet returned from France. She needed to buy time for another petition to reach him. What she intended was tantamount to rebellion and she quailed at the thought, but the alternative was begging for John's mercy, and that she would never do.

Hesitantly she approached the door to the chamber, wondering how much the guard in the passage had heard through the four inches of oak. The pikeman, standing three paces from the door, came to attention as she slipped out and closed the door behind her. If the man had heard her cry out, he had chosen to ignore it; his face was impassive.

"Count John's order is that he not be disturbed under any circumstances," she said firmly.

"Yes, milady," the guard replied calmly.

"Do you know if Fulk le Brun is standing watch tonight?"

"Black Fulk, milady?" the guard said with a laugh. "He's not on watch, and my guess is that he'll still be gaming with the others in the great hall."

Isabelle nodded regally and walked away, suppressing the urge to hurry. One hour to prepare for the journey, another half hour for Fulk to bribe or overpower the gate house watch, and that would give them at least a seven-hour head start on their pursuers. With luck she would make it to Milford Haven and out to sea before John could stop her. And if she could reach Kilkenny, there she would make her stand.

Shortly after dawn, the castellan of Pembroke burst in on John, who was on his knees in the latrine, vomiting. John barely registered the news of Isabelle's escape. Each fresh convulsion of his stomach sent pounding waves of pain coursing through his head and intensified the agony in his swollen testicles. Only after servants had cleaned him up, changed his clothes, and helped him to bed could he begin to think. Then he sent for Roger Poole.

Poole was John's chamberlain, a clever and ambitious man whom John trusted as much as he did any of his retainers. John's court entourage of young, sycophantic noblemen served to amuse him and massage his ego, but it was men like Poole—lowborn and totally dependent on his patronage—who did his work for him. Particularly the dirty work.

John shifted on the pillows supporting him in the wide, canopied bed that had been built for the late Earl of Pembroke and took another sip of honeyed wine, trying to wash away the aftertaste of vomit that stubbornly lingered in his throat. He disliked the idea of receiving Poole while still in bed, but he was unable to stand without experiencing intolerable pain in his groin.

He suppressed the anger that surged through him at the thought of what the girl had done to him, concentrating on the problem her escape

38

posed, so that he could instruct Poole immediately. John never allowed his chamberlain to do his thinking for him. He used his men; he didn't ask them for advice.

A charge of attempted rape did not worry him, for Isabelle de Clare could prove nothing; he could dismiss her accusations as the wild imaginings of an unstable, hysterical girl. But Ranulf de Barre's unexpected refusal to surrender Kilkenny to Meiler fitz Henry, coupled with the girl's flight, threatened to expose his maneuvering in Ireland. It was a small threat to be sure, but John never took chances.

For nearly a year he had been quietly ceding control of the de Clare lands in Leinster to willing barons—in return for their secret support of his ambitions. John wanted to be King.

He was the youngest of the four sons Eleanor of Aquitaine had borne Henry II, but the two eldest had died, and now only Richard stood between him and the Throne. John pursed his lips petulantly. He had done his best with his mother, but she had always favored Richard, in whom she persisted in seeing the future King of England.

To bolster Richard's claim as Heir Apparent, Eleanor had made him Count of Poitou, declaring him heir to the Duchy of Aquitaine, the great fertile region in the south of France that she held in her own right. Richard now ruled the Aquitaine with an iron hand, and even John acknowledged that he had proved his capacity to govern.

Richard lacked his father's political finesse and cunning, but he understood the use of power and had the necessary appetite for war. He loved combat, and he was a skillful, charismatic field commander. But Richard left his father cold, and his strength inspired Henry's distrust.

John detested the sweaty, dangerous game of knightly warfare, and he had seen an easier route to power. From his earliest years he had fawned upon his father, cultivating his love, if not his respect; and John, not Richard, now received the affection the King had once reserved for his eldest son, Henry.

John smiled slightly with satisfaction. His cultivation of his father was slowly but surely bearing fruit. Two years ago the King had installed John as Lord of Ireland, carving out a separate inheritance for him. And, ignoring the royal counselors, Henry had steadfastly refused to publicly declare Richard his heir.

Perhaps Henry merely wanted to keep Richard off-balance, for he had never suggested to John that he might try to circumvent the order of succession; but Richard had begun to fear that the King planned to disinherit him, and Richard's fear became John's hope.

It was an open secret that young King Philip of France was trying to drive a wedge between Richard and the King, and if Richard should be seduced into rebellion, the civil war that followed might leave John undisputed heir to the Throne of England.

When Henry had made John Lord of Ireland, he had given John what he wanted most: an independent power base. His domain provided the opportunity to subvert greedy barons with unofficial grants of land and promises of more to come, enabling him to secretly build support for an eventual bid for the Crown.

Yet John's hopes would come to nothing if his father discovered his ambition; the King would turn from him, as he had from Richard. That was the risk the girl's escape presented. The danger was slight, but John intended to meet it. Although physical danger frightened him, he thrived on the risks of intrigue, which stimulated his facile, manipulative mind. When Poole appeared in his chamber, he had his instructions ready.

The chamberlain bowed and said dryly, "I take it, sire, that Lady Isabelle refused to sign the letter."

Poole was a sandy-haired, nondescript man in his thirties whose unremarkable face and figure rendered him invisible in a crowd.

"Exactly how did she get out?" John replied coldly, unamused by Poole's ironic tone.

"The gate house watch claims to have been overpowered by one of the late Earl's retainers, sire. I was told he's a great hulk of a man, but I suspect that the guards were simply bribed. It would appear that you were too liberal with the girl's allowance. She's a cool one," Poole added with the barest hint of admiration. "She even took her hawk with her."

"Well, she certainly isn't fool enough to try to cut eastward across my own lands," John said, "and north is out of the question. The Welsh princes had no love for her father, and she'd fetch a hefty ransom. That leaves Milford Haven and the sea. I assume she's bolted for Kilkenny."

"Or she might cross to Dublin and seek shelter with Lord Meath. He is no friend of yours, sire."

"Friend or not, he is my vassal. If she's gone to Dublin, she'll be no better off than in Kilkenny. Either way we'll have her back. I want you to ride to Milford Haven directly.

"If the girl has sailed for Ireland, you will transmit orders to all harbormasters there to seize her should she try to leave again. Send a messenger to Meiler fitz Henry, informing him that the girl may try to slip into Kilkenny and ordering him to seize her. You will sail for Dublin to see Meath. If she has fled there, bring her back. If the girl has gone to Kilkenny, persuade Meath not to interfere if she tries to enlist his aid."

Poole cleared his throat. "If Meiler storms Kilkenny while Lady Isabelle is there, sire," he said diffidently, "she'll be in danger. Shall I caution him?"

"She has fled my protection," John replied stonily. "The risk is on her own head."

If Poole disapproved, he gave no sign of it. As always, his eyes were devoid of emotion.

"What tack shall I take with Meath, sire?"

John smiled thinly. "Simply explain the situation, Poole. The poor girl is obviously deranged and plagued by delusions—one of which appears to be the fear that I'm trying to rob her of her lands. We won't rest until she's in our custody again—for her own safety and well-being.

"You will carry two documents for Meath's benefit. The first, a direct order from me to surrender the girl at once if she is in his custody. The second, an order for Meiler fitz Henry to withdraw immediately from Kilkenny. You will show that order to Meath and request him to transmit it on our behalf. That should convince him that the girl's fears are groundless."

"The order for Meiler fitz Henry, sire," Poole said, "shall I prepare it with or without the confirmation code?"

John allowed himself another smile. "Without it, of course."

John's secret orders were always transmitted orally, and the recipient was advised to ignore subsequent orders in writing unless they contained a specified word code. John had already authorized Meiler fitz Henry to seize Kilkenny, and the rapacious baron would press the siege regardless of the written order to desist, knowing that John would continue to turn a blind eye.

"And if Lord Meath remains unconvinced, sire? He was a good friend of the girl's father."

John's face hardened. "I am Meath's liege lord. Remind him of the penalty for treason."

"I will, sire," Poole said, bowing and retreating. "If you will permit, I shall withdraw now and prepare the letters for your signature and seal."

John nodded and dismissed his chamberlain with a wave of his arm. As Poole left, John lay back on his pillows with a sigh and closed his eyes, satisfied that he had the situation in hand. He was sure the girl had fled to Kilkenny. Meiler would subdue the castle, hang Ranulf de Barre, and seize the girl. And if the affair did somehow come to the King's attention, John's version would be the one he would believe. If necessary, John could make Meiler fitz Henry the scapegoat.

Now that the need for thinking was past, John again became aware of the dull ache in his swollen testicles, and he cupped his hand protectively over his groin. "Bitch," he muttered viciously. There would be ample time to take his revenge once the girl was in his custody again—plenty of time.

Slowly John's facial muscles slackened, and his lips parted salaciously as he let the possibilities run through his mind. As his imagination took hold of him, he felt his loins stir with sadistic anticipation.

4

Isabelle de Clare awoke slowly, clinging to sleep, unwilling to leave its refuge. A cock crowed, robbing her of the hope that it was not yet dawn, and she opened her eyes. The soft yellow glow of the all-night candle on the stand beside her bed was already dissolving in the gray light filtering through the translucent cloth window screens that covered the arrow slits in the stone walls of her chamber.

As the bells of nearby St. Canice Abbey rang Prime, she rolled onto her side and pulled the fur-lined down coverlet tightly about her, wishing she were in her own bed, safe and secure as she had been as a child, with nothing to fear from the day. These moments just after waking were the worst, and she knew she should rise at once to face the day, but still she lingered under the covers, wishing, wishing . . .

The heavy oak door to her chamber swung open, and Matilda, her lady-in-waiting, swept in, carrying a basin of steaming water, a towel, and Isabelle's chemise and stockings. "Good morning, milady," she said, depositing the basin and towel on a small trestle table beneath the arrow slit which caught the first rays of the sun.

"Morning, Mattie," Isabelle said huskily, not quite able to match the older woman's brisk, cheerful tone.

Already the sounds of the castle coming to life were drifting up from the courtyard. A barking dog had started the chickens and geese squawking and honking, and now men added to the noise: the splitting of firewood, the castle's marshal cursing his varlets, who were bringing the horses out of the stables for exercise, the ringing of the armorer's hammer on the anvil. The day was upon her.

Matilda came over to the bed, and for a moment Isabelle thought she meant to chide her again for sleeping without the bed curtains drawn. Instead Matilda bent down and kissed her on the forehead—something she had not done for many years.

Matilda, the spinster daughter of a landed knight, had been the one constant in Isabelle's life for as long as she could remember. It seemed as if she had always looked as she did now, a short, plump woman with a soft, smiling face. As Matilda had grown older she had taken to wearing a wimple instead of letting her dark braids hang free, and the headcloth, drawn in folds around the chin, hid the graying of her hair.

Matilda laid the chemise and stockings on the coverlet at the foot of the bed. "Put these on now," she said. "I warmed them by the fire in the hall just before I came up."

Isabelle managed a wry smile. "What did the men think of that?"

"Those Welsh ruffians?" Matilda sniffed. "Not a thing. They've all just come off the second watch and are already snoring, dead to the world. God, what a noise."

With that, Matilda bustled out of the chamber, and Isabelle rose naked from the bed and hurriedly slipped the linen chemise over her head, grateful for the warmth that still clung to it. She pulled on the white, woolen stockings, fastened them with ribbons sewn in above the knees and pushed her feet into a pair of soft leather slippers dyed scarlet and lined with felt.

Spring was slow in coming, and the night had been cold. Goose bumps rose on her bare arms. For once she missed the service of a full complement of maids to help her dress. The sheer frivolousness of the thought brought a brief smile to her lips. Her situation could not be so desperate if she could still be distracted by a chill in the air.

Shivering, she reached for her *pelisse*, which hung on a pole projecting from the wall beside the bed. It was a white, ankle-length gown of fine wool, trimmed with ermine and lined with squirrel fur covered by silk. The *pelisse* was put on over the head, and it had a slit neckline to permit the arms to slip into long, tight-fitting sleeves.

She closed the neck slit with a gold brooch and walked to the water basin, her feet rustling in the fresh rushes carpeting the floor. Her falcon was stirring on its wall perch, and she talked to the bird as she washed, the meaningless chatter helping her to shut away the fear that assaulted her afresh each morning.

The *pelisse* had warmed her, and she was no longer shivering. She carefully dried her hands and face to avoid the chapping that plagued her and moved aside the window screen. The falcon spread its wings and flapped restlessly, demanding attention, the tiny silver bells attached to its legs tinkling softly.

Isabelle checked that the cup attached to the perch still held water and added the hawk's morning dose of medicine for the molting season. Now that she had washed her hands, she permitted herself to stroke the bird. Like others of her class, she was fastidious about personal cleanliness, but when it came to handling a prize falcon, cleanliness became a fetish.

The sunlight streaming in through the arrow slit threw a bright yellow rectangle against the opposite wall. Her chamber occupied half the area on the top floor of the frontier castle's three-story, rectangular stone keep. It was a bare room, devoid of wall hangings or any other adornment, and furnished only with the canopied bed, a folding stool with a canvas seat, and two ironbound chests containing her clothes and jewels. The bare, rough-hewn wooden beams above supported the conical wooden roof and fighting platform on the tower's battlements.

Isabelle was unaffected by the stark aspect of the tower's interior. As her eyes swept over the well-laid stonework she felt only satisfaction and pride in her father. Many of the frontier castles in Ireland could boast only a wooden tower, and few of the stone towers had walls as thick as these. This cold, cheerless keep had not been built for a woman's taste or comfort; it was a fighting man's citadel, and without its strength she would not have dared to risk her men's lives in what she knew was a desperate gamble.

Through the arrow slit Isabelle could see the river and virgin pine forest stretching limitlessly into the distance, and she imagined herself on the parapet, able to look in all directions. Her father's lands stretched beyond the horizons—lands won by his courage and daring and by the loyalty and blood of the handful of Normans from the Marches of South Wales who had followed him.

As a child she had listened in awe to the story of his conquests in Ireland, and she recalled it now, drawing from it a heightened awareness of her responsibility and the strength to shoulder it. Her father, Earl Richard de Clare, had married the daughter of the Irish King of Leinster, and when the Earl had died, Leinster had become Isabelle's legacy.

Prince John, her guardian, should have held her lands in trust for the sons she would one day bear, and his betrayal of that trust had left Isabelle no choice but to fight as best she could for her rights and the rights of her unborn sons. That had been her father's way, and she knew no other.

Isabelle's mother had died in childbirth, and the bond between the

Earl and Isabelle, his only child, had been far stronger than it might otherwise have been. Though her father had died while she was quite young, she felt its pull still. His face had long since blurred in her recollection, but she remembered his gentle voice and delicate, almost feminine hands, which had seemed so remarkable in a warrior.

Even as a child Isabelle had guessed that her father would have wished for a son to carry his name and to defend his legacy; but the Earl had never even hinted that he regretted Isabelle, and she had loved him all the more for it. . . .

Isabelle heard Matilda ascending the stairs, and with a pang of childish guilt she realized that she had forgotten to use the twig of green wood Matilda had placed beside the washbasin. Quickly she fetched the twig and began rubbing the freshly cut, pulpy end of the stick over her teeth, grimacing as she worked it into the gums. It would not matter to Matilda that they lay under siege; come hell or high water, teeth had to be polished.

Matilda entered the room, carrying a goblet of spiced wine and a small round load of bread on a silver tray, and Isabelle smiled inwardly. She had expressly forbidden Matilda to pack anything that was not strictly necessary, but she had forgotten that to Matilda style was essential.

Once again Matilda conveyed her disgust at the lack of furniture by making a show of looking for a place on which to set the tray. She sighed heavily and finally deposited it on the bed. "I'll fix your hair while you have breakfast," she said, extracting a brush, a comb, and coils of silver thread from a cloth bag that hung from the girdle about her waist.

Isabelle obediently came to the bed and sat down. She was too nervous to be hungry, but she was always thirsty in the morning. She picked up the cup and sipped the wine slowly, as she'd been taught. Had she been alone, she would have gulped it down like a man.

"Mulled wine is just the thing for you," Matilda said, as she had said nearly every morning for as long as Isabelle could remember. "It puts color in your cheeks and sweetens your breath. Now have some bread, milady. You never eat enough bread in the morning."

Isabelle winced as Matilda combed out a tangle in her hair, which hung down her back to her waist, but the old woman ignored her protest. When she had combed Isabelle's hair to her satisfaction, she began plaiting it into two thick braids, weaving in the silver thread.

"Oh, Mattie," Isabelle sighed. "You never stop trying to improve on nature. You can embroider rough cloth to your heart's content, and all you'll get is gaudy homespun."

"Don't talk nonsense, child," Matilda said sharply, but then she continued in a gentler tone. "You're more beautiful than you know. I don't know why you listen to the idiotic songs of those bleating trouvères. Half of them are fairies. Do you actually believe that men have eyes only for pallid blonds with flat chests and tiny, pouting mouths?"

Isabelle was about to reply when she caught the faint ringing of ax blades biting into tree trunks somewhere in the distance. She stiffened and cocked her head. In other circumstances it would have been an innocuous sound, but not now—not to the defenders of a castle under siege.

"Finish quickly, Mattie," she said tensely. "It's time I made my appearance; Ranulf will be expecting me."

"Patience, milady. It takes time to do this just right."

"Then never mind the thread," Isabelle said, starting to rise. "I'll—"

Matilda gripped Isabelle's shoulder firmly and forced her back onto the bed. "A few minutes longer will make no difference, milady, and it is important that you carry on with style—no matter how you feel inside. That is what Sir Ranulf and the men expect of you; it's what they need. You know that better than I."

Isabelle shifted restlessly but then nodded, acquiescing. "You're right," she muttered.

"Of course," Matilda replied in a matter-of-fact tone. "I'm almost finished, anyway. Your hair is like burnished copper, dear, and silver is just the thing to set it off."

Matilda tied off the braids with a pair of scarlet ribbons, went to the chest at the foot of the bed and took out a flowing *bliaut* of scarlet silk, not unlike a modern dressing gown, with wide, trailing sleeves. Isabelle slipped it on over the *pelisse*, and Matilda tightened the laces that drew the *bliaut* in at the waist, emphasizing her figure, and added a girdle of silver rope, tied in front with one end hanging down to the floor.

Isabelle's white, fur-lined cape also hung on the wall pole, and Matilda took it down and draped it over Isabelle's shoulders, fastening the gold clasp chain and making final adjustments to make sure the cape and *bliaut* hung correctly. The final touch was a delicate silver headband.

"How do I look, Mattie?" Isabelle asked.

"Like what you are, milady," Matilda answered with a nod of encouragement.

Lady Isabelle de Clare took a deep breath and, accepting for yet another day the burden of her responsibility, lifted her head and went out to greet her men.

Ranulf de Barre paced slowly along the inner fighting platform of the wooden palisade surrounding the castle courtyard, trying to relieve the early-morning stiffness in his joints. He envied the youngsters who had come on watch with him for their freedom of movement, which they took for granted. The air was still, crisp, and clear, and once he would have found its mild chill invigorating, but Ranulf was feeling his age.

The old knight turned and looked toward the distant camp of their enemy, Meiler fitz Henry. The castle had been built on a promontory rising above the forest and jutting out into the river far below, beside which lay the village of Kilkenny. The villagers had recently cut a fresh clearing out of the forest beyond the marshland bordering the river, and it was in this field that the warlord had established his camp.

The camp was more than a mile and a half away, but Ranulf could see enough to know that time was working against him. The tents dotting the clearing grew more numerous each day, as Meiler's recruiting efforts added to his force, and apparently an engineer had arrived. In the center of the camp, work crews were hewing tree trunks into heavy timbers with the obvious intention of constructing a trebuchet—a simple, but effective, siege catapult.

Meiler fitz Henry had not expected resistance when he had come down from the north to take Kilkenny with only a token force; but when Ranulf had refused to surrender custody of the castle, Meiler had lost no time preparing a siege. His force now numbered at least two hundred.

Excluding the castle's varlets, Ranulf could muster only thirty fighting men, but fifteen of these were Welsh archers, handpicked masters of the longbow, and until the trebuchet was built, Ranulf had no fear of a daylight assault.

The old frontier castle did not conform to the standard motte-and-bailey design. Its stone tower keep and wooden outbuildings were surrounded by a single wooden palisade, and it was protected on three sides by the sheer cliffs dropping down to the river, allowing the defenders to concentrate on the forward wall.

To reach the wall, attackers had to cross a deep, dry moat, and the long, steep slope leading up to the castle from the forest was devoid of

48

cover. Ranulf's archers could cut an attack force to pieces before they could scale the palisade.

But a night attack would be chancier, and soon Meiler would have his trebuchet. Already woodsmen were felling trees to clear a track through the forest so that the catapult could be hauled from the camp to the base of the slope before the castle. Ranulf had no doubt that the old wooden stockade could be breached, and when that happened, they would be forced back into the stone tower. . . .

"You look worried, Ranulf."

The old knight started. "You should wear bells, Rusty!" he snapped, turning toward Isabelle. "You're as quiet as a cat."

"Worried *and* grouchy," Isabelle said with a slight, nervous smile.

Ranulf reddened. "I'm sorry, milady," he said, remembering his place. His voice grated harshly; like many knights who had survived to his age, he had ruined his vocal cords in battle.

Ranulf had pledged to serve Isabelle de Clare as faithfully as he had her father, but sometimes he forgot that she was no longer the mischievous little girl who had fled to him so often for protection against a tutor's wrath. She had a quick mind, but as a child she had preferred mock swordplay with her father's pages to her tutors' lessons.

Yet only he could still think of her as a child, Ranulf reflected as he looked at the striking young woman beside him. The copper-colored hair, the freckles, and the impish, turned-up nose were the same, but the skinny little tomboy was no more.

And as she looked at him the seriousness in her green eyes was not a child's gravity but an adult's grim understanding. "Well?" she prompted, her voice husky like her father's.

Ranulf glanced about to be sure none of his men was within earshot, but the nearest of them had tactfully moved away. In the confines of a castle, privacy was as cherished as it was difficult to obtain.

"It appears Meiler is building a trebuchet."

"I know."

"Well, that gives us two—maybe three—weeks before he forces us back into the tower. The well in the keep is reliable enough, so we can probably hold out for months. But Meiler will make life hell for us in there, and eventually he'll either undermine the walls or scurvy will drive us out. He's cutting down our options, milady."

Isabelle looked toward the enemy camp, and her tongue flicked out to moisten her lips, a nervous mannerism she had inherited from her mother. Her parents' blood had melded evenly in their only child, Ranulf thought, in her emotional makeup as well as in her appearance.

"And no word from Meath," she said needlessly.

Ranulf shook his head. "Even if the messenger got through, it's too soon to expect a response."

For a moment longer Isabelle continued to stare out at Meiler's camp, unconsciously biting her lower lip, but then her expression hardened. "I won't give up Kilkenny now—not without a fight."

"I'm not suggesting surrender, milady," Ranulf said carefully, "but *you* could still slip out and try to get through to Meath yourself. Meiler hasn't invested the castle because he knows there will be no relief force, but once he discovers your presence here, or drives us into the tower, you'll be trapped."

Isabelle shook her head sharply. "No. By now John has undoubtedly guessed my whereabouts, and he'll have his agents out in force. If our courier can't get through, what chance have I? When John intercepted my petition, we lost the first round, Ranulf, but we may still win. If our message reaches Lord Meath, he will surely bring our case before the King; and even if our man has failed, it still makes sense to hold out here as long as we can. Word of the siege is bound to spread; sooner or later Meath will hear of it."

Ranulf shifted uneasily, unsure of how to respond. Isabelle knew her own mind, and he couldn't fault her reasoning, but Ranulf could not be so cold-blooded about it. At all costs he wanted her out of harm's way.

When he had decided not to yield Kilkenny, he had known full well that he and his men might pay with their lives, but he had been determined to force John's theft of Isabelle's lands out into the open. It had never occurred to him that Isabelle might flee Pembroke and join him, and he had been horrified when she'd appeared without warning and slipped into the castle.

Ranulf had never dreamed she would be so reckless, and her explanation had been puzzlingly vague. Only the guilt he felt for drawing her into danger had prevented him from giving her a tongue-lashing.

If something went wrong and they were overrun before they could establish themselves in the keep, Meiler might lose control of his undisciplined Irish auxiliaries. Ranulf had seen men flushed with victory and blood lust run amok. . . . No, she could not stay. He should have sent her north days ago, as soon as she had rested from her flight from Wales.

Ranulf made up his mind and was about to speak when a cry from the watchman on the tower's battlements distracted him. A small party of horsemen was emerging from the forest at the base of the slope before the castle. Meiler fitz Henry, mounted on a richly caparisoned coal-black charger, was in the lead, followed by his knights and their squires. Beside Meiler rode his standard bearer, carrying Meiler's saffron banner emblazoned with a black falcon.

"What the hell?" Ranulf growled. "They're decked out as if for tournament."

Meiler's knights were also mounted on their chargers, which were draped with bright ceremonial caparisons. The knights' jewel-studded reins and saddles sparkled in the sunlight, and their shields gleamed with new paint.

It was Isabelle who guessed the implications. "I think this is for my benefit," she said softly. "Meiler must have heard from John. He knows I'm here."

"Son of a—" Ranulf growled. Then he hastily moved to screen Isabelle from view. "He can't be sure," he said urgently. "If he doesn't see you—"

"It doesn't matter, Ranulf," Isabelle interrupted, reaching out and grasping Ranulf's rough hand. She smiled slightly and shook her head. "Old friend, did you really think you could persuade me to leave you to fight my battle?"

Her voice was steady, and in that moment Ranulf realized that he'd underestimated the tenacity of his young mistress. Face-to-face with her enemy, Isabelle was entirely her father's daughter.

Although the watchmen had not sounded the alarm, the men off watch were running to join the archers on the wall, who had unslung their bows and were selecting the straightest arrows from their quivers. But in the courtyard below, the blacksmith continued his hammering, and the marshal yelled at his varlets to carry on with their chores.

Ranulf grunted sourly as Meiler reined in his horse just out of bowshot and his men fanned out behind him. "Just a little closer, you bastard," Ranulf muttered, "and we might waste an arrow on you."

"Hello, the castle!" cried Meiler's standard bearer, his voice carrying clearly up to the stockade. "My lord, Sir Meiler, salutes Lady Isabelle and begs to know why she resists the command of her guardian, Count John, to surrender custody of Kilkenny."

Isabelle compressed her lips and stepped past Ranulf so that she was clearly visible to the eyes below. "Is your lord's voice so tender that he cannot speak for himself?" she called out. "Or is it that the words would stick in his throat?"

Ranulf grinned in spite of himself, wishing he could see the expression on Meiler's face. The Marcher lord would not relish being goaded by a woman in front of his men. But to Ranulf's surprise, Meiler kept his temper. "If Your Ladyship grants me leave to approach," Meiler called, "we may yet settle our differences in a peaceful manner."

"Come forward if you wish, Sir Meiler," Isabelle responded without consulting Ranulf.

As Meiler spurred his charger up the slope, Ranulf called to his archers, "No man pulls his bow without my command!" Then he lowered his voice and grumbled, "A parley will gain us nothing, milady."

"I know," Isabelle said calmly, managing a smile, "but I haven't seen him since I was a child, and I'm curious to know if he's really as ugly as I remember him."

Meiler fitz Henry was a burly knight, and his saddle creaked under his weight as he reined in his stallion at the edge of the dry moat. *Ugly* was too strong a word, but there was little charm in his swarthy, beetle-browed face. His head sat low on his shoulders, and black curls of oily hair poked out from beneath his mail coif.

"Your Ladyship," Meiler said, bowing his head formally, "I bid you a good morning."

"Sir Meiler," Isabelle responded coldly, "you trespass on my father's land."

"Not so, Your Ladyship. I have orders from Count John, entrusting the custody of Kilkenny to my protection. When I arrived ten days ago to fulfill my duty, the former castellan, who stands beside you, unlawfully denied me entry."

"Your order, Sir Meiler," Isabelle replied haughtily, "is but one of several my guardian has seen fit to issue in the past year. He has been parceling out my father's lands as if they were his own. But I will stand for it no longer."

"That is not your prerogative, Lady Isabelle!" Meiler snapped. "You are the Count's ward until you marry. By law and custom it is your guardian who decides how best to safeguard your inheritance."

"A responsibility for which he has shown a fine disregard!" Isabelle shot back. "I am not a fool to be despoiled so easily. My father fought for these lands, and if my guardian will not defend them, then I have no choice but to defend them myself. I will not surrender Kilkenny until the King hears my petition and decides on the justice of my grievance."

"*John* is Lord of Ireland," Meiler responded, "not Henry. Count John is my liege lord, as he is yours, and he has commanded the surrender of Kilkenny to me."

"And we dispute the lawfulness of the command," Ranulf interjected harshly. "The King is the final arbiter in all his dominions, and we will not yield Kilkenny until the case is heard in a royal court."

Meiler's thick eyebrows rose, and Ranulf had the uncomfortable feeling that Meiler had been waiting for just those words. What was the bastard up to?

"The King is in France and we are here, Sir Ranulf," Meiler said with a self-satisfied smile. "Yet I have no wish to deny Lady Isabelle the justice she seeks." He paused, and his smile widened into a gap-toothed grin. "You are her knight. Let us put her case before the highest arbiter of all. Meet me now in single combat as her champion, and let God decide the outcome."

So that's his game, Ranulf thought, *humiliate me in front of my men and draw me into a one-sided duel for a cheap victory*. Ranulf smiled. It was a feeble ploy, but as close to cleverness as Meiler could come.

Isabelle didn't take it so lightly. Ranulf heard her sharp intake of breath. "Oh, *gallant* knight," she said with heavy irony. "How bravely you choose an opponent. But are you sure his beard is gray enough?"

Meiler ignored the jibe. "And what do *you* say, Sir Ranulf," he sneered. "Do you have the courage to defend your lady's claim to this castle?"

"Easy, Rusty," Ranulf said quietly as Isabelle clenched her fists in fury. "I've too thick a skin to be drawn out so easily. He dishonors no one but himself."

"Well, Sir Ranulf?" Meiler shouted. "Do you accept my challenge, or do your shrink from defending the justice of your lady's cause?"

There was complete silence on the wall as Ranulf's men tensely awaited his response, and Ranulf let the silence stretch out. "Not today, I'm afraid," he said at last in an offhand tone. "My arthritis is giving me a bad time."

At that, a pikeman on the far end of the stockade wall snorted, and the tension dissolved in general laughter. Meiler flushed darkly.

"Your mockery is born of cowardice, Sir Ranulf! Not today, you said. Then I will come tomorrow to repeat my challenge, and the day after, and the day after that. But then I will waste no more breath, and we shall take this castle by storm. In the meantime let your men reflect on the courage—or the lack of it—of the man who leads then."

Meiler pulled on his reins to turn away, but Ranulf was in no mood to let him go so easily.

"A moment, Sir Meiler!" Ranulf cried. "I have a question to put to you."

Ranulf barked an order in Welsh, and his archers drew their longbows.

"My question is this," Ranulf grated, "how do you expect to get back down the hill?"

Meiler looked up in confusion at the fifteen steel-tipped shafts trained on his heart, and his face paled. "What treachery is this?" he yelled, the anger in his voice failing to mask his sudden fear.

"Treachery?" Isabelle said innocently, picking up her cue. "I gave you permission to approach, Sir Meiler—if you *wished* to. I did not guarantee your safe return. Neither you nor your men carry a flag of truce."

"That was understood!" Meiler burst out, hastily lifting his shield. But he knew it was no protection; a longbow shaft at close range could penetrate four inches of solid oak.

Isabelle gave him a saccharine smile. "In the interest of sport, we'll give you a bit of a head start. Your horse appears swift; perhaps he can carry you to safety in time. But I would go quickly, Sir Meiler," she said sharply. "I would go now!"

With an animal snarl, Meiler wheeled his horse about and dug in his spurs, and Ranulf signaled his archers to stand down. Instead of arrows, the men sent whistles and catcalls after the fleeing knight.

Ranulf laughed along with the rest, but it was gallows humor. If Kilkenny fell, he could expect no mercy from Meiler fitz Henry.

5

Ranulf de Barre cursed the rain. Without moonlight the darkness enveloping the stockade was impenetrable, and the tattoo of wind-driven raindrops on the heavy canvas hood of his rain cloak was loud in his ears. If the bastards had any imagination, Ranulf thought grimly, they would come now, under cover of the storm, when his archers would be least effective.

He had been standing very still, staring out into the darkness, listening, straining to detect that first telltale clink of metal on metal, or the snort of a horse, but now he had to move, lest his arthritic joints lock up. The old knight grunted with pain as he forced his body into motion.

The silent castle was all but blacked out. The bright night-combat torches would not be lit unless the enemy attacked, and the standard torches burning on the outer wall cast little light into the castle's interior. Ranulf had to feel his way along the stockade's fighting platform.

His shoulder and chest muscles were tiring under the weight of his hauberk. There had been a time when he could have worn the armor for sixteen hours without fatigue, but no longer. Had it been a day watch, he could have laid aside his armor, but a night attack would come with too little warning.

Ranulf had ordered his men to sleep in their fighting armor, their swords girded and their longbows strung. They would be stretched out and snoring by now, warm and dry in the great hall of the keep. They were young men and needed sleep more than he. Fulk le Brun, another old veteran, was standing the tower watch. Ranulf twisted his head to look back up at the stone tower at the rear of the castle courtyard, but despite its whitewashed walls, the keep was only visible as an ill-defined mass merging with the night.

Ranulf stiffened as he picked up the sound of horses' iron-shod hooves clattering over a granite outcropping that cut across the open slope just below the dry moat surrounding the stockade wall. "Horseman coming!" cried Fulk from the parapet of the keep.

"Hello, the castle!" called the approaching rider. He did not shout, but his voice was clearly audible, a resonant baritone that carried through the wind and rain.

Ranulf focused his eyes in the direction of the voice and made out the shadowy form of a horse and rider on the very edge of the dry moat, barely illuminated by the flickering torch above the main gate.

"Who are you?" Ranulf challenged.

"I am called William Marshal. I request shelter and rest within your walls."

That drew a laugh from the old warrior. "God's blood, man, don't you know we're under siege? We need fighters, not guests."

"I must speak with the castellan, Ranulf de Barre. I have come a long way to see him."

Ranulf frowned. He couldn't place the stranger's name, but somewhere he had heard it. "*What* are you? A trouvère? A messenger? What?" he demanded, his eyes restlessly sweeping the darkness. He hadn't forgotten the enemy.

"I am a free knight, recently returned from the Holy Land."

Ranulf's frown deepened, and he held his breath, listening. If this was a diversion, it was an odd one. The stranger was not one of Meiler fitz Henry's cronies, for although he spoke with an Anglo-Norman drawl, his grammar had the polish of the Continent. Perhaps he was a mercenary in Meiler's pay.

"A knight? Traveling alone, without even a squire? State your business or clear out."

"I will speak with Ranulf de Barre."

"You're speaking to him now," Ranulf growled.

"I have much to tell you," replied the stranger. "But I will not do so sitting my horse in the rain."

The undertone of aggressive self-assurance beneath the fatigue in the stranger's voice was unmistakable. He was either a knight, as he claimed, or a consummate actor.

And then Ranulf remembered where he had heard the stranger's name.

"I saw a knight called William Marshal fight in the great tournament at Joigni in '77," Ranulf called out. "Are you that knight?"

"That was a long time ago. I may have been at Joigni."

Ranulf felt the tug of professional curiosity. The knight Ranulf had watched that day had been the best man with a sword and lance he had ever seen. Hadn't Marshal ridden with Prince Henry? Once, years afterward, he'd heard Marshal's name again. There had been a scandal involving young Henry's wife. . . .

Ranulf grimaced sourly; he was woolgathering like an old man. "I wouldn't open our gate to Christ Himself this night," he shouted. "You found your way up here from the village. Find your way back and seek shelter there."

The stranger did not reply. The gusting rain dimmed the torch, obscuring the horse and rider, and for a moment Ranulf thought the knight had gone.

"Your son is dead, Sir Ranulf," said the stranger out of the darkness. "I have brought you his sword."

The torch above the sally port in the stockade's eastern wall had been lighted, and it hissed and sputtered in the downpour. Ranulf's fingers curled around the trigger lever of his crossbow as the stranger, mounted on a palfrey and leading a charger and packhorse, rode through the narrow gateway into the torchlight. The knight was shrouded in a black rain cloak, but his chain-mail leggings were visible. He was a big man, built for combat, and he was fully armed.

"Welcome to Castle Kilkenny," Ranulf grated. "I am Ranulf de Barre." There was no cordiality in his voice, and the crossbow was aimed at the stranger's chest.

"William Marshal," the knight said.

Ranulf's squire stepped forward to take the palfrey's reins, and the two archers Ranulf had awakened to cover the entrance heaved the timbers barring the sally port back into place.

"Give me a hand with my shield, son," Marshal said to the squire, and as the boy took the shield, Ranulf saw that Marshal's left forearm was bound in a splint. "Broke my wrist getting off the boat in Waterford," Marshal said. "Damned gangplank was rotten."

With a tired grunt Marshal dismounted, and the short leather boots he wore over his chain mail sank a full two inches into the mud. Ranulf was above average height, but Marshal was even taller. Two hundred and thirty pounds with his armor on, Ranulf estimated, and from the look of him, not an ounce of fat.

Now Ranulf was sure this was the knight he'd seen at Joigni; even after ten years he remembered him. Marshal had taken out ten of the best knights on the field that day, and broken wrist or not, he was dangerous.

Marshal pushed back his hood so that his face was no longer in shadow and walked toward Ranulf, careful to stop just out of arm's reach of the crossbow. "My manservant broke his shoulder," Marshal said, "and I had to leave him behind."

It was a long trip up from Waterford, and Marshal's face was etched with fatigue; that much of his story tallied, Ranulf noted. Although closely trimmed beards were in fashion, Marshal was clean-shaven, and that also fit. Beards inside a helmet could become intolerable in the desert heat, and many returning pilgrim knights retained the habit of shaving.

"I suppose you have a right to be cautious," Marshal said, looking pointedly at the crossbow.

Ranulf nodded grimly. "I learned of my son's death two months ago. Meiler fitz Henry may have heard the news as well, and he's fond of tricks."

"Perhaps," Marshal said tiredly, his mouth turned down at the corners. "I don't know the man."

Marshal had a high forehead and a broken nose that gave him a hawklike profile. His deep-set brown eyes, glinting in the torchlight, were framed by projecting eyebrows and prominent cheekbones. His was a hard face that fatigue could not soften.

But Ranulf could detect neither guile nor cruelty in his expression. They left their stamp, and Ranulf had lived too long to be easily fooled. Women remained a mystery to Ranulf, but he knew men.

"You may have my sword if you wish," Marshal added. "Crossbows make me nervous."

Ranulf didn't believe that last statement, for he suspected that to a man like Marshal, nervousness would be only a word. But the offer of the sword removed the last of Ranulf's doubts. "That won't be necessary," he said, lowering the crossbow and disarming it.

"Jean," Ranulf said to his squire, "see that Sir William's horses are taken care of, and then attend us in the great hall. We'll be wanting food and drink. Griff, Peter—take over my watch on the wall."

Marshal shivered as he followed Ranulf de Barre up the steps of the wooden platform before the keep and across the drawbridge to the raised entrance. The fatigue of the long, damp ride was catching up with him. Ranulf pushed open the massive oak door, and they entered the smoky gloom of the tower's great hall.

Two mastiffs rose from their place by the fire and trotted across the hall to investigate the stranger. "They're good dogs," Ranulf said. "Can kill a boar between the two of them."

Marshal nodded absently. A strange sense of déjà vu had gripped him as he had stepped across the threshold. Although many of the keeps the Normans had built throughout Britain in a century of occupation were similar, no two were completely alike; yet something in the stark architecture of this tower evoked lost memories. The keep seemed hauntingly familiar, filling Marshal with an uneasiness he could not understand.

Shrugging off the feeling, he walked toward the warmth of the fire. The tower's builder had designed a strong keep but a primitive one, and the smoke holes above the open hearth were insufficient. Much of the smoke drifted up to the blackened rafters, where it collected in a thick cloud and eddied out through the arrow slits of the overhead gallery. Mingling with the acrid wood smoke was the pungent scent of unwashed bodies. Ranulf's men lay snoring on straw pallets in the shadows, apparently undisturbed by the knights' entrance.

Ranulf came over to the fire, walking on bandy legs bowed from too many years in the saddle. Eustace had borne little resemblance to his father, Marshal noted. Ranulf was a barrel-chested man, with thick-shoulders, and age had only toughened his leathery, gray-bearded face.

"How did you get past Meiler's pickets?" Ranulf asked in his harsh, gravelly voice.

"I paid a villager to guide me. He took me up to the forest line along an old, overgrown track. If your enemy has pickets out, they're stretched pretty thin. I take it he doesn't anticipate a relief force anytime soon."

"There will be no relief," Ranulf said curtly.

Marshal cocked an eyebrow and looked about him, his eyes probing the hall's dark recesses. "Two men on the wall," he said quietly, "one on the parapet, and these men in here. Cutting it a bit fine, aren't you?"

"We can hold."

For the time being, perhaps, Marshal thought to himself, looking curiously at the tough, grizzled castellan. What kind of fight had he ridden into? Marshal was unfamiliar with the local dialect, and he had learned very little from the villagers. The rainstorm had given him the chance to slip into the castle, but getting out again might not be so easy.

According to Eustace, Ranulf held Kilkenny from the King, which made a siege impossible to understand. And why did Ranulf de Barre expect no relief? "Just what claim does this Meiler fitz Henry have to Kilkenny?" Marshal asked.

"You're a cool one," Ranulf replied. "Not many men would ride into the middle of a siege they knew nothing about."

Marshal waited for Ranulf to respond to his question, but the old knight remained silent. Marshal blinked wearily; he was exhausted, his broken wrist was throbbing, and he was in no mood for verbal fencing. Perhaps Ranulf still didn't trust him.

"I told you why I came," Marshal said, drawing the sword slung from his waist and extending it hilt first toward Ranulf. The blade, which gleamed orange in the firelight, was deeply dented and chipped along both edges. "This was your son's," he said. "He used it to save my life."

Marshal had handled the sword countless times in the ten months of his journey back from the Holy Land, but as he looked at it now, the memories came flooding back with remorseless clarity. He should have found a way to shield Eustace from the madness of that day. The boy had not been ready. He should have found a way. . . .

Ranulf stared in silence at the sword for a moment before he took it in his hands, and Marshal saw his shoulders slump as if suddenly burdened by a great weight. Ranulf had said he knew his son was dead, but perhaps until now, Eustace's death had been an abstraction.

"I gave Eustace this sword," Ranulf said hoarsely. "Just before he left Ireland. A man is supposed to be proud when a son dies bravely, but pride can't make up for the loss."

Marshal remained silent. What was there to say? He had no experience of the love between a father and son.

"You knew him, then?" Ranulf asked.

Marshal nodded. "He was my squire, but he died a knight, Sir Ranulf. I knighted him myself before our last battle."

Something like a sigh escaped the old knight. "So he had that much at least. He wanted it so damn much. Not every man is born for battle, and I tried to tell him . . ."

Ranulf took a deep breath, and his spine stiffened. "Where the hell is that squire of mine?" he growled. "I know you're tired, Sir William. Food and rest is what you need; we can talk tomorrow."

"I'm not too tired for talk," Marshal lied.

"Are you sure?"

Marshal saw the desire in Ranulf's eyes, and he nodded.

"Then we'll talk," Ranulf said. "There's much I'd like to know."

The fire in the great hall had burned low, and Marshal rose to add fresh wood. One of Ranulf's dogs lifted his head, yawned, and went back to sleep. Tending fires was servants' work, but this garrison was of fighting men only, and Ranulf's squire, who had attended them, had gone off to dry and polish Marshal's chain mail before it rusted. Marshal staggered as dizziness swept over him, and he cursed silently. Wine always hit him hard when he was tired, and he knew that he would pay for his carelessness in the morning.

Ranulf's squire had helped the two knights free themselves of their hauberks and then had brought them bread, wine, and a bowl of congealed, warmed-over stew. Not bothering to have a trestle table set up, they had piled straw before the fire and sat down on the floor. Clad in their tunics and linen breeches, with mantles draped over their shoulders to keep the chill off their backs, they had eaten their fill and fed the rest to the dogs.

The flat, round loaves of bread had been stale, and the spice in the stew had barely masked the flavor of the nameless boiled meat, but Marshal had not cared. Even court life in France, where he had feasted on the finest foods available, had not cultivated his palate. For Marshal, food was little more than an antidote to hunger.

Marshal tossed a log onto the embers, and the fire crackled back to life, spraying sparks. Ranulf, who had been sitting for a long time in silence staring at the fire, looked up, his sorrow masked behind flinty eyes.

"I thank you for coming here," he said. "I'm in your debt."

Marshal sat down heavily. His eyes stung from the smoke and the need for sleep. "The debt was mine," he said, finding the words hopelessly inadequate. Eustace had not simply saved his life; the boy had died in Marshal's place, fighting in a battle in which he should have taken no part.

"Maybe," Ranulf said, "but not every man would come so far out of his way."

Marshal shook his head, but he let it pass. Ranulf poured fresh wine into the cup they shared, drank some, then passed the cup. He had been drinking steadily but without apparent effect. The wine had eased the throbbing in Marshal's wrist, but already he felt the onset of a headache.

"I'd assumed until now that Eustace was killed with all the others at Hattin," Ranulf said. "God, what a disaster. It's still hard to believe it could happen."

Marshal nodded grimly and looked into the fire. One month after he'd left Palestine, the Grand Master and Guy de Lusignan, King of Jerusalem, had led the kingdom's army into an obvious trap before the Horns of Hattin, ten miles from where de Maille and his men had been wiped out. Saladin had annihilated the Christian army of ninety thousand men in a cataclysmic two-day battle, and shortly afterward he'd taken Jerusalem.

Marshal took a token sip of wine and set the cup down. *I should have killed the bastard*, he thought bitterly.

"What are your plans now?" Ranulf asked.

"Before I left for the Holy Land, I promised the King I'd return to his service. From here I'll be going directly to his court," Marshal said with a sense of detachment.

For him the future was a blank, and he still felt suspended in an emotional limbo somewhere between Palestine and the homeland to which he'd returned. The short time he had spent on the family estates in England before crossing to Ireland had not acclimated him, and the visit had only reminded him of how far he had drifted from his older brothers. They had never been close, and Marshal's only real ties to his family had been severed long ago by the deaths of his mother and his uncle, who had trained him as a knight.

Marshal looked forward to joining Henry's mesne, for the King's service offered him the best chance to acquire land of his own. His years with Prince Henry had gained him nothing beyond a reputation, and it was time to win a permanent place in the world before it was too late. But his hopes remained abstract, without clear definition.

"I don't need to tell you that I wish you luck," Ranulf said, leaning back in the straw. "You can rest up tomorrow and slip out tomorrow night. The sooner you get out of here, the better—before Meiler decides to tighten his siege."

"Why should he, if you expect no relief?"

"He'll have his reasons."

"Look," Marshal said. "Don't you think it's time you told me what's happening here?"

Ranulf shook his head. "It's not your concern. Do yourself a favor and ride on out of here tomorrow night without looking back."

But Marshal was no longer willing to be put off. He liked this gruff, hard-bitten veteran, and he couldn't simply ride away. He stared at Ranulf until the old knight met his eyes. "What is Meiler fitz Henry's claim to this castle?" he asked.

"Count John, our exalted Lord of Ireland," Ranulf growled, "has given him leave to seize Kilkenny."

"What! I thought you held Kilkenny for the King."

"This isn't the King's land. All of Leinster belongs to the House of Pembroke."

"But Eustace told me that Pembroke died years ago. Didn't his lands revert to the Crown?"

Ranulf shook his head sharply. "The Earl had a daughter, Isabelle de Clare. She's heiress to all the Pembroke lands in Wales and in Ireland. I received custody of Kilkenny from the King's hand to hold for her for the duration of her minority."

Marshal frowned, trying to clear his head. "She can't still be a child."

"Hardly. She should have married long ago; she's already nineteen. But she's too rich a prize, and Henry has been holding her in reserve."

"Then how does John come into this?" Marshal asked impatiently. "He can't interfere with a ward of the King." He still did not understand what was going on, but one thing was certain: By resisting a royal order, Ranulf was courting a charge of treason.

"Lady Isabelle is John's ward, not Henry's," Ranulf said. "The bulk of her holdings are here in Ireland, and Henry gave her to John as ward when he made him Lord of Ireland. John has been giving her lands to his cronies, and by God, this is where it stops! We're not giving up Kilkenny before Lady Isabelle's case is put before the King."

Marshal stared at Ranulf in disbelief. "My God, man, you're playing with fire."

Ranulf's expression hardened. "I don't need you to tell me that," he said. "I may be old, but I'm not senile."

"You could have fooled me," Marshal responded sharply, his concern emerging as anger. He saw at once that Ranulf hoped to force

John's misuse of the heiress's lands out into the open, but this was the wrong time for such a gamble.

"What is John getting in return for the fiefs he's been handing out?" Marshal asked. "Promises of future support?"

Ranulf nodded grimly. "So you *have* heard what's been going on in the last few years."

"Enough," Marshal said bleakly. The rumors had reached as far as the Holy Land, and Marshal had confirmed them during his brief stay with his brothers in England. Henry, it was said, was slipping and could no longer control his sons.

At the age of nineteen, Henry of Anjou—Duke of Normandy; Count of Anjou, Maine, and Touraine; and pretender to the Throne of England—had burst upon the European political scene by marrying Eleanor of Aquitaine, the cast-off queen of Louis VII of France.

In acquiring the Aquitaine, Henry had taken his first great step toward forging an empire that would encompass Britain and half of France—an empire he was strong and clever enough to hold for a third of a century. But in Eleanor, eleven years his senior and as intelligent as she was strong-willed, he had found a woman too much like himself, a queen who had her own ambitions and vision of the future.

A breach between them had been inevitable, for only one could rule, and when it came, it was deep, bitter, and enduring. The Queen withdrew to her own court at Poitiers, in the heart of Aquitaine, to raise the four sons she had borne the King; and when the boys came of age in turn, they were Eleanor's sons, not Henry's, jealous of their father's power and impatient to have their own.

In 1173, Prince Henry had rebelled against his father. The rebellion was supported by King Louis of France, who was anxious to curb the English king's power, and by Eleanor; but young Henry was more puppet than leader, and his father snuffed out the revolt.

Henry loved his namesake, and he forgave the prince as quickly as he had crushed the rebellion. Eleanor was not as lucky. She had been captured en route to the French court in Paris, and Henry sent her to England under permanent house arrest.

Ten years later Prince Henry tried again. King Louis had died three years earlier, and this time the prince was supported by Louis's son, Philip. Again Henry crushed the revolt, and again he forgave his wayward son. Shortly thereafter Prince Henry died of fever, and he was soon followed to the grave by his brother, Geoffry of Brittany, leaving two brothers as potential heirs to the Throne of England: Richard and John.

John was everything Richard was not. Richard was tawny-haired, tall, stocky, and powerful—physically a larger version of his father. John was short, slight, and dark with neither the strength nor inclination for knightly combat. Where Richard bellowed, John whined; where Richard challenged, John conspired; and where Richard forgave, John exacted revenge. Devious and indolent, John still behaved like a spoiled child. Yet John was reportedly Henry's favorite.

It was an open secret that John was using his power and privileges as Lord of Ireland to curry favor, in the hope of supplanting his brother as heir to the Throne; but Henry, worried and preoccupied by Richard's strength and ambition, turned a deaf ear to the whispers against John.

And that was what made Ranulf's resistance to John so dangerous. Years ago Henry would have looked beyond a charge of treason to investigate its cause; he would have listened to a plea for justice. But now the King appeared determined to ignore his youngest son's intrigues.

"You could swing for this," Marshal said grimly.

"They'll have to take Kilkenny first."

"So?" Marshal snapped with deliberate sarcasm. "How much time does that give you? A month? Two months? Through the summer, if you're really lucky. And then you'll hang. You can't defend your lady's rights from the end of a rope."

Ranulf's leathery face hardened into a stubborn mask. "It's not your problem."

Marshal expelled his breath in a hiss of frustration. His head was pounding now. "Why didn't Lady Isabelle find an intermediary to bring her case before His Majesty?"

"She tried; we're not fools!" Ranulf snapped. "She sent her priest to beg the intercession of the Bishop of Llandaff, but John intercepted him. In all probability the man is dead."

Marshal nodded grimly. From what he'd heard, John was probably ruthless enough to eliminate the priest and clever enough to get away with it. If so, he was prepared to go to any lengths to hide his maneuvering in Ireland from the King.

"We sent a messenger north to the Lord of Meath," Ranulf said, "but we can't be sure he'll get through. Nevertheless, Meath is bound to hear of this siege if we hold out long enough. He and Earl Richard were friends; he'll care enough to find out what's happening here."

"And even if he does," Marshal responded sharply, "what makes you think the King will side with you? You're committing treason, old man; that's the line John will take. Do you think the King can afford to tolerate rebellion?"

"I received Kilkenny from the King," Ranulf grated, "and John never bothered to secure my homage. Technically he isn't my liege lord, so my resistance cannot be considered treason."

Marshal said nothing. Technically Ranulf was right, but he didn't need Marshal to tell him that the argument was parchment-thin. And Ranulf undoubtedly had no friends at Court; there would be no one to argue on his behalf.

"There's no other way," Ranulf said stiffly, responding to the grim look on Marshal's face.

But there was another way, Marshal knew.

He turned away, resisting the impulse to become involved. It *wasn't* his problem, damn it, and the last thing he wanted was to make an enemy of John. Perhaps he could have ignored the instincts of a lifetime and let it go. Perhaps. But as Marshal stared into the fire he was seeing Eustace astride the roan, shielding Marshal with his sword as the last of his blood poured down his side and splattered onto the dusty earth. The debt was there, not to be denied.

"There is another way," Marshal said at last. "You could negotiate an honorable surrender with Meiler and come out of Kilkenny with me. End your resistance now, before it's too late. I have the ear of the King, Ranulf. I was father in chivalry to his son, and he will listen to me. I can promise that your lady's case will be heard."

Marshal thought he saw hope flare briefly in Ranulf's eyes, but the moment passed and the old knight's eyes were again flint-hard and unreadable.

"That's a generous offer," Ranulf said finally.

"Accept it, Ranulf. Accept it in payment for the debt I owe your son."

Ranulf did not respond at once. Thoughtfully he scratched his wiry gray beard. "An honorable surrender may no longer be possible," he said slowly. "Not if Meiler believes he has the upper hand."

"You have nothing to lose by trying. Let me negotiate with him— as an outside party. He knows he can take this castle eventually, but he also knows the cost."

"There are complications—"

"What complications?" Marshal said impatiently. "Your mistress would not want you to make a hopeless stand when an alternative is open to you. In any event, you can't consult her. John must be determined to keep this quiet; he'll be holding her incommunicado at this point."

"That's the complication," Ranulf said with a thin, humorless smile. "John is not holding her at all."

Marshal's eyebrows shot up in surprise. "Where is she, then?"

Ranulf pointed a blunt forefinger toward the ceiling. "Sleeping right above us. Lady Isabelle bribed her way out of Pembroke Castle, crossed over to Ireland, and slipped in here five nights ago."

6

Marshal awoke with a start from a wine-drugged sleep, jolted into consciousness by the castle alarm. On the tower's parapet, the watchman was hammering on a sheet of copper, the blows sounding like thin, high-pitched thunderclaps. Marshal sat up too suddenly, and he groaned aloud as a wave of pain slammed against the inside of his skull. His queasy stomach contracted, and he gritted his teeth against the spasm, swallowing back the acid that rose in his throat.

He took a deep breath and then another, waiting for the pain in his head to subside to manageable proportions. Marshal had slept in his robe on a pile of straw against one wall of the great hall, and while he had slept, someone—presumably Ranulf's squire—had set up a canvas screen to give him a measure of privacy. Marshal's two baggage chests had been placed nearby. His shield rested against the wall, and his own sword and armor had been laid out on a cloth on the floor.

The screen shielded him from the sunlight streaming into the hall through the arrow slits, but it was the wine that had kept him from awakening at first light. He guessed that it was at least an hour after dawn. From beyond the screen he heard men who had come off watch at dawn cursing sleepily as they gathered their weapons and stumbled out of the hall, leaving him alone.

Mercifully the tower watchman ceased his hammering, and Marshal sighed with relief. He tried to discern what was happening from the shouts drifting faintly in from the courtyard. The orders were in Welsh, of which he understood too little, but he detected no sense of urgency. An attack might be imminent, but it was not yet under way. Probably an overanxious tower watchman, Marshal thought sourly.

Marshal eased himself into a kneeling position to offer his morning prayer. He was sure there would be no Mass to hear in the chapel, for Ranulf was not the type to suffer a priest in a castle under siege. Marshal's view of religion was practical, and his prayer was short and to the point. "Please, oh, Lord," he murmured, "if I must fight today, take away my hangover first."

One of Ranulf's mastiffs had come over to Marshal, and now the dog licked his ear. Marshal irritably pushed the dog away. He hastily added a routine devotional to round out his prayer and got to his feet.

At that moment Ranulf's squire burst into the hall. "Alarm, sire!" he cried breathlessly, runnng toward Marshal.

"Softly, son, softly," Marshal said, closing his eyes and massaging his forehead.

"I'm sorry, sire."

"What's happening out there?" Marshal asked with his eyes still closed.

"Meiler's army is advancing through the forest, sire. Sir Ranulf and Lady Isabelle are on the forward palisade and ask that you join them at your convenience."

Marshal nodded and opened his eyes. The sunlight from the arrow slits diffused in the hall's smoky gray haze, but even that dim light seemed far too bright. "Was that the entire message?"

"Yes, sire—I mean no," the boy stammered, reddening. "Lady Isabelle asked me to convey her apology that she was unavailable to greet you upon your arrival."

"Never forget the details of a message, son—even the courtesies."

"Yes, sire."

"And never run if you don't have to. It sets a bad example for your men. Let them do the running."

"Yes, sire," the squire said again, now thoroughly chagrined.

"What's your name?" Marshal asked.

"Jean d'Erly, sire."

Marshal didn't recognize the family name, but that was not surprising. If Ranulf held a fief of his own from the House of Pembroke, it would be small, and he would not have a baron's son as squire.

Marshal looked at the boy, appraising him as automatically as he had instructed him. It did not matter that this was Ranulf's squire; the boy aspired to knighthood, and it was the duty of every knight to evaluate and guide the young men who might one day join their fellowship.

Jean d'Erly was tall and straight, with thick black hair that contrasted sharply with his fair, clear skin. He was fit and alert, and Marshal had noted that he was excited, not frightened, by the alarm. That was a good sign; an eagerness for combat was one essential quality that could not be instilled.

"All right, Jean. How long before Meiler has his troops in position?"

"Their encampment is almost two miles away, sire. Half an hour, perhaps a little longer."

"Plenty of time, then, whatever your enemies have in mind. Are you free to attend me?"

"Of course. I'll bring a washbasin for you and whatever else you require."

"I'm not hungry, but I'm thirsty as hell. Is your well clear?"

"Yes . . ." the squire said uncertainly.

"Is it or isn't it?"

"Yes, it is, sire, but—do you want to drink water?"

"Yes," Marshal said, ignoring the astonishment in the squire's eyes. "And some beer as well. Water to kill the thirst and beer to settle my stomach."

"Excuse me, sire, but you look as if you might have a headache."

"What of it?" Marshal said in irritation.

"I could bring you a dead man's tooth to hold."

Marshal smiled slightly. "Thanks, son, but that remedy's never worked for me."

Marshal turned away and walked toward the latrine chamber, built into the thick stone wall at the rear of the hall.

"Be careful of the splinters in the seat," the boy called after him, but Marshal didn't need the warning. He had discovered the dangers of the latrine's wooden seat the night before.

Marshal slowly climbed the stone staircase that spiraled up through the tower's wall to the parapet, his chain mail clinking softly in time to his measured steps. His headache was subsiding, but he had to rest at intervals to keep it under control. Before he went out to meet Ranulf and the mistress of Kilkenny, Marshal wanted to gauge the situation for himself.

He had to squint against the sunlight as he emerged onto the parapet. The storm had passed in the early hours of the morning, pushed aside by a front bringing the first warm air of spring. To the north, broken rain clouds hugged the horizon, but overhead the sky was clear. The red-

and-gold Pembroke banner flying from the peak of the tower's conical wooden roof flapped lazily in a soft southerly breeze. The clear air was a relief after the dank atmosphere of the tower.

The young watchman, standing on the catwalk encircling the base of the roof, touched his cap and said something in Welsh which Marshal didn't understand. In reply, Marshal summoned up a greeting in English. Like the others of Ranulf's garrison Marshal had seen, the watchman carried the Welsh longbow, and he had the well-developed chest and sinewy arms necessary to draw it.

Ranulf must have anticipated the possibility of a siege, Marshal thought, to have recruited so many longbowmen for his small garrison. Tactically it was a shrewd move that maximized defensive power with a minimum of mouths to feed, but Marshal was unimpressed. Sound tactics could not make up for a suicidal strategy.

He stepped to the edge of the stone parapet and looked out over the forest spreading out below them. In the distance a long column of men and carts crawled toward the castle along a narrow track from Meiler's encampment. The men and horses were largely screened from view by the overhanging treetops, but to Marshal it did not have the look of an assault force ready to storm the castle.

As Marshal had expected, it had been a false alarm. Ranulf had said that Meiler was building a trebuchet, and the warlord would certainly wait for his catapult. The castle's forward stockade wall cut across an open slope, dropping steeply down to the forest line. In front of the wall was a wide, dry moat screened by sharpened stakes and piles of brambles. As long as the stockade was intact, Ranulf's longbowmen would have no difficulty stopping a daylight attack.

Had not Meiler had an engineer to build a catapult, he might have tried to destroy the defenses with fire arrows, either directed against the stockade itself or into the cluster of wooden buildings within. Only the keep was of stone. Abutting the tower was a wooden chapel, and the kitchen and bake house. Other wooden buildings were built alongside the stockade walls adjacent to the cliffs: a smithy and stable, a granary, and on the opposite side of the courtyard a long wooden building that served in peacetime as a barracks.

Ranulf had guarded against the threat of fire. The roofs of the wooden buildings had been covered with hides to retard ignition, and scattered throughout the compound and spaced along the fighting platform of the stockade were barrels filled with water to fight a blaze before it could spread.

Ranulf's garrison was well provisioned. A cacophony of barnyard noises drifted up from the courtyard. Chickens and geese, some wandering free but most locked in rows of stacked cages, cackled and honked, and from the barracks hall came the lowing of cattle that had been herded in from pens outside the stockade. The granary was overflowing, and Marshal assumed that the storeroom on the ground floor of the keep was filled to capacity.

But frontier castles like Kilkenny had been built to hold rebellious Irishmen at bay, not to withstand Norman siege engines—particularly a trebuchet. The trebuchet was designed for massive loads, and it threw them in a high arc. Once Meiler hauled the catapult into place at the bottom of the slope, he could bombard the antiquated stockade above him with boulders or with firebombs and destroy the wooden wall in a single day.

The defenders' retreat to the keep was already prepared. Narrow bridges extended from the near walls of the stockade to a wooden platform halfway up the tower, from which an outer wooden staircase rose to the parapet. Men on the ground, retreating to the tower from the courtyard, would raise the drawbridge after them, and those coming across from the wall would cut the ropes securing the bridges to the tower. Yet once the garrison was forced into the keep, surrender was only a matter of time.

And now, it appeared, Meiler was moving to prevent Lady Isabelle's escape. Two knights and a half dozen mounted *serjants* had emerged from the forest, followed by skirmishers on foot, carrying slings and Irish battle-axes. Behind them came workmen with picks and shovels. Ox carts trundled in their midst, piled high with poles and tent canvas. Meiler was preparing to dig in.

Several carts, Marshal noted, were loaded with fire-hardened stakes, which would be driven into the ground in a defensive line to protect the tents against a sortie from the castle. This was an unnecessary precaution, and it indicated that Meiler overestimated the strength of Ranulf's garrison. Perhaps that would make it easier for Marshal to negotiate a surrender.

Marshal sighed and gingerly rubbed his eyes. His head still ached, and he felt sluggish from lack of sleep. God help him if his head didn't clear soon; he would need his wits about him today. Marshal grimaced as a part of him rebelled against his entanglement in the affair. Meiler was just the first obstacle. He had promised to present Lady Isabelle's case before the King, but he could not promise success. If he failed, Ranulf most certainly, and perhaps his lady as well, would pay the price. It was a responsibility he did not want.

Yet even as he chafed under its burden he knew that he had no real choice. It was not just that he owed a debt to Eustace; Ranulf was defending his lady's rights. Marshal could not turn his back and ride out of Kilkenny and still call himself a knight. Some knights could, when it suited them, ignore their sacred oath to defend the right, but Marshal could not.

Marshal saw Isabelle de Clare standing beside Ranulf on the forward wall. Meiler fitz Henry was not the only unknown quantity he would have to deal with. The girl certainly possessed courage, but John must have cut her off from her late father's advisers. Almost any other course of action would have been better than the one she had chosen.

The sunlight glinted on copper-colored hair, and Marshal groaned inwardly. A young woman could be unpredictable enough, but a redhead . . . Marshal sighed and turned to leave the parapet; it was time to meet the mistress of Kilkenny.

Isabelle stood beside Ranulf on the stockade's fighting platform, looking toward the forest, pretending to watch the approach of Meiler's siege column; but out of the corner of her eye she was studying Ranulf. *Please, my faithful old friend, don't fail me now.*

"Bloody false alarm," Ranulf said. "Meiler's not fool enough to attack now without the trebuchet. He must be preparing to dig in and seal off your escape, milady. John doesn't intend to let you slip away from him a second time."

"I wish you had awakened me last night," Isabelle said tensely.

"I thought it best to let you sleep, milady."

"I'm no longer a child, Ranulf!"

"I know that, milady. I just thought . . ." Ranulf's voice trailed off in a grunt of resignation. He didn't understand her irritation and was in no mood to try to fathom a woman's preoccupation with irrelevancies.

Isabelle caught herself gnawing on her lower lip and stopped. She needed more than Ranulf's obedience, she needed his confidence; and the stranger who had slipped into Kilkenny the previous night had managed to rekindle Ranulf's doubts. If only she had been present when Ranulf had talked with William Marshal.

Apparently they had talked through the night, blithely settling her fate between them, as men were so quick to do, and Ranulf had come to her at first light to tell her of Marshal's presence and of his offer. Caught off-guard, Isabelle had played for time, not giving Ranulf a direct answer. But she had no intention of surrendering.

Isabelle shivered imperceptibly. John had driven her to this desperate gamble, and no one could persuade her to surrender voluntarily to his custody again—not Ranulf, and certainly not the meddlesome William Marshal. But how could she refuse Marshal's offer without some plausible reason and hope to retain Ranulf's trust?

Marshal had already won Ranulf's confidence; the old knight spoke of him in a way that he had once reserved for her father. Isabelle had observed how quickly bonds could form between warriors, and Marshal was more than a famous knight. If half of what she had heard as a girl were true, there were few knights who could equal him on the battlefield. That would weigh heavily with Ranulf, even if it meant little to her.

She knew nothing of Marshal's character, only of the legends that had grown up around him, and she had no faith in legends. Marshal was a stranger. How could she blindly entrust her fate to him?

"Where is your William Marshal?" Isabelle asked irritably. "Jean said he was up and about, and that was half an hour ago."

"Probably up on the parapet, milady," Ranulf said, his eyes on the lead elements of Meiler's column just now emerging from the forest. "Checking out the situation from the highest vantage point. It's what I'd do."

Isabelle turned and looked up at the tower in time to glimpse a figure in chain mail turn away and disappear from view. "You were right, Ranulf, but he's gone now. Come," she said peremptorily, "it's time I met our famous guest."

Ranulf nodded and called to the men who should have been off watch to stand down. "I'll have to tell the tower watchmen not to sound the alarm by day without an order from me," he said to Isabelle.

It was an indirect acknowledgment that she was still committed to holding Kilkenny, but Isabelle knew Ranulf didn't understand her coolness to Marshal's proposal. He couldn't understand without an explanation—an explanation she daren't give.

Ranulf preceded her down the ladder to the courtyard. The ground was still muddy, and he offered her his arm as she stepped off the ladder onto the narrow walkway of planks that had been laid out for her. As she walked toward the keep with Ranulf trudging beside her through the mud, the old knight leaned toward her and said, "Try to look a little more cheerful, Rusty. The man *is* on our side, you know."

Isabelle saw Marshal emerge from the entrance to the keep, and she slowed her pace so that he would have time to come down to their level before she reached the steps to the drawbridge. She did so automatically, without hauteur, out of consideration for a guest. Because of her rank, if they met while he was still on the steps above her, Marshal might feel awkward.

He was a big man, as she had expected, but as he strode across the drawbridge and came down the steps to the courtyard, he moved with a surprisingly light-footed grace. Whatever else he might be, she noted, he was not vain, for the burnished steel of his chain mail was not lacquered, and the white surcoat he wore over his armor was without embroidery.

"Lady Isabelle," Ranulf said as Marshal came up to them, "may I present Sir William Marshal, formerly companion to the Templars and now returning to His Majesty's service."

The unaccustomed formality in Ranulf's voice struck Isabelle as comically out of character.

She smiled politely and stepped forward to grasp Marshal's hands in welcome. Ranulf had told her that Marshal's wrist was broken, and she saw the splint poking out from his mailed sleeve.

"You are most welcome, Sir William," she said, tilting back her head to look up at him.

"I thank you, Lady Isabelle," Marshal replied, bowing with just the right amount of deference. But as he straightened up, Isabelle was sure she saw a suppressed wince of pain, and she noticed that his eyes were bloodshot. So the great knight has his weaknesses, she thought wryly. With Ranulf as a drinking companion, he'd been overmatched.

"And I thank you, Sir William," she said, "for coming so far to bring solace to Ranulf, my faithful knight. I deeply regret that I could not receive you properly last night."

Marshal smiled. "Believe me, I am grateful enough that last night's welcome did not include a crossbow bolt."

Isabelle was surprised that his smile revealed no missing teeth. Few knights who rode the tournament circuit professionally could boast a full set. Despite the scruffy beard stubble on Marshal's cheeks, his face made a good impression—intelligent and forceful. He had brown hair receding from a high forehead and a broken nose, which Isabelle decided was to his advantage, for it saved him from being too handsome. His thick, projecting eyebrows, prominent cheekbones, and strong jaw would have given him a fierce look, had it not been for his disarming smile.

Marshal was appraising her as well, and Isabelle found his direct gaze strangely disconcerting. He had held her hands a trifle longer than politeness demanded, but now he released them. He has the courtier's touch, she thought, suddenly recalling the rumors she'd heard as a girl. There had been talk linking him to Prince Henry's young wife, Marguerite of France. Isabelle felt a flash of irritation she didn't understand.

She turned to Ranulf and said lightly, "It appears that we are not in danger of attack at the moment, so you gentlemen can shed your armor. We will dine in the open, I think, and a touch of festivity would not be amiss. We'll forget the rationing today and eat a proper meal in Sir William's honor."

"Yes, milady," Ranulf said without hesitation.

Isabelle was surprised that Ranulf did not object, but only momentarily. Meiler's trebuchet would be completed long before they exhausted their livestock, she realized, and once they were driven into the tower, only the provisions they could hold in the keep would be of use.

"In the meantime," Isabelle said, "I will have a bath prepared for Sir William, and he can—"

"I hope the need for a bath is not too obvious," Marshal interrupted with a smile.

"No, of course not," Isabelle said too quickly, and then flushed. That she should be flustered by Marshal's harmless joke surprised and annoyed her, which only made her cheeks burn more hotly.

Marshal gave no sign that he noticed. "A bath would be wonderful, Lady Isabelle," he said easily. "And then, perhaps we could talk. Ranulf has explained the situation here, and I—well, if I can, I would like to be of service to you. At your discretion, of course."

Isabelle was not reassured by the proviso. Was he really prepared to defer to her judgment, or was he simply approaching her carefully, as one might deal with a difficult child? She saw now that Ranulf's trust in Marshal was due to more than an affinity between warriors. There was a self-assurance to the man, unmarred by arrogance, which in other circumstances would have inspired her confidence.

"I would of course value your counsel, Sir William," she said in a carefully neutral tone, "and we deeply appreciate your offer of aid. When you have refreshed yourself, Ranulf and I will await you in my chamber."

Isabelle saw a flicker of surprise as Marshal registered her deliberate reserve, and once again Marshal was appraising her. But although his look was probing, it was not detached; there was genuine concern in his eyes. She had suspected Marshal's offer of help to be, at least in part, a gratification of his ego—the noblesse oblige of a hero of the lists. But she could detect neither condescension nor self-importance in the man. Marshal was not at all what she'd expected.

Marshal shifted on the stool in the wooden bathtub that had been prepared for him behind his screen in the great hall and closed his eyes. Lady Isabelle had sent her lady-in-waiting to wash his hair, and now that the woman had departed, he could relax. Marshal never felt comfortable when women attended him in his bath, but it was an idiosyncrasy he had been unwilling to reveal.

Without decent Saracen soap, the bath would be only partially effective in cleansing his body, but the steaming water had eased the stiffness in his muscles and taken away the last of his hangover. He felt human again.

He slid farther down into the water so that he could soak the stubble on his jaw. He shaved as infrequently as possible, and he could have let his whiskers grow for another few days; but he had seen the girl's eyes focus on the stubble, and he wanted to make himself more presentable. It was a matter of courtesy, he told himself, due her as a lady of high degree.

He would be more persuasive if he made a favorable impression, and now he knew that persuasion would be necessary. Lady Isabelle was clearly not ready to accept his proposal. Why? he wondered. He could understand her reluctance to trust a stranger, but Ranulf must have explained that her continued defiance was likely to end in disaster.

Marshal picked up the dagger he'd brought from Palestine and began to scrape his jaw. The dagger's blade was of blue Damascus steel, and it held a keener edge than any European shaving knife, yet even so, shaving was a painful ritual.

It was ironic, he thought, that the very richness of Isabelle de Clare's inheritance should hold her hostage in the social limbo of an unmarried heiress. If she were free to choose, she could have her pick of eligible bachelors, not to mention the barons who would willingly put aside their wives to take her hand. With the lands she could bring to a marriage, she would be desirable even if she had been an ill-favored girl.

And this Isabelle de Clare certainly was not. Her broad forehead and generous mouth did not conform to the courtly standards of beauty, nor did her freckles and turned-up nose, but Marshal preferred the open vivacity of her features and manner to the pouting, narrow-faced blond belles of the French courts.

Marshal smiled wryly to himself, admitting the immediate and visceral attraction he had felt toward the girl, but he had long since learned to suppress such feelings toward highborn women beyond his reach. Despite his fame, Marshal's prowess had gained him no fiefs of his own. He was still a landless knight. Other men could walk the line between flirtation and indiscretion, but Marshal knew from bitter experience that he could not.

Marshal ascended the spiral staircase to the chamber above the great hall, taking the stone steps two at a time. The bath had refreshed him, and he felt energetic and purposeful. The reluctance and worry that had gnawed at him earlier had vanished with his hangover. He was sure that he and Ranulf could persuade Isabelle to surrender Kilkenny, and he was reasonably confident that he could successfully plead her case before the King. She was defying her lawful guardian, but Count John's misuse of his trust was too flagrant to overlook.

Marshal's optimism evaporated as he reached the level of the second floor and heard Ranulf's gravelly voice explode in anger. Ranulf's words were muffled by the thick oak door to Lady Isabelle's chamber, but Marshal understood them well enough: "Why won't you listen to reason, milady!"

Marshal heard no response, and he knocked on the door. Isabelle called for him to enter, and Marshal walked in. The girl was sitting on the bed, rigidly erect, looking very small and vulnerable in the empty, stone-walled chamber, but there was nothing tremulous in her demeanor. Her green eyes were hard and uncompromising. Ranulf stood nearby, his hands clasped behind him, and though his voice had been angry, there was only confusion and worry in his eyes.

"Perhaps I've come at an inopportune moment," Marshal said.

The girl shook her head. "No, Sir William. It was your proposal we were discussing."

Isabelle's voice was controlled, but Marshal caught an undertone of accusation that took him by surprise.

"That is all it is, Lady Isabelle," Marshal said. "A proposal for you to consider."

"A proposal to surrender," Isabelle said coolly.

"With honor, and with safe conduct for you and your men. It is true that you would almost certainly be required to return to Count John's custody, but I would proceed immediately to the Royal Court to present your grievances to the King. As I understand it, you are without an advocate and are hoping for the intercession of Lord Meath."

"You understand correctly, Sir William."

"But you cannot be sure your messenger got through to Meath— or of Meath's response. I know that you hope the news of this siege will eventually reach him, but would you not prefer to exchange a possibility for a certainty? I stand ready to present your case, and I—"

"Why?" Isabelle interrupted.

Marshal saw that the abrupt question had slipped out before the girl had considered it, and her eyes flickered as she regretted it an instant later; but Marshal would not let it go by. The implication nettled him. "Because you have been wronged, Lady Isabelle. That is reason enough for any knight who remembers his oath."

Isabelle took a deep breath and nodded. "I apologize, Sir William," she said as gracefully as could be expected. "The question was unworthy."

Marshal cursed inwardly; he was bungling the situation. For some reason the girl felt on the defensive, and he was only making matters worse.

"Lady Isabelle, I have no intention of interfering in this affair against your wishes."

Isabelle's tongue flicked out to moisten her lips, and she glanced at Ranulf uncertainly. She was obviously afraid of losing Ranulf's support, but she was even more afraid of something else. What?

"I can assure you, Lady Isabelle," Marshal said, "that neither Count John nor anyone else in the realm can prevent me from reaching the King. I have a safe-conduct from His Majesty and a written order commanding my presence at Court. You can be sure your case will be presented, and I suggest that I can serve your interests better than could Lord Meath.

"The King would be suspicious of any case brought against his son by a baron with a power base in Ireland; he would be bound to look upon it as a challenge to John's authority as Lord of Ireland. I firmly believe that my proposal offers you the best chance for justice."

Ranulf nodded in agreement and looked to Isabelle. For a moment there was silence, broken by a rhythmic thumping from above, as the watchman on the parapet idly tapped his pike on the scaffolding. Isabelle's expression had not changed; it was clear that she still resisted the idea. Her fingers plucked restlessly at the folds of her robe. Why was she resisting? What the devil was she afraid of?

"I take your point, Sir William," Isabelle said at last. She took a breath and added, "And I would welcome your intercession on my behalf—with heartfelt thanks—for I do believe His Majesty would listen to you. But could you not go now, leaving us to hold Kilkenny? Why must we surrender?"

"Rusty, you know very well why!" Ranulf burst out in frustration.

To Marshal it was a measure of the old knight's worry that he slipped and used her nickname in front of a stranger.

"You would be undercutting your own position, Lady Isabelle," Marshal said. "Count John's misuse of his guardianship is against all custom. But to hold Kilkenny in defiance of his order is rebellion, and that places you outside the law."

Again Marshal saw uncertainty in the girl's eyes. It was clear that she understood their argument, yet something still prevented her from giving her assent. She compressed her lips and shook her head.

"If you feel you cannot represent us while we still hold Kilkenny, Sir William," she said, "you may withdraw your offer of advocacy, but I have no intention of surrendering."

Ranulf expelled his breath in exasperation. "I am your liege man, milady," he rasped, "and I owe you counsel as well as service. I am bound to say that your decision is irrational. In fact, it's stubborn and reckless! Pride should have its limits!"

Isabelle stiffened as if in anger, but there was a hint of desperation in her eyes. She blinked rapidly, and Marshal saw that she was holding back tears. Ranulf was wrong, he realized. The girl was neither reckless nor foolish, and pride was not the reason for her stubbornness. Isabelle de Clare was frightened.

"You may withdraw, sirs," she said hoarsely, turning away.

"As you wish, milady," Ranulf said curtly. He bowed stiffly and strode from the chamber.

Marshal followed him to the door, but then he stopped and closed it, remaining in the chamber.

"I would like to be alone, Sir William," Isabelle said, her face still averted.

"You *are* alone, Lady Isabelle," Marshal said quietly. "That's just the trouble. What is it that you won't tell Ranulf?"

The girl looked up at Marshal and shook her head quickly—too quickly. Her face was very white, and in that instant Marshal guessed the truth.

7

"My God," Marshal breathed. "It's John you're afraid of!"

Isabelle's eyes widened in alarm, and she stood up, stretching out her arm toward him. "No, you must not think that!"

But it was there, plain in her eyes. Marshal would have had to be blind not to see it. A wave of revulsion swept over him, followed an instant later by a rush of white-hot anger. No wonder she had not dared tell Ranulf. If the old knight found out, he would track down John and kill him with his own hands, or die trying.

"What happened?" Marshal demanded, his pulse hammering at his temples.

"You're wrong, Sir William!"

With an effort of will Marshal mastered his anger. The last thing he wanted was to strip the girl of her dignity. Slowly he shook his head. "I'm not wrong, and if I am to be of service to you, I should know the truth."

Isabelle swallowed convulsively and shook her head, unwilling to speak. Several seconds passed before she finally yielded. "Ranulf must never know," she said, her voice barely above a whisper. "If he found out . . ."

"I'll tell him nothing, Lady Isabelle. You have my word."

"It was not as terrible as you may be thinking," she said, taking a deep breath. "He didn't—he didn't succeed. It was late at night and I was alone with him. He was furious that I refused to sign a letter instructing Ranulf to surrender Kilkenny, and he was drunk—very drunk. He told me that he'd stopped my priest from carrying my petition to the King, and he hinted that he'd had Father Bertrand killed—"

Isabelle broke off and bit her lip uncertainly. "Now I think he may have simply wanted to frighten me. Would he dare to kill a priest, Sir William?"

"I don't know," Marshal said hoarsely. "I hope not."

"Still, I refused to sign, and when I tried to leave him, he—he attacked me."

Marshal felt the blood draining from his cheeks. He was no innocent and he knew of barons who had taken advantage of their wards, but that did nothing to quell his rising anger and disgust. The bastard! The slimy little bastard!

Isabelle was no longer looking at Marshal. She stared straight ahead, as if seeing it all again in her mind, and her words came tumbling out in a rush.

"He was so drunk that I managed to kick free of him. I hurt him— hurt him badly. And while he was helpless, I took his head by the hair and slammed it against the floor."

Isabelle looked up at Marshal, her eyes blinking rapidly, and then stepped back and dropped tiredly onto the bed. "And that was all. He lost consciousness and it was over."

"And you told no one?"

"No. Not even Mattie. I didn't want to . . ."

Marshal nodded, finding it difficult to speak, imagining the girl's terror and what it must have cost her to keep the secret locked inside her to protect those who would have sought to avenge her.

Isabelle suddenly compressed her lips and shook her head. "I shouldn't have fled Pembroke. John was so drunk, he may not even remember what happened."

"Lady Isabelle, I—"

"God, I've made a mess of things! You're right, Sir William. Of course I'll agree to an honorable surrender. If John hadn't been drunk, he would never—"

"No!" Marshal burst out, horrified that the girl was blaming herself. "You won't be returned to John. Not as long as I live to prevent it."

Despite Meiler's siege line, it should be possible to bring the girl out of Kilkenny by night, but there was another possibility that Marshal preferred. Rage burned like a hot iron in his gut, and the urge to strike back at John was not simply a desire, it was a need. John was out of reach, but Meiler fitz Henry was not—and Meiler was John's man.

Isabelle was looking at Marshal strangely, and he tried to recompose his expression. He was not adept at masking his feelings, and his thoughts now were ugly. "If you permit," he said stiffly, still fighting to control his anger, "I'll leave you now to speak with Ranulf."

"But don't you think—"

"I think we can find a way to keep you out of John's hands, Lady Isabelle, and secure your safety and rights. John may be Lord of Ireland, but Henry is still king."

"But what will you tell Ranulf?"

"I'm afraid I'll have to let him believe his mistress is simply too stubborn to listen to reason," he said, trying to smile.

"It won't be hard to convince him," Isabelle said bleakly.

"And that's just as well. It took great courage not to tell him, Lady Isabelle—the kind of courage that would make any knight proud to serve you."

Marshal meant what he said, and Isabelle knew it. Her cheeks colored under his direct gaze, and she looked away.

"When we've worked out some sort of plan," Marshal said, "we'll submit it for your consideration."

Isabelle shook her head and rose from the bed. "I give my consent now to whatever you and Ranulf decide—on one condition. You must consider the risk to yourselves."

"Neither one of us is reckless," Marshal said.

Isabelle smiled tentatively. "I hope that's true, Sir William." She stepped toward him and took his hands. Her fingers were feverishly hot. "Trusting that it is," she said huskily, looking up at him, "I place myself in your hands, and gratefully so."

This time it was Marshal who flushed.

By the time Marshal found Ranulf in the tower's cellar storeroom beneath the great hall, he was confident that he had calmed down enough to fool Ranulf. Marshal didn't like deceiving him, but Isabelle was right: Ranulf couldn't be told.

A single torch burned on the wall beside the stairwell, soot curling upward from its oily flame. The torchlight barely illuminated the dungeon's recesses, and Marshal had to wait a moment for his eyes to adapt to the gloom. The musky odor of rats' nests hung in the air.

With the exception of the torture chamber, the cellar was undivided. Wine casks and beer barrels lined one wall, and small barrels containing cheeses were stacked against another. Additional stores for the siege were distributed haphazardly throughout the room, and Ranulf was opening barrels at random to check for spoilage. There were supplementary stocks of salted fish in brine, smoked and salted meat, barrels of flour, and barrels of raw grain to feed the fowl that would be brought into the keep at the last minute.

Checking the provisions was the responsibility of the steward, but Marshal guessed that Ranulf had sent away his steward, as well as the castle's priest. Ranulf resealed the cask he had opened and came over to Marshal. The end of a cherry twig protruded from the corner of his mouth.

He shifted the chewing stick to the other side of his mouth and asked, "Did she change her mind?"

Marshal shook his head. "She won't surrender to Meiler."

"Shit."

"My thought precisely," Marshal said with feigned exasperation.

Ranulf grunted sourly. "We'll get you out of here tonight, then. Unless you want to try to slip through Meiler's siege line, we'll lower you down to the river by rope. Then we'll use the same hoist to lower a skiff we have on hand for just this situation. You can row downriver all the way to Waterford. I only wish Lady Isabelle would go with you."

"She won't," Marshal said. "Not as long as there's a chance of being intercepted. If Meiler takes her hostage, you'd be forced to surrender, and she doesn't want to see you hang. As long as she remains here, she can hope to bargain for your life if surrender becomes inevitable."

"Well, that doesn't leave us much choice. We'll just have to hang on here as long as we can and hope that you can persuade the King to intervene."

"I don't like the idea of leaving her here."

"God's blood, man," Ranulf growled. "You just told me she won't go with you."

"I know," Marshal replied coolly, "but we may have another option."

Ranulf bit off the end of his stick and spat out the piece of pulp. "I'm listening."

"Before we turned in last night, you told me that Meiler has been challenging you to single combat. Will he come again today?"

Ranulf frowned in puzzlement, then his eyes narrowed and he shook his head sharply. "Forget it, Marshal. Bad idea."

"Will he come?"

"Look. You're the best man with a sword and lance I've ever seen—but not with only one good arm."

"Will he come?"

"I'm telling you to forget it! You don't know Meiler. He's one tough son of a bitch, and he's good. Too good. He might even be able to teach you a trick or two."

Marshal said nothing, waiting Ranulf out.

"For Christ's sake, Marshal—yes, God damn it, he'll come. He said he'd come three days running, and this is the third. He's having too much fun baiting me to quit now. But you—"

"When?" Marshal cut in impatiently.

"Sometime around Terce. I think it's his way of working up an appetite for dinner."

"Does he come armed?" Marshal persisted, ignoring Ranulf's resistance.

Ranulf shook his head. "He did the first day, but not after that. You'd have plenty of time to say your prayers."

"I already said mine this morning," Marshal said with a slight smile, "and it was answered."

Ranulf spit out another piece of wood. "Terrific. You won't mind if I say a prayer or two for us? If you go down, we go down with you."

"Then don't take the chance," Marshal replied. "But if I defeat Meiler today, we can bring your lady out of here without the risk of pursuit."

Ranulf's eyes dropped to the splint on Marshal's wrist. *"If* you can take him," he said.

"I think I can."

"With that arm? It will never take the strain, Marshal. Even if you get through a pass or two with lances, it won't hold up when Meiler closes with you. He uses a mace, not a sword, and he's as strong as an ox. He'll batter down your shield arm and then go to work on your skull."

"Who said I'd let him close with me?"

"Unseat Meiler? No one ever has."

"He's never run into me."

Ranulf laughed, an explosive, coughing bark. "You can't be accused of false modesty, I'll say that much."

Marshal didn't smile. "It's what I do, Ranulf."

The old knight bit through his chewing stick again, and he threw it away. He looked up at Marshal thoughtfully.

"Well?" Marshal asked. "What's it going to be?"

"You tempt me. You know that, don't you? I would give a lot to see that bastard knocked on his ass. The question is, can you really do it?"

"Try me."

Ranulf drew in his breath, held it for a moment, and then expelled it in a long hiss. "All right," he said finally, "you've called it, and that's what it will be: all or nothing."

The blaring of three unskilled trumpeters announced Meiler's appearance before Castle Kilkenny. As the discordant fanfare sounded, Meiler, accompanied by his knights and standard bearer, started up the hill. All morning long his men had labored to set up a new encampment stretching three hundred yards along the edge of the forest, blocking the approach to the castle, but now all work stopped. The men of Meiler's small army watched his progress up the hill, grateful for the chance to rest and hoping for entertainment.

"Trumpets, no less," Ranulf remarked dryly to Isabelle, who stood beside him on the forward wall.

"Will he take the bait?" Isabelle asked, unsure of the answer she wanted to hear. She was amazed that her voice sounded so calm.

"He'll take it, all right—hook, line, and sinker."

"But won't he be suspicious when we accept his challenge?"

"Maybe, but I doubt it. He'll think we're desperate. Anyway, it doesn't matter. Even if he smells a rat, he's trapped by the show he's putting on."

All of Ranulf's garrison, including the cooks and varlets, had lined the forward wall, drawn by the rumors they had heard, and Ranulf was content to allow the breach in discipline. Seeing the number of men on the wall, Meiler reined in short of the point from which he usually threw out his challenge, but he didn't hesitate long. He put his spurs to his horse and continued up the slope.

Isabelle surreptitiously brushed her damp palms against her silk *bliaut*. She was glad she would have to shout to Meiler, for it would help to mask her anxiety. Now, dismayed by what she had set in motion, she wished with all her heart that she had never fled Pembroke.

If Marshal's wrist failed him, as Ranulf had warned her it might, Meiler would surely kill him. Kilkenny would fall to Meiler, and Ranulf would be the next to die. And all she had to fear, she thought bitterly, was a return to John's custody.

John was a drunk and a lecher, not the boogey man. She had wanted to be worthy of her father, but where had her courage been when she had turned down Marshal's original plan? John was vindictive enough to punish her, but he could not go too far—not once Marshal presented her appeal to the King.

Fear, not pride, had prompted her refusal. How could the groping of a drunken weakling have frightened her so? Once she had told Marshal what had happened, she had seen it in a different light—as simply a loathsome incident. John would not dare try again; there were limits to even a prince's power.

Yet the effect on Marshal had been just the opposite. His emotions had played across his face as plainly as words on parchment. She had seen his initial shock, followed by the anger boiling up inside him.

When he had returned to tell her that he intended to answer Meiler's challenge, she had begged him to consider that Meiler would certainly demand a fight to the death. Again she had seen the ominous glint of anger in his eyes, and she had realized that Marshal hoped for nothing less.

For the first time in her life she had glimpsed the power—however unwitting—that a woman could have over a man's emotions. It was as if she had pressed a lever on a machine, precipitating action she had no idea how to stop.

Meiler was shouting up to the castle. "I call upon you to yield to your lawful lord's command, Lady Isabelle, and surrender Kilkenny to me!"

Isabelle stepped forward, prepared to answer, but then she hesitated, seized by the desire to halt the rush of events before men died because of her misjudgment. She could still ask for a parley, returning to Marshal's original plan—now, before it was too late.

Ranulf gripped her arm, seeing her hesitation but not understanding it.

"Answer him, milady," Ranulf pressed.

But it *was* too late. The time for second thoughts was past.

Isabelle drew a breath and lifted her head. "I answer you as I have before, Sir Meiler," she shouted. "The King placed Kilkenny in Sir Ranulf's hands, and only the King can relieve him of that duty."

"Then let him defend that claim before God!" Meiler cried. "I challenge him one last time to decide the issue in single combat. Sir Ranulf! Do you find sufficient courage today, or will you continue to hide behind your wall?"

Ranulf smiled and released Isabelle's arm. "Dangle the bait, milady," he said, and Isabelle nodded.

"It is I who deny you entry to Kilkenny," she shouted, "not Sir Ranulf. Dare you meet a champion of my own choosing?"

Meiler's response was immediate. "If he be a knight, Lady Isabelle. But I believe Sir Ranulf is the only knight among your company, and I will not dishonor my lance with the blood of a *serjant*."

Isabelle cupped her hands to her mouth to be sure her challenge reached Meiler's troops at the bottom of the hill. "My champion is a knight, and a true one, Sir Meiler, as you shall discover to your sorrow if you have the courage to meet him. Unlike Sir Ranulf, his hair is not gray!"

Meiler's horse reared as the burly warlord angrily jerked on the reins, and Ranulf chuckled deep in his throat. "That should do it," he muttered gleefully.

Isabelle glanced at him in astonishment. This was no game they were playing. Had he forgotten Marshal's injury?

"I will meet your champion, Lady Isabelle," Meiler yelled, "and gladly—if he exists."

"So he thinks we're bluffing, does he?" Ranulf grinned. "Well, the son of a bitch is in for a surprise."

It *was* a game to them, Isabelle thought, a deadly game that these men loved to play. She swallowed to relieve the dryness in her throat and continued as Ranulf had instructed her. "My champion will meet you one hour from now," she cried, "on the level below this slope. He offers you three passes with the lance, to be followed by combat with sword, ax, or mace. This will be single combat with only squires in attendance, and to the victor goes Kilkenny Castle."

"Agreed, Lady Isabelle! As I myself will be hostage to the outcome, I could by right demand a hostage of you; but I will settle for your word of honor that Kilkenny will be surrendered to me *unconditionally* when I defeat this nameless champion of yours."

"He means to hang you, Ranulf," Isabelle said anxiously.

"Of course," Ranulf said. "Agree, milady."

"I do so promise, Sir Meiler," Isabelle shouted. "Upon my honor and the honor of my father."

"And you, Sir Ranulf? Do you pledge your word as well?'"

Ranulf's face darkened at this fresh insult. "I give you my word," he shouted hoarsely, "though a knight who understood honor would not demand my separate assurance. And now I will make a demand of my own. Let your own knights swear before God to honor the outcome of this combat, and let their oaths be heralded before your troops!"

"It will be done," Meiler shouted back, and laughed. "I am glad that you refused to meet me yourself, Ranulf. I prefer to see you finish your days at the end of a rope."

Marshal prepared himself for battle in the courtyard, beneath the roof of an open shed attached to the stable. He preferred the light and the scent of hay and manure to the gloom of the great hall, with its dank odor of charred firewood. Isabelle and Ranulf had retired to the keep, and the men and boys of the garrison were avoiding the area around the stable. The long trestle tables that had been set up for a dinner in the open stood unused; the cooks had served up a hasty meal, which everyone had eaten individually or in scattered groups.

A heavy, uneasy silence had descended on the castle, and the buzzing of the flies around the stable's manure pile seemed unnaturally loud. The waiting would be hard for Ranulf's garrison, Marshal knew; their fate had been placed in the hands of a knight they did not know—a knight with an injured arm. Marshal examined the splint on his wrist. Jean d'Erly had reinforced the splint and added padding beneath new bindings. All that could be done to protect the wrist had been done, but would it be enough?

Marshal brushed the thought aside. He had made his decision. He might have tried to slip out of Kilkenny with the girl, as Ranulf had suggested, but there was the danger of pursuit if Meiler guessed that Isabelle had escaped. The shipping out of Waterford was irregular, and it might take days to obtain passage out of the port. To leave her behind, under siege, seemed no less dangerous.

Marshal had rationalized his decision, but he had not really tried to weigh the risks against each other. The naked truth was that Marshal was driven by anger. He wanted to neutralize Meiler fitz Henry once and for all, and he wanted to do it with cold steel.

Marshal had stripped to his linen shirt and breeches, and although the sun was strong, the air beneath the shed roof was cool. That suited

Marshal; he would be sweating soon enough. He knelt on a low mound of straw, crossed himself, and began a litany, going through the motions of prayer, but his mind remained focused on the coming duel, envisioning Meiler's attack.

A man who used a mace enjoyed battering an opponent. If, as Ranulf said, Meiler had never been unhorsed, he would be good with the lance; but he would be satisfied to break lances in a standoff, looking forward to the moment when he could close with his enemy and hammer him down.

If it came to that, Marshal could try to fight him on his right hand, sword to mace, but Meiler would soon notice the splint and force combat shield to shield. No, he couldn't allow Meiler to close with him, and he couldn't rely on textbook lance play. If he could not take Meiler on the first or second pass, he would have to try the French shift.

As skilled as Marshal was, he had only used the dangerous maneuver once in earnest, and that had been years ago. He was still as strong as he'd been then, but he was not as sure of his speed. The timing had to be perfect. . . .

Jean d'Erly came out of the stable and looked at Marshal expectantly, his eyes bright with excitement. Marshal rose and casually brushed the straw clinging to the knees of his breeches. His show of calm was a bit of theater for the boy's benefit; Jean was excited enough for them both.

"Your horse is saddled, sire."

"Bring him out, then," Marshal said, "and I'll have a look at him."

Jean brought out Marshal's charger and tethered him to a shed post. Marshal walked over and patted the chestnut stallion's head. "Not a pretty beast, is he, Jean? Too thick a neck, and the skull of a draft horse."

"It's his age that worries me, sire," the boy said hesitantly.

Marshal nodded. "That's why I was able to pick him up for a song in Waterford. For the long term you'd be right to worry, but this old devil will hold up for a lance pass or two, and he responds well to knee commands. He knows all the moves, and that's what I'll need today."

"What's his name, sire?"

Marshal shrugged. "No idea. He's just a horse, son—a tool, and an expendable one at that. Don't make a pet of your charger; someday he may have to die for you."

Marshal checked each of the stallion's shoes and then tested the saddle girth. He still used his unpainted Templar saddle with a simple saddle blanket. The rig was not much to look at, but it was strong and reliable. Jean had done a proper job, and Marshal nodded approvingly. "He hasn't been watered recently, has he?"

"No, sire, not since early this morning. Are you sure you don't want caparisons?"

Marshal shook his head. "You know there's no point. They won't stop a lance, even if Meiler is fool enough to go for the horse instead of me."

"I know, sire, but . . ."

Marshal smiled. "You'd like to see a touch of class."

Jean reddened, and he brushed back a shock of black hair that immediately fell across his brow again.

"That's okay, son, I understand. But this isn't a tournament, and we're not putting on a show for the ladies in the loges. If Meiler is unimpressed by my appearance, so much the better. Have you checked out my lances?"

Jean nodded. "The grain is solid, sire, but one is slightly warped."

"Badly enough to make a difference?" Marshal asked, knowing the answer.

"I don't think so."

"Good. I'm glad you're coming out with me, Jean."

"Thank you, sire," the boy said, beaming. "It's a great honor for me."

"Let's hope you think so when it's all over," Marshal said with a wry smile. "Has Sir Ranulf provided you with helmet and hauberk?"

"Yes, sire. I have my gear in the stable. I wasn't sure . . ."

"Well, bring it out here, boy. It's about that time."

Grinning, the squire dashed into the stable. Not every knight permitted his squire to appear beside him armed, but Marshal found this conceit idiotic. In his opinion, only a fool required another man to ride into hostile territory unarmed.

The squire's excitement brought a wan smile to Marshal's lips as he remembered how it had been for him when he was young—his impatience to prove himself in battle and the early thrill of combat. He could remember the joy of those wild, rough-and-tumble years, but the joy of combat for its own sake had slipped away with his youth. Now there was only controlled tension, calculation, and the grim determination to get the job done. When the fighting began, excitement would come with the rush of adrenaline, but it would be reflexive, born of the instinct to survive.

Jean carried out his armor, shield, and sword, piled the equipment beside Marshal's in the straw, and turned to help Marshal dress for battle. First the chain-mail leggings were piled up over the baggy breeches and fastened to a cord around the waist. Next came the thickly padded, quilted tunic, followed by the hauberk. After the boy had laced the mailed sleeves and coif to the hauberk, Marshal slipped his lightweight, white Templar surcoat over his armor, and Jean knelt to attach Marshal's plain steel spurs.

Jean quickly put on his own armor, and Marshal helped him with the laces. He set the squire's open-faced, conical helmet on the boy's head and rapped it sharply with his knuckles. "Tie that down well. You don't want it to fly off at the first blow."

Marshal picked up his sword, buckled it around his waist, and slipped on a pair of thin leather gloves. He had roughened the palm of the right-hand glove and smeared it with pine pitch. He would not be wearing chain-mail gauntlets; for what he had in mind, a sure grip on the lance was essential.

"You won't carry your shield, Jean," Marshal said, "and you'll tie your sword to the back of your saddle. You haven't been knighted, and I want those men out there to know it. You're not to mix into the fight, no matter what happens. If Meiler's squire comes to his master's aid, let me take care of him. You stay out of it. You're to fight only if *you* are attacked—which is not very likely—and fight only if you can't make a run for it. Meiler's knights have sworn to stay clear of this, and I don't want you giving them an excuse to break their oaths. Understood?"

"Yes, sire."

"Don't forget! Now fetch your horse."

Marshal's charger had been standing patiently, but as Marshal mounted him, the aging stallion came to life. Marshal looped the reins about the saddle pommel and touched his spurs to the horse's flanks. The stallion responded instantly, and Marshal cantered him around the compound, shifting the horse left and right with knee commands alone.

Several onlookers had appeared to watch the performance, and Marshal was sure his preparations had been discreetly observed all along. As he rode back to the stable and reined in, Jean whistled appreciatively and Marshal nodded.

"He'll do, won't he? Let's have my helmet and shield."

Jean handed up Marshal's shield and then the helmet, which Marshal sat before him on the pommel. As the squire placed Marshal's lances in canvas slings attached to his own saddle, Marshal glanced critically at the palfrey the boy would be riding. The bay gelding was smaller and less powerful than a war-horse, but it looked swift enough to carry Jean to safety, and that was what counted.

Across the courtyard the door to the keep opened, and Ranulf and Isabelle walked out across the drawbridge.

"This is it," Marshal said, feeling his stomach muscles tighten. "Mount up, boy."

Marshal turned his charger and rode toward the keep, followed a moment later by Jean. As they crossed the courtyard Marshal's war-horse began to prance. "One of us is looking forward to this, at least," Marshal muttered with a faint smile.

Ranulf and Isabelle had done what they could to demonstrate their confidence, and despite Marshal's renewed tension, he was affected by the gesture. They were both dressed as if for an appearance at court. The old knight was resplendent in red and yellow: a silk, saffron-colored tunic; short scarlet boots; and a scarlet cloak edged with ermine. Around his neck he wore a heavy gold ceremonial chain, and he'd gone to the extreme of combing his thinning hair and tough, wiry beard.

It had become the fashion in tournaments for a knight to wear his chosen lady's colors, and Isabelle had turned that around. She was dressed entirely in blue and white. Over a white pelisse, its tightly fitting sleeves extending to the wrist, she wore a filmy, sky-blue *bliaut*. The blue gown extended behind her in a long train, and its wide, trailing sleeves billowed in the soft breeze. Her cape was white, and on her head she had placed a simple crown of intertwined silk cords of blue and white.

But it was the girl herself, not her attire, who captured Marshal as he reined in beside the drawbridge. He was no stranger to elegance, nor to youthful beauty. What struck him was the absence of self-awareness in Isabelle's manner. Like Ranulf, she had dressed with care only to do Marshal honor, and the concern he saw in her eyes as she tried her best to smile convincingly was not for her own safety.

"May God give you strength, Sir William," she said in her low, husky voice. "I have said a prayer for your victory."

"Thank you, Lady Isabelle," Marshal said formally, but then, on impulse, he lightened his tone. "That makes two of us," he said with a smile.

"Hell, more than two," Ranulf said. "There isn't a man here who hasn't gotten religion in the last hour."

Isabelle tried to stifle the laugh the two men had surprised out of her, and it emerged as a girlish giggle. She recovered her dignity, but Marshal was glad to see that her eyes were no longer quite so grave. The jesting wasn't bravado; it was simply a way to release some of the tension.

Isabelle was holding a long blue scarf, and now she bent down and gave it to Marshal. "Ranulf said you asked for a scarf of mine."

Marshal nodded and wrapped it around his left wrist. "Meiler will assume I'm wearing a token of yours, Lady Isabelle, and it may prevent him from noticing the splint."

"But I do have a token for you, Sir William," Isabelle said, and from the voluminous sleeve of her *bliaut* she withdrew a pair of spurs of red gold. "These were my father's. I've kept them with me ever since he died. I know he would want you to have them."

Out of the corner of his eye Marshal saw Ranulf begin to smirk.

Marshal ignored him. "I'd be honored, Lady Isabelle."

From the edge of the forest below the castle came a fanfare of trumpets, and the watchman on the parapet shouted that Meiler was making his appearance.

"Better get a move on," Ranulf growled impatiently.

"There's no need to dismount, Sir William," Isabelle said quickly, running lightly down the steps to the ground. "It will only take me a moment to put these on for you."

"No," Marshal said in embarrassment. "Jean can—"

But Isabelle was already at his side, unfastening his spur. Ranulf was grinning broadly now, displaying a set of chipped, yellowed teeth. Marshal glared at the old knight, but Ranulf's grin only widened. "My true knight," Ranulf mouthed silently, and his belly shook with suppressed laughter.

8

"Raise the portcullis and open the gate," shouted Ranulf, who stood on the platform roof of the timber gate house.

Marshal lowered his helmet over his head and lashed it down as Ranulf's men winched up the heavy iron grate blocking the passage through the gate house to the outer doors. His nostrils twitched at the enveloping stink of the sweat-stained helmet liner. He slipped his left arm through the shield loops, and Jean, mounted beside Marshal and carrying his banner, handed him a lance.

Two of Ranulf's men ran into the passage, unbarred the great double doors of the main gate, and swung them open. Marshal touched his spurs to his charger's flanks and rode forward, followed by Jean. As Marshal passed beneath the murder hole in the roof of the passage, Ranulf shouted down a final farewell: "Try not to break your other wrist!"

Marshal's answering grin, hidden by his helmet, was only fleeting. As he rode out through the gate, his eyes locked on the figure of Meiler fitz Henry waiting for him below, and he barely registered the sharp, clear notes of the garrison's trumpeter saluting him from the parapet.

Meiler and his squire were waiting at the southern end of a grassy flat lying between the bottom of the slope and the stakes of Meiler's siege line. The field was one hundred yards long and no more than thirty yards wide, bounded on one end by the castle's outlying corral and cattle pen, and on the other by a large garden, walled by thick hedges.

Meiler was offering no excuse for Isabelle's champion to deny him combat; he had withdrawn his troops from the area adjacent to the impromptu battlefield. His men were clustered at the far ends of their encampment, close to the forest line, and screened from access to the field by knights and *serjants*. In the center of the field Meiler had stationed a mounted herald.

As Marshal eased his prancing stallion down the slope, the incoherent crowd noise washing up to him from Meiler's troops became a rhythmic chant: "Mei-ler. Mei-ler. Mei-ler." Perhaps Ranulf's men were cheering as well, but Marshal couldn't have heard them over the concerted bellowing of the siege army.

Marshal and Jean rode out into the northern end of the field and turned to face Meiler, and the crowd's chant broke into a roar of jeers and catcalls. Marshal glanced at Jean. The boy's dark eyebrows were drawn together, and his eyes were angry. That's right, son, Marshal thought; stay angry. Keep your head, but stay angry.

Meiler's herald was riding toward them, but Marshal looked past him to where Meiler waited astride a magnificent coal-black stallion. His saddle was draped with yellow and black silks, and he wore a yellow surcoat over black-painted armor. Ranulf had said he was as strong as an ox, and he looked it. The burly warlord radiated arrogance.

The sight of Marshal's banner instead of the triangular pennant of an ordinary knight must have come as a surprise, but Meiler was apparently unworried. Even at a distance of one hundred yards Marshal could see his opponent's broad grin. He wore the old Norman helmet, with nothing but the steel nasal to protect his face. It was easier to fight in than the helmet Marshal wore, but it meant that Meiler was contemptuous of the additional protection of a steel cylinder.

Good. Meiler was a man accustomed to victory and confident that he could hammer down anyone daring to ride against him, and Marshal was relying on that confidence. A man who trusted to overpowering strength could fall prey to finesse.

The herald drew up before Marshal. He was a sallow-faced youth with a short, thin beard. Meiler had decked him out in a bright red robe, but the herald's tunic was soiled and greasy, and the smell of him drifted in through the eye slit of Marshal's helmet.

The herald addressed Marshal. "My lord, Sir Meiler, would have your name announced—unless you prefer to die anonymously," he sneered.

"I meet him in the name of Lady Isabelle de Clare," Marshal replied, loudly enough to carry over the continuing roar of the onlookers. "That will suffice."

The herald nodded curtly and rode back to the center of the field. He lifted the trumpet slung from his saddle and blew a single long blast to quiet the crowd. "Be it known," he cried hoarsely, "that Sir Meiler fitz Henry has graciously agreed to meet the champion of Lady Isabelle de

Clare in single combat, so that God may vindicate his right to custody of Castle Kilkenny. Three passes of the lance will be followed by combat with hand weapons of choice. This combat shall be to the death. No man shall intervene on behalf of either combatant, and all men present are bound by the outcome.

"In assurance of this, Lady Isabelle de Clare and Sir Ranulf de Barre have so sworn, as have the knights of Sir Meiler's banner. At the next sounding of this trumpet, the combat shall commence!"

The herald's last words were nearly lost in the renewed roar from Meiler's army, and Marshal's lips drew back in a grimace of anticipation. As the herald rode off the field, Marshal shifted his shield higher on his shoulder and tightened his grip on his lance. His attention was riveted on Meiler, and he didn't hear Jean d'Erly's shout of encouragement. The herald reached the edge of the field, turned his horse, and lifted his trumpet.

Marshal took a deep breath, and then another, as his pulse quickened and his lungs demanded oxygen, and he let the anger that had been simmering inside him boil up. Across the field, Meiler's shield rose and his lance swung down. The roar of the troops clustered behind the siege line swelled abruptly as Meiler dug in his spurs an instant before the herald's trumpet blast, and his stallion surged into a gallop.

For a full two seconds Marshal held his own mount in check, feigning hesitancy, letting Meiler come, knowing that he could give his own horse a shorter run and still meet Meiler at full speed. The warlord was charging him in textbook fashion, bent low, with his shield at the optimum angle. Unless Marshal's aim was perfect, his lance would glance off harmlessly.

Now! Marshal dug in his own spurs, and the old stallion lunged to the attack. The horse knew what was expected, and Marshal let him run straight out, his concentration focused on the exact spot where he would have to strike Meiler's shield. He watched for a last-moment shift in its angle, and the alteration came a split second before impact. Marshal shifted his aim a fraction to the left to compensate. He had adjusted his own shield to minimize the shock to his wrist, and he did not alter its slant. Let Meiler think he was dealing with an amateur.

The aim of both knights was true, and their lances struck simultaneously, rocking both men back in their saddles with bone-jarring force an instant before the ashwood shafts snapped in two with a thunderous crack. Marshal's shield slammed back against his splint, and tears spurted into his eyes. He cried out in pain as the stallions drove past each other, the sound of his agony lost in the animal roar of Meiler's men, yelling for blood.

Grinding his teeth against the stabbing pain in his wrist, Marshal dropped the splintered haft of his lance, took the reins in his right hand, and slowed his mount, turning the horse in front of Meiler's squire, who was staring at him with wide eyes.

"What's the matter, boy?" Marshal yelled hoarsely. "Did you think your master would drop me on the first pass?"

At the far end of the field, Meiler had also made his turn, and they cantered past each other, twenty yards apart. Meiler was no longer grinning, but Marshal could see that he was unhurt. The roar of the onlookers continued unabated.

"Give me the warped lance," Marshal shouted to Jean as he drew up and turned to face Meiler for the second pass.

"How's your wrist, sire?" Jean cried, handing Marshal the lance. "Christ! He's coming at you!"

Meiler had seized a fresh lance as he turned, and now he was charging back down the field. Marshal lowered his lance and galloped to meet him, bracing himself for a second shock to his pain-torn wrist. The gap between the charging horses closed with lightning speed, and this time the horses met almost head-on. As the lances struck the opposing shields, driving the riders back in their saddles, the force of impact actually slowed their mounts' forward momentum before the lances splintered.

An involuntary shriek of pain was torn from Marshal's throat, and for an instant he was afraid he would faint. The roar of the crowd rose to an incredible level as Meiler's men saw Marshal pitch forward in his saddle as the two chargers swept by each other. Tears blurred Marshal's vision. He grasped the reins in his right hand and blindly wheeled his charger about, unwilling to allow Meiler to get the jump on him on the last pass; it would have to be the French shift now, and he needed a full run.

Marshal was gasping with pain as he reined in and picked up the third lance—pain that knifed up from his wrist through his entire arm. He had known he couldn't stand up to the battering of Meiler's mace, but he'd been sure that he could take out Meiler with a lance. Too sure. He hadn't reckoned with the pain that assaulted him now, crowding out thought and all other sensation.

Grinding his teeth, he seized the lance and, with an effort of will, took an extra second to find just the right point to grip it. He was unaware that he was groaning, and oblivious to the sudden shock in Jean d'Erly's eyes. Meiler was taking his lance now, turning his horse—slower this time.

Blot out the pain, damn it! Concentrate on what you have to do. Concentrate! Across the field, Meiler's lance swung down into attack position, and his stallion lunged forward.

"Jesus, he's hurt," Ranulf said tightly as he watched Marshal turn his horse and ride back to pick up the third lance. "God, I warned him his wrist couldn't take it!"

Isabelle didn't trust herself to speak. Her throat had constricted, choking off her involuntary cry when she had seen Marshal reel after the second pass, and the naked ferocity in the roar of anticipation from Meiler's army had chilled her to the core. The horde of Irish auxiliaries jostling each other behind the screen of Meiler's knights seethed with blood lust.

Ranulf was gripping the pointed ends of the stockade pilings with his gnarled fists. If his hands had been at his sides, Isabelle would not have been able to resist the urge to slip her hand into his, as she'd done so often as a child. She felt as helpless as a child, and that magnified her fear. Below, on the field, which had been churned and muddied by the chargers' tearing hooves, a man was fighting for his life, and she could do nothing but watch!

Ranulf was no less impotent, and his desperate frustration showed in his face. His teeth were clenched, making the cords in his neck stand out, and Isabelle could see his pulse beating. He had seemed confident until the second pass, believing in Marshal—perhaps because he had to, but believing nonetheless. Now he stood rigid, his feet planted wide, gripping the pilings as if he meant to tear them from the earth.

"Marshal, you've got to do it this time." Ranulf growled through gritted teeth. "You've got to finish him now!"

Isabelle's anxiety flared into anger. "How?" she burst out. "What is he supposed to do?" She heard the desperation in her voice, and she didn't care. Marshal and Ranulf had been so damned determined to play their bloody game, and now they were going to pay for it with their lives. Yet a part of her anger was directed at herself. She should have stopped them! She could have, but she hadn't had the will.

Ranulf tore his eyes from the field below and looked at Isabelle. "I don't know what he'll do," he said hoarsely, shaking his head. "But he must have something up his sleeve. He knew what he was up against, and still he was determined to go. He must have something!"

"But, he's hurt, Ranulf! You saw it, and they know it too! Listen to those animals screaming down there."

The old knight had no time to answer. Marshal and Meiler fitz Henry had couched their lances and spurred their horses into the final charge. The two stallions raced toward each other along the dark track of torn-up sod marking the line of the first two passes, the pounding of the war-horses' hooves lost in the unremitting roar from the siege line.

Isabelle gasped. Marshal had been charging Meiler almost head-to-head, as he had on the second pass, but as the galloping stallions neared the center of the field, Marshal veered to the right, as if he'd suddenly lost his nerve. Instantly Meiler turned his mount to intercept him, the warlord's lance poised to strike Marshal from the side at a fatal angle.

As Meiler moved left to cut Marshal off, Ranulf gave a wild shout of exultation as he realized what Marshal intended. What happened next occurred in the space of three heartbeats, and Isabelle was never to be sure how much she actually saw and heard and how much her imagination filled in later to bring clarity to the blur of action.

Marshal's stallion abruptly swerved back to the left, and Meiler found himself bearing down on his enemy on the wrong side, unprotected by his shield and too late to alter course. With blinding speed Marshal swung his lance across to the right-hand side of his body, relying only on the strength of his right arm to absorb the impact when the lance struck. As the two horses flashed by each other, Marshal's lance tip caught Meiler squarely in the chest and swept him from the saddle.

The roar of Meiler's army died instantly, and the metallic crash as Meiler hit the ground carried clearly up to the castle. For a moment there was stunned silence, and then pandemonium broke out along the stockade wall. Ranulf was yelling incoherently at the top of his lungs, as were his men, who were waving their arms, slapping each other on the back, and literally jumping for joy; but Isabelle felt hot tears streaming down her cheeks, and they were not tears of joy.

The weeks of strain and moments of raw fear had taken their toll, and Marshal's sudden victory released a torrent of delayed anger, as if a dam had broken inside her. Her pent-up hatred of John and of the man who lay helpless on the field below swept her away, and now it was she who wanted blood.

Meiler lay on his back with the breath knocked out of him. First one leg twitched and then the other, and he feebly raised an arm, grasping in thin air for something to seize hold of to pull himself up. In those seconds of shocked silence among Meiler's company, no one rushed to his aid. Meiler's squire sat unmoving on his horse, as did his knights. It had happened too quickly for the onlookers to absorb before it was too late to intervene. Marshal had already turned and was bearing down on Meiler with his lance.

Meiler, still partially stunned, lay helpless, without the means to defend himself. His stallion had galloped off the field with Meiler's mace still slung from the saddle pommel, and the warlord's shield and lance lay twenty feet away. For a moment Isabelle thought that Marshal would drive his lance into his prostrate enemy, and she clenched her fists in fierce anticipation. She felt no pity for the man who had sought to terrorize them all, who would have gladly killed Marshal and executed Ranulf; she wanted him to die.

But abruptly Marshal reined in his mount. Meiler had lifted his head and managed to raise himself onto his elbows, staring at Marshal as he advanced on him deliberately and pinned him to the ground with the point of his lance. The cheering from the castle wall died away, and in the sudden hush the men on both sides awaited Marshal's decision.

"Kill him," Isabelle hissed. "Kill him!"

Ranulf turned and stared at her. "No, milady, he won't," Ranulf said. "If he meant to, Meiler would already be dead."

"Do you yield, Sir Meiler?" Marshal demanded loudly, his powerful baritone breaking the tense silence.

"Yes!" Meiler cried hoarsely, and a sound like a collective sigh drifted up from the soldiery, followed by a low, incoherent muttering—whether of relief or of discontent, it was impossible to say.

Isabelle shuddered as her rage spent itself, and slowly her tension drained away, leaving her with a slack, empty feeling of anticlimax. Marshal said something to Meiler and backed up his horse. The warlord slowly got to his feet, removed his helmet, and turned to face his troops.

"I hereby surrender my claim to Kilkenny," he called out bitterly, "until such time as the matter is brought before His Majesty, the King. My chamberlain shall pay off all enlisted auxiliaries at once; and all knights, *serjants*, officers of my household, and men in my service shall retire without delay and return home."

Meiler turned back to Marshal, and Marshal spoke to him again. Isabelle saw Meiler shake his head vehemently, and she heard his growl of protest, but Marshal raised his lance, and the warlord immediately nodded in assent.

"My squire and I," he announced, "shall remain in Kilkenny as the 'guest' "—Meiler spat out the word—"of Lady Isabelle de Clare, to insure the proper execution of my orders."

"Marshal, you bastard," Ranulf chortled, "what a malicious sense of humor you have!"

Grinning, Ranulf turned to Isabelle, and suddenly she found herself smiling in return as it finally came home to her that they had won. She took a deep, shuddering breath of relief. The future was still uncertain, but for the moment, at least, she was free.

"Rusty," Ranulf said, shaking his head, "I had no idea you were such a bloodthirsty devil," and Isabelle laughed, intoxicated by the belated rush of relief flooding through her.

"Just be glad Marshal had a cooler head than you," Ranulf said seriously. "I wouldn't have minded seeing that arrogant bastard skewered, but it's better for you that he's alive. Killing him would not have helped your case in court."

Isabelle looked down at Marshal, still astonished that he had spared Meiler, who would cheerfully have killed him if their positions had been reversed. Perhaps Marshal was cool enough to choose the politically wiser course, but she had seen the anger burning in his eyes and found it difficult to understand how it could be quenched so quickly.

Meiler's lieutenants were already shouting orders to their men, organizing the retreat, and Jean d'Erly and Meiler's squire had ridden over to join Marshal and his captive. One of Meiler's knights led out the warlord's charger and handed the reins to Marshal, who gestured for Meiler to mount.

As Marshal started up the slope with Meiler in tow, Kilkenny's garrison roared its approval, and Ranulf turned and shouted up to the trumpeter on the parapet. "When Sir William comes through our gate, Tom, I want the longest, loudest fanfare you've ever blown!" The trumpeter grinned and waved in acknowledgment.

"I didn't think he could do it," Isabelle said huskily. "I thought . . ."

"So did I," Ranulf grated. "And I knew what he could do. I hoped he had a surprise for Meiler, but the French shift . . ." Ranulf shook his head in wonderment. "That's something you hear about but never see, and now that I've seen it, I still don't believe it. If his charger had reacted a split second too late Meiler would have run him down. And to swing the lance to the offhand side and land on target in one motion . . . Christ. By rights, the impact should have torn that lance right out of his hand."

The afternoon sun was in Isabelle's eyes, and she raised her hand to shield them from the glare. Marshal's exhaustion and pain were evident in the way he sat his horse. He was leaning back heavily against the high cantle of his saddle, his right hand gripping the reins of Meiler's mount, which he had looped around the lance resting on his stirrup. He held his own reins slackly in his left hand, the splint resting on the pommel, and his left shoulder sagged. Isabelle wished she could see his face, but it was still hidden by his helmet.

Meiler's face was fixed in a fierce scowl. Behind him rode his dazed squire, who stared blankly straight ahead. Bringing up the rear was Jean d'Erly, grinning from ear to ear. As the party approached the gate, Jean spurred his mount forward and drew up alongside Marshal. "Open the gate!" Jean cried triumphantly. "Open for Sir William Marshal and Lady Isabelle's 'guest'!"

"God's legs," Ranulf said to Isabelle. "That kid is never going to be the same."

Nor am I, old friend, Isabelle thought to herself. *Nor am I.*

As Marshal rode into the courtyard and Ranulf's men swarmed down from the wall to surround their triumphant champion, the sharp, clear blast of the trumpeter's horn cut through their cheers. Ranulf was tone-deaf, and he had no appreciation of the trumpeter's inspired virtuosity as the young man's fanfare climbed the scale, but it was as loud as a single trumpet could be, and that was enough to satisfy the old knight.

Ranulf looked up at the parapet, and the veteran *serjant*, Black Fulk, made a sign to him. Certain now that at least the tower watch would be maintained, Ranulf ushered Isabelle down from the gate-house roof and led her through the throng to Marshal. Jean d'Erly had swung down from his saddle and rushed to assist Marshal in dismounting. Prodded by Jean's example, Meiler's own squire belatedly did the same for his master. Jean unlashed Marshal's helmet and lifted it off as Ranulf and Isabelle came up to them.

Marshal's face was haggard, and his attempt at a smile to Isabelle was less a smile than a grimace. He was cradling his broken wrist in his right arm. As Isabelle looked up at him, she realized that she had no idea how to express what she was feeling. Gratitude, relief, admiration—the words were totally inadequate.

"Thank you, Sir William," she said simply, hoping he would understand. "Thank you for all of us."

"Here, here," Ranulf said, provoking a fresh outburst of cheering from the men pressing in around them.

Isabelle, still unable to find the right words, thought to convey something of the depth of her feeling with her eyes, but Marshal glanced away, looking toward Meiler, who stood with his squire, surrounded by hostile stares.

Isabelle stiffened and approached the warlord, and the men around them fell silent. A look of resignation had replaced Meiler's scowl. "I am your prisoner, Lady Isabelle," he said tonelessly.

Isabelle ignored the silence pressing in on them and looked into Meiler's eyes for a long moment without speaking. A residue of the hatred that had gripped her on the wall stirred deep inside her, and she glanced at the spot where Marshal's lance had gashed Meiler's chain mail. The lance tip must have penetrated to some extent on impact, for the rent was stained the color of rust by blood that had seeped through the armor.

If she, and not Marshal, had held the lance pinning her enemy to the ground, she believed she would have driven it home. As she met Meiler's eyes again, a faint, ironic smile of understanding played across his lips. He knew what she was thinking.

"Not my prisoner, Sir Meiler," Isabelle said icily. "I prefer the word chosen by my champion. Consider yourself my 'guest.' That has a far more pleasant ring."

"As you wish, Your Ladyship," Meiler responded dryly.

"Yes," Isabelle agreed. "As I wish. But do not think I mock you, Sir Meiler. You will be confined to the dungeon at night, but by day you will have the freedom of the castle."

If Meiler was relieved that he would not be left to rot in the tower's cellar, he was too proud a man to show it.

"Tomorrow we will celebrate our victory," Isabelle added. "Unless you cannot stomach a feast in honor of the knight who defeated you, I would be pleased to have you attend."

"I can stomach food under any circumstances, Lady Isabelle," Meiler answered calmly. "And I remind you that custody of this castle is still undecided. Count John may not be content to share my defeat."

9

The night of Marshal's victory, Isabelle went to bed far later than usual. Only reluctantly had she left the great hall, where the men were getting a head start on the celebration to be held the next day. The singing, gambling, and drinking had been going on for hours and was still in full swing when Isabelle's exhaustion forced her at last to retire.

Marshal had wanted her to leave Kilkenny immediately, but he had finally yielded to her insistence that one day's delay would make no difference, and Ranulf had reluctantly concurred. Suppressing a yawn, Isabelle entered her chamber, preceded by Matilda, who carried a candle lantern to light their way. The odor of wood smoke and the sound of raucous laughter drifted up the stairwell and followed them into the chamber.

Matilda removed one of the lantern's translucent horn windows to light the all-night candle by the bed. As the candle flame flared, suffusing the chamber with a soft yellow glow, Isabelle walked to the trestle table and sat down heavily on the canvas seat of the folding stool. Despite her fatigue, she wondered if she would be able to fall asleep. She was still keyed up, and her body seemed to hum with nervous energy.

"How much did you win, Mattie?" she asked as Matilda came over to loosen her hair.

Matilda opened her fist and proudly displayed a handful of silver pennies. "The odds were two to one against you, milady," Matilda said, and hiccuped. "You should have seen poor Fulk's face when he had to pay up," she added, her tongue tripping over the words.

Isabelle smiled. She had never seen Matilda tipsy before. This had been a rare day in all respects. "You were luckier than you know," she said, stifling another yawn. "Sir William very nearly finished me when he brought out his bishop at the end."

"He never had a chance, milady, and you know it. You are a

106

murderous chess player. Winning Fulk's money was like taking candy from a baby."

"I thought you considered wagering a sin," Isabelle said, still smiling.

"Certainly not." Matilda sniffed, stepping behind her mistress and untying the ribbons on Isabelle's braids. She seemed to be having difficulty manipulating her fingers. "The priests don't approve, but they hate anything that's fun. At worst it's indiscreet for a woman to gamble." Matilda giggled. "And you, milady, were being discreet enough for both of us."

"What's that supposed to mean?"

"Nothing, milady," Matilda said innocently, but as she unbraided Isabelle's hair, Isabelle sensed that Matilda was grinning.

"All right, Mattie," Isabelle said impatiently, "out with it."

"I just thought that when Sir William offered you a game of chess, you might have invited him to play the game up here—away from all the noise. But no, you were the very soul of discretion."

"Noise has never disturbed my game," Isabelle said, deliberately missing the point, but she felt her cheeks flush. It was not difficult to guess what Matilda was driving at, and she wondered how many others had had the same thought. Had Marshal?

"Of course you were right, milady. Very proper," Matilda said, patting Isabelle's shoulder. "And I suppose your game might actually have suffered. Up here, alone with him, it might have been even more difficult to concentrate."

"Don't be impertinent!"

"I know it would have been difficult for me." Matilda sighed, blithely ignoring Isabelle's tone. Then she chuckled deep in her throat. "I wouldn't have minded washing more than his hair this morning, if he weren't so shy. Yes, I do believe I could become accustomed to that chore. I think—"

"I'm tired, Mattie," Isabelle interrupted. "I'm going to bed now."

"Not before I've brushed your hair, dear," Matilda said, preventing Isabelle from rising. "One hundred strokes a night makes the hair shine bright."

"And ladies who've been drinking, talk without thinking," Isabelle responded tartly. She wouldn't admit it, but Matilda was embarrassing her.

As a girl, Isabelle had always confided in Matilda. Neither the

King nor Count John had bothered to see to it that Isabelle was raised in the customary manner for a young lady of her rank, and she had grown up on her family estates surrounded by men and boys, with Matilda her only intimate female companion.

Matilda had been part mother and part older sister to Isabelle, and it was Matilda to whom Isabelle had turned for solace and advice in the first years of her sexual awakening, sharing the joys and sorrows of her adolescent infatuations with a handsome squire or the occasional silver-tongued trouvère.

But this was different. Isabelle was no longer a girl, and Matilda, however tipsy, was speaking to her woman-to-woman about Marshal; it was a new experience for Isabelle, and it made her uncomfortable. Marshal had been at the center of her thoughts all evening, to the exclusion of almost everything else, and the feelings he aroused in her were bewildering, in large part because she found herself unwilling to talk about them.

Isabelle's youthful crushes had not altered her straightforward view of men, and the strength of her attraction to Marshal had taken her by surprise. His gallant courage and skill on the battlefield had, of course, been dazzling, but it was the sound of his voice—deep, resonant, and surprisingly gentle—that lingered now in her mind; his voice and his ready, infectious smile. She had been able to talk with him that evening as if they were longtime friends, and it seemed incredible that only that morning he'd been a stranger.

Matilda began to brush Isabelle's hair. "I've seen Sir William before, milady," she said.

"Yes, you told me."

"At the Queen's Court in Poitiers. I saw him myself only once or twice, but I heard all the gossip. He was thinner then—more boyish, of course. All the ladies were in love with him."

"Don't talk nonsense, Mattie."

"But that was the fashion then, milady! And still is, I imagine," Matilda added wistfully. "The French courts are civilized, and they permit a lady to enjoy the attentions of her true knight—within certain limits, of course."

"Of course," Isabelle said with a smile.

Matilda still pined for the days she had spent at Eleanor's Court. That had been before the Queen had made the mistake of supporting her son, Prince Henry, in his first abortive revolt against his father. The King and his son had been reconciled, but Eleanor had been banished to England under house arrest, ending forever her reign as queen of the most fashionable Court of Love in France.

Matilda had wiled away many a rainy afternoon telling Isabelle of those Courts of Love, presided over by Eleanor on the dais, flanked by her daughter from her first marriage to King Louis of France, Marie of Campagne, and her daughter-in-law, Marguerite of France, wife of Prince Henry. With the heroes of the tournaments and ladies of high degree arrayed in the court before them, these three high priestesses of Courtly Love would rule on questions of principle and adjudicate disputes of love brought anonymously before the Court.

Could true love exist in a marriage?

Judgment: Possibly, but love and marriage were basically incompatible.

Could a lady's true knight breach his sacred silence to come to his lady's defense if he heard her charms disparaged?

Judgment: Not without incurring the lady's displeasure, but she should forgive him eventually.

Even as a girl, Isabelle had thought it all sounded childish—an excuse for posturing and gossip.

"There were all sorts of rumors about Sir William in those days," Matilda said admiringly. "And some in later years as well."

"Yes," Isabelle said dryly. "I suppose there were."

"Of course, the rumors may have been the result of wishful thinking, milady. Marshal was never the flirtatious type, and I doubt that the ladies I knew had any luck in that direction—not even the Queen. And if anyone could have claimed Marshal as her true knight, Eleanor could have."

"Why do you say that?" Isabelle asked, unable to resist her curiosity.

"Because there was a bond between them, milady, going back to a time just after Sir William was knighted. He was only modestly equipped at the time, as he had no independent means, and his uncle, Patrick, Earl of Salisbury, took him into his household.

"The Lusignans were in rebellion at the time, and Earl Patrick crossed to France with the King to help him put down the revolt. Knowing that the Lusignans were no match for him, the King had allowed Eleanor to come with him. Having occupied Lusignan Castle, the King left her there under Earl Patrick's protection while he pressed on in pursuit of the

Lusignans. Unknown to anyone, a war party under Guy de Lusignan slipped past the King at night and headed for the castle, in the hope of capturing the Queen.

"They tried to ambush her while she was riding outside the castle with her escort, but they were spotted while they were still some distance away. Earl Patrick sent Eleanor and the rest of the escort fleeing back to the castle, but he and Marshal stood their ground to delay the raiders. Neither of them was fully armed, and only Marshal was wearing a hauberk.

"The Earl was trying to mount his charger when he was killed by a lance thrust in the back, and Marshal barely had time to seize a pike and place his back against a hedgerow. Crying challenges to keep the knights from pursuing Eleanor, he fought them on foot, with neither shield nor helmet, cutting down their horses one after the other. They say he fought like a boar cornered by dogs.

"He put fifteen men out of action before one of Lusignan's knights came up behind the hedge and drove a lance into Marshal's thigh. Guy de Lusignan was furious that his knights had turned aside to fight Marshal, allowing Eleanor to escape, and he had Marshal thrown on a horse and carried off for ransom. Had he known that Marshal was a landless knight, he probably would have killed him on the spot. When they discovered their mistake, the Lusignans continued to hold Marshal, but they left him to tend his own wound, not caring whether he lived or died.

"But Eleanor cared. His allegiance had been to his uncle, not to Eleanor; and after the Earl fell, Marshal could have surrendered with honor. Yet he fought on.

"Eleanor ransomed him and kept him with her until his wound had completely healed. Then she equipped him with the finest arms and horses that money could buy, giving him his start in tournament. Once he had established a reputation, it was through Eleanor's influence that he became Prince Henry's tutor in chivalry.

"But that was years ago, milady. He may have been the Queen's knight once," Matilda said with wine-enhanced pride, "but now he is yours."

"You're being ridiculous, Mattie, and that's enough brushing," Isabelle said dismissively, and stood up.

"Am I?" Mattie persisted as she helped Isabelle undress. "Marshal risked his life for you today, and whether you acknowledge it or not, there's now a bond between you. You chose him as your champion, milady, and he served you magnificently. He *is* your true knight, and you must reward him."

"I know better than you how much I owe him," Isabelle said sharply, slipping into bed. "But you do him a disservice by implying that he expects a reward—a reward that you know very well I am powerless to give. I am not Eleanor of Aquitaine."

"I wasn't speaking of gifts of land or money," Matilda said coyly.

"What, then?" Isabelle asked, instantly regretting the question.

Matilda smiled knowingly. "You must have seen the way he looked at you this evening. Your chastity is reserved for your future husband, milady, but your love—that is something you should give to the man of your choice."

At that Isabelle groaned and turned on her side, pulling the coverlet over her head. "Go to bed, Mattie!"

Marshal stopped trying to reconstruct the sequence of moves that had led to his defeat. Now that the game was over, he could no longer summon the energy to concentrate. He rubbed his eyes tiredly and gathered up the discarded chess pieces that lay scattered among the remains of supper.

"You don't like losing, do you, Marshal?" Ranulf said, belching alcohol fumes.

"Not particularly," Marshal said, giving Ranulf the answer he expected. Actually Marshal didn't mind losing to a better player, and the girl was good—very good.

Ranulf sat beside Marshal at the head table on the raised dais at the lord's end of the great hall, facing the long trestle table for the enlisted men, which ran lengthwise down the center of the hall. Ranulf was sprawled in the canopied ceremonial seat Isabelle had vacated, a wine cup grasped none too securely in his hand.

Marshal stretched out his legs and leaned back in his chair, easing the stiffness in his body. He was no longer as resilient as he'd been at twenty, and he would have to sleep soon. Yet he wanted to stay awake a while longer. With fatigue clouding his mind like an opiate, he felt no compulsion to think ahead; for the moment, at least, he could savor the satisfaction of his small victory and the pleasure he found in Isabelle de Clare's company.

Tomorrow, he knew, sore muscles and stiff joints would remind him that time was working against him. His strength, speed, and endurance would not last forever. If he was to win with his sword something enduring for himself, he might not have many more years in which to do it. And in the cold light of morning, when reality reasserted itself, he would have to forget the smiling green eyes and flame-red hair of a girl forever beyond his reach.

Ranulf reached over and clapped Marshal on the shoulder. "Cheer up, my friend. At least you didn't lose any money."

"I never bet on my own game," Marshal said absently, as a cold sense of loneliness descended on him suddenly—a loneliness that had attacked him at odd moments throughout his adult life, always when he least expected it.

Friends he had always had, but there were times when that was not enough, when he missed the deeper ties of family and home—the sense of belonging somewhere and to someone.

"I hope you didn't mind my betting on Her Ladyship," Ranulf said, jingling a bag of coins, "but I've seen her play."

"Quite all right," Marshal said, raising his voice to carry over a sudden swell in the noise level.

A few of Ranulf's men were slumped over their table, overcome by wine, but most of them were clustered in a sweating pack at the table's far end. They were throwing dice, and the gambling was hot and heavy. The hall resounded with the yelling of the kibitzers, the triumphant cries of the winners, and the groans and curses of the losers.

"Poor old Fulk," Ranulf laughed, gesturing at the *serjant*, who, Marshal knew, had helped Isabelle escape from Pembroke. "He never learns; he just can't gamble worth a damn."

Fulk was a dark, slack-jawed giant, with long, powerful, almost simian arms. From the puzzled scowl on his face it was clear that the dice were running against him, and his jaw muscles were working furiously.

"What's he chewing on?" Marshal asked.

"Chunk of rawhide. Half the time he forgets and swallows the damned thing. But he isn't as dumb as he looks."

Marshal shook his head. "I hope not."

"He's one hell of a campaigner," Ranulf said with drunken affection. "We were together when the Earl took Waterford. Christ, that was eighteen years ago."

Marshal could see that Fulk would be a formidable enemy, and he understood why Isabelle had relied on him. His type was to be found in many baronial households—unimaginative but unswervingly loyal. His devotion to the late Earl had clearly been transferred to Isabelle, for when she was near, Fulk's watchful, protective gaze never strayed from her for long.

"I'm telling you, Marshal," Ranulf said, hiccuping and belching simultaneously, "those were the days! The land was here, just waiting for men with the guts to take it and the will to hold it," he said. "The Danes had never tried to push inland from the seaports they'd settled; they were content to let the wild Irish tribes war among themselves. Until we brought in civilization, the people here were living in the dark ages. No law to speak of, and no idea of what to do with the land. They still reckon their wealth in cattle, and left to their own devices, they'd only clear the forest for pastureland."

"Then, of course, the King made *his* move," Ranulf grumbled. "He came over with an army of his own, including a siege train, to be sure the Earl and the other Marcher lords did homage to him for the lands *we'd* taken—the land we'd won with our own sweat and blood."

Marshal smiled. "That's the way it works, Ranulf. That's civilization for you."

Ranulf grunted, drained his cup, and set it down on the table with a bang. "The King skimmed the cream right off the top. He took Wexford, Waterford, and Dublin into his own hands, along with about a third of the territory Earl Richard claimed as his."

"Your earl must have come out all right," Marshal said without much sympathy. "Henry never squeezed a man too hard."

"Oh, he gave something in return," Ranulf said sourly. "The lands in Wales he'd seized from Earl Richard years before on the pretext that the Earl's father had supported King Stephen in the civil war."

"Leaving Richard de Clare the richest baron in the realm," Marshal said pointedly. "That's not bad, Ranulf, not bad at all."

"It wouldn't be so bad if the King hadn't handed over Ireland to John. When John came over two years ago with an entourage of teenage courtiers to receive homage from the Irish chieftans, he damned near provoked a rebellion. The chieftans came to his court in Dublin to do him honor, and John and his pimply-faced court laughed in their faces. Christ, some of his courtiers even started pulling on the chieftans' long beards.

"And now he has Normans pitted against each other. His agents are all over the place. I'm telling you, Marshal, John must have been weaned on intrigue."

Ranulf looked up sharply as a snarling dogfight erupted over a bone tossed to one of Ranulf's mastiffs. "Tom!" he yelled. "Throw some water on those damned dogs before they tear each other apart!"

Marshal yawned and rubbed his eyes.

"You look beat," Ranulf said. "You can sleep in my room in the barracks hall. We've moved out the livestock and cleaned up the place, but the stink's still there."

"I prefer that to the smoke in here," Marshal said, suppressing another yawn. "And that latrine is getting pretty ripe. When's the last time the pit was cleaned out?"

"What do you care? You're getting out of here soon."

"I wish we were leaving tomorrow," Marshal said worriedly. "John may have wanted to keep this quiet up to now, but once he learns what's happened here, he'll go straight to the King—to protect himself. I want to get to the King first."

"One day won't make any difference," Ranulf said easily. "Meiler's henchmen will return home, as they were told. None of them has the imagination or initiative to send word to John."

Marshal nodded, but still he itched to be on his way with Isabelle. Neither she nor Ranulf would be safe from John's wrath unless he could persuade the King to intervene; and now that Meiler had been neutralized, this last obstacle loomed larger in his mind. He had to get to Henry first.

"If I were John," Marshal said, "I'd have alerted my customs agents to watch for Lady Isabelle—to make sure she remains bottled up in Ireland."

"It's a possibility," Ranulf agreed. "We'll have to disguise her, that's all."

Ranulf's tone was casual, and it made Marshal uneasy. He sensed that both Ranulf and Isabelle, buoyed by his victory over Meiler, had too much confidence in him.

"Did you have any trouble with bandits on the way up from Waterford?" Ranulf asked.

"Nothing I couldn't handle, but I didn't have a lady with me."

"I'll give you Fulk, Jean, and five others. In these parts that qualifies as an army. What are you going to do when you get to England?"

"If I knew where the King would be, I'd take Lady Isabelle straight to him; but I don't want to be wandering around the countryside with her. I'll take her to the Queen. Eleanor has no great love for her youngest son, and she'll appreciate a fresh face. Lady Isabelle's rank is certainly high enough to suit her, and neither John nor the King should complain.

Once Lady Isabelle joins the Queen, she'll be on ice. She won't be able to bribe her way past the guards watching Eleanor the way she did in Pembroke."

"She'll have to leave Matilda behind for the time being," Ranulf said. "Smuggling one woman aboard ship will be enough for you to handle. But she'll want to bring Fulk; he's something of a talisman to her. Besides," he added with a crooked grin, "I wouldn't want to be the one to deal with Fulk if we tried taking her out of here without him."

"That's fine with me," Marshal said.

Ranulf cleared his throat tentatively. "You could use a squire, couldn't you?"

Marshal looked at Ranulf in surprise. "Are you offering me Jean?"

"If you'll take him. He's a good, straight lad. He's quick and he's eager. He has the makings, Marshal."

"And what about you?"

Ranulf grimaced. "I won't find a boy as good as Jean, but hell, I'm past it and you know it. Let's face it, with you he'll have a shot at the big time."

"Have you mentioned this to him?"

Ranulf shook his head. "I didn't want to get his hopes up. You know damned well he'll jump at the chance."

"All right," Marshal said without hesitation, "I'll give him a try— *if* you're sure about this."

"I'm sure. I hate the thought of breaking in a new squire, but I'm sure. One more thing. How long do you want me to hold Meiler?"

"That's up to you. A few weeks should be enough. Even if he breaks his word and musters another siege force, that will take time. By then you should have received word of the King's decision, and that will settle things—one way or the other."

Ranulf turned and placed his hand heavily on Marshal's shoulder. "Listen, my friend, however it goes, we owe you. Have you got that?"

"I've got it."

"Good," Ranulf said, refilling his wine cup. "Now, if you're not going to take this opportunity to do some serious drinking, you'd better get to bed. The lady of the castle is going to have you up early tomorrow for some hawking."

"What!"

"I don't think there's any risk. My scouts tracked Meiler's knights far enough to be sure they're heading home."

"And what if they double back?"

Ranulf shrugged. "As I said before, they don't have that much initiative, but if you're worried, you'll have to explain it to Her Ladyship. I'm going to have my own hands full tomorrow. My wife will be coming back from St. Canice Abbey. I'll tell you one thing, Marshal. I thank God Meiler didn't take it into his head to burn down our manor. If my wife had to move in here with me, there'd be hell to pay."

10

Marshal reined in his horse, and Isabelle halted beside him. "Don't look so worried, Sir William," she said. "Meiler's men are long gone."

Marshall nodded absently, studying the lay of the land. They were riding along the east bank of the river a mile south of the castle, following a narrow strip of dry ground between the marshland bordering the river and the virgin pine forest on their left. It was just after dawn. Fog shrouded the river's glassy surface and rose in ghostly fingers from the marsh.

The early-morning stillness, the mist in the half-light, and the great fir trees of the limitless, primeval forest created a scene of enchantment and mystery, but Isabelle could see that the effect was lost on Marshal. He sat stiffly erect in the saddle, listening, his restless eyes probing the dark forest.

He had not wanted her to venture outside the castle, and now she wished she had not pressed him so hard. The hunting party had the air of a war patrol. Fulk and Ranulf's marshal were riding point, fifty yards ahead, and Jean trailed at the same distance. They were fully armed, and Marshal's armor lacked only the enveloping steel helmet. Two young Welsh riders kept pace on the left flank, threading their way through the trees thirty yards inside the forest.

Despite these precautions, Marshal had not relaxed for a moment, and Isabelle felt a pang of guilt. She was sure that Ranulf was right and that Meiler's men would not have doubled back; but Marshal was not sure, and she regretted forcing him to go against his own better judgment. Hawking was a passion for her, and she had not immediately appreciated the depth of his concern.

"Let's ring up your bird, Lady Isabelle," Marshal said, managing a smile, but there was a hint of impatience in his voice.

For a moment Isabelle considered giving up the hunt, but the falcon she carried on her gloved hand was stirring with infectious anticipation. Now that they had come this far, surely one flight could do no harm.

Eagerly Isabelle unhooked the short tether binding the bird to her wrist, and the falcon spread its wings in response. She removed its hood, and the hawk lifted its head, its fierce eyes flashing. Isabelle's heart beat faster. Her falcon was a magnificent peregrine she had trained herself, and part of the reason she had been so anxious to come out this morning was to show off her hawk to Marshal.

She stroked the falcon affectionately. "I think she bears a distinct resemblance to you, Sir William," she said impulsively. "The same coloring, the same—"

"Beak?" Marshal interjected with a smile.

Isabelle laughed self-consciously. "Well, I wouldn't have put it that way," she said with a sidelong glance at him.

Marshal did have a hawklike profile, but now she was flustered, thinking the remark revealed how keenly aware of him she was—of everything about him.

When she had arisen at first light, she had been torn between her desire to see him as soon as possible and her wish to take the time to make herself attractive. Matilda's suggestive chatter the night before had embarrassed her at the time, but she had awakened with a secret excitement and a rush of anticipation.

Did he sense the intensity of feeling he aroused in her? A part of her wanted him to know, and the other part quailed at the thought. What would he think if he knew? How could she possibly compare with the sophisticated, worldly women he must have known at Court?

"All right, Isolt, catch us a nice fat heron!" she cried, launching the hawk.

Isolt's powerful wings dug sharply into the air, and the falcon climbed in a swift spiral, its wings beating rapidly, the tiny bells attached to its legs tinkling in the stillness. Isabelle smiled with pleasure as the hawk spread its wings and tail feathers to catch an updraft, and she felt the familiar exhilaration as the bird spiraled higher and higher, riding the air current, until it was only a speck against the sky.

This was the thrill of hawking for her: watching the hawk she had trained soar into the sky, an extension of herself, her spirit carried aloft on its wings.

"Fulk!" she shouted excitedly, waving in the direction of the river, and Fulk turned his horse and rode out into the marsh to flush the game.

Isabelle spurred her horse forward and called over her shoulder, "Come on, Sir William! And try to stop frowning!"

In a few moments she came abreast of Fulk, whose horse was splashing through the marsh at the river's edge, and she had to slow down. Ranulf's marshal had kept ahead of her, maintaining his point position, and as Marshal caught up with her she saw him turn to check that Jean was following at the correct distance.

Again she felt guilty, but then a pair of herons hidden in the mist-shrouded marsh reeds were startled into flight.

"There!" Isabelle cried, digging in her spurs.

The herons rose to a height of fifty feet above the marsh and flew downriver, with Isabelle in full chase. She overtook the point rider and raced past him.

"Take care, Lady Isabelle! Slow down!" she heard Marshal cry, his horse pounding over the treacherous terrain in pursuit.

Abruptly the hawk dropped into view, streaking down on the unsuspecting herons. The falcon dropped a wing, veered, and then plummeted, wings folded, toward its prey. At the final instant the falcon's talons shot forward, and it struck the trailing heron with a sound like the punch of a fist. The stunned heron dropped like a stone into the marsh, and the falcon swooped down to deliver the coup de grace with its deadly beak.

Isabelle swung her horse into the marsh, riding toward the spot where the falcon had disappeared in the reeds, and closed in on the sound of the hawk's bells. Fulk and Marshal rode up, and Fulk dismounted to retrieve the heron.

"Easy, now," Isabelle said, her cheeks flushed with the excitement of the chase. "Don't frighten her."

Fulk nodded and gently lifted the dead heron out of the water, with the falcon still jealously hanging on. Isabelle whistled softly to the hawk and coaxed it back onto her glove. She tethered it, slipped on the hood, and fed the falcon some bits of fresh pigeon meat.

"It's a fine kill, milady," Fulk said approvingly, tying the heron to his saddle and remounting.

"Let's try farther downriver!" Isabelle said happily. "We'll bag another for the feast."

Marshal shook his head. "We've come too far from the castle already, Your Ladyship."

Still caught up in the excitement of the hunt, Isabelle started to protest, but she checked herself as she noted the worry in Marshal's eyes. She glanced back at the castle, which was nearly out of sight beyond a bend in the river, and she was surprised by how far they had come.

"You're right, Sir William," she said quickly. "One heron is enough," and she turned her mare upriver.

Marshal began to relax as soon as they turned back. He trusted Ranulf's judgment enough to know that an ambush was unlikely, and now that they were returning, his anxiety ebbed away. But he was not at peace with himself.

He should have insisted that Isabelle remain within Kilkenny's walls; an hour's sport was not worth the risk, no matter how slight. Yet he had found himself unable to resist the antipication in the girl's eyes when she had appeared before sunrise in the great hall with her hawk.

It was a small warning, but a warning nevertheless. He would have to keep a tighter rein on his attraction to Isabelle de Clare. If he allowed his feelings to warp his judgment, things could end badly for both of them.

He smiled self-derisively. It had not been as easy to ignore her charm as he had thought, for she was unlike other women of her class. She had a distinctive beauty of which she seemed strangely unaware, and her manner melded a man's directness with a natural femininity that was unmarred by affectation.

Marshal was not simply drawn to her as a man to a beautiful young woman; he *liked* this courageous, unaffected girl, and that made him wary. It would be far too easy to be captivated by Isabelle de Clare, he thought; and perhaps because he wished it were otherwise, Marshal failed to realize that he already was.

They were still a mile and a half from the castle when the two young Welshmen suddenly burst upon them from the forest. Marshal had his sword out in an instant. One of the boys babbled excitedly to Isabelle, but Marshal didn't understand a word. He only knew the boys were scared.

"What's he saying, Lady Isabelle?" Marshal cut in as the other men converged on them, reining in and drawing their swords. His voice

120

was controlled, but inwardly he cursed himself for allowing Isabelle to leave the castle.

"Goblins!" Isabelle responded, her face going white.

"What!"

"Goblins," Isabelle said again. "The forests here are supposed to be full of them!"

"That's right, sire," Jean confirmed loudly, and Marshal shot him an angry glance. Now all the men, including Fulk, were eyeing the forest nervously.

"But what exactly did they *see*, Lady Isabelle?" Marshal said impatiently. He was tempted to order a dash for the castle walls, but if this was an ambush, they might ride straight into it.

"They didn't see anything," Isabelle said anxiously. "They just heard noises—strange noises."

"What noises? Men on foot? Horses?"

"Neither. They're sure there are goblins in there, Sir William. Goblins hate the sun, but the forest is so dark. . . ."

"It's an ambush I'm worried about," Marshal said, turning to Fulk. The *serjant* could be relied on to protect Isabelle with his life if necessary. "I'm going into the forest," he said. "Count to thirty and then move out. Keep your weapons at the ready and hold the pace to a trot so I can stay ahead of you on the flank. If men are lying in wait up ahead, I want to flush them out."

Marshal was uneasy about leaving Isabelle's side, but the fear of goblins he saw in the boys' eyes forced him to take the flank.

He turned his horse and moved into the forest, its darkness closing over him. The scent of pine was heavy in the air. There was no undergrowth, and the soft tread of his horse's hooves on the thick carpet of fir needles barely disturbed the silence. He rode in as far as he could without losing sight of the light at the forest's edge and turned to ride parallel to the riverbank.

The gaps between the massive, primeval trees were wide and the riding was easy, but Marshal suppressed the temptation to press forward too quickly. He eased his left arm out of the sling he was wearing and slipped it through the loops of his shield, wishing now that he had his helmet.

As his horse trotted forward, Marshal's eyes restlessly scanned a wide arc, and his ears strained to pick up any strange sounds. At regular intervals he looked upward, for he'd known knights who had died because they forgot that men could climb trees.

He started as a squirrel chattered at him from a branch directly above his head, and he deliberately eased his grip on his sword. There was no reason to be jumpy. Without undergrowth for cover, he would see an ambusher as soon as the man spotted him. How much time had passed? One minute? Two? He picked up the pace a bit, anxious to stay ahead of Fulk.

The sound that had frightened the boys must have been fairly close to them or Marshal would have heard it too. He rode for another fifty yards and then reined in a for a moment to listen. Nothing. Behind him and to his left he heard the snort of a horse. The others were catching up with him. Marshal was about to touch his spurs to his mount's flanks when he heard something else—off to the right. A dry slither, followed by a strange, whistling sigh. There was a pause, and then the sound came again.

Marshal cocked his head, waited, and got another fix on the noise. He turned toward it and move deeper into the forest, sure that was what the boys had heard. It had an eerie quality that he could not place, but goblins? Marshal had no idea what sounds a demon might make. Maybe the boys knew something he didn't; the Welsh reputedly knew more about such things.

Marshal crossed himself for good measure, but he kept going, following the sound ever deeper into the forest gloom. Slither—sigh. Slither—sigh. Gooseflesh rose on his arms as his imagination worked on him.

Slither—sigh. He was close now—very close. He should see it any second. Marshal caught a flicker of movement ahead and gently reined in, willing his horse to remain still.

The next sigh Marshal heard was his own, and it was an involuntary sigh of relief. The "goblin" was an emaciated hunchback dressed in a filthy patchwork of black woolen rags, dragging the carcass of a freshly killed doe across the needle-carpeted forest floor.

The man's head was swathed in a greasy tangle of hair and beard. It was impossible to judge his age, but he was clearly nearing exhaustion. He was an asthmatic, and the whistling sigh Marshal had heard was just the first and loudest of the man's gasps for air every time he dragged the carcass another few feet.

Bent over as the man was, and too exhausted to raise his head, he didn't see Marshal watching him. A leather sling hung from a cord about his waist, and Marshal assumed he'd killed the doe with a stone to the head. It must have been an incredibly lucky shot, Marshal thought grimly. Bad luck for the deer, and worse luck for the man. The man was obviously not a professional poacher, or he would be using a more effective weapon, and he had to be desperate to risk killing a deer so close to the castle.

Leinster was a palatinate, exempt from the King's justice, but that would not save the man's life. Justice was administered by the palatine lord alone, but the laws were the same—and the strictest was the forest law. Forest game was reserved for the lord, and the penalty for taking it was death without appeal. The man had killed one of Isabelle's deer, and for that he would have to die.

The man was dragging the deer deeper into the forest. Perhaps he was a charcoal burner with a family to feed. Perhaps they were starving, but that wouldn't matter to a court. Maybe he was ignorant of Norman law, but that mattered even less.

Marshal swallowed back the bitter taste that rose in his throat. It made no difference that he was not in Isabelle's service; he was sworn to enforce the law wherever he might be, and he'd caught the man red-handed. The only mercy he could show would be to kill the wretch now, sparing him the mental torment of a trial and certain execution. Marshal was less than thirty yards away, and he could attack and kill him before the man realized what was happening.

The man seized the deer's forelegs to drag the doe another few feet, and Marshal drew his sword. He had no choice. Here, alone, with no one to know, he was all the more honor-bound to do the right . . .

The man was dragging the carcass out of sight, and Marshal still hadn't moved. Now he could no longer see him, but he could hear the man, hidden by the trees, wheezing for breath. As he listened to the receding sounds, Marshal, his sword still poised, slowly realized that he wasn't going to attack. His duty was absolutely clear to him, but he simply couldn't bring himself to do it.

With a grimace of self-disgust, he sheathed his sword, turned his horse, and rode back toward the river.

The victory feast was held outdoors in the courtyard before the keep. The banquet tables, covered in white cloth, were arranged in a *T* on a wide, green carpet of freshly cut rushes. Isabelle's canopied chair was centrally placed at the head table, and her guests were seated at varying distances from her according to rank. Knights and ladies were served at the head table, and everyone else sat at a long row of tables forming the spine of the *T*, with the priest and castle officers sitting nearest the head table.

Despite the best efforts of Ranulf's wife, the feast did not begin on time. The bells of St. Canice Abbey had long since rung Sext when the trumpeter finally sounded the call to the feast in the early afternoon. The knights, ladies, officers, and enlisted men converged on the tables, waited impatiently for the end of the priest's long-winded blessing, and then sat down and proceeded to gorge themselves.

It was difficult to believe that only the day before the castle had been under siege, stripped of nonessential personnel, the courtyard filled with the stink and barnyard noise of livestock and cluttered with the paraphernalia of war. The return to a peacetime footing had already begun on the afternoon of Marshal's victory. Word that the siege was over spread quickly, and Ranulf's steward and butler returned to organize the small army of retainers streaming back to the castle.

Ranulf's wife, Madame de Barre, escorted by Ranulf's priest and the chamberlain, returned from the abbey while the hawking party was hunting downriver, and she immediately plunged into the confusion of cleaning operations and preparations for the feast. The steward resented her intrusion into his domain, but she enforced her demands with an iron will. Ranulf's wife was a tiny, birdlike woman who looked like a nun in her simple white gown and wimple, but she wielded her tongue like a whip.

Unsatisfied with the steward's initial efforts, Madame de Barre ordered a second cleaning of the barracks and the keep's chambers, the removal of the manure piles from the courtyard, and the raking of every inch of ground. Next she had the excess stocks of grain carted down to the town for distribution. There was not enough to compensate for the losses to Meiler's scavengers, but the example was intended to prompt St. Canice's tight-fisted abbot to open his own ample storehouses.

All this was accomplished amid the frenetic swirl of activity around the bakery and kitchen, where varlets and cook-house assistants toiled under the demanding supervision of the steward, who, in turn, was driven by the lash of Madame de Barre's tongue. Prodigious quantities of fresh meat and poultry sent up from the castle slaughterhouse were dressed and cleaned and variously stewed, baked, and roasted. The domestic fare was augmented by the game and fish brought in during the morning by the castle's huntsmen and the local fishermen.

Having tasted the butler's souring wines, Madame de Barre had sent to the abbey for several cartloads of wine, and a variety of spiced and honeyed wines were prepared, gallons at a time. For cruder palates, barrels of beer were stacked outside in readiness.

She had intended to cut down the walkways suspended between the stockade fighting platform and the tower, but when Ranulf refused, she ordered varlets to drape them with brightly colored bunting she miraculously conjured up, probably from her own manor, from which she had also drawn additional cutlery, cups, platters, and table linen.

The whirlwind transformation of the castle's appearance and the spur-of-the-moment feast were an impressive feat, but Marshal was in no mood to enjoy the festivities. Preoccupied by the incident in the forest, he would have preferred to skip the whole thing. Marshal believed in the rule of law, and he despised those who did not. In his own mind he shared the poacher's guilt. By letting the man go free, he had abetted a capital crime, and his conscience gave him no peace.

"More wine, sire?" Jean d'Erly asked.

Marshal turned to look up at his new squire and frowned. "If it pleases the *lady*," he said pointedly.

Jean cleared his throat in embarrassment. "Would you care for more wine, madam?" he said to Matilda, who was seated on Marshal's left and sharing the cup with him.

Matilda smiled up at Jean and nodded. As the squire poured wine from his pitcher, he was clearly aware of Marshal's scrutiny, and he took care not to spill a drop.

Jean moved away to serve the others at the head table, and Matilda whispered, "Don't be too hard on the boy, Sir William. He's trying very hard."

"He has to learn, Lady Matilda," Marshal said, lifting the cup with both hands and extending it to her. Matilda's rank did not entitle her to be addressed as Lady Matilda, but it was permissible to bend the rule, and Marshal knew that she appreciated the gesture.

"I'm sure he's thrilled to be your squire," Matilda said. "I'm sure I would be. The Royal courts are nothing if not exciting."

Matilda chattered on, as she had throughout the banquet, and Marshal, half listening, nodded at appropriate intervals, grateful that he was not required to hold up his end of the conversation.

He had taken something from nearly every dish brought to the tables by the parade of varlets streaming back and forth from the kitchen. The courses had followed one another in a staggering array: stag, beef, mutton, trout, eels, rabbit, duck, heron, pork pies, chicken pies, custards and pastries, nuts, dried fruits, and honey bread.

He had eaten mechanically, without real appetite, and although Marshal normally enjoyed music, he barely registered the surprising skill of the local flute and harp players performing off to one side. He had, however, noted Isabelle's performance. Although she was seated on Marshal's right, they had exchanged few words, for she was fully occupied with entertaining her "guest," Meiler fitz Henry.

Throughout the banquet she had engaged her enemy in courteous conversation, plying him with questions about his exploits. She had overcome his initial, surly reserve and actually managed to draw him out. Now she was asking the warlord about his family, and Meiler was responding. Marshal considered it a bravura performance, for he had seen the hatred flickering in her eyes when she had accepted Meiler's surrender.

Meiler must have seen it, too, which made it even more surprising that she could persuade him now to put aside their enmity for the sake of civility. There was still something of the coltish, volatile girl in Isabelle de Clare, but she could, when it suited her, display the style and wit of a great lady.

"Ranulf!" Madame de Barre snapped, her sharp voice knifing through the drunken clamor rising from the enlisted men's table. "Control your men!"

Marshal smiled and leaned back to look toward Ranulf, who was seated at the far right-hand end of the head table. Isabelle had placed Madam de Barre between Ranulf and Meiler, but from the dogged look on the old knight's face Marshal guessed that Ranulf would have preferred the company of his enemy.

The pikemen and archers were becoming unruly, hurling chunks of meat and bread across the table at each other, and Ranulf decided on the simple expedient of ending the feast. He caught Isabelle's eye, and she nodded.

"Father!" Ranulf yelled to the priest. "Let's have the benediction."

The priest rose to his feet unsteadily and, forgetting his linen napkin, wiped his greasy fingers on his cowl. He was a thin young man, and the wine had hit him hard. He started to speak, but his words were lost in the drunken shouts and laughter from the far end of the tables. He was about to raise his voice when he was quite obviously struck by a wave of nausea. Covering his mouth, he hurriedly made the sign of the cross and rushed away.

Isabelle laughed, shook her head, and rose from the table, bringing the banquet to an unceremonious end.

"Fulk!" Ranulf shouted. "I don't want those men to go to sleep now, or too many will be hung over to stand watch. Organize a stone throw and wrestling—and set up some archery butts on the forward slope. I'll put up five sous prize money for the winner of each contest."

Isabelle turned to Marshal and looked up at him with a smile. "Are you going to participate in the stone throw, Sir William? It only takes one arm."

"I think I'd prefer a quiet stroll, Lady Isabelle," he said with a smile, noting that Matilda had moved away as soon as Isabelle had turned toward him.

"We could walk down to the garden," Isabelle said. "If you don't mind company."

"Of course not."

Looking at her, Marshal wondered why he had never thought freckles were attractive on a girl. The thought was only fleeting, for out of the corner of his eye he saw Meiler fitz Henry, who had managed to drift away, walking toward the courtyard stable. The stockade gate was open, and the two guards manning the gate house looked none too alert.

Marshal excused himself and went over to Ranulf, who was staring, glassy-eyed, at his wife, clearly not listening to whatever she was saying. Ranulf had not yet adjusted to the renewal of marital bliss, and he'd been using wine as an anesthetic.

"I think your hawk is about to fly the coop," Marshal said, gesturing toward Meiler.

Ranulf gaped for a moment, and then his eyes snapped back into focus. "Son of a bitch!" he growled, and started yelling for the men who were supposed to be guarding the warlord.

II

"I'm surprised you didn't put on your hauberk, Sir William," Isabelle teased as they walked down the long slope toward the castle's garden. Jean, mounted on his gelding, trailed them at a discreet distance. He carried Marshal's sword and shield and was leading two horses for Isabelle and Marshal. "Are you always this cautious?"

"Always," Marshal said, nodding in response to a black-clad old man who bowed to him and Isabelle as he passed.

The townsfolk who had shared in the feast at rude tables set out in front of the gate were streaming back down the hill, many of them staggering from a surfeit of beer. Bread, beef, and mutton had been their fare, with beer instead of wine, but for many it was the first time their bellies had been full since the previous year's harvest. The poor who were too old, sick, or crippled to make the short journey up to the castle would receive the leftovers collected from the tables.

"People around here are certainly partial to black," Marshal remarked.

Every man, woman, and child he had seen was dressed from head to foot in primitively fashioned black woolens. The men's costumes were curious. Instead of hooded mantles, they wore tightly fitted patchwork caps attached to short, knee-length capes, and their hose and breeches were all one piece. But what struck Marshal most was the total absence of any color but black.

"They don't dye their clothes black," Isabelle said with a smile. "It's the wool. They only raise black sheep here."

Marshal shook his head. "Ranulf was right when he said this territory is backward. What you need here is trade. If I were . . ."

"If you were what?" Isabelle prompted. "A lord in Ireland?"

"I suppose that's what I was thinking," Marshal admitted. "I'd do what your father probably meant to do if he'd lived—construct inland

128

ports along the rivers, build up some river traffic, and use trade instead of arms to stabilize the region."

"I'm not sure that was in his mind," Isabelle mused. "I think he was an adventurer at heart. At least that's the way Ranulf talks about him."

"A man can tire of adventure, Lady Isabelle. It's a young man's game."

"And do you feel old, Sir William?" Isabelle asked with a sidelong glance.

Marshal smiled. "Sometimes."

"You have no land of your own?"

"Not an acre. I was a fourth son. My father was the King's Marshal under Stephen, and he saved his lands by switching sides in the civil war, but his holdings were modest. When he died, there was too little to carve up. I knew from the start that I'd have to make my own way, and maybe one day it will add up to something."

"You'll receive a grant from the King," Isabelle said confidently. "After all, what knight banneret in his service has not? All it takes to make you a baron," she said, snapping her fingers, "is a word from the King."

"That's right," Marshal said with a laugh. "That's all it takes."

They were approaching the entrance to the garden, which was situated on a knoll beside the river and surrounded by a high, thick hedge.

"From what I hear," Isabelle said lightly, "the King has stored up a rich supply of marriageable heiresses. Who knows, he might even give you my lands."

With that, she slipped through the arched gateway in the hedge and disappeared into the garden, sparing Marshal the necessity of a reply. Marshal looked back at his squire, who had halted partway up the slope to keep watch. Jean waved to assure Marshal that he was alert.

The late-afternoon sun was behind Marshal, and the low angle of its rays illuminated the castle's whitewashed keep, casting it in sharp relief against the horizon. Once again Marshal was gripped by déjà vu and a haunting uneasiness. He was sure that somewhere, sometime long ago, he must have been in just such a castle and had looked at it at the same time of day from a similar angle.

Unaccountably he shivered, then turned away and entered the garden. It was surprisingly large and elaborate for a frontier castle and designed for pleasure as well as utility. The largest area was reserved for vegetables, herbs, and spices, but there were small groves of fruit trees and also extensive beds of flowers, some of which were beginning to bloom.

Isabelle had vanished, and Marshal grimaced. To his right was a labyrinth, its hedge walls grown to the same thickness and height as the hedge surrounding the entire garden. She must have gone into the maze, and he would have to follow. *Claustrophobia* was not a word in his language; he only knew that he hated garden labyrinths.

The path between the labyrinth's walls was little wider than Marshal's shoulders. At first the path curved in a wide arc, but then it turned sharply in the reverse direction. As Marshal strode along the path, it twisted and turned, endlessly doubling back on itself, with multiple side exits, most of which eventually led to a dead end.

Despite the open sky above, Marshal felt the walls closing in on him as he went deeper into the maze, and he walked more quickly, anxious to reach the center. But the design was too clever for him and he became disoriented. As he found himself in the same cul-de-sac for the third time, cold beads of sweat began to dot his forehead.

The walls seemed to be squeezing out the air he was trying to breathe, and he could barely resist the urge to smash his way straight through them. Marshal closed his eyes to fight down his rising panic. That was what it was, he knew. Panic. But why? It was only a goddamned garden maze. He wasn't trapped. He wasn't trapped!

"It's a pretty good maze, isn't it?"

Marshal opened his eyes. "Yes, Your Ladyship," he said, feeling sweat running down over his ribs.

"Come on," Isabelle said, walking forward to take his hand. "I'll show you the way. There's a turning farther on that looks like a dead end. That's what fooled you." Isabelle laughed. "You certainly don't have much patience. I heard you barging around in here like an angry bull. My father loved labyrinths. He ordered them planted almost everywhere he built a stronghold."

The maze ended at a gate opening into a long hedge-walled corridor leading directly out of the garden. Isabelle opened the gate, and Marshal followed her out to a rock ledge overlooking the river. The sun still shone on the rolling forest beyond, tinging the green with orange. The river below lay in shadow, its dark, mirrorlike surface occasionally broken by a surfacing fish.

Isabelle spread out her robe and sat down, clasping her arms about her knees, and Marshal sat down beside her. From the direction of the castle .came isolated shouts of Ranulf's archers on the slope, but the sounds were muted and only emphasized the peaceful stillness hanging over the river.

For a long while they said nothing, and Marshal wondered what Isabelle was thinking as she looked out over the forest. Was she thinking about him? Marshal smiled inwardly. He'd been with the Templars too long. Finding himself alone with a beautiful woman after so many years was like swallowing brandywine on an empty stomach.

When Isabelle finally spoke, she caught Marshal off-guard. "What did you see in the forest this morning?" she asked.

"What makes you think I saw anything at all, Lady Isabelle?" Marshal responded lamely.

Isabelle turned toward him, smiled, and shook her head. "Dissembling is not one of your talents, Sir William."

"I didn't see any goblins."

"But something was out there. When you caught up with us, you acted—I don't know—differently."

Marshal remained silent. He knew that his evasion was arousing her curiosity even more, but he didn't want to lie to her, and he had no wish to discuss the incident in the forest. He would wrestle with his own conscience alone.

"You don't want to tell me, do you," Isabelle said.

"No, Lady Isabelle," Marshal replied more bluntly than he'd intended. But Isabelle did not appear to take offense, and to Marshal's surprise she did not press him. Instead she changed the subject.

"Ranulf told me that you're worried John may have alerted his customs agents at Waterford to watch for me," she said. "He suggested I diguise myself as your manservant until we reach England. With the right clothes I think I could pass for a boy."

"I think that's a good idea," Marshal said. "It may take a little practice, though—acting like a servant, I mean. Your voice is all right, but we'll have to dirty your face up a bit. You're a little too pretty to be a boy."

Isabelle bowed. "Thank you, sire."

"Of course, the freckles will help," Marshal said without thinking. "Most women cover them up with powder."

"Do you think I should?" Isabelle said quickly.

"No—no, of course not, Lady Isabelle! That's not what I meant," Marshal said in confusion.

Isabelle smiled slightly and nodded, but Marshal was sure the damage had been done, and he silently cursed his clumsiness. He liked those freckles of hers.

"And what will you call me?" Isabelle asked. "You'll have to drop the 'Lady Isabelle'."

"What about Rusty?"

"How did you know that?" Isabelle laughed.

"I heard Ranulf use it."

"You did? When? Oh, it doesn't matter. Rusty it will be," she said with pleasure. "I've always preferred my nickname, anyway."

"Well, you'll have to change back when we reach England," Marshal said. "I don't think you'd care for the rude comfort of wayside inns, and if we're to make use of castles along the route to Winchester, we don't want to deal with the complication of a disguise. We'll just say that the Queen has invited you to visit her. The lack of an entourage for a lady of your rank will seem odd, but we should be able to invent a plausible excuse."

"What's she like, the Queen?" Isabelle asked.

Marshal thought for a moment and said, "Regal. Eleanor of Aquitaine is a woman fit to rule a kingdom and forever disappointed that she could not."

"Is she bitter?"

"No, I don't think so. Eleanor is too much of a realist to be bitter. I haven't seen her in over six years, but I doubt she's changed very much."

"Are you sure she'll consent to my staying with her?"

"That's the only thing I *am* sure of," Marshal said firmly. "She'll welcome your company, Lady Isabelle. Some of her ladies-in-waiting are even older than she is. Young ladies don't care to share imprisonment, even with a queen. She'll welcome you, and she'll keep you safe from John."

"You're not going to tell her about that?" Isabelle said in alarm.

"One of us should. That's the whole point of my bringing you to her."

"But I'd feel so . . . uncomfortable if she knew."

Marshal smiled and shook his head. "If you think she'll be shocked, you're wrong. We're talking about a woman who has borne the children

132

of two kings and has had more than her share of consorts. Eleanor is a woman of the world, and she knows her sons."

Isabelle nodded, but she was clearly still uncomfortable with the idea of telling a queen that her son was a lecher and would-be rapist.

"You know the Queen well, don't you?" Isabelle asked.

"Well enough," Marshal said, "within limits. A queen doesn't confide in a landless knight."

"But Mattie said . . ."

"Yes?" Marshal prompted with a smile. "What sort of stories has she been telling you?"

"She said that—well, she said there was a bond between you."

Marshal laughed. "She flatters me. Ladies-in-waiting don't always sift the wheat from the chaff when they pick up their gossip."

Marshal leaned back on his elbows and stretched out his legs. "What else did she have to say about me?" he asked.

Isabelle unconsciously bit her lower lip, and Marshal grinned. "That bad?"

"No," Isabelle said, looking away from him. "Mattie told me that all the ladies in Eleanor's court were in love with you."

"Well, *that's* certainly true," Marshal deadpanned. "Of course, I was younger and handsomer then."

"As a matter of fact," Isabelle said airily, "that's exactly what Mattie said—that you were better-looking then."

They were drifting into flirtation, and it made Marshal uneasy. The more he had tried to resist his growing attraction to Isabelle, the stronger its pull had become.

He was too experienced and objective to be flattered or surprised that Isabelle might feel drawn to him. He had appeared out of nowhere to rescue her from a siege, and he had defeated her enemy before her eyes. That in itself was enough to turn a girl's head, and Marshal discounted its significance.

He had known too many women who, when they looked at him, saw the legend and not the man—a legend trouvères, starved for fresh material, had embellished out of all proportion to reality. How could he expect Isabelle to appreciate what he knew: that behind the mystique of knightly combat there was simply sweat and muscle, experience and timing.

For Isabelle a flirtation might be a harmless diversion, but not for him. It would be too easy to fall in love with her. Marshal had made that kind of mistake once before, and once was enough for a lifetime.

"Is Marguerite of France very beautiful?" Isabelle asked abruptly, startling Marshal. It was as if she'd read his mind.

"Yes," he said after a moment. "Very."

High above the river an eagle appeared, sweeping in a majestic arc across the sky, and Isabelle tilted back her head to watch it. "I'd like to have an eagle of my own one day," she said. "I know they're supposed to be flown only by kings, but that's not laid down in law, is it?"

Marshal shook his head. "It's only custom," he said, guessing that this was not the question she wanted answered. Matilda might have told her about Marguerite, or she could have heard the rumors elsewhere; the scandal had dogged Marshal for years.

But Isabelle didn't ask, and there was a long silence between them before Marshal decided to break it. "You were asking about Marguerite of France," he said.

Isabelle shook her head, and her tongue flicked out to moisten her lips. "I'm sorry," she said. "It's really none of my business."

Marshal smiled slightly. "Do you know that no one has ever asked me—directly, to my face?"

Isabelle looked at Marshal in surprise. "But I thought you went before the King himself."

"Oh, I heard the rumors, and I brought them out in the open when the Prince and his father held Christmas court together. That was back in eighty-two," he said. He remembered it all quite clearly, but now it seemed surprisingly remote, as if it had happened in another life. "I demanded the right to face my accusers in judicial combat, but no one would come forward."

"That," Isabelle said with a wry smile, "doesn't surprise me."

"The point is, Lady Isabelle, that no one has ever put the question to me."

"But I—I have no right to ask."

"Yes, you do," Marshal said quietly, "because I want you to know. There was nothing improper between myself and Marguerite of France."

Isabelle looked gravely at Marshal. "But were you in love with her?" she asked huskily.

"Marguerite was the future Queen of England and the wife of my liege lord. I had no right to be in love with her."

"Even as—as her true knight?"

134

Marshal grimaced. "I don't think you believe in that sort of nonsense any more than I do."

Isabelle dropped her eyes. "No, I suppose not." Then she looked up at him through lowered lashes and said, "But either you were in love with her or you weren't. What does 'right' have to do with it?"

Isabelle was holding his eyes, and Marshal knew it was time to put a stop to what was happening. They faced a long journey together, and it would be difficult enough without additional complications.

"Right has everything to do with it," he said. "Love is for those who can become man and wife. For others it can only lead to bitterness."

Isabelle's eyes flickered, but still she held his gaze, and Marshal felt that she had not understood what he meant to say. "Lady Isabelle, outside the garden you joked that the King might give me your hand in marriage. But that could never happen. You're quite beyond my reach."

Color flared on Isabelle's cheeks, and she quickly looked away. "I never meant to imply . . . and I was asking about Marguerite of France just now, Sir William, certainly not about myself."

Seeing her reaction, Marshal suddenly felt like an utter fool, and a flush of his own spread up from his neck to his face. He had misread her completely. His sense that she was attracted to him had been nothing but his own imagination and conceit. She might be grateful to him, but that was all.

Marshal's own embarrassment was nothing compared to his chagrin at having embarrassed and perhaps insulted Isabelle, and impulsively he tried to make amends.

"Please accept my apologies," he said quickly. "I didn't mean to imply anything on your part. I . . . well, I suppose I was voicing my own feelings—that I wished I were a baron who could hope, through the King's favor, to win your hand. But I am not such a baron and never will be."

Isabelle, still not looking at him, sighed theatrically. "And I thank you for those pretty words, Sir William. If I understand you correctly, you're saying that you might love me if that were possible but that unfortunately it's not. You *do* have the courtier's touch."

Marshal sighed inaudibly and felt his tense stomach muscles slacken, relieved that Isabelle had the kindness and wit to let him off the hook gracefully, dismissing his words as courtly flattery. Or perhaps she believed that's what they'd been. She had no way of knowing how far she'd thrown him off-balance; he could hardly believe it himself.

Yet his relief was mixed with a disappointment far deeper than he would have thought possible, and he knew that what he'd said to her was true. He *did* wish she were not beyond his reach.

Isabelle had turned toward him, and now she moved onto her knees, so that she was kneeling beside him. She looked into his eyes and smiled, very slowly. "Or is it possible," she said in her low, husky voice, "that you were not speaking as a courtier—that you actally meant what you said?"

Marshal swallowed, and he felt his pulse begin to race. He knew he should ignore the feeling sweeping over him, that he should deflect the question with a smile and a clever reply. But like a man seized by vertigo on a precipice, he stepped off the edge.

"Milady," he said hoarsely, "if it would do any good, I'd ride into hell itself to win your hand."

Isabelle looked at him in silence for a moment longer. Then she placed her hands lightly on his shoulders, leaned forward, and kissed him softly. The touch of her lips lingered long after she had risen and left him sitting alone on the ledge.

12

Isabelle glanced anxiously at the Danish guards blocking the approach to the ship in which Marshal had secured passage. The Danes were posted at the shore end of a stone jetty thrusting out into Waterford Bay. No shore watch had been evident when Isabelle had landed at Waterford only ten days before, and the guards' presence now was ominous. It was more than likely that they were on the lookout for her, as Marshal had feared.

Marshal had not allowed Isabelle to leave her room at the inn in which they had spent the night until the last possible moment. Fulk and Jean had stowed most of Marshal's and their own gear aboard ship and then had fetched Isabelle from the inn.

Dressed as a manservant, Isabelle had led the packhorse carrying the last of their luggage down to the waterfront. Her hair was hidden beneath a skullcap, and her cheeks were smudged with soot. She had thought she could pass for a boy easily enough, but now that the moment was at hand, she was no longer sure.

Isabelle swallowed back her anxiety, determined not to lose her nerve. Marshal, she knew, had been on edge from the moment they had entered the port city, but he gave no sign of nervousness now as he chatted amiably with the Norman officer in charge of the guard detail.

"Ready, milady?" Jean asked in a stage whisper, and Isabelle nodded.

A manservant would be expected to shoulder a share of the luggage, and Fulk lifted an ironbound oak chest and lowered it onto Isabelle's back, waiting until she had a firm grip before releasing it. Although they had all but emptied the chest for her benefit, its bulk was almost too much for her.

"Are you all right, milady?" Jean whispered worriedly.

"Yes," Isabelle hissed through gritted teeth, "but let's go quickly!"

Jean and Fulk swung the last of the luggage onto their shoulders and signaled the boy from the inn to take the packhorse. Their ship was too small to accommodate their horses, and they would buy fresh mounts in England. With Isabelle trudging between Jean and Fulk, they went down the rocky slope to the jetty.

As they approached the guards, Isabelle heard Marshal begin a ribald story to divert the officer's attention, but the rawboned, blond guardsmen understood too little French to be distracted. Bent under her load, Isabelle could see only the ground in front of her, but she sensed the Danes' eyes on her, and suddenly her disguise seemed hopelessly transparent.

Her heart pounded wildly as she passed through their midst, and at any moment she expected one of them to reach out and snare her. The chest's iron bindings were biting into her shoulders, but she dared not shift the burden for fear of losing her grip and dropping the empty chest at the guards' feet.

But no one tried to stop her, and as she followed Jean out onto the spray-washed jetty, she breathed a constricted sigh of relief. If the guards had not seen through her disguise, it was unlikely that the sailors and dockworkers on the jetty would take any notice of the slight-figured boy struggling under the weight of his master's chest.

Isabelle's relief was short-lived. Behind her, she heard Marshal following them out to the ship, and he was beginning another off-color story. Apparently the Norman officer had decided to see Marshal off.

Already Isabelle's arms and shoulders were beginning to ache, and she had hoped to be able to put down the chest for a moment; but with the Norman so close behind her, she couldn't risk calling attention to herself. Luckily their ship was the nearest of those moored beside the jetty, and she willed herself to make it to the ship without resting.

The early-morning sun still lit the bay, but the wind was stiffening, and dark clouds were building on the landward horizon. A storm was coming, and had Isabelle not been preoccupied with the present danger, she would have quailed at the prospect of crossing the Irish sea in the tiny cargo ship awaiting them; it was hardly more than a Viking ship in design.

Yet Marshal had had no choice. The ship's master was the only captain in port at the moment who was willing to accept a bribe to bypass the ports in South Wales under John's control and make the longer run to England.

Jean had heard Marshal's voice, too, and he quickened his pace, anxious to stay well ahead of the customs agent. Breathing hard, Isabelle struggled to keep up.

"Watch your step, milady," Jean said as they finally reached the gangplank. He spoke softly to be sure he was not overheard by the sailors standing nearby, who were prepared to cast off as soon as their passengers came aboard.

Isabelle looked anxiously at the treacherously narrow gangplank, which was rising and falling in response to the rocking of the ship on the swell. There was not even a single guard rope.

Jean walked quickly up the swaying gangplank and stepped aboard, and now it was Isabelle's turn. For an instant she couldn't move. Even without the chest's weight precariously balanced on her back, she would have hesitated. Fulk was close behind her, and with a pang she realized that he was moving to assist her—automatically, without considering how it would look.

Quickly Isabelle stepped onto the plank and staggered up the incline, praying that she would not lose her balance and topple into the water. She would have made it without incident, but just as she reached the ship's gunwale, the gangplank dipped suddenly and she felt the chest slip sideways.

Desperately she lurched forward and tripped. Jean's arm shot out to steady her, but he was too late. She fell headlong to the deck, the chest crashing onto the planking beside her amid a burst of raucous laughter from the crew. She had landed facedown, and as she lay on the deck, grimacing in pain, she found herself staring at the hairy toes of a sailor.

"Hurt, are you, laddie?" she heard him say as he moved to help her. Too late, she realized the danger as he slipped his hands under her chest to lift her bodily to her feet.

"What the hell!" he burst out, recoiling with surprise. Then he laughed coarsely and hauled Isabelle to her feet.

"Boys, lookee here!" he yelled. "We've got a girl on board!" And before Isabelle could resist, he plucked the cap from her head, freeing her braids.

Isabelle looked in fright toward the Norman officer beside Marshal on the jetty, and she saw his expression change as he registered the color of her hair. They *were* on the lookout for her.

Marshal saw it too. "Fulk! Jean!" he cried, throwing back his cloak. As Marshal drew his sword, the Norman froze, his face a mixture of anger and dismay.

Fulk, at the top of the gangplank, tossed the chest he was carrying onto the deck, unslung his longbow, and nocked an arrow with incredible speed. He drew the bow and held it drawn, the muscles in his gorillalike arms and shoulders bulging under his tunic, the arrow trained on the Norman officer.

"If you or your men try to stop us," Marshal growled to the officer, "you'll be the first to die."

The Danes at the end of the jetty, drawn by the commotion, were running toward the ship, and the white-faced officer bellowed for them to halt. Jean had drawn a dagger and was covering Fulk's back. The startled sailors on board had been slow to react, but as Marshal came running up the gangplank, sword in hand, some of them produced knives, and others scurried in search of whatever weapon came to hand.

Isabelle's momentary shock fell away as she saw the danger. If the captain and crew turned against them, they were lost. "We're not pirates!" she cried out, pulling free of the sailor who had picked her up off the deck. The captain stood on the steering platform in the stern. "Captain!" she called peremptorily, running toward him, "I am Lady Isabelle de Clare, and I order you to cast off at once!"

Her title and her commanding tone had the desired effect. The sailors in her path did not try to hinder her, and the captain, confusion evident in his weather-beaten face, gave her time to reach him.

"Captain," she said, seizing his hand and pressing a fistful of silver coins into his leathery palm. "Please cast off."

Isabelle saw him unobtrusively heft the silver in his hand, gauging its worth, and as Marshal, scything the air with his sword to force the sailors back, came running aft, the captain let him come.

Marshal leapt up onto the steering platform and flashed a grin at Isabelle as he spotted the money in the captain's hand. "You need hesitate no longer, Captain," he said softly, thrusting his sword under the captain's chin. "Your incentive is in your hand, and your excuse before the law is in mine. The customs agent can see that you are at my mercy."

The captain gave Marshal a sly wink and cupped his hand to his mouth. "Linesmen cast off," he shouted. "Oarsmen to your stations."

Then he turned to look at the glowering officer on the jetty and shrugged in a show of helplessness. The sailors on the jetty slipped the moorings, scampered aboard, and pulled in the gangplank. Fulk still stood at the gunwale, his bow drawn, holding the Norman and his men at bay.

"Mind your helm," the captain snapped to the gaping seaman manning the steering oar. "Steer for the harbor mouth."

As the oarsmen pulled the ship away from the jetty, Fulk finally let his bow go slack, but the Norman officer waited until the ship had moved well out of bowshot before shouting after them: "I know your name, Sir William Marshal, and it won't be long before Count John knows it, too, you bloody bastard!"

The wind was blowing off the land, and the captain ordered the oars shipped and the sail raised. Minutes later the ship was running before the wind toward the open sea.

Marshal had sheathed his sword and was talking with the captain, who was in a jovial mood. The silver Isabelle had added to the exorbitant sum Marshal had already paid gave him more than enough reason to be happy—happy and content to remain ignorant of the circumstances surrounding his passengers' bizarre flight from Waterford.

Isabelle stood at the port rail, watching Waterford's walled city recede into the distance. The ancient, needlelike Viking tower, rising like a stone spire above the town, gradually lost definition as its gray outline merged with the cloud mass building behind it.

Isabelle's spirits were flying too high to be affected by the threatening weather. Overhead, the sun still shone, and she relished the salt-laden wind on her cheeks. They had beaten John at Kilkenny, and now they had beaten him again. Buoyed by exhilaration, she felt as if she, not the ship, were sailing on the wind.

The captain left the steering platform to go forward, and Marshal came over to stand beside her. "You did well, Lady Isabelle," he said quietly, his voice inaudible to the steersman through the singing of the wind in the rigging and the sound of the sea against the hull.

"Thank you, Sir William," Isabelle said, smiling up at him, amused that he continued to address her formally.

This was the first time they had been alone, even for a moment, since she had left him in the garden at Kilkenny, and he had maintained a discreet distance during the ride to Waterford—presumably out of the desire to preserve her reputation.

Marshal was looking at her with concern. "It's not over yet, Lady Isabelle," he said. "Once John learns of your escape and knows you're in my company, he's bound to realize that I will present your case before the King. My guess is that he will try to reach the King before me, and if he does . . . well, I've heard that His Majesty dotes on him."

Isabelle nodded, managing to assume an appropriately solemn expression, for she did not want to worry Marshal more by appearing foolishly unconcerned. Yet she *was* unconcerned, and she wished she could reach out and smooth away his worried frown. She wished she could convince him, as she was convinced, that it would be all right.

She couldn't escape the feeling that all of this had been meant to happen. Marshal's journey from the Holy Land had taken the better part of a year, and yet he had appeared unbidden at Kilkenny at precisely the right moment. A few days earlier and she would not have been there; a few days later and he would have been denied entry by Meiler's siege line. Could that be anything but God's hand at work?

And how could her feeling for him have grown so quickly if they had not been predestined to meet? Alone with him in the garden at Kilkenny, she had flirted shamelessly, feeling the giddy rush of excitement of an adolescent infatuation; but underneath had been an attraction far deeper and more enduring than she had imagined possible, and it had grown stronger with each passing day.

She could no longer recall with clarity her first impression of Marshal, and looking at him now, it seemed as if she had known him all her life. His features, the sound of his voice, his gestures, they no longer registered individually. They had become an indissoluble part of the man as a whole—a man she knew she loved as she could no other, a man God *must* have given her to love.

What had she to fear from John or anyone? *What God hath joined together* . . .

Marshal reached out to steady her as the ship's bow suddenly lifted on the first heavy swell of the open sea. Isabelle felt her stomach lurch in response, and she tightened her grip on the rail.

"You'd better go forward, Your Ladyship," Marshal said. "You'll be more comfortable near the mast."

Isabelle frowned and looked at Marshal questioningly, wondering why he persisted in his formality. She was about to ask when a second wave hit the bow and the stern dropped precipitously. The question was blotted from her mind as the deck beneath her rose again with sickening speed and her stomach heaved.

Isabelle's euphoria did not survive the storm that chased their boat across the Irish Sea, a storm that terrified her and prostrated her with seasickness. As she lay hour after hour, retching on the deck, soaked with spray and the wash of waves cascading over the gunwales, she was certain that the groaning mast would snap at any moment and that the ship would founder. Her relief when they finally reached port was immeasurable.

Yet for Isabelle the sea voyage was only the beginning of a miserable journey. Marshal turned the long ride eastward from the coast into a forced march, driven by his determination to keep a step ahead of John. Isabelle would have cheerfully endured the fatigue and the wind and rain that followed them day after day across England, had it not been for the way Marshal treated her.

He was invariably courteous—too courteous. Day after day he used a screen of formality to maintain a discreet distance between them. It was as if he were trying to pretend that those moments in the garden at Kilkenny had never happened. In vain, Isabelle waited for him to acknowledge with words, or even a look, what had passed between them—what she had thought had passed between them.

As desperately as she wanted an explanation, her pride prevented her from asking, and she began to respond to his insufferable courtesy with a mask of cold indifference, hiding the ache she felt inside. If Marshal wanted to forget Kilkenny, she was determined not to let him see how much it hurt her. . . .

They were approaching Winchester at last, and Isabelle gazed bleakly through the driving rain at the painted battlements of the castle in which Eleanor was held. Blue and red were the Queen's favorite colors, and the blue-tinted whitewash on the castle walls and towers and the crimson paint on the towers' conical roofs silently proclaimed Eleanor's presence.

Thirty yards ahead, Marshal turned in his saddle and called back to Jean d'Erly, who was riding beside Isabelle—riding where Marshal should have been. Fulk, taciturn as always, brought up the rear, his longbow carefully wrapped in oiled cloth to protect it from the rain.

"I'll have to go on ahead to announce your coming, Lady Isabelle," Jean said apologetically. "Cheer up, Your Ladyship," he added, his dark, serious eyes wide with concern. "You'll be warm and dry soon, and you'll feel better then."

"Jean!" Marshal called again, and the squire spurred his horse forward.

As Jean rode on toward the castle, Marshal turned back to accompany Isabelle, his face shrouded by the hood of his rain cloak. "We're almost there," he said needlessly, turning his horse to ride beside her.

"So I see," Isabelle said, fighting back tears.

The love she had been so certain was meant to be had been no more than a pitiful, girlish illusion. In the garden that day he had simply thought to entertain her with the games of court, not realizing that she might take his words seriously. God, what a fool she'd been!

"Let me hold that for you," Marshal said, reaching for the pole supporting the small, tentlike canopy shielding Isabelle from the rain.

"Don't trouble yourself, Sir William," she said stiffly.

"Rusty, I—"

"*Lady Isabelle*, if you please, Sir William. That's the way you want it, isn't it?"

"It's not the way I want it," Marshal said softly. "It's the way it is."

Isabelle shook her head and looked away, determined not to cry. Despite everything, she still wanted to be near him; and if it was possible, she would have prolonged their miserable journey. *And he knows it*, she thought. *It's not just the threat of John that's driving him; the man fairly itches to be gone.*

"Rusty, I've behaved like a fool," Marshal said suddenly.

"You flatter yourself," Isabelle responded icily. Now, at the last moment, he apparently wanted to give her an explanation, but she no longer wanted to hear it.

The dirt road they were following ran across a stretch of low-lying pastureland before it wound past a cluster of tenant farms on higher ground and up a long slope directly to the castle gate. Three heavily loaded mule-drawn carts trundled toward them, straddling the narrow road, and the villeins driving the carts started to move off into the soggy ditch in deference to the lady and her knight.

"Please make way for them, Sir William," Isabelle said, turning her horse off to the side and reining in. "If we force them into the mud, they'll never get out again."

The villeins didn't understand Isabelle's French, but they appreciated the favor. "God bless you, milady," said the man hunched on his perch on the lead cart, giving Isabelle and Marshal a toothless grin as he went by. "And you, as well, sire."

The rain had streaked the villeins' dirt-smeared faces, and Isabelle felt the urge to tell them to lift their heads and give the rain a chance to wash their faces. She commanded enough English to do it, but she knew the men would think she was trying to torment them.

"I wanted to—I wanted to talk to you," Marshal said to Isabelle, "but I couldn't find the right words."

"In all this time?" Isabelle responded. "You can stop looking for those words, Sir William. I found them on my own."

"I should never have said what I did that last afternoon in Kilkenny," Marshal went on lamely.

"Oh, so you *do* remember that," Isabelle said, urging her horse back onto the roadway. She had intended her response to be cold and firm, but the voice she heard was very small. Marshal was only confirming what she'd already guessed. Why should his words cut her so? "I've been wondering when you'd work up the nerve to take back what you said," she added.

"Take it back?" Marshal said with a surprise that should have been obvious. "I can't . . ."

But Isabelle, no longer able to suppress her tears, was not listening. She dug in her spurs and cantered ahead. The wind caught her rain canopy and twisted the pole from her hand. She let it fall by the wayside. She wanted to reach the castle and get it over and done with—once and for all.

She heard hoofbeats pounding up behind her, but before she could urge her mount into a gallop, Marshal caught up with her and seized the bridle.

"Listen to me, Rusty!" Marshal pleaded. *"Listen*, for God's sake! I can't take back my words, because they were true. I said that I wished I were a highborn baron who could hope to marry you, and I meant it. But in the garden that day you only listened to the first part of what I said and not the second, and I made the mistake of letting it go by. I'm *not* that baron and never will be."

"How convenient for you," Isabelle shot back, not daring to believe him, no matter how much she wanted to.

"Don't you understand?" Marshal demanded. "There is no future for us together, no matter what I might want. Your marriage will be a matter of politics. I could love you, Isabelle de Clare, but that's bloody well irrelevant. Can you get that through that stubborn red head of yours? *Irrelevant!*"

Isabelle's hood had fallen back on her shoulders, and she blinked against the rain blowing into her face. Marshal was staring at her fiercely, and the intensity she saw in his eyes finally made her believe him.

"Do you understand me now?" Marshal demanded, and Isabelle nodded, unable to speak, smiling and crying at the same time.

"When will I see you again?" she asked.

"I don't know," Marshal said gruffly, taking the reins of her horse to lead it. "But by that time, madam, you will probably be married to the next Earl of Pembroke and have assumed your rightful place beside him as countess."

As Marshal led Isabelle up to the curtain walls of Eleanor's castle prison, trumpeters atop the gate house announced their approach. Jean d'Erly was waiting with the castle's first squire to greet them at the gate and escort them through the outer courtyard to the inner court of the castle's shell keep.

Rain pelted Isabelle's face as she looked up at the battlements and the men-at-arms staring down at them in curiosity, and she was aware of the contrast between the cool rainwater and the hot tears streaming down her cheeks. She was crying silently, and she made no attempt to hold back the tears.

They were not tears of sadness. She was sure now that he loved her, and for the moment that was all that mattered.

13

The Queen chose to receive Marshal in one of the chambers she occupied in the southwest tower of the keep, and to his surprise he found no one in attendance. Perhaps because of the rain, or more probably because of Eleanor's advancing age, a fire blazed in the chamber's hearth, overheating the room.

As Marshal approached, Eleanor did him the honor of rising from her high-backed chair to greet him. Marshal kneeled before her, and she grasped both his hands and bade him rise. She lifted her face to him, and he dutifully kissed her on both cheeks.

"Welcome home, Will," she said, smiling up at him.

"Thank you, Your Majesty," Marshal said, grateful for the warm reception.

He had always liked Eleanor, and she had favored him with her friendship in times past. He had been away for many years, and he was relieved to find that neither advancing age nor a decade of imprisonment had greatly changed her. The Queen he had known would not turn Isabelle away.

"You've injured your arm, I see," Eleanor said. "Anything serious?"

"No, Your Majesty."

"Good. I trust Grenville provided you with all you require in the way of comfort and refreshment."

"Yes, Your Majesty."

Eleanor nodded. "He's a conscientious soul, and I'm afraid he doesn't enjoy the role of jailer."

Still smiling, Eleanor stepped back and gave Marshal a measuring look. "You've changed quite a bit, you know," she said. "It's not just that you're older. The last time we saw each other you still had a devil-may-care air about you. Did the Holy Land take that away, along with your beard?"

"It's been at least six years, Your Majesty. Those were different times."

Eleanor smiled wryly. "Less serious, you mean—in the service of a playboy prince."

"I didn't mean—"

"Don't apologize. We both know that my oldest son was a disciple of Pan, not Mars. But thinking back, you were changing even then— growing more serious. I believe the King saw it too. That's why he allowed you to rejoin my son in eighty-three, during that pitiful second attempt at a revolt. Henry must have known that you'd put a damper on it. You were the only one who was not out to use the boy."

"You haven't changed, Your Majesty," Marshal said with a smile.

"Ah, gallant as ever, Sir William."

Marshal shook his head. "The beauty lingers, Your Majesty," he said truthfully. Age had thinned Eleanor of Aquitaine, taking the voluptuousness from her oval face, but she was still a handsome woman. Her once raven hair was doubtless completely gray by now, but it was covered by her wimple. Eleanor had been a black-eyed beauty, and her dark eyes still retained much of their youthful flash.

Seeing her again brought back a flood of memories, and for the first time Marshal truly felt that he'd returned home. But it would not be as easy to pick up the threads of his life as it might have been. First he would have to deal with the threat John still posed for Isabelle, and then— then he would have to try to forget her.

Marshal cursed himself for having made their final journey together a misery for both of them. Why had he tried to evade the issue, to pretend that nothing needed to be said? Why had he waited until the very last moment to speak to her?

Eleanor took Marshal's hand and led him to a window seat built into a wide-angled recess in the wall. They seated themselves on red silk cushions and leaned back against the upholstered wood paneling covering the stone. Both the richness of Eleanor's clothing and the furnishings of her chambers testified to the King's desire to maintain her in comfort and style.

The ceiling and walls were fully paneled and decorated with murals and silk tapestries. The floor was strewn with fresh rushes and spring flowers, but beneath the rushes, the floor was elaborately tiled.

Although the decor was little different from that found in a chamber occupied by any lady of title, the craftsmanship in the tapestries and wood carvings was quite rare, and the windows of Eleanor's chamber were sealed with stained glass—the first Marshal had seen in a private dwelling.

Eleanor read Marshal's thoughts. "My husband keeps me comfortable," she said. "Sometimes I think he may even feel a little guilty. And speaking of the King, does he know you're here?"

"No, Your Majesty."

"Well, he will soon enough. He keeps a close watch on me."

"And you on him, Your Majesty?"

Eleanor laughed. "I *am* glad you're back, Will, I truly am."

"Thank you, Your Majesty. It's good to be home."

"Were you with the Templars?" Eleanor asked, eyeing Marshal's white robe and tunic.

"I rode with them, Your Majesty."

"Thank God you didn't join the order. What a loss that would have been to the ladies of the realm. And speaking of ladies, I'm sure you didn't drag the richest heiress in England across half the country to my gate for no reason. But if you've eloped with the girl, there's nothing I can do to help you."

"It's not anything like that, Your Majesty," Marshal said quickly.

Too quickly, he realized, as he saw Eleanor pick it up. She was too subtle to cock an eyebrow or respond overtly in any way, but Marshal was sure she had registered his overreaction to her remark and had already filed the information away.

Simply and succinctly, Marshal described the sequence of events that had brought him to Eleanor.

The Queen's sigh when Marshal had finished was genuine. "I always thought I would love my youngest son best," she said, "but Johnny was such a *nasty* child. I'm afraid manhood hasn't improved him. . . ."

Eleanor's voice took on a harder edge. "It's a pity his father doesn't see the boy's defects. Remember that when you see the King, Will. And stick to the issue of the girl's property rights. That John tried to rape his own ward will carry little weight with Henry; my husband would be the last man on earth to find *that* shocking."

Marshal did not take Eleanor's warning seriously, for he had a higher regard for Henry's moral judgment than Eleanor did; but he had already decided not to risk accusing John of a crime that could not be proved.

"Then Lady Isabelle can remain here with you?" Marshal asked.

"Of course. You knew that, or you wouldn't have brought her here. She can stay as long as the King permits—assuming, of course, that I don't find her insufferable." Eleanor smiled. "Will I?"

"No, Your Majesty," Marshal said, smiling in return. For the time being, at least, Isabelle had found a safe haven.

Marshal was beginning to perspire slightly, and he unconsciously wiped his brow with the back of his hand. Now that he had accomplished what he'd come for, he itched to be on his way again. He had to reach the King ahead of John.

"Do you find it too warm in here?" Eleanor asked.

"A little, Your Majesty."

"Then take off your robe. There's no need for formality between us after all these years. And I have a bit of advice for you: Give that robe away. The King will not want to be reminded of the Templars."

"Oh?" Marshal said, removing his robe and draping it over his arm. Until this moment Isabelle had dominated his thoughts, but now he forcibly cleared his mind. He didn't understand Eleanor's last remark, but the Queen was not the type to wander off on conversational tangents, and he recognized the change in her tone. She wanted to talk politics, and Marshal knew it would be wise to listen.

Despite the isolation the King had imposed on her, Eleanor of Aquitaine continued to spin her webs, which, fragile though they were, continually threatened to entangle her husband.

"You've heard about the Saladin tithe, haven't you, Will?"

"Yes, Your Majesty. Even the churchmen are howling in protest."

The Saladin tithe was the special tax the King had levied to support a Crusade to save Jerusalem. The fall of Jerusalem had galvanized Western Europe and induced Henry and young Philip of France to declare a truce in their long-smoldering border war and to take the Cross jointly.

"Clever of the King to agree to the Crusade, don't you think?" Eleanor said. "I doubt he ever intended to go himself. Richard was to be his stand-in."

So that was why Henry had underwritten the Crusade so generously, Marshal thought. Two birds with one stone. Not only would Henry be rid of Philip for a while, but also he would obtain a respite from Richard. And all it would cost was money.

"Unfortunately," Eleanor continued with evident satisfaction, "His Majesty has been mousetrapped by his own proverbial efficiency. Last month word came that Philip has broken the Truce of God. The French are ravaging Berry and have taken Châteauroux, and Henry has no money to fight a war with Philip. He's already given the proceeds of the Saladin tithe to the Templars, and they won't give it back."

"Why did Philip attack?" Marshal asked.

"Does the pretext really matter?"

"I suppose not, Your Majesty."

The provinces of Berry and the Norman Vexin had been the focus of a desultory border war between Henry and the young King of France ever since Philip had ascended the throne. It was not simply a territorial dispute; the roots of the conflict lay in the thirty-year power struggle between the Plantagenets and the Capets.

As King of England, Henry was the peer of the King of France, but as Duke of Normandy and Count of Anjou, Maine, and Touraine, he was nominally a vassal of the French Crown. The French royal domain extended over only a limited area centered on Paris, and the French king did not have the resources to enforce his will directly on his powerful, independent vassals.

Philip's father, Louis VII, had maintained a semblance of authority by playing off his vassals against each other, but with the ascendancy of Henry of Anjou, the power balance had shifted inexorably to the English King.

Louis was forced to look beyond his own lifetime for a restoration of Capetian power, and he sought that restoration through marriages of state. He arranged the marriage of his daughter, Marguerite, to Prince Henry, the designated heir to the English Throne; and he betrothed his infant daughter, Alais, to Richard, whom Eleanor had made heir to Aquitaine. The marriage and betrothal were potentially rich prizes for the Capets, and in return for his agreement, Henry exacted a stiff price.

As Marguerite's dowry, Henry received control of the Norman Vexin, a key border territory that had long been disputed by the Dukes of Normandy and the Capetian kings. Henry also took immediate custody of the child, Alais; and of her dowry, the province of Berry. Louis had exchanged yet a further reduction in his real territorial power for the promise of a return to Capetian greatness in the future, envisioning a day when his son, Philip, would preside over a Capet family trust, with his influence extended through his sisters to the Angevin domains and England.

Mercifully for Louis, he did not live to see the collapse of his grand design, which shattered on events and Henry's antipathy toward Richard. When Prince Henry died in 1183, Marguerite returned to Paris—without her dowry. Philip had only recently inherited the Throne of France, and when Henry refused to part with the Vexin, Philip could do no more than complain.

Philip was equally unsuccessful in the matter of Richard's marriage. Richard was now presumptive heir to the Crown of England, and his marriage to Alais could still salvage something of Louis's dream. Philip demanded that the long-promised marriage take place at last, but Henry, wary of Richard and unwilling to see him allied by marriage to Philip, procrastinated endlessly.

Henry continued to hold the Vexin, the province of Berry, and Alais herself, and the Capets had nothing in return. For five bitter years Philip had chafed with frustration, and now it appeared that he had run out of patience. By breaking the Truce of God, he had incurred the wrath of the Church—a grave step for any monarch—and Marshal took this to mean that Philip now felt strong enough to win back in war what his father had lost through diplomacy.

"The King will not have an easy time with Philip," Eleanor said. "Philip is twenty-three now—a man, not a boy—and he's far more determined than his father to recoup the losses the Capets have suffered at our hands. This may be much more than a border skirmish this time, Will, and the King no longer has the money to fight a prolonged war. The Saladin tithe emptied his coffers."

"The King doesn't need mercenaries if his vassals on the Continent remain loyal," Marshal responded.

"*If*," Eleanor said with heavy emphasis. "A number of barons across the Channel are looking toward fresh leadership."

Marshal raised his eyebrows. "Looking toward Richard?" he asked, and Eleanor nodded.

It was no secret that Eleanor hoped Richard would one day humble the King, and rumors of Richard's disaffection were rife, fed by the growing perception that Henry was losing his grip on the kingdom. But the Queen was not in the habit of idly voicing her hopes and dreams, and Marshal had the feeling that Eleanor wanted something from him. What?

"Will, are you absolutely determined to enter the King's service?" she asked abruptly.

"That was my promise to him, Your Majesty," Marshal said, startled by the question.

"In return for what?"

"Nothing, Your Majesty," Marshal replied, certain that Eleanor already knew. He suspected that there was little of interest to Eleanor that she did not manage to discover.

"Precisely," Eleanor said. "Not even a promise of his own—or so I've heard. You've been gone for years, Will. Even the King could not hold it against you if you changed your mind. You've always been loyal to the Plantagenets, despite the opportunities you might have had elsewhere on the Continent—even in Paris. I wouldn't want to see you change that loyalty, but there is more than one Plantagenet in the realm."

Suddenly Marshal realized what Eleanor was driving at, and it stunned him. She was asking him to desert the King and join Richard— in anticipation of his revolt. He had thought she knew him better than that.

"There's no need to tense up, Will," Eleanor said, reaching out and gripping Marshal's arm. "What I'm suggesting is for your *own* good. Do you believe me?"

"Yes, Your Majesty," Marshal said, but he was stretching the truth.

Eleanor had always liked him, and he liked her in return; but he never forgot that Eleanor of Aquitaine was first and foremost a queen—a queen who yearned to influence events. Eleanor's favor never ran counter to her own purposes.

"You know as well as I do that Richard will be the next King of England," Eleanor said, "whether or not my husband formally recognizes him as heir."

"That may be true, Your Majesty," Marshal replied, finding it difficult to match Eleanor's calm. "But the King is unlikely to relinquish the Crown while he lives."

"If it's left up to him," Eleanor responded. "As I said before, this time he may find Philip more than a match for him on the battlefield."

"Surely you're not suggesting, Your Majesty, that Richard might side with Philip against the King," Marshal said, but he knew that this was precisely what she was suggesting.

"I don't know everything that is in my son's mind," Eleanor replied, and that, at least, Marshal believed. They supported each other, but Richard was his own man. "But I know," Eleanor continued, "that the King will lose Richard if he does not soon declare him to be his heir. If my husband drives Richard away, he will be making a fatal mistake."

The threat of civil war between Henry and Richard had been brewing for years, and Eleanor clearly thought it was about to boil over. Philip appeared to be spoiling for a fight with Henry, and if Richard joined him . . . Even the poorly organized rebellion of young Henry in 1173 had triggered a rising of barons that had threatened the King's hold on his empire, and Richard posed a far more formidable threat.

"You're suggesting I back the strongest horse," Marshal said woodenly.

Eleanor nodded. "For your own good, Will. For your own good."

But Marshal was not as certain of the outcome of a civil war as the Queen appeared to be. Henry of Anjou had confounded his enemies for a third of a century, and aging or not, he was still a king to be reckoned with.

At worst, Marshal would have assessed the odds against Henry at fifty-fifty, but he was not gambling on the outcome. Marshal had pledged his word to the King that he would return to his service, and that he would do. It was not just a matter of a promise; to Marshal, treason was anathema.

Eleanor had been watching him, and now she shook her head. "A man can have too many scruples, Will. If you never bend, life can break you."

"I don't break easily, Your Majesty," Marshal said, and there was a hint of coldness in his voice. He was not willing to be pushed. Why, he wondered, was Eleanor so anxious to have him defect to Richard? One knight more or less could not possibly make a difference.

"Your father knew when it was time to switch sides," Eleanor said quietly. "I thought you might have learned from his example."

The remark caught Marshal off-guard, and he felt a flash of anger. "I did, Your Majesty," he responded coldly. "I learned some things I'll never forget."

Marshal's tone was clear enough, but if the Queen took offense, she did not show it. "Well," she said smoothly, lifting a gloved hand to indicate that she intended to rise. "I think we've exhausted the subject. The King is probably still in London," she said as Marshal assisted her to her feet, "at Bermondsey Manor. But you know how he is. If you want to catch him there, you'd better leave soon."

"With your permission, Your Majesty, I'll leave immediately."

"Immediately?" Eleanor said, arching her eyebrows. "Without presenting your lady to me? Surely you intend to say good-bye to her."

"We've said our farewells already, Your Majesty, but of course I should present—"

Eleanor cut him off with a gesture. "That's not necessary, and perhaps it is best for you to go at once." She paused and held Marshal's eyes for a long moment. "I do wish you only good luck, Will. I hope you realize that."

"Thank you, Your Majesty."

"And where did Grenville put the lady?"

"In the tower on the north wall of the keep, directly across from this one, Your Majesty."

Eleanor nodded. "That will do for the moment, I suppose. Grenville has been dragging his feet on the refurbishing of the apartments in the *palais*. I think he feels more comfortable with me cooped up in here. The poor man hasn't grasped the simple fact that the *palais* is inside the keep, the keep is inside the castle, and the castle is inside England. Ah, well, it always takes me at least six months to break in a new jailer."

"If Your Majesty permits . . ." Marshal said, bowing and starting to retreat.

"You may kiss me good-bye," Eleanor commanded. "And, Will— do it properly this time," she added, lifting her face to him and closing her eyes. Marshal kissed her lightly on the lips.

Eleanor smiled and sighed wistfully. "I was still beautiful when we first met, wasn't I?"

"I thought so, Your Majesty," Marshal said truthfully.

Eleanor shook her head. "What a pity I was always so chaste with you. Looking back, I don't understand why."

"Good-bye, Your Majesty," Marshal said, bowing low.

"*Au revoir*, Will. And when you see my husband, give him my love."

For the third time in the last hour Isabelle moved to the window overlooking the outer courtyard as she heard the sharp clatter of horses coming out through the gate to the keep. The castle's great outer courtyard abutted the western wall of the town, and Isabelle's window offered a panorama of Winchester, with the Conqueror's palace and the cathedral rising above a tightly packed jumble of burghers' houses and shops, but Isabelle's eyes were fixed on the two horsemen riding out across the courtyard's muddy cobblestones.

The rain had driven to shelter most of the chickens, dogs, and pigs, but the courtyard teemed with people. The castle walls enclosed a village in miniature: the chapel, barracks for the lower-ranked castle servants, kitchens, bakery, armory, smithy, carpenter shop, stables, hawk house, livestock pens, and storehouses. The servants were unloading carts from the town and surrounding farms and continually crisscrossing the courtyard as they plodded through their chores.

As Marshal appeared, followed by Jean leading their packhorse and Marshal's charger, a path through the confusion opened before them, and the knight and his squire picked up a retinue of half-naked urchins who had been playing by the courtyard fountain. Marshal rode directly for the main gate, but Isabelle refused to believe that he would leave without looking back.

She was sure she understood him now. The legendary William Marshal was afraid of something, after all—afraid of losing his heart to a woman he could not have. He thought to sever the tie before it grew too strong—to cut it quickly, once and for all.

Isabelle knew full well how powerless she was to control her future—that the King would choose her husband—but that simply didn't matter to her now. She loved Marshal, and she wanted his love in return. The future would have to take care of itself.

Marshal was approaching the outer gate now, and the guards were saluting him; in a moment he would be gone. Isabelle held her breath, willing him to turn and look back. He had to look back; he *had* to. The gateway was clear and Marshal touched his spurs to his horse, but at the very last moment he reined in and turned, looking up toward the tower where he knew Isabelle might be. He raised his arm high over his head and waved once. Then he was gone.

Isabelle smiled a slow, secret smile. He had not found it easy to cut the bond between them, after all, and if it was in her power to prevent it, he never would.

"How does it feel to be rescued by the most famous knight in the realm?" came a woman's voice from behind, startling Isabelle.

She turned to see a tall, slim, oval-faced woman standing on the threshold of the chamber. The purple, ermine-trimmed robe the woman wore declared her rank, but even without it Isabelle would have known she was facing Eleanor of Aquitaine. *Regal* had been Marshal's one-word description, and it fit.

"Your Majesty," Isabelle said, sinking to her knees.

"Get up, child," Eleanor said, coming into the chamber. "A curtsy will do in future. It appears we will be seeing a lot of each other."

"Yes, Your Majesty," Isabelle said.

"You *are* a beauty," Eleanor said with a measuring look. "And there's just enough of the devil in your eyes to tempt a man. I can't say I blame my son much."

Isabelle felt her cheeks redden.

"Do I shock you, dear?" Eleanor said innocently.

"Not nearly as much as Count John did, Your Majesty," Isabelle responded coolly, and Eleanor laughed.

"Touché. Now I know we'll get along. From what Marshal told me, I didn't think you were the fluttery type, but I like to see for myself."

The statement did not seem to require a response, and Isabelle remained silent.

"You're very lucky to have Sir William as your advocate, Isabelle. I'm sure you were impressed with his battle prowess, but in this case his sword alone could win you nothing. The King has no patience with ladies who undermine his policy. I can testify to that."

"I am only asking to be secured in my rights, Your Majesty," Isabelle replied. "I seek to undermine nothing."

"What you seek and what you do are two different things. The King made my Johnny Lord of Ireland for a purpose—to try to prove his princely qualities and to enhance his standing among the barons. His Majesty won't take kindly to a charge of malfeasance against John, let alone of rape. That's why I said you are lucky. Marshal will not make it easy for the King to decide against you."

"I'm not sure I understand, Your Majesty."

"It's a matter of Marshal's rather odd character, my dear. He has two exceptional traits, which can be viewed as virtues or as flaws, depending on your point of view. The relevant one in this case is his fetish for justice and the law. If you kill his friend and you are within the law, you have nothing to fear from him; but if you murder his enemy in violation of the man's feudal rights, Marshal will hold it against you. Strange, don't you think?

"The King knows that Marshal will never serve him if he flouts the law, and he wants to take Marshal into his mesne. My husband wants

Marshal at his side, Isabelle, and that may be your strongest card. I only hope, when the time comes, that our knight can champion his own cause as effectively."

"Your Majesty?"

"It's not important," Eleanor said dismissively. "I'm sure you're not interested in the musings of an old woman."

"Oh, but I—"

Isabelle broke off as she saw the momentary flicker of acknowledgment in Eleanor's dark eyes, as if an unspoken question had been answered.

Eleanor smiled. "Yes, I suppose you *are* interested—at least as far as Marshal is concerned."

Isabelle saw no point in denying it, but she was puzzled by Eleanor's apparent interest in her feelings. Why should the Queen care what she felt toward William Marshal?

"I'm thinking of the second of the odd traits I spoke of," Eleanor continued. "His loyalty. I'm afraid he carries it to extremes. Stormy times are coming, and a man should be prepared for sudden shifts in the wind, but Marshal, left to his own devices, will probably hold to his chosen course no matter what. Even strong ships can founder that way."

Eleanor waited a moment, but when Isabelle did not respond, she said, "We have Marshal in common, you and I. He once risked his life for me, too, you know. The time may come when we may have to put our heads together to help our stubborn champion—assuming, of course," she added briskly, "that His Majesty does decide to take you under his wing. My Johnny is a clever boy. For your sake, I hope Marshal reaches the King before he does."

14

John's eyes narrowed as William Marshal appeared in the garden of Bermondsey Manor and started up the gravel path to the arbor where the King, flanked by John and the Lord Chancellor, awaited him. John had been seventeen when Marshal had left for the Holy Land, and he remembered Marshal well, but the towering figure striding up the path was even more imposing than John remembered, the broken-nosed, hawklike visage even fiercer.

But John was unimpressed. Marshal's sword arm would avail him nothing here. This would be a battle of wits, and it was a battle John had already won. He smiled inwardly as he saw Marshal recognize him. *That's right, you meddling bastard, I got here first.*

John was certain that the version of the Kilkenny affair he had given the King would shield him from any charges the girl might make through Marshal; having protected himself, he was concerned only with revenge. He had been careful not to attack the King's favorite knight directly—dismissing Marshal's role as unwitting, overzealous meddling—and Henry was annoyed with Marshal, not genuinely angry; but that was enough for John's purposes. He knew Marshal and what motivated him; he knew how to get even.

The King started to rise to greet Marshal, caught himself, and remained seated, his eyebrows drawing together in a deliberate frown. "So you've come back to us at last, Marshal," he said, his voice grating with the hoarseness of age.

As Marshal went to one knee before Henry, John could see that he was taken aback by the change in the King, for Henry had aged far beyond his years.

When Marshal had left for the Holy Land, the King had still been robust and muscular. Now he was obese, his skinny legs appearing almost atrophied in relation to his swollen torso, and his once reddish-brown hair and beard had gone completely gray. The sagging flesh of his florid face was etched with strain and disappointment. Only Henry's gray eyes were the same—still alert and probing.

"I returned as soon as my pilgrimage on behalf of your late son was completed, sire," Marshal said.

"But not without a detour to Ireland," Henry said irritably, gesturing for Marshal to rise.

As Marshal stood up, he glanced at John, and John caught a flash of anger—perhaps even hatred—in his deep-set eyes. John returned the look with a sly half smile. So the girl *had* told Marshal everything. Good; without that, revenge might not have been possible.

"Damn it, Marshal," Henry growled, "I thought you'd outgrown your recklessness."

"I did what I thought best to secure Lady Isabelle's safety, sire. Her castle at Kilkenny was under siege, and she was in jeopardy."

Marshal was handling himself well, John noted with ironic detachment; he spoke as firmly as possible without sounding impertinent. It was a very fine line.

"That's the usual result of rebellion," Henry responded sarcastically.

"Rebellion, sire?" Marshal said. "Lady Isabelle has taken refuge with the Queen at Winchester, which places her entirely in your power. That is the act of a supplicant, not a rebel."

"Rebellion against *me*," John interjected coldly, "not against the Crown of England. I am her lawful guardian and Lord of Ireland, and she has defied me openly."

Marshal looked at John and cocked an eyebrow. "And you would elevate a girl's defiance to rebellion, sire?"

The Chancellor chuckled softly, and John glanced sharply at his half brother. Geoffry Plantagenet, Bishop of Lincoln and Royal Chancellor, was a thin, ascetic-looking man in his mid-thirties, with dark, wiry hair lying close to his scalp. He bore no resemblance to Henry, but he was the King's bastard son.

Geoffry owed his position to his keen mind and utter devotion to his father; and John was always careful in his presence, for the Chancellor was the King's most trusted adviser. But John would remember that short, derisive chuckle as he remembered similiar slights in the past, and one day there would be a reckoning . . . .

The King was not amused by Marshal's jibe. "This is no laughing matter," he snapped.

"I agree, sire," Marshal said. "Lady Isabelle fled Pembroke Castle because—rightly or wrongly—she believed it was the only way to bring her complaints before your court. I appear before you now, sire, not only to offer my allegiance and service to you but also to plead on her behalf. You know me well enough to trust that I would not do so lightly, and I know my King well enough to trust to his sense of justice."

It was a good speech, John acknowledged as he saw the King's expression soften.

"You were the best of my son's knights, Marshal," the King said, smiling for the first time, "and perhaps the very best we have. I have long awaited your return, but I would not ask you to serve a king you thought unjust. I will hear you now."

Marshal glanced at John, clearly expecting him to try to block a hearing of Isabelle de Clare's complaints, but John remained silent. *Talk away, Sir William. It will do you no good.*

Succinctly and dispassionately, Marshal related how he had come to Kilkenny and why he had intervened on the girl's behalf. Ranulf de Barre must have briefed him well, John thought, for Marshal was able to list the castles and lands in Leinster that John had already ceded to willing barons.

But to John's surprise, Marshal made no mention of the girl's last night in Pembroke, and John's estimate of Marshal's intelligence rose a notch. Just as John had been loath to attack Marshal directly, Marshal was apparently unready to accuse him without conclusive proof.

"I therefore request, sire," Marshal said in conclusion, "that you take custody of Lady Isabelle and her lands and exonerate Sir Ranulf of any charge of treason. Sir Ranulf has never sworn allegiance to Count John, and he received Kilkenny Castle from your own hand. He was therefore within his rights in refusing to surrender it."

"I agree that Sir Ranulf was *technically* within his rights," the King said, "and I will not call him to account this time. But he must proffer his allegiance to Count John as Lord of Ireland at once."

"Yes, sire," Marshal said, his relief evident in his voice, and John felt a smile tugging at his lips.

Marshal thought he had won.

"As for the girl," the King said, and John wet his lips in anticipation, "she is unhappy with the way her guardian has administered her lands. That's all her 'plea' amounts to."

"But, sire!" Marshal burst out, reacting with shock to the King's dismissive tone. "You mustn't—"

Henry peremptorily raised his hand, cutting Marshal off. "Her mistaken belief that my son has violated his trust is nothing more than a misunderstanding of his motives—a misunderstanding that Count John has already explained to me to my satisfaction."

John could barely resist grinning openly as Marshal's face darkened with anger, and again Marshal started to protest.

"It may interest you to know, Sir William," Henry said sharply, overriding Marshal, "that Count John did *not* authorize Meiler fitz Henry's siege of Kilkenny. In fact, as soon as he learned of the siege, he sent a written order for Meiler to withdraw at once. In future you would do well to take the wild imaginings of a distraught, headstrong girl with a grain of salt."

"But, sire, there can be no justification for the parceling out of Lady Isabelle's lands!"

"You're making a mountain out of a molehill, Marshal," Henry snapped. "Even if it were true that the barons who have taken custody of Lady Isabelle's castles in Leinster mistakenly believe that they have title to the surrounding lands—and Count John assures me that this is not the case—they would be disabused of that notion when the time came for her to marry. She will marry when I see fit, and when that time comes, her entire inheritance will pass into her husband's control. I see absolutely no reason to burden myself with her custody at this time."

No longer able to resist, John smiled, but he contrived to make it a smile of amused tolerance rather than one of triumph. But triumph was what he felt, for he knew that he had read Marshal correctly. He could see the dismay and worry in Marshal's face as he realized that the de Clare girl would now be returned to John.

John could not afford to proceed too harshly against her—at least not at once—but neither the girl nor Marshal could be sure of his restraint. Neither would know when or how he might choose to exact revenge, and that in itself—the never-ending fear and uncertainty—would be the sweetest revenge of all. To a man like Marshal, it would be a torment. . . .

Abruptly the Chancellor spoke up, and his words shattered John's complacency.

"Sire," Geoffry said. "Taking custody of Lady Isabelle would hardly be a burden. In fact, it would be highly advantageous. The income from her estates is considerable, and we are facing the prospect of war with nearly empty coffers. Surely the Royal Treasury has greater need of funds than Count John."

John ground his teeth as he saw the King's expression suddenly turn thoughtful. Marshal was looking gratefully at the Chancellor, who was staring into the middle distance, as if totally detached. "You bastard!" John wanted to snarl, certain that Geoffry had intentionally taken Marshal's side. Money was a powerful argument, and John could see that Geoffry's remark was having its effect.

"Sire!" John implored, grasping his father's shoulder. "Don't undercut my authority. Lady Isabelle *must* be returned to my custody—if only for appearances. She has defied me openly, and if you take custody of her now, it will be seen as a rebuke to me."

The King looked up at John, and John held his eyes, calling on his father's affection and demanding his support. As Henry started to nod in assent, John knew he had retrieved the situation.

"Sire," Marshal said quickly, "I would be the last to ask you to undercut Count John's authority. If he feels that Lady Isabelle should be returned to his custody against her will—if he insists on calling her defiance rebellion against his authority—then let the matter be settled in his own court, according to law and custom."

John looked at Marshal in astonishment, taken aback by his sudden capitulation. Why was he giving in? Was he simply playing for time? John's lip curled. If so, it made no difference. Marshal had blundered, and John had no intention of letting him take back his hasty words.

"I will agree to present the case in my own court, sire," John said, "for that is where it belongs."

The King was frowning and he shot John a warning glance; but John ignored it, assuming that Henry simply did not relish deferring to a lesser court.

"Are you sure about this?" Henry said.

"Yes, sire," John said firmly, "I accept Sir William's proposal."

Marshal's expression had become uncharacteristically impassive, and John suddenly sensed a trap he did not see.

"You *are* sure?" the King asked, watching John coolly, and John recognized the look; Henry was testing him, intentionally loosening the reins and giving him his head. But what trap could there be? In his own court John would have his way.

"I'm sure, sire," John said.

"Very well," Henry said, "so be it." Then he looked up at Marshal, and John thought he detected a glint of wry amusement in his father's eyes. "I don't suppose, Sir William, that you intend to withdraw as Lady Isabelle's advocate."

"No, sire," Marshal replied evenly, "I will appear in Count John's court on her behalf—as her judicial champion. And I will demand trial by combat."

John's stomach muscles knotted, and he felt the color drain from his face as the trap sprang shut on him. How could he have missed it! Marshal had found a way to bring his sword arm into play, after all, and John had given him his opening. There was no one in John's court—not even his own champion—who would stand a chance against Marshal.

"Furthermore, sire," Marshal said coldly, fixing John with an icy stare, "I would feel compelled to speak out more fully in Lady Isabelle's defense than I have up to now, and I would be prepared to prove *any* countercharge I might make—before God in judicial combat."

John swallowed hard as he absorbed the implied threat. With Marshal as the girl's champion, a charge of attempted rape would go unanswered, and John would stand convicted in his own court—a blot on his character and dignity he simply could not tolerate. . . .

The look of pure hatred that John shot Marshal was so fleeting that only Marshal caught it. An instant later John smiled disarmingly and spread his hands in a gesture of royal beneficence, and it was this swift change of expression that brought home to Marshal just how dangerous the young prince was.

"Sire," John said, "Sir William is a true and gallant knight, but I fear he misreads my purpose. I could not countenance what I perceived as Lady Isabelle's defiance of my authority, but now that she—through Sir William—has agreed to accept the judgment of my court, there is no need for a trial. I am completely satisfied.

"As the Lord Chancellor has quite properly pointed out, you have far greater need of the income from Lady Isabelle's estates than I. With Philip of France threatening war, I can do no less than to surrender the wardship to you, sire."

The King settled back with a sigh and smiled warmly. "Well spoken, my son," he said with satisfaction. "Well spoken, indeed."

"Thank you, sire," John said smoothly.

Still smiling, the King looked at Marshal and Geoffry in turn, as if to say, "You see, gentlemen, the boy is learning." Marshal couldn't understand the King's affection for the weasely prince he had spawned, but John's hold on him was undeniable.

Cold trickles of nervous sweat still rolled down over Marshal's ribs. John had very nearly won, and he would have if the Chancellor had not intervened at the crucial moment, driving a wedge between John and his father's own interests. Henry had known at once that Marshal would demand trial by combat; he had seen the trap, but he had let John walk into it.

Glancing at the Chancellor, Marshal saw some of his own relief mirrored in Geoffry's eyes. Why? Why should Geoffry have cared enough to intervene? But the question was washed away on the tide of relief sweeping over him. Isabelle was finally safe; that was all that mattered.

The King looked up at Marshal. "Now that this business is settled," he said dryly, "I trust there are no further impediments to your accepting service with me."

"No, sire," Marshal said. "I'll serve you, and serve you gladly."

Grunting with the effort, Henry rose from the stone bench on which he was seated and gripped Marshal's shoulder. "God's legs, it's good to have you back, Marshal. Just seeing you again reminds me of happier days."

"Thank you, sire."

Out of the corner of his eye, Marshal saw John smiling benignly, and he knew that he had made an enemy for life.

"As of this moment," the King said, "you are captain of my household knights, but I'll demand far more of you than that title implies. You will attend all baronial councils, and I expect you to speak your mind."

"I will do as you ask, of course, sire," Marshal said diffidently, "but surely your barons will resent the intrusion . . ."

"Of a landless knight?"

"Yes, sire."

"Perhaps," Henry said, "if they're fools. But in any event, the question is moot. While you were in Prince Henry's service, you could receive no grants from me, and my son had no lands of his own to give. Yet in serving my son you served me, and your reward is long overdue."

The King sat down again and gestured to the Chancellor. Geoffry smiled broadly and nodded.

"Sir William," he said formally, "in recognition of your service to the Royal Family and in anticipation of future service to the Crown, the King has awarded you title to the land of Cartmel in Lancashire. The income from Cartmel is modest—thirty pounds a year—and would be insufficient to maintain you and the knights who will follow your banner.

"Therefore His Majesty appoints you guardian of the heiress, Helwis of Lancaster. You will henceforth enjoy the income from her estates, and if you choose, you have the King's permission to marry the lady and become the seigneur of her lands."

Caught completely by surprise, Marshal was unable to think of an appropriately elaborate reply. "Thank you, sire," he said. "I didn't expect . . ."

"We can see that, Marshal," Henry said with a grin, "but I'm not known for my largesse. These grants are not gifts; they're compensation, and you won't find your service with me a sinecure."

"I didn't expect it to be, sire," Marshal said distractedly, struggling to adjust to the abrupt change in his fortunes. At a stroke he was no longer a landless knight, and Henry had opened for him the way to the baronage.

Isabelle's words came back to him: "All it takes is a word from the King."

Henry and the Chancellor were smiling at him, and Marshal tried to appear as pleased as he knew he should be. He now possessed what he'd desired for so long—land of his own, and the King's permission to marry a lady of title—but instead of pleasure, he felt only aching regret. The lady would not be Isabelle de Clare.

What was the matter with him? He'd known from the start that Isabelle de Clare was hopelessly beyond his reach, and because of that he had made their final journey together a misery. Why couldn't he face it now? Forcibly Marshal turned his thoughts back to the present—back to reality.

"I've heard, sire," Marshal said, "that Baudouin de Bethune and Hugh de Harlincourt joined your mesne some time ago. With your permission, I'd like to ask them to follow my own banner."

"Of course. You three made a formidable team in the old days, and I wouldn't have it any other way. Besides," Henry added, "I'd prefer them to drain your purse instead of mine."

Abruptly the King's smile vanished. "They're both in France right now," he said grimly. "I sent them to accompany the Earl of Essex to Paris. I assume you've heard that Philip has invaded Berry and taken Châteauroux."

"Yes, sire, but not the reason for it."

"Reason!" Henry snorted. "*Excuse* is the word—an excuse to stab me in the back. I sent Essex to Paris to demand an explanation, and the answer just reached me two days ago. It seems the Count of Toulouse made the mistake of picking a quarrel with Richard, and Richard responded in predictable fashion by taking several of Toulouse's castles. Toulouse apparently complained to Philip, and Philip used the appeal as a pretext for his raid into Berry."

"But, sire," Geoffry put in quickly, "Toulouse is a vassal of the French Crown, so Philip would be bound to support him."

"Then he should have moved against Richard, not the King," John snapped. "He knows damned well that Richard acted on his own."

"Precisely," Henry concurred. "It's simply an excuse to break the Truce of God. He probably heard that our treasury is drained and thinks he can get away with it. Damn the Templars! They know Philip has double-crossed me, and they won't give me back a penny. Not one damned penny!"

"Philip may still withdraw of his own accord, sire," Geoffry said, "once you make it clear to him that Richard acted on his own."

"Oh, I'll give him a chance to withdraw," Henry growled. "The question is, what if he stays in Châteauroux?" Henry looked at Marshal and said, "My council met yesterday. Their advice was to drive Philip out of Berry by force."

Marshal was inclined to agree, but the contrasting attitudes of John and the Chancellor caused him to hesitate. He knew only the outlines of the current political situation, and he had as much reason to trust the Chancellor's judgment as he had to suspect John's. John was clearly spoiling for war, and Geoffry just as clearly wanted to avoid it.

But Marshal was sure that King Philip would only dig in his heels if Henry showed restraint, interpreting that restraint as weakness.

"I agree with your council, sire," Marshal said. "Philip must be driven out."

"But if we go to war, sire," Geoffry protested, "it will strain our remaining resources beyond the limit. We can't pay our mercenaries for more than a few months in the field."

"All the more reason to hit Philip at once, and hit him hard, sire," Marshal said. "To convince him *and* your own barons in France that you're as strong as ever. Give Philip a quick, sharp jab that will take the wind out of him."

Henry compressed his lips and nodded in satisfaction. "Exactly. I've already sent out orders to muster Welsh archers at Portsea, and we should be able to cross the Channel by the end of the month."

"But let's not strike without giving Philip a clear warning, sire," Geoffry said urgently. "We must send another embassy to Paris—"

"Another one!" John said, cutting in. "God's blood, there's been enough talk already. It's time for cold steel!"

"And can we look forward to you leading the troops, sire?" Geoffry said sarcastically to John.

"Enough!" Henry barked. "I already told you, Geof, that I'd give Philip a chance to withdraw on his own. I'll send the Archbishop of Rouen to Paris—to remind Philip just whose side the Church is on. But I'm not going to ask Philip to withdraw; I'm going to *tell* him. I'm going to give him an ultimatum: Either Philip withdraws immediately or, by God, I'll renounce my allegiance to the Crown of France."

Startled, Marshal glanced at the Chancellor, wondering if this was what Geoffry had been afraid of. If Henry renounced his nominal allegiance to Philip, the war that followed would be no mere border skirmish. It would be prolonged and costly. Again Marshal noted the contrast between Geoffry and John. The King's threat of an ultimatum had brought a glint of satisfaction to John's black eyes.

"That's an extreme measure, sire," Marshal said worriedly.

"Extreme or not," Henry grated, "it's what I'll do. If Philip won't deal fairly with his vassal, the Duke of Normandy, we'll see how he likes war with his peer, the King of England!"

Shortly thereafter the King dismissed Marshal, and as Marshal left the garden, John allowed his smiling mask to slip from his face. If Marshal thought he could humiliate a prince of the realm and get away with it, he would soon learn otherwise. Marshal's small victory would only cost him more dearly in the end; John would see to that.

"You made the right decision on Richard de Clare's daughter, sire," Geoffry said, meeting John's eyes with a challenging look. "We need a man like Marshal as never before."

John stared coldly at his half brother. Now he knew why Geoffry had intervened: The Chancellor had feared the King might lose Marshal.

"What would you think of sending him with the Archbishop to Paris, Geof?" Henry said. "He was with my son at the Paris Court years ago, and he knows Philip."

"That's a good idea," the Chancellor agreed readily. "The Archbishop is a fine talker, but I'm not sure he listens well. We want to be sure of Philip's response."

"I'm more concerned that the Archbishop might try to soften the ultimatum," Henry said. "I can rely on Marshal not to mince words."

The Chancellor frowned and shifted restlessly on his feet.

"What's gnawing at you, Geof?" Henry said in annoyance.

"Are you really determined to go so far as to renounce your allegiance to Philip, sire?"

"You know I am."

"It's certain to make Philip think twice, sire, but if he refuses to back down, we'll face an open-ended war."

"So be it," Henry growled. "We may have no funds for mercenaries, but neither does Philip. Our baronial forces are more than a match for his, and I'm sick of his incessant snapping at my heels. I mean to put an end to it once and for all."

Geoffry cleared his throat. "We're a match for Philip, sire, only as long as the barons across the Channel continue to support you."

Henry's eyes narrowed. "What exactly are you worried about? Richard?"

"We can't ignore the fact that Philip has been courting him, sire. That's probably the reason Philip was so careful not to attack his lands."

"Richard is my *son*," Henry said sharply. "And he knows which side his bread is buttered on."

"But *does* he, sire?" Geoffry said, seizing on the opening. "You could make sure of that by declaring him to be your heir and allowing him to marry Alais. You'd cut the ground right from under Philip."

"Like hell I would! By making Richard Philip's brother-in-law, I would create the very alliance you're warning me against."

"And if you don't, sire, you risk driving Richard into Philip's arms."

The King's face hardened, and he got to his feet and began to pace. His knee had been smashed years ago by a horse's kick, and he limped badly.

"I won't force Alais to marry Richard," Henry said with an involuntary grimace of distaste. "I couldn't do that to the girl."

John smiled inwardly. Unlike Geoffry, he had no doubt that Henry could prevail against both Philip and Richard. If Richard did rebel, he would be defeated, and the King would not forgive him as he had his eldest son so many years ago.

"She's not a girl, sire," Geoffry protested. "She's twenty-seven years old."

"Damn it, Geof, I won't do it! Alais deserves better than to be forced into a marriage with a man who prefers boys to women."

"God's blood," John put in, "for years it's been Richard who's refused to marry her."

"But he's changed his tune, sire," Geoffry said desperately. "And I'm sure it's because of the rumors."

"What rumors?" Henry demanded. "That I've taken Alais as my mistress?" He paused to draw a breath. Even the brief exertion of his pacing had winded him. "If Richard believes that, he should be even less willing to marry her."

"Not if he thought you intended to marry her yourself, have children by her, and disinherit him."

"That's bloody nonsense," Henry snorted. "Is that the latest slander out of Paris?"

"I'm afraid so, sire."

"Richard's not stupid enough to believe that," Henry said flatly.

But he might be, John gloated silently; Richard just might be that stupid.

"If you won't give him Alais, sire," Geoffry persisted, "you should at least declare him your heir and require your barons to do him homage as the future King of England."

"I'll not make *that* mistake again!" Henry burst out, and John had to suppress a smile of satisfaction. "I did that for young Henry, and he thanked me by trying to take my Crown."

Breathing heavily, Henry returned to the bench and sat down, staring out across the Thames at the White Tower, its massive, whitewashed walls gleaming in the afternoon sun. The river swarmed with galley barges and single-masted merchant ships with square, brightly colored sails, bringing cargo to London's teeming wharves.

The Tower of London was the Conqueror's monument, but the burgeoning city itself was a monument to Henry, for it mirrored the economic growth his thirty-year reign had given England. The city's tightly packed shops and houses seemed to be jostling each other for space, straining at the confines of London's high walls. London was congested and filthy, its narrow streets darkened by overhanging second stories and thronged with noisy crowds, but it pulsated with the excitement and profit that drew travelers like a magnet from all over Britain.

"I built an empire," Henry said, half to himself. "I was strong enough to build it, and I'm still strong enough to hold it. I'll let *no one* take my Crown."

Two nights later John sat alone in his chamber at Bermondsey Manor, awaiting his chamberlain, Roger Poole. Moonlight streamed in through an open window, and John had lit no chandles. He did not fear darkness, as did so many men of his time; he was a creature of the night. Without the distraction of the light and sounds of day, he found it easier to think, to plan—to dream.

Never before had his dreams seemed closer to reality. War with Philip was coming soon—perhaps only weeks away—and Richard, John was sure, was about to make the mistake of his life. Henry would crush both Philip and Richard, leaving John undisputed heir to an even stronger kingdom.

Events were moving inexorably in his favor, proving his mother wrong. It was he, not Richard, who was destined to be king. The thought of Eleanor's coming disappointment added to John's anticipation, for the knowledge that she did not love him was like a running sore that refused to heal. He longed to wound her in return.

Poole's knock on the chamber door came just as the sand in John's hourglass ran out. Punctuality was a sign of subservience that Poole unfailingly observed.

"Come!" John called, and Poole entered, raising the lantern he carried.

"Do you mind if I light a candle, sire?"

"If you must," John said, and Poole walked to the all-night candle standing beside the canopied bed and lit it with his lantern.

"I have seen to it that your household is prepared to follow you to France whenever you wish, sire. I understand that His Majesty will be assembling his army at Alençon. Will you be joining him there?"

"No. I will be traveling to Count Richard's court at Poitiers. It is vital that he support my father in the coming conflict, and I intend to do my best to encourage my brother to do his duty."

"Of course, sire," Poole said with a perfectly straight face. "As to the other matter—concerning William Marshal. I thought that might be the reason for your summons, and I have a suggestion for you to consider."

John's breathing quickened; he was sure that Poole was about to give him the means for revenge. He had not forgotten Isabelle de Clare, and one day there would have to be a reckoning with her, but first he would deal with the insufferably arrogant William Marshal.

"I would have thought it would take more time," John said, "to find the right man."

"An infinite amount of time, sire—for what you originally had in mind."

John frowned. "What are you saying?" he snapped. "Have you found a man or not?"

"Sire, you asked me to find a replacement for your court champion—a knight who surely could defeat Marshal in single combat—but that request was unrealistic. There are few knights in England or in France who might successfully challenge him, and each one is a baron of substance. A king might prevail on such a knight to act as his champion, but you, sire, are not yet a king."

John held back his rising anger. Poole had never failed him yet, and he could not deny the truth of what Poole was saying.

"Well?" John demanded impatiently. "What *do* you have in mind?"

"A combat challenge is out of the question, sire, and Marshal is also beyond your reach politically. He has the King's favor, and there is no doubt that he will serve His Majesty faithfully and with distinction. But this knight has wronged you, sire—grievously so—and he should be made to pay the price. There is one—and only one—way to strike back at him."

John gazed stonily at the mild-looking man before him. Poole, he realized, was suggesting an assassin.

"I have a man in mind who should suit your purpose, sire," Poole said. "He is a knight—not a cutthroat who might betray you for the sake of a greater reward. His name came to my attention when he recently applied for service with the King. But now that Marshal is captain of the King's household knights, his employment would be quite impossible. As I understand it, there is no love lost between them.

"If you should choose to take this knight into your own service, sire, I could see to it that he be apprised of the wrong Marshal has done you and of the rewards to be expected for redressing that injury—by whatever means, however drastic. From what I have heard, he would require very little prodding."

"*Discreetly* apprised," John said coldly. "Discretion would be absolutely essential."

"Of course, sire."

It was not what John had desired; he had wanted Marshal humbled on the field of battle for all to see. But what Poole was suggesting was far better than nothing, and vengeance could not always be perfect. John hesitated only long enough to assess the risk to him if something went wrong, but he could see no danger at all.

"What's this knight's name?" John said, making up his mind.

"Gerard de Ridefort, sire—formerly Grand Master of the Templars."

FAMILIARIS
REGIS

15

Gisors, France—August 1188

Marshal surveyed the enemy camp from a vantage point high on the slope of the fortress hill overlooking the River Epte. Above him the great tower keep of Gisors Castle jutted against a hazy sky. The keep was surrounded by a massive curtain wall, and encircling the gleaming, whitewashed stone fortress was an outer palisade of wood that encompassed an area sufficient to accommodate the bulk of King Henry's army if it was forced into retreat.

Philip had responded to Henry's ultimatum by requesting one last parley at Gisors, on the border between the Norman Vexin and Philip's royal domain, and Henry had agreed. But both kings were prepared for war if the conference failed, and their armies now faced each other across the Epte.

Henry's forces were dispersed among thick shade groves on the Norman side, but Philip's army was encamped in an expanse of open, dusty fields, and his troops sweltered in the oppressive August heat. The day was barely two hours old, and already men were sweating, even in the shade. The torpid, humid air lay on the land like a steamy blanket, and the horizon was washed out in a gray haze.

Far below the castle, near the riverbank, a great elm spread its limbs over the English king and his entourage. The elm was the time-honored site for meetings between French kings and the Dukes of Normandy, and there Henry sat serenely in the shade, sipping English ale, awaiting the appearance of his liege lord, Philip of France.

Henry believed that Philip's request for a parley meant that the young French king would back down rather than precipitate an all-out war, but Marshal was not so sure. In Paris, Philip had not even blinked when the Archbishop of Rouen had delivered Henry's ultimatum. Marshal could not escape the feeling that Philip was coming to Gisors, not to accede to Henry's demands but to present demands of his own.

Baudouin de Bethune and Hugh de Harlincourt, Marshal's old comrades-in-arms, had come up the hill with him to scout the French camp. They were among the knights of Prince Henry's mesne who had joined the King's household following the Prince's death, and they had eagerly transferred to Marshal's banner. He was glad to have them at his side again.

Marshal turned to Bethune. "What's your count, Bo?"

"About three thousand foot and four hundred cavalry," Bethune said.

"I make it about the same," Harlincourt agreed.

The two knights were a study in contrast. Bethune was a tall, slim, fair-haired man with blue, mischievous eyes and tightly curled blond hair. Harlincourt was shorter and chunky, with dark, straight hair and chipmunk cheeks, and his brown eyes looked forever serious, even when he smiled. What the two knights shared was a lust for combat and the skill to win.

Marshal twisted around in his saddle and looked back at Jean d'Erly, who waited a short distance away with the other two squires. "Jean," Marshal called. "How strong is the enemy?"

"Three thousand, three hundred, and twenty-two pikemen, sire. Two hundred and sixty-five *serjants*, and one hundred seventy-one knights."

"Impudent monkey," Marshal growled under his breath, but he couldn't quite suppress a smile. Jean trained hard, and Marshal's stern discipline had not dampened his spirits.

"Give the boy a break, Will." Bethune grinned. "At least he's awake enough to sass you. As I recall, your reputation as a squire was for sleeping and eating."

"Any way you slice it," Harlincourt said seriously, "they've got us outnumbered. It's just as well we have the castle to back us up."

"Is all this for real?" Bethune asked. "Or are they just bluffing down there?"

"It's for real," Marshal said grimly, and rubbed his gritty eyes. The humid heat had robbed him of sleep and given him a throbbing sinus headache.

"Good," Bethune said with satisfaction. "God knows Hugh and I could use the action. I'm telling you, Will, there were times in the last five years when I wished I'd taken the Cross myself."

"You wouldn't have like it," Marshal said. "Too few eligible women."

"Well, there's that, I suppose," Bethune said doubtfully, "but God, it's been dull! You'd think the Old Man would have let us enter a tournament once in a while, just so we wouldn't get rusty."

"Amen to that," Harlincourt put in.

Marshal smiled and shook his head. "You don't look rusty to me," he said, eyeing Bethune's gilded armor and flaming red surcoat. Baudouin de Bethune had always been the flashiest knight in Prince Henry's mesne, but there was plenty of strength and daring behind the flash.

Marshal had found his friends surprisingly unchanged, as if he alone had aged. Bethune, of course, with his smooth, apple-cheeked face would probably look boyish forever; and Harlincourt had looked middle-aged at sixteen. But it was not simply a matter of appearance. These two still itched for glory—in war or in the occasionally deadly mock warfare of the tournament—and to some extent Marshal envied them this passion that he could recall but no longer feel.

Marshal remembered the excitement and anticipation in the hours just after dawn as the knights had gathered in the lists, the impatience for the opening charge of the opposing teams that began the melee. The tournament could rage all day, with knights returning again and again to the refuge of the lists to rest and repair their equipment, riding out again as soon as possible to plunge into the sprawling battle that ranged over the countryside. Sometimes a tournament engaged hundreds of knights at a time, supported by squires and occasionally even by squads of infantry.

King Henry had suppressed tournaments in England, deeming them a waste of money and lives, but in France they had steadily gained in scale and grandeur, becoming pageants where ladies, as well as knights, could act out their fantasies of chivalry. In time the onlookers outnumbered the combatants, and the beauty of the noblewomen clustered in the loges and pavilions overlooking the lists could excite as much interest as the battle itself.

Marshal had loved it all, and he could not pinpoint the time when he had first realized that the joy of combat for its own sake had slipped away from him.

The old excitement was no longer there; but as Marshal looked out at the enemy he found himself hoping that the war—if it was inevitable—would begin here at Gisors. It would release the tension that had been building in him for weeks as his responsibilities had grown, and it would absorb him mind and body, helping him to close the small chapter of his life that he'd not yet put behind him.

Isabelle was safe, her inheritance secure. He had fulfilled his promise to her, and it was high time he forgot the copper-colored hair and smiling, innocently seductive eyes of a girl he could not have. Those images belonged to the past, as ephemeral as a desert mirage. Soon, he hoped, they would begin to fade.

"You'll get action soon enough, gentlemen," Marshal said, "but I want discipline from our knights. And that goes for you two as well. Anyone who can't resist charging into the enemy on his own will find himself riding with our *serjants*. We will attack in units and withdraw in units."

Bethune looked at Harlincourt and winked. "I'm afraid the Templars made an old maid of him, Hugh."

Marshal turned sharply on Bethune, and the knight held up his hand and laughed. "Don't worry, Will, we'll play it your way. Hell, it's the only game around."

Harlincourt pointed down toward a distant party of horsemen riding along the riverbank. "Look," he said, "the lion stirs."

Marshal nodded. The powerful, tawny-haired knight riding in the lead was immediately identifiable, even without the crimson banner emblazoned with three golden lions that his standard bearer carried. Richard had arrived late the previous evening, having marched up from Poitiers at the head of one hundred cavalry and eight hundred foot, and he had brought Count John with him. For the time being, at least, Henry was supported by both his sons.

Marshal squinted up at the sun, estimating its angle. "We have another hour yet before Philip comes across," he said. "I think we should go down and renew our acquaintance with the Count of Poitou. He's the wild card in this game."

Marshal watched Richard's stately progress along the riverbank as the Count returned from his inspection of the opposing lines. His palfrey, a white gelding, was as impressive as most war-horses and was draped in crimson silks. Richard periodically lifted his arm in regal acknowledgment of the scattered cheers of the soldiery he passed, and Marshal noted that the cheering came from both sides of the river. Whatever else Richard might be, he was a born leader of men.

When the Count of Poitou was still one hundred yards away, he caught sight of Marshal's blue-and-white banner, which Jean d'Erly carried, and he spurred his mount into a canter, followed immediately by his entourage. As Richard rode up, he was grinning.

"Welcome home, Will!" he cried heartily, reaching out to grasp Marshal's hand. "Bethune. Harlincourt. Good to see you. So the old team is taking the field again. It's about time!"

"Thank you, sire," Marshal said.

"God's legs, Marshal, what's it been? Five years? You're looking healthy enough. I'll bet Saladin is glad to have seen the last of you."

"You're looking fit yourself, sire," Marshal said. Richard, at thirty, appeared to be at the peak of his strength and assurance.

Richard laughed and slapped his belly. "I've been putting on some weight lately, but if this little rumble with the Franks develops into something, campaigning will slim me down soon enough."

Richard was heavier than Marshal remembered him, but there was muscle beneath the fat. As his father had as a young man, Richard relied on exercise to hold down his weight. He was a taller, handsomer version of the King, with the same ruddy complexion but with tawny, rather than reddish, hair. The Count's powerful arms were exceptionally long, giving him a three-inch advantage in reach over men of equal stature, and he had the skill to make use of it.

Richard was every inch a warrior, powerful and recklessly brave, but there was a disturbing softness to his round face, particularly in the eyes and in the lines of his mouth; and in contrast to his father, who invariably looked disheveled, Richard's appearance was a shade too neat. His carefully combed hair and beard were too precisely trimmed, and he was fastidious about the fabric and cut of his cloaks and surcoats.

Richard's eyes turned serious. "What went wrong out there, Marshal? At Hattin, I mean."

Marshal shook his head. "I wasn't there, sire."

"Thank God you weren't," Richard said. "We lost too many good men in that disaster. But you must have some idea, and I need to know." Richard pointed to the green cross embroidered on the shoulder of his yellow surcoat. "Jerusalem has to be saved, and I'll be going out there soon. The reports of the battle have been sketchy, but you must have formed an opinion. I asked Ridefort—thought I'd get the story straight from the horse's mouth—but the fellow clammed up on me."

"*Gerard* de Ridefort, sire?" Marshal said in astonishment, not believing he'd heard correctly. "The Grand Master?"

"The former Grand Master," Richard said. "Didn't you know he'd returned? My brother took him into his mesne two months back."

Marshal shook his head dumbly, forgetting the courtesy due Richard's rank, as again he tasted his hatred of Ridefort.

Richard looked at him curiously. "Ridefort is a Lusignan by blood, isn't he," he said, shaking his head. "God's eyes, Marshal, twenty years is a long time to hold that kind of grudge."

Marshal's expression hardened. "You asked my opinion on the Battle of Hattin, sire," he said coldly. "Well, I'll tell you. There are only two inviolable rules of warfare with the Saracens: Never let your heavy cavalry advance too far ahead of your infantry; and never forsake your water supply.

"Saladin refused to cross the desert separating his army from ours, and King Guy and the Grand Master didn't have the sense to wait him out. Instead, they marched out to meet him across ten miles of waterless hell. With the Turks harassing them, it might as well have been a hundred. Once our men left Suffariya Wells, they never had a chance."

Richard looked speculatively at Marshal and then nodded, but Marshal wondered if the Count accepted his verdict. Saladin had beheaded the four hundred Templars and Hospitalers he had captured at Hattin, but he had spared the lives of Guy de Lusignan and Gerard de Ridefort, presumably in recognition of their bravery.

Apparently the Templars had not been as charitable. Marshal doubted that Ridefort would have left the order voluntarily—not at the cost of the power he had wielded. So he was John's man now. They were a good match, Marshal thought grimly.

"What about the Saracens' weapons?" Richard asked. "Is it true that their steel is superior to ours?"

"It's true, sire," Marshal said, still distracted by the surge of bitter memories. He slipped the dagger he carried from its sheath and handed it to Richard. "Their blades are stronger and hold a keener edge."

Richard examined the blue-hued blade, the polished surface of which was covered with an intricate tracery of spidery lines, the hallmark of Damascus steel. He tested the blade edge with his thumb and whistled appreciatively. "Did you take this off a dead Saracen?"

182

"No, sire. I bought it at a bazaar."

Richard hefted the dagger and held it to the sun so that the blade flashed, and he grinned. "I fancy this, Marshal. Would you care to make me a present of it?"

"I'm afraid not, sire," Marshal said firmly, running his hand over his jaw. "It's my only decent shaving blade."

Richard looked surprised, and then he scowled petulantly. He made no move to return the knife until Marshal held out his hand.

"You'll get your own in Palestine, sire," Marshal said.

Richard, who was used to being given whatever happened to catch his eye, irritably slapped the knife into Marshal's outstretched palm. "If and when we finally do mount our crusade," he muttered.

Marshal gestured toward the French camp across the river. "Over there is the man who stands in the way," Marshal said. "While your father was draining his treasury to support a fresh crusade, Philip was making plans of a different sort."

Richard's face darkened. "I know, and I don't understand it. I was sure Philip would . . ." His voice trailed off, and he shook his head. "The Capets have always been a slippery lot. We'll just have to teach Philip a lesson he won't forget."

"My thought, exactly," Marshal said, satisfied that he had managed to score a point off Philip; but he was under no illusions. Richard's holy zeal could be all too easily quenched by his ambition to be king.

The time set for the conference was at hand, and the trumpeting of heralds from across the Epte signaled King Philip's approach. The barons, knights, and bishops waiting under the elm with Henry stirred in expectation and relief. Most of them had been standing for the past three hours while the King, comfortably seated on a cushioned throne, had held court.

Henry was in an expansive mood; he had argued religion and philosophy with his bishops, battle tactics with his mercenary captains, and engaged all and sundry in discussions ranging from horse breeding and crop rotation to the proper medicine for a molting hawk. It was a flashback to the Henry of younger years, in whose Court, observers had complained, school was held every day.

Flanking the King were Richard and John, seated in their own ceremonial chairs, with their hangers-on interspersed among the nobles attending Henry. The princes' entourages mirrored their masters. Richard's men were battle-hardened knights. John's young retainers were creatures of the court who aped his foppish tastes. Richly attired in the latest fashion, they had soft hands and softer minds, and their smiles and high-pitched laughter always came on cue.

Watching Richard and John, Marshal was struck by the perversity of physical inheritance, which had produced flawed caricatures of the princes' parents. Richard, who resembled his father, had Henry's strength and boldness but neither his intelligence nor his political savvy. John had his mother's black hair, black eyes, and oval face, but the dynamism in her features was washed out in his visage, mirroring his indolent personality; and in John, Eleanor's craftiness had emerged as sneaky malevolence.

The King looked toward Marshal, standing with Bethune and Harlincourt behind the barons in the front rank, caught his eye, and winked.

"The Old Man's in a good mood," whispered Bethune.

"But for how long?" Marshal said softly.

Henry certainly had the advantage over Philip in staging. The Crusader's Cross was conspicuous on the breast of his surcoat, and the bishops surrounding him proclaimed the Church's support of the English King. In this particular quarrel Henry had managed to occupy the moral high ground. Rome's call for a Crusade to save Jerusalem was the principal reason Richard now sat beside his father in common cause against the violator of the Truce of God.

But Henry, himself, had proved that the Church's support was no substitute for military and political strength. Philip's father, Louis of France, had tried in vain to gain advantage in his protracted struggle with Henry by supporting Thomas á Becket's cause, but Henry had prevailed in spite of the Church's opposition, even weathering the storm loosed by Becket's martyrdom.

Marshal sensed that now the tables had been turned. It was the young French king who was bold enough to scoff at the Church's condemnation, and Henry was the aging monarch who, feeling his power slipping away, grasped at bishops' skirts for support.

"What the hell did you do to Count John?" Bethune muttered under his breath.

John, whose black eyes rarely left his father's face in his fawning attention to the King, had caught Henry's wink and was looking at

184

Marshal. As Marshal glanced toward him, John's sly, sensuous lips twitched into a half smile that failed to touch his eyes, and he bestowed a regal nod.

"I cost him the revenue of a rich wardship," Marshal answered without moving his lips.

"You'll have to tell us about it sometime," Bethune said. "If looks could kill . . ."

But Marshal wasn't listening, for he had caught a glimpse of Gerard de Ridefort standing behind John in the outermost rank of knights. Ridefort was staring at him, and as their eyes locked, Marshal could almost feel Ridefort's hatred beating against him in waves.

Abruptly Ridefort was blocked from view as the crowd shifted in response to the appearance of Philip on the opposite bank of the Epte. All eyes turned toward the river, and at a signal from Henry, his heralds trotted their horses toward the river to form a line of trumpeters to salute Philip. The French horses splashed across the river ford, the spray sparkling in the sunlight, and as Philip reached the near bank, thirty Norman trumpets blared in fanfare.

Mounted on a prancing, snow-white charger, the King of France rode up toward the elm, followed by a retinue of knights in silvered and gilded armor, whose surcoats and silk saddlecloths blazed with the colors of the rainbow. Philip came unarmed, dressed entirely in white and gold. His surcoat and lightweight cape were of white silk, trimmed with ermine and richly embroidered with gold thread. His boots gleamed with gilt lacquer, a rope of gold thread girdled his waist, and on his head he wore the gold Crown of France.

Henry, who had been slouching, straightened up. His own crown had been resting in his lap, and now he placed it on his head and picked up his scepter. In so doing, he made it clear that he was meeting Philip as the King of England, not as Philip's vassal, the Duke of Normandy.

As Philip rode into the shade beneath the elm and reined in, Henry did not rise. The packed gathering waited tensely to see how Philip would respond, for no chair had been provided for the French king. To stand before Henry on his throne was unthinkable, and if Philip seated himself on the ground, he would have to look up to the English king.

Philip was only twenty-three, but he had been King of France for eight years; he could not be flustered. He solved the dilemma neatly by not dismounting, forcing Henry to look up to him. It was a trivial point, but everyone knew Philip had won the first round in the contest of wills.

"Good morning, Henry," Philip said with a relaxed smile, breaking the brief silence that followed the conclusion of the trumpet fanfare. "It's a pity we have to meet with our armies at our backs—all these thousands forced to sweat in this accursed heat."

Philip was a slight young man with light brown hair and high color in his cheeks, who carried himself with a stylish elegance that contrasted sharply with the rough-cut manner and appearance of his aging antagonist. As Philip looked over at Richard and smiled warmly, it occurred to Marshal that Philip might be particularly appealing to a man of Richard's blurred sexual proclivities.

"A pity, you call this?" Henry spat. "Jerusalem is in mortal danger—or had you forgotten? We both took the Cross at this very spot only seven months ago, and I kept my faith. But while I was bending every effort to prepare for the Crusade, you were raiding into Berry—attacking my lands without provocation."

"You've already had my answer on that," Philip replied calmly. "As for the Crusade, I am as ready for it as you are."

"Then prove it!" Henry barked. "Give up Châteauroux and retire at once from Berry."

A fine trickle of sweat started down from Philip's right temple, and he delicately wiped it away with his little finger. "And why should I withdraw?" he said with the same unflappable calm. "They are my lands, after all."

"Your lands!" Henry thundered. "Berry has been ours for twenty-five years—given freely by your father as Alais's dowry."

"Twenty-five years," Philip said, drawing out the words with heavy emphasis, and he exchanged a long look with Richard. "My father ceded Berry to you as dowry for a *marriage*, Henry, not for an empty promise."

"She will be married at the proper time," Henry said. "I will keep my pledge, but I will not be stampeded."

"Stampeded!" Philip said sarcastically. "My sister has languished in your custody for *twenty-five years*. What, pray tell, are you waiting for? Why, sir, won't you marry her to Richard?" Philip paused and looked again at Richard. "We *all* wonder why."

"I repeat," Henry said stubbornly, "I will keep my pledge."

For the first time Philip elected to show impatience, and he compressed his lips. "Will you, now? As you kept your pledge with regard to the Vexin, I suppose. You promised my father that the Vexin

186

would be returned to Marguerite if her husband died. Instead, she sits a widow in Paris with a paltry yearly pension."

"A pension you accepted five years ago," Henry shot back.

"I was a boy then, and easily hoodwinked. I am a boy no longer."

"Hoodwinked?" Henry burst out. "The Vexin has been Norman from the time of the first duke, as you very well know. And *I* was a boy when your father forced me to cede him the Vexin in return for recognition of my ancestral rights in Normandy and Anjou. When he gave the Vexin as Marguerite's dowry, he was simply returning what was rightfully ours."

Philip sighed theatrically and shook his head. "Yes, you always have a ready excuse to explain away your broken promises."

"Enough!" Henry said peremptorily. "I didn't agree to meet with you to go over old ground. We swore to put aside our differences for the sake of Jerusalem. It was a holy oath, which I have kept and you have broken. I charge you now, Philip of France, to declare before this assembly that you will withdraw from Berry to restore peace between us, so that we may work together to save Jerusalem."

Philip looked down at Henry and nodded slowly, and for a moment he had the assembly believing he was about to yield. "I will withdraw from Berry," he said, and paused for effect, "if you will announce—here and now—the date on which my sister, Alais, shall wed your son, Richard."

"By God, sir, you try my patience," Henry thundered, shifting angrily in his seat.

Philip stared down at him, unmoved. "And you try mine, but if there is a reason why Alais and Richard should not at long last be married, perhaps you'd care to share it."

"That's my business!"

"No, sir, it is not yours alone. It concerns both our houses—and certainly your son, Richard."

"I ask you again," Henry said, breathing heavily. "Will you withdraw from Berry?"

Philip smiled slightly. "No."

In the heavy silence that followed Philip's refusal, Marshal heard Bethune sucking air through his teeth.

"Damned molar's gone rotten," Bethune whispered. "Can you see any swelling, Will?"

Marshal shook his head. "Don't worry," he said under his breath.

"The way things are going, there will soon be a few thousand Franks over there, anxious to knock it out for you."

Slowly the King of England rose from his throne. "Is that your last word, Philip?"

"For the time being," Philip replied flippantly.

Henry's face darkened. "Then I, Henry, Duke of Normandy, Count of Anjou and Maine, do hereby renounce my allegiance to you, Philip of France, and I will henceforth defend my lands on this side of the sea as my own."

"Then you have given up your right to those lands," Philip replied coolly, "and I take them back into my own hand."

Henry laughed bitterly. "You can try."

"Yes," Philip said. "I certainly will."

16

Philip launched his war against Henry with a joke.

Following the breakup of the parley, the French and Norman armies remained in place all day, in an apparent stalemate; the Franks had superior numbers, and the Normans had Gisors Castle to back them up. But an hour after sunset Marshal was abruptly summoned to a council in Henry's command tent at the bottom of the fortress hill.

The King sat sprawled in his chair, flanked by Richard and John. He breathed heavily in the muggy air, which was thickened even further by the incense burning in and around the tent to hold mosquitoes at bay. Moths fluttered about the two candles illuminating the tent's interior, and the light flickered each time a moth immolated itself in one of the flames.

"Now that we're all here," Henry said irritably as Marshal entered, "we can get started."

To Marshal's surprise, only the Chancellor and William Earl of Essex were with the King and his sons. Essex, ten years Marshal's senior but still in his prime, was the leading member of Henry's baronial council. Apparently Henry had not wished to convene a full war council, and Marshal's inclusion in this select group was sobering proof of the trust Henry placed in him.

"It appears, gentlemen," the King said, his deep voice rumbling with suppressed anger, "that war amuses the King of France. I just received a message from him, challenging me to settle our differences with champions. He proposes to decide control of Berry and the Vexin by the outcome of a combat between two knights from each side."

"But that's an interesting idea, sire," Essex said enthusiastically. "It would save—"

"Please allow me to finish," Henry snapped, mopping his fleshy face with a sodden handkerchief. "Philip offers as his own champions the

Counts of Clermont and Flanders, but he proposes that they fight William fitz Ralph and William de la Mare."

Richard burst out laughing, and John started to join in until he noticed that the King was not smiling. It was obvious that Philip was simply tweaking the tail of the Plantagenet leopard. Although the Counts of Flanders and Clermont were two of France's leading duelists, fitz Ralph, the Seneschal of Normandy, was sixty-five years old, and de la Mare was notoriously incompetent with sword and lance.

"It's only a joke, sire," said John, still trying to suppress a grin.

"I *know* it's a joke, damn it, and I see it's infantile enough to amuse you."

John's grin vanished instantly. "Simply ignore it then, sire," he said quickly, trying to reingratiate himself. "His proposal is not worthy of a response."

Richard shrugged nonchalantly and nodded in agreement.

"We certainly can't accept, sire," Essex said, obviously puzzled by Henry's annoyance, "as Philip knows full well. If the joke amuses him, so what? Let is pass, sire."

If anyone but John had made the suggestion to ignore Philip's jest, Marshal would probably have accepted it along with the others; but the very sight of John disgusted him, and he distrusted anything he said. It was also clear that Henry wanted something more. If he'd been content to let the joke pass, he wouldn't have called for advice. In contrast to Richard, who appeared amused by Philip's flippancy, Henry was angry and frustrated.

Marshal found the contrast ominous. Richard's partiality toward the young French king was all too obvious in the detached amusement with which he viewed his father's discomfiture, and Henry's frustrated anger smacked of weakness. The concern Marshal saw in the Chancellor's expression confirmed his feeling that the wrong tone was being set.

"So you would let Philip amuse himself at the expense of your King's dignity?" Henry said angrily.

"What do you suggest, sire?" Essex asked calmly.

"I've asked for *your* counsel, gentlemen!" Henry snapped, plucking restlessly at the folds of his tunic, which stuck in places to his bulky, sweating torso, "and I'm still waiting for it."

For several seconds there was an awkward silence, and no one ventured a suggestion. When Marshal saw that no one was going to speak, he made up his mind.

"I disagree with Count John, sire," he said. "We shouldn't let Philip's joke pass—and not simply because it affronts your dignity. His jest is an affront to every Christian in Europe, and it should not be ignored." Marshal paused and looked directly at Richard. "Philip has chosen to war against the king he swore to join with in Crusade, and now he laughs about it. Jerusalem is in the hands of Saladin, and Philip sits across the river making jokes. It's obscene!"

"And just what do you propose?" John said, breaking in churlishly. "We can't accept the challenge, and refusing it would make us look foolish."

Marshal felt his lip begin to curl, and he could not quite suppress the reflex. "Count John is wrong, sire," Marshal said. "We *can* accept the challenge—and impale Philip on his own barb. He has issued a public challenge, and he has named *his* champions. But it is not his right to name ours. As the challenged party, sire, you are free to name your own champions. I suggest you accept the French King's challenge and pick a team that can win. Then we'll see who ends up laughing."

"God's balls, Marshal, you're the man for me!" Henry exclaimed happily, slamming a fist into his palm. "That's exactly what we'll do!"

Essex slapped Marshal on the back. "You *have* hit the nail on the head!"

Everyone save John was grinning with approval.

"Well, Marshal," the King said, "who should make up our team?"

"The choice is yours, sire, but Essex and I should make as good a pair as any."

"What the hell!" Richard cried, his face flushing with sudden anger. "You can't leave me out of this! I'm a match for any knight in France—including you, Marshal—and by God, I stand ready to prove it—here and now, if you wish."

"More than a match," John put in, his voice rising in pretended outrage. "Marshal, you insult my brother!"

"Silence!" the King barked, and John wilted.

But Richard remained tense, his weight balanced on the balls of his feet, his hand on his sword hilt.

"I meant no insult, Count Richard," Marshal said easily. "Your participation would be quite impossible. We can't risk the heir to the Throne in a duel when there are others who can serve as well. As far as your skill and courage are concerned, they are as well-known . . . as your temper."

Richard blinked and then smiled self-consciously. He waved his hand in a gesture of dismissal. "Sorry, Marshal. My mistake," he said, his anger gone as quickly as it had come.

Marshal had deliberately referred to him as the heir to the Throne, and he hoped Richard had registered Henry's acquiescence. John, taking his cue from Henry's and Richard's smiles, nodded solemnly, as if he, too, were satisfied.

But Marshal had had his fill of John's sniping. He looked at John and said dryly, "Of course, I see no reason why the second in line for the Throne should be denied the honor of championing the King's cause. Perhaps you would care to take my place on the team, Count John."

At that, even Henry joined in the ensuing laughter. Still chuckling, he heaved himself to his feet and threw off his cloak, which a servant hastened to retrieve. Henry patted John good-naturedly on the shoulder and then limped to his cot. With the servant's help he removed his tunic and sat down heavily, the cot's frame creaking in protest. The servant knelt before him and stripped off his boots and stockings. Clad only in his sweat-stained linen shirt and breeches, Henry lay back with a sigh.

"Well, that's that," he said with satisfaction. "Marshal, you will see to it that Philip receives our answer tomorrow morning. And now, gentlemen, off with you. My guess is that the fur will start to fly tomorrow, so we'd best turn in."

Geoffry, the last to leave the King, caught up with Marshal not far from Marshal's tent.

"A moment, please, Sir William," Geoffry said. "I'll be returning to England tomorrow, and I wanted to speak with you before I left. I'd like to remain with the King, but His Majesty wants me to try to raise more money."

"I wish you luck," Marshal said. "We'll need every penny you can dredge up."

"What do you think our chances are?" Geoffry asked.

"Against Philip?"

"Yes."

A full moon flooded the countryside with ghostly light, illuminating the Chancellor's pale, narrow face, but his eyes remained in shadow. Marshal did not need to see his eyes to feel the tension he knew Geoffry

192

kept bottled up inside. Alone among Henry's sons, Geoffry, the bastard, clearly loved his father.

"Philip is no match for us at this point," Marshal said, "and he must know it. That's what bothers me."

"Precisely," Geoffry hissed. "It's Richard he's counting on. That's why he asked for the damned parley—to harp on Alais in front of Richard. You've heard the rumors, I'm sure."

"About the King and Alais?"

"Yes."

"Are they true?"

"The King has no intention of marrying her and disinheriting Richard. That much I'd swear to. But it's what Richard believes that counts."

"I assume you've tried to persuade His Majesty to publicly declare Richard his heir."

"Of course," Geoffry said in exasperation. "The King is as determined a man as ever, but he's losing his objectivity. He's becoming increasingly inflexible. Unfortunately Richard doesn't understand that. He sees the King's gray hair but fails to realize that the King is aging in other ways as well. Richard looks for a rational explanation of the King's refusal to acknowledge his rights where there are none, and sooner or later he may come to believe the rumors."

Marshal made no comment, for there was nothing to say. If Geoffry, the closest of Henry's advisers, could not persuade the King to placate Richard, no one could. Marshal was struck less by what Geoffry had told him than by his sense that the Chancellor was desperate for someone to talk to. It confirmed what he'd come to suspect in the short time he'd been with the King: Henry was losing the support of his baronage.

Advising the king was not simply a baron's right. It was considered an obligation, for the skills and attitudes the barons developed in ruling the fiefs they held from the Crown were those required of the king himself. Each barony was a kingdom on a smaller scale. The barons patterned their households and local administrations after the king's, and they understood his problems.

As long as the barons believed that their fortunes were intertwined with the king's, their advice and support were given willingly. Now, however, Henry's barons were beginning to hedge their bets. Reluctant to be tied to Henry's policies, more and more of them were finding excuses to absent themselves from his councils.

"Is there any chance at all of finding enough money to hold our mercenaries through next year?" Marshal asked. With a mercenary army, Henry could hold his own, even if Richard defected.

"None whatsoever," Geoffry said.

Marshal had known what Geoffry's answer would be, but still he had to suppress a sigh of frustration. "Well, then," he said, "we'll just have to draw enough blood in the next month or two to make Philip reconsider this war he's so eager for. If we hit him hard enough, we should be able to win enough time to replenish the treasury."

"If Richard remains in the fold."

"Yes," Marshal said grimly. "*If.*"

They both understood the implications. A war with the King of France could not seriously endanger the King, even if he should be defeated. At most he risked losing prestige and territory. But if Richard turned against him, it would mean civil war, and no one could say how it might end.

"Well, I'm glad of one thing," the Chancellor said, reaching out impulsively to grip Marshal's arm. "I'm glad you're with us."

"I know," Marshal responded dryly.

The Chancellor laughed softly. "Is it that obvious?"

"It's in the air. Quite a few of the rats seem to be leaving the ship."

For a long moment the Chancellor was silent, and then he said, "Any regrets, Will?"

Marshal shrugged. "Not if we win."

Geoffry smiled and shook his head. "You'd like to be that cynical, wouldn't you? I've got bad news for you, Marshal: You'll never make it."

After Geoffry left him, Marshal remained where he was, letting his thoughts settle; but as he stood alone in the moonlight, something made him look toward a nearby grove of trees. Perhaps he'd caught the sound of movement, but he could not be sure, and the darkness in the wood was impenetrable. Yet he sensed that he was no longer alone—that someone was watching him.

For a moment he was tempted to investigate, but then he shrugged off the feeling, certain that it was his imagination, and walked to his tent.

The following day was even more oppressive than the first. Not a hint of a breeze stirred the thick, humid air, and by mid-morning it was ninety degrees in the shade. A French attack was not expected, but the Franks were too close to ignore, and Marshal had ordered his knights to don their hauberks despite the heat.

"What's up?" Hugh de Harlincourt asked as Marshal approached the cluster of tents housing the King's mesne. Harlincourt was lounging in the shade, his chunky body propped against a tree trunk.

"The King's acceptance of Philip's challenge has been delivered, and Essex and I are going down to the river to await a response."

Harlincourt laughed. "I love it; it's positively Arthurian. I didn't think the Old Man had a romantic bone in his body."

Marshal shrugged. "Nothing will come of it, Hugh, but now that we've shoved the joke back down Philip's throat, I'll enjoy watching him choke on it. Essex said—"

Marshal broke off as a howl of pain burst from inside Bethune's tent. "What the hell is that?" he asked as the howling continued.

"Bethune," Harlincourt said with a sneer. "What a baby! When he saw the size of the tongs the medico brought with him to pull that tooth of his, Bo damned near fainted."

Abruptly the howling stopped, and Marshal smiled. "Sounds like he just did. Where did my squire disappear to?"

"Can't you hear them?" Harlincourt said, gesturing in the direction of a wood from which came the sounds of youthful hooting and cheering. "He's practicing with the other squires. In this heat, no less. Oh, for the eagerness of youth!"

"What's happening with the challenge?" Bethune called, emerging from his tent. He was holding his jaw and spitting blood.

"You tell him," Marshal said to Harlincourt, and went off to fetch Jean d'Erly.

In a clearing in the wood, ten squires from the King's mesne were tilting at a quintain. They had attached an old shield to a wooden beam that pivoted on a post driven into the ground. One after the other, they charged the shield with blunted lances, endeavoring to strike the small target circle painted in the center of the shield.

Marshal was pleasantly surprised that the squires had summoned the energy for a workout in spite of the deadening heat, but his approval evaporated as he came near enough to see that they were not wearing their armor. The squires had stripped to their linen shirts and breeches.

Marshal was not just annoyed, he was angry. The other squires might do as they pleased, but Jean was *his* squire and bound by *his* rules. And his cardinal rule was to wear armor whenever an enemy was near.

As it happened, Jean was about to take his turn at the quintain, and Marshal let him make his run. Thinking back on it later, Marshal knew he should have called Jean over at once. The delay only allowed his anger to build.

Jean couched his lance and made his run at full gallop, riding with the skill and ease of a natural horseman. The squire preceding him had missed the target altogether, but Jean's lance struck the shield squarely in the circle, sending the pivot arm spinning. At any other time Marshal would have applauded the performance, but not now.

Jean grinned and raised his lance in triumph as he turned his palfrey and acknowledged the cheers of his fellow squires.

"That's three in a row, you lucky bastard!" yelled Harlincourt's squire.

"Jean!" Marshal barked, startling the group, and Jean immediately rode across to him and dismounted. He guessed that Marshal had seen his run, and he was smiling broadly; but as he registered Marshal's expression, his smile vanished.

"Carry on," Marshal called to the others. He knew his rising anger was excessive, but he was in no mood for restraint. "Not a bad run," he said tightly. "You've got the touch, Jean."

"Thank you, sire," Jean said uncertainly. His black hair was slick with sweat and plastered against his scalp, save for the recalcitrant shock that was forever falling across his forehead. "I was lucky."

"I think not. You're a natural."

"Is something wrong, sire?"

Marshal compressed his lips, took the reins of Jean's horse, and swung up into the saddle. "Let's go," he said curtly, gesturing for Jean to precede him.

Jean looked up at Marshal in confusion and then turned and walked ahead of him through the wood toward the mesne's tents. As soon as they were out of sight of the clearing, Marshal drew his sword. At the sound, Jean spun around apprehensively.

"We're going to play a little wargame, boy," Marshal said. "Just the two of us. Think of me as one of those French knights across the river."

"I—I don't understand . . ."

Marshal smiled thinly. "It's simple. I'm going to attack you, and you are going to defend yourself—with that lance you're carrying, I suppose. Of course it won't do you much good. Too bad you're not wearing your iron."

Jean's eyes widened as he realized his mistake. "I'm sorry, sire, but it was so hot I thought—we all thought—"

Marshal raised his sword and spurred forward. Jean stumbled backward with a startled cry and brought up his lance to parry the blow he couldn't quite believe was coming. Marshal's sword flashed down, its tip so close to Jean's nose that the boy felt the whiff of the blade's passage, and snapped the lance shaft like a matchstick.

"Sire! What are—"

"I think you'd better make a run for it," Marshal cut in harshly, raising his sword again, and Jean turned and ran.

Marshal hesitated for a moment and then coldly pursued the boy through the wood. He caught up with him as they came in sight of the tents, and again his blade flashed down. He struck Jean across the shoulder blades with the flat of his sword, knocking the boy headlong onto the ground. It was a carefully calibrated blow that drew no blood, but Marshal knew Jean would feel the welt it raised all day.

Marshal reined in and turned to face Jean, who struggled, panting, to his feet. "None of the other squires were wearing hauberks, sire," Jean cried, fighting back tears of anger and humiliation. "Surely in this heat—"

"I don't give a damn about the other squires!" Marshal snarled. "You're my squire, and you'll damned well do as you're told while in my service. Do you understand that?"

Jean swallowed hard. "Yes, sire."

"As for the heat, we're all sweating like pigs, but what of it? Do you think the enemy only attacks when it's convenient? The enemy is right across that damned river, and if I'd been a Frank, you wouldn't be feeling any pain now—none at all—because, God damn it, you'd be dead!"

"Hey, Will!" Bethune called from fifty yards away. "You having a problem?" Bethune and Harlincourt had watched the scene and were looking curiously in their direction. No other knights or squires were near, and the servants moving about the tents had pretended not to notice.

Marshal expelled his breath in a hiss, sheathed his sword, dismounted, and handed the reins to Jean. "Just where did you leave your iron?"

"At the corral, sire, with the other squires' armor," Jean said huskily, and Marshal felt a pang of guilt, wishing he'd not let his anger carry him away. The last thing he wanted was to break the boy's spirit.

"All right, saddle my charger and get yourself suited up. The Earl of Essex and I are going down to the river to answer a challenge. I'll explain on the way. We'll be meeting the Counts of Flanders and Clermont, and you should take a good look at them. They're two of the best knights in France."

Ordinarily Jean would have questioned Marshal excitedly, but now he showed no interest and refused to meet Marshal's eyes. "Shall I lay on your new silks?" he asked stiffly.

Marshal nodded. "You might as well. This time we *are* putting on a show."

Jean cursed as he bent over and struggled into his hauberk, wincing at each fresh stab of pain from his bruised back. Marshal's stallion, which Jean had draped in new blue-and-white silks that trailed to the ground, restlessly pulled at its tether nearby. Normally Jean would have prepared his master's charger with anticipation and a sense of pride, but now he felt demeaned and surly. His throat was as dry as dust, and the odious stench of the corral's manure pile filled his nostrils.

He jumped as he felt hands grasp his hauberk and help him pull it down over his shoulders. "Thanks," he said, straightening up with a sigh, and he turned, expecting to see one of the other squires. Instead, he looked up into Bethune's mischievous blue eyes.

"You're not hurting too bad, are you, son?" Bethune said.

"No, sire. I suppose not."

Bethune grinned and spat a clot of blood onto the dusty ground. "It can't hurt as bad as my jaw does right now. Christ, I don't think I'll be able to chew for a week. Come to think of it, that may not be too bad. I'll just go on a diet of wine and beer."

Jean smiled uncertainly, wondering why Bethune had sought him out.

"You think Sir William came down on you too hard, don't you," Bethune said quietly.

"Your squire isn't wearing his hauberk, sire," Jean said, challenge in his eyes. "Do you intend to beat him?"

"Maybe I should," Bethune said. "I'm sure he'd appreciate your reminding me."

Jean swallowed and dropped his eyes. "I'm not always this stupid, sire."

"I know," Bethune said. "If you were, I wouldn't have bothered speaking to you. But I wanted you to understand why Sir William did what he did."

"I wasn't wearing my hauberk. That's why."

"But do you know why he didn't just bawl you out—why he rode you down and humiliated you?"

"No, sire, I don't."

"Because he likes you, Jean, and because he knows you're going to make a fine knight one day—a fighting knight."

Jean shook his head.

"It's true, son, believe me. You've seen that mess of scar tissue on Sir William's thigh. Well, he got that in a fight when he was only twenty-one. The party he was with was ambushed by the Lusignans, and his uncle was killed—speared in the back while trying to mount his horse.

"Sir William loved that man and looked up to him like a father—the only real father he ever had. The point is, Jean, that his uncle died because he wasn't wearing his hauberk. They were in hostile territory, but they weren't expecting trouble. It was hot that day—very hot—just like it is today."

Marshal and the Earl of Essex sat astride their silk-draped chargers at the riverbank, waiting in the blaze of the noonday sun for a response to the message they had sent across to the King of France. Their coifs were pushed back and their squires held their helmets, but they were fully armed. Within a quarter-mile radius there was an unnatural quiet as the Norman knights and soldiery, in the shade, and the Franks, sweltering in the sun on the opposite bank, watched and waited with them.

The Earl eased himself in the saddle and looked across at Jean d'Erly. "The last time your master and I fought side by side, he wasn't much older than you are now. A cocky young buck he was, but after that fight I had to give him a talking-to. I'll wager he's never told you about it."

"No, sire," Jean said, smiling.

Marshal glanced at Jean, surprised that the boy had recovered his spirits so quickly.

"Well, he fought bravely enough, but he forgot the first rule of knightly combat. He has passed that on to you, hasn't he?"

"I'm not sure, sire."

Marshal grinned. "Make sure of your booty," he said, remembering.

"That's right," the Earl said sternly. "Make sure of your booty. Sir William must have put at least three knights out of action in that little combat, but he didn't take the time to capture a single one of them. He didn't even seize a horse. Battles aren't worth winning if you don't come away with a profit. Ransom, horses, equipment—in that order."

"That fight was at Driencourt," Marshal said. "What—twenty years ago?"

"Damn near," the Earl agreed. "And we were up against Flanders that day. Never did get a crack at him myself. Now, maybe I will."

"Not a chance, sire," Marshal said, wiping the sweat out of his eyes. "Philip won't bite."

The Earl shook his head regretfully. "Probably not. It's too bad, because it's a damned good idea—the civilized way to settle things," he said, lifting a skin of diluted wine to his lips. "How long do you plan to sit out here in the sun, Marshal? We could just as easily wait in the shade."

"The men on both sides know what's going on, sire," Marshal said. "Let them have a good look at us. Philip is going to back down, and I want to rub it in; it's the only fun we're going to get out of this charade."

The Earl grunted noncommittally, but then he raised his hand to shade his eyes and smiled with satisfaction. "Here comes our answer. No banners, but I do believe that's Flanders—and Clermont too."

"Banners or not, everyone will know who they are soon enough," Marshal said with satisfaction. "I'll bet Philip isn't laughing anymore."

The two French Counts, tall, powerfully built men with the unmistakable look of seasoned warriors, rode up to their side of the river ford. Leaving their squires on the bank, they crossed to the river's midpoint and reined in. It was clear that they wanted to avoid a shouted conversation, and as neither Marshall nor the Earl intended to embarrass the Counts personally, they rode out to meet them.

"Essex, Marshal, good day to you," said the Count of Flanders casually.

Flanders was about the same age as Marshal, and at the height of his power and prestige. Some years back he had flirted with rebellion, but now he was Philip's principal war counselor. Despite a pockmarked face and thinning hair, he was a darkly handsome man with a grace and style that matched his king's; but beneath the courtly manner and carriage it was not hard to detect a hard edge. He was as tough as he was courteous and intelligent.

"I understand that you'd like to pick a fight with me and Clermont here," Flanders said.

"No, sire," the Earl responded. "We are acting on behalf of our King. His Majesty has accepted King Philip's proposal of a combat between champions, and Marshal and I are his choices. King Philip, I understand, has chosen you."

"Surely you realize that King Philip was only jesting," said the Count of Clermont with an uncomfortable smile.

"No, sire," the Earl said with a perfectly straight face. "Our King received a challenge and has accepted it. That's where the matter stands as far as we are concerned."

"Twisting the knife a bit, are you, Essex?" the Count of Flanders said with a good-natured grin.

The Earl shrugged and returned the grin.

"Well," the Count of Flanders said, "if you two were looking forward to a fight, I'm sorry to disappoint you. His Majesty has withdrawn the challenge—once and for all."

"That's a pity," the Earl said. "It might have been interesting."

"Interesting, perhaps," Flanders said, "but I for one am not crazy enough to go one-on-one with Marshal, here, no matter what my King may have said. I can't speak for Clermont, but I'm getting a little old for that kind of risk."

The Count of Clermont laughed softly. "You can speak for me. I might try you, Essex, but with Marshal in the picture . . . I must say, Marshal, you were a tough enough customer before, but you've come back from the Holy Land looking even meaner."

"Thank you, sire," Marshal said with a smile, "if that was intended as a compliment."

"Simple fact, Sir William. Simple fact."

"Then King Philip's refusal to go through with his challenge is absolutely final?" Marshal said.

"Absolutely," the Count of Flanders replied. "To quote His Majesty, this damned joke has gone far enough."

"Well," Marshal said dryly, "let's not forget that it was his joke to start with."

"Quite," the Count of Flanders said curtly. "Now, unless you have further business to discuss, we'll bid you adieu. Another few minutes in this sun and I'll be tempted to jump into the water, armor and all."

As Marshal and Essex returned to their side of the river, someone in the Norman ranks called out to them. "Has Philip withdrawn his challenge?"

"Yes!" Marshal shouted back, and as if on signal, a horde of foot soldiers poured out of the woods and ran down to the river, hooting and yelling like madmen. Within minutes three hundred men had lined the riverbank and taken up a rhythmic chant: "Chick-en-shits! Chick-en-shits! Chick-en-shits!"

The Earl shook his head. "Those poor bastards baking in the sun over there must be fed up. They're in no mood to take this sort of thing for long. Philip probably doesn't intend to attack, but my guess is that there'll be trouble before the day is out."

Marshal smiled and nodded. "I wouldn't be surprised."

17

Marshal was asleep and dreaming when the French attacked in the middle of the afternoon.

He lay on his back in the shade near his tent, his head pillowed on a tree root. In his dream he was riding in the midst of a party of solemn-faced knights, one of whom was leading Marshal's horse. The horse was huge, and Marshal's feet couldn't reach the stirrups. He had to hold on to the saddle pommel with both hands to keep his balance.

He was frightened of the grim, towering knights surrounding him, and unaccountably helpless. But although he read danger in the knights' stony faces, he didn't know its origin. He kept asking where they were taking him, but no one answered. They just rode on at a funereal pace, ignoring him and avoiding each other's eyes. On a hill in the distance, silhouetted against the sky, was a stone tower keep surrounded by a wooden palisade—

"Wake up, sire!" Jean d'Erly cried, shaking Marshal's shoulder. "They're coming across the river!"

Marshal's eyes flew open, and he was on his feet before his mind cleared. Jean slipped Marshal's sword belt about his waist, and Marshal buckled it as he strode to his charger, tethered a few feet away. Fifteen knights of King Henry's mesne were already mounting up. Everyone had expected an attack.

As the dregs of sleep drained away, Marshal found himself grinning, relieved to be free of the nightmare and looking forward to action. After the slow buildup of tension, waiting for the war he had known was coming, combat would be a release.

From the direction of the river, which was screened from view by the woods, came the blare of trumpets and the rising roar of yelling men rushing into battle. As yet it sounded as if only a few hundred were engaging, but the noise was swelling minute by minute.

Marshal swung up into the saddle, and Jean handed up Marshal's shield, mailed gloves, and helmet. Marshal pulled the mail coif up over his head and tightened the laces, but he did not put on his helmet; his knights followed his example.

Hugh de Harlincourt, who had been keeping watch by the river, galloped up on his palfrey. "Infantry's coming across at the main ford at our center," he reported, dropping from his saddle and mounting the charger his squire held ready for him. "A hundred or so Franks started across on their own, and our archers cut them down in the river. Our captains are pulling the Welsh back now, and the French are pouring across and engaging our pikemen."

"What about the deep ford downriver?" Marshal asked.

Harlincourt shook his head. "So far they're only crossing at the center. This isn't a planned attack, Will. Some of the Franks just got tired of our boys' insults and decided to try to shut them up. But Philip will have to throw in reinforcements at once, or lose a chunk of his army. The Welsh are back at the line of trees, screened by our infantry, and using the French coming across the river for target practice."

At that moment Bethune, who had been at his post at the King's command tent, rode up. His blue eyes were frosty with anger. "Damn, Will, the King's ordering a general retreat. The right flank is to fall back to the town walls; the left and center are to retreat to the fortress. Philip is moving cavalry forward now, and Richard is leading out his knights to cover the retreat in the center."

"It's the right move," Marshal said sharply, raising his voice so all could hear him. "If the French are stupid enough to attack fortified positions, we'll have a field day, and if we don't retreat, we play into their hands; they outnumber us three to two. Bethune, Harlincourt, Clifford, Quency, and Preux—you stay with me. The rest of you are to fall back to the fortress with the King."

Marshal's directive was instantly greeted by cries of protest from the knights he hadn't named.

"That's my order, damn it," Marshal barked. "Now get your squires moving! You've got time, so don't leave any equipment or pack animals behind."

An orderly retreat in the event of a French attack had been planned from the beginning. The bulk of the Norman army's stores were inside the fortress, with additional supplies in the walled town. The soldiers emerging from the woods and moving up the steep slope toward Gisors

204

Castle were bringing their wagons and pack animals with them. The withdrawal was proceeding quickly and smoothly, and the roar of men fighting and dying was still confined to the immediate battle zone in the army's center, between the river and the line of trees.

Bethune mounted his charger and hastily armed himself. A grin had replaced his angry look as soon as Marshal had given his orders, and Harlincourt's normally serious eyes were bright with anticipation.

"All right, let's get down to the river," Marshal said calmly, spurring his horse forward. "Hugh, carry the banner."

Harlincourt took Marshal's banner from Jean d'Erly and gave the disappointed knights being left behind his chipmunk grin. "Tough luck, boys. Better you than me!"

But the grins of the five knights following Marshal faded as he led them diagonally through the woods, downriver, and away from the battle. They had to ride slowly at first, threading their way through the masses of infantry streaming back from the river toward the town walls.

"Where the hell are you taking us, Will?" Bethune complained. "The fight's over there. Listen, there goes Richard!"

They all heard the concerted yell—"Lionheart!"—rise above the frenzy of battle cries as Richard led his knights in a charge somewhere far to their left, but Marshal's response was to veer farther downriver.

"I've got a hunch," Marshal responded. "I'm heading for that deep ford. If I'm wrong, we can still cut back upriver."

As the press of infantry retreating past them lessened, Marshal moved the pace up to a trot, feeling his own excitement build. He felt healthier and stronger than he had in months, and it was good to be riding into a fight with his comrades again. For the first time in many years he was feeling some of the old, joyous anticipation.

Through the trees ahead, he saw the sparkling flash of the river and the light of the open fields beyond. As they neared the edge of the wood fifty yards from the river, he held up his hand and reined in. Across the river, the masses of Philip's infantry and cavalry swirled in apparent confusion, but Marshal saw at once that the captains were marshaling their units and keeping them under control.

Philip had already thrown sufficient forces across the river to support the contingents that had made the initial, unplanned thrust, but he clearly had no intention of pressing the attack. He was holding back the bulk of his army.

The woods cut off Marshal's view of the restricted battle that was raging a half mile upriver, in the vicinity of the Elm of Gisors, but they were close enough to hear individual cries for help and shouted orders above the bedlam of yelling, screaming, and clashing steel. Bodies and parts of bodies were floating lazily downriver by the dozens, amid wooden shields and broken pike shafts. The gently flowing water was streaked with blood.

Marshal and his knights viewed the ghastly flotsam with indifference. To them, dead foot soldiers were simply the refuse of battle.

"Just what are we doing here?" Bethune demanded impatiently. "We're missing all the action."

"Not for long," Marshal said, pointing toward a detachment of knights emerging from the milling throngs of men and horses on the far side of the river.

Harlincourt shaded his eyes and squinted. "That's Flanders in the lead. They're heading right toward us!"

"I knew it!" Marshal said with satisfaction. "The fox is up to his old tricks. They're going to cross here and hit Richard in the flank."

Bethune grinned. "You're right. That's the same stunt he pulled at the tournament at Lagni."

The Count of Flanders, one of France's leading patrons of chivalry, held a highly practical view of tournaments. He and his team habitually remained aloof from the battle, until most of the combatants had exhausted themselves. Then he would charge with his knights into a flank and win an easy victory.

"Clermont isn't with him," Marshal said, "but it looks like he's brought along Clermont's knights. Twenty men to our six. Is that enough action for you, Bo?"

"It'll do, Will. It'll do."

"All right, gentlemen, here's the drill. We'll hit them with lances as they're coming out of the water, and make a stand with swords on the riverbank. That ford is narrow as hell, and they won't be able to spread out. Lace your helmets!"

Grinning, the knights lowered their helmets over their heads, lashed them down, slipped on their mail gauntlets, and took lances from their squires.

"Just like old times," Harlincourt said happily, his voice muffled and metallic behind the helmet.

The Count of Flanders had reached the opposite bank, and his knights were probing the river's depth with their lances to be sure of the ford's location. The Count raised his hand and started across. The knights rode two abreast, the leaders continually sounding the bottom. The river current was barely perceptible, but the ford was so deep that the water rose above the riders' stirrups.

"Any deeper and they'd be swimming," Bethune said.

"If the fight takes us into the water," Marshal cautioned, "try to stay upriver of the ford. Spread out now. We'll go out abreast in a single echelon on my order."

Marshal watched the knights' approach tensely, waiting for just the right moment to attack. When the Count and the knight riding beside him were ten yards from the near bank, Marshal raised his hand and lifted his shield into position.

"Now!" he shouted, digging in his spurs.

Marshal and his five companions burst from the woods in line, their stallions surging into a gallop. In unison their lances swung down into attack position, and Marshal's knights honored him with their battle cry, shouting his name in a single, bloodcurdling yell. "Mar—shal!"

The French knights saw the Normans pounding toward them and frantically spurred their mounts forward, but Marshal had timed the charge perfectly. The Count of Flanders and the knight beside him reached the bank when the Normans were still forty yards away, and the Count had only seconds to make a choice. He made the wrong one.

Marshal's lips drew back from his clenched teeth in a triumphant grin as he saw the Count rein in. Instead of instantly countercharging, the Count waited for the knights coming up immediately behind him to form a line of six against six. Too late, their lances swung down and their spurs dug into their chargers' flanks. As the French started forward, Marshal and his men crashed into them at full gallop, sweeping four of the six from their saddles as if they were quintain targets.

The instant Marshal's lance drove his opponent from the saddle, he swung the lance tip to the offhand side as his charger's momentum carried him down the embankment, and he buried the lance in the chest of the next horse in line. The rider flung himself free of the saddle, only to be trampled under the water by Bethune's stallion.

"Out of the water!" Marshal bellowed, drawing his sword. "Hold the bank!"

But Marshal's own horse had carried him too far into the river, and he was immediately surrounded by the French knights surging forward in a packed mass and pressing in around him. He swung viciously at a

Frenchman on his right, catching the knight with a backhand blow across the side of the helmet that dented the steel plate and sent the man reeling. It was Marshal's last decisive sword stroke.

Blades struck at him from all directions at once, caroming off his shield and ringing on his helmet with deafening clangs. In the midst of the plunging, thrashing horses, Marshal could not maneuver for position.

He finally managed to wheel his horse about, and as his charger turned back toward the bank he glimpsed his knights holding their position, their swords flashing down on the French and beating them back into the river. Marshal winced as a sword blow from behind rang off his helmet and bit into his shoulder armor. Before he could react, two more jarring blows struck his helmet, and suddenly he couldn't see.

The first blow had severed the leather thong tying down his helmet, and now it had twisted around on his head. Another vicious sword stroke caught him in the side of the head, denting his helmet and knocking it further askew. Blindly he swept his sword left and right, sometimes striking a shield and sometimes scything air, but the jarring blows to his head kept coming, numbing his mind.

Worse, with the helmet's breathing hole out of position, he was sucking in his own exhalations, and he realized that he was suffocating.

"To Marshal! To Marshal!" came a cry from the riverbank, and a moment later Marshal recognized Bethune's voice yelling at him from somewhere close by. "Get the hell out of here, Will!"

"Go!" he heard Harlincourt thunder at him above the shouts and clanging of steel on steel.

But Marshal was completely disoriented now, and although the sword blows had abated, he couldn't guide his horse.

"Give me your reins, sire!" yelled Jean d'Erly, close on Marshal's right hand, and Marshal felt the reins torn from his grasp. Suddenly he pitched forward as his stallion unaccountably foundered beneath him. The saddle rolled, throwing him into the river. It happened too quickly for him to feel fear, but he knew he would sink like a stone.

Just as the water closed over his head, a hand seized the back of his mail coif and lifted him to the surface.

"I've got you, sire," he heard Jean cry, and he was dragged, coughing and choking, through the water to the river bank, held like a puppy by the scruff of the neck. Dimly he heard Flanders bellowing to his knights to retreat.

* * *

Marshal stood with the King and Richard on the parapet of Gisors Castle's gate house, looking out across the Epte. It was a half hour past sunset, and clouds darkened the sky. Heat lightning flickered silently on the horizon.

"Wind's picking up," Richard said. "Looks like this storm will clear the air."

"Why the hell did he chop down the elm?" the King said morosely. "What was the point of that?"

Far below them, barely visible in the fading light, lay the fallen Elm of Gisors. Enraged and frustrated by the Normans' retreat, French foot soldiers had attacked the only target left to them—the giant tree. They had hacked it down with battle-axes. From a distance it was the only visible sign that the short, sharp engagement had taken place. The French had retired, carrying away their dead and wounded, and the Normans, reoccupying their encampment, had buried their own dead. The men who had fallen in the river had been washed downstream.

"I doubt that Philip ordered it done, sire," Marshal said, finding it difficult to speak clearly. His lips were split, and the right side of his jaw was bruised and swollen from the battering his face had received in the fight at the river. "His men were just taking out their frustration. They took heavy losses coming across, and they accomplished nothing. We took one or two hundred casualties, and I estimate they lost twice that number."

Leaning on his elbows against the parapet wall, Henry nodded woodenly and continued to stare out at the elm, as if reading an evil omen in its fall. Again Marshal was struck by the contrast between Henry and his son. Richard was relaxed and good-humored in the wake of the initial, inconclusive clash with Philip, but Henry seemed depressed and drained of energy. And there was no good reason for his morose lethargy.

"Our spies report that Philip will begin pulling back his troops as soon as darkness falls," Marshal prompted. "He'll undoubtedly start releasing his levies over the next few days; the grape harvest is due."

"He must not relish stalemate any more than I do," Henry said sourly, and Marshal suppressed a frown of impatience.

Until now, the King had seemed determined to teach his young opponent a lesson. Now, suddenly, he seemed to lack the will to follow through. But the King who had deliberately challenged Philip to war was the King Marshal had known, and Marshal was sure that the old fire was still there inside that bloated, tired body. It was up to Marshal to fan the flames into life again.

Marshal waited for Richard to point out the obvious, but the Count of Poitou remained silent.

"If Philip disbands his army, sire," Marshal said, "we don't have to settle for a stalemate."

Henry looked up, and Marshal saw a glint of interest in his eyes. "What have you in mind?"

"You know the French, sire. They campaign from spring until the harvest, and then retire from the field. Neither Philip nor his father ever relied on mercenaries as heavily as we do, and my guess is that it won't occur to Philip that we're not bound by the same rules.

"We can fight until the money runs out, and I suggest we do just that. Let Philip see us disband our forces, but issue secret orders for our men to reassemble next week—farther south. If we raid in force across the Epte, we'll catch Philip with his pants down—and do him a lot more damage than he did to you by chopping down that tree."

Henry straightened up and slapped the parapet stone with the flat of his hand. "Sounds good," he said firmly. "What do you think?" he said to Richard, but the question was only a matter of form.

"It's a good plan," Richard said, "and we can make it even hotter for Philip if I slip down to Poitiers and then cut into Berry toward Châteauroux. I think we can afford to split our forces."

The King nodded in agreement, and Marshal could think of no way to object, because the tactic was sound. Yet he didn't like the idea. So far Richard had fully supported his father against Philip, adopting the view that it was Philip who stood in the way of a fresh Crusade, but Marshal wondered how long his loyalty would last once he was no longer physically in Henry's camp.

The wind was gusting heavily now, ruffling their hair, and Henry, his optimism and energy renewed, took a deep breath and grinned up into the black sky. The lightning flashes were coming closer, accompanied by the rumble of rolling thunder.

"We'd better get off this parapet," Henry said jovially. "I'd hate to have lightning do Philip's work for him. Let's go down to the great hall and speak to the barons. If they're not already too drunk to listen, they may be interested in hearing what we have in store for the King of France."

Because of the storm, the King, his older barons, and the few bishops who had remained behind after the breakup of the parley sheltered in Gisors Castle for the night; but Richard, the fighting barons, and Marshal weathered the storm in the encampment with their men. John and his entourage stayed in the castle.

Marshal was surprised to find his tent empty when he returned; Gilbert, his manservant, should have been waiting to attend him. The rain trench around the tent was overflowing and the rushes on the floor squished underfoot, but either Jean or Gilbert had safely stowed his oak chest and armor on improvised platforms of brushwood.

The torrential rain had soaked Marshal to the skin, and he stripped down immediately, toweling himself vigorously to remove what sweat and grime he could. Soon, he hoped, he would have a chance to bathe; he itched, and he was sure he smelled like a goat. Wearily he dropped naked onto his cot and pulled a sheet over himself. As he was reaching to put out the candle lantern hanging above him, Jean pulled aside the tent flap and came in, dripping wet. He was out of breath and panting.

"What have you been up to?" Marshal said, propping himself up on his elbows.

Jean's boots and breeches were caked with mud, and there was blood on the sleeves of his tunic.

"I sent Gilbert to try to find the carcass of your horse, sire," he said excitedly, "and he found it just before dark. It washed up on our side of the river a mile downstream."

"Why? What were you after?"

"It didn't make sense to me, sire—your mount dying under you like that. I was almost certain it hadn't been wounded in the fight, and I was right," he said triumphantly, holding out his hand and displaying his find. "Your horse wasn't killed by a French knight; it was brought down by this, sire. I dug it out of the carcass."

"Where was the wound?" Marshal said, staring at the steel cross-bow bolt in Jean's hand.

"In the chest, sire," Jean said angrily. "The bolt was discharged from our side of the river. One of our men must have tried to pick off an enemy knight. It's a disgrace, sire, and the blackguard nearly killed you!"

Marshal considered the implications of the steel bolt, gleaming evilly in the lantern light, and he felt a tingle in his spine as he reached a chillingly different conclusion.

"I owe you one, son," Marshal said. "You saved my life today."

Embarrassed, Jean looked away and shifted restlessly on his feet.

Marshal smiled crookedly with the undamaged side of his mouth. "You did well, but I don't want you to take that kind of risk again."

"I know a squire is supposed to stay out of a fight between knights, sire," Jean said quickly, "but I didn't draw my sword."

"That might not make any difference in the heat of battle. You have to stay clear. There are some knights who would cut you down like a foot soldier."

"I understand, sire."

"Good," Marshal said, wishing more than ever that he'd not punished Jean that morning. "How's your back, son?"

"It hurts like hell, sire," Jean deadpanned, and Marshal laughed, certain now that Jean had taken it in stride.

"Then you'd better turn in and get some rest. You can sleep on your stomach."

"May I ask you a question first?" Jean said.

"What?"

"You told me that the Counts of Flanders and Clermont are two of France's foremost knights, and I heard Sir Hugh and some of the other knights talking late this afternoon. They said Flanders and Clermont were afraid to fight you."

"Just talk, Jean. Just talk. It was Philip's decision," Marshal said, downplaying the incident. He demanded respect and obedience from his squires, but he tried to discourage the hero worship so many squires were prone to. A squire would be a knight one day, and no knight, Marshal thought, should stand in another's shadow.

"I also heard Sir Hugh say that Count Richard challenged you this morning—at the Barons' council."

Marshal frowned. "That's how rumors start," he said. "Count Richard did nothing of the kind."

"But if he had, sire," Jean persisted, "could you take him?"

"I don't know," Marshal said truthfully. "Maybe, but I hope I never have to find out. Now get out of here and let me get some sleep."

Jean extinguished the lantern, plunging the tent into darkness, but as he turned to leave, he said confidently, "You could beat him, sire, I *know* you could."

As Marshal lay back on his cot listening to the crash of thunder and the rattle of raindrops on the tent, it was not Richard he was thinking about.

212

"Ridefort," he said into the darkness.

There had been no crossbowmen in the wood where they had waited to ambush Flanders; there had been no infantry at all. Jean had assumed that the bolt had not been meant for Marshal, but he had not been present at the parley. Jean had not seen the look in Gerard de Ridefort's eyes.

18

Isabelle stifled a yawn as Master Edmond Orri, the premiere troubador of Aquitaine, launched into the final aria of the romance of Tristan and Isolde. Edmond, a renowned poet and singer, was also an accomplished actor, and he gave life to the dialogues woven into the tragedy's narrative. But his rendition of the epic in prose, verse, and song was three hours long, and Isabelle ached to rise from her cushioned bench and relieve the stiffness in her back.

The Queen had commanded the performance to celebrate the refurbishing of Winchester Castle's *palais*, and it was held in the great feast hall before the Queen, the Bishop of Winchester, and a large gathering of lesser knights and noblewomen. The pillared hall, with its high arches and vaulted, frescoed ceiling, swallowed up sound, but Edmond's rich, powerful voice filled the air. He was a tall, blond, dynamic man who appeared no less larger than life than the heroic figures depicted on the bright new tapestries covering the walls.

As Edmond sang the tragic last lines of his tale of ill-fated love, Isabelle saw that many of the ladies were silently weeping. She started to yawn again but caught herself as Edmond's piercing blue eyes sought her out—as they had repeatedly during his performance.

At supper the previous evening, Eleanor had seated Isabelle next to the troubador, and he had danced with Isabelle more often than with any other lady present, provoking jealous looks from the neglected women, and smiles of detached amusement from the Queen.

Isabelle had been flattered, and although the air of professionalism in Edmond's attentions had not escaped her, she had found them a welcome diversion. For a time after she had come to Winchester, the restricted life she led as the Queen's lady-in-waiting had been a comfort; but as she had become accustomed to her newfound security and past terrors receded from her mind, she began to chafe with boredom.

And with boredom came melancholy. Four months had passed since she had watched Marshal ride out of Winchester Castle. She had thought then that the future would take care of itself; but as the empty weeks had stretched into months and she received no message from him, she had begun to fear that Marshal's own resignation to their separation might be self-fulfilling.

She longed to find a way to take her destiny into her own hands, but she was as powerless and as isolated as the Queen—even more isolated, for the devious Eleanor had her private sources of information. Isabelle did not even know precisely where Marshal was, or how he might be faring.

The Queen, herself, was a daily reminder of the King's ultimate power over their lives. Isabelle had always known that she could marry only at the King's pleasure; but knowing and feeling were very different, and now Isabelle felt her helplessness.

At last Edmond's song ended, and as the final note died away, the audience burst into applause and stood for a prolonged ovation. Isabelle's smile of relief was indistinguishable from the others' smiles of pleasure, but it vanished abruptly as the cheers turned to cries for an encore.

Edmond bowed to Eleanor and smilingly shook his head, spreading his hands in an apologetic gesture of fatigue, with which Isabelle heartily concurred.

"That was extraordinary, Master Edmond," said the Queen as the applause subsided, "but surely you would not let us down from the heights so abruptly. Vespers is not far off, and I know you are tired, but could you not favor us with one last, short piece?"

"Your Majesty," Edmond replied, brushing back his yellow hair from his damp forehead, "I thank you for your kind reception of my art, but I *am* tired, as I know you will understand, and my throat is as dry as dust."

"But that is easily remedied," Eleanor said briskly, snapping her fingers, and a servant hurried forward and thrust a wine cup into Edmond's hand.

The troubador drank deeply and then bowed to the Queen's request. "A short piece, then, Your Majesty. I could recite a rather witty *tenso* for you and your gracious company. It poses and answers the question, Should a lady display her affection by asking her true knight to go abroad and win renown, or should she simply ask him to love her always in his heart?"

The Queen frowned and shook her head. "I think we would prefer a song, Master Edmond—a little *chanson*."

"Ah," Edmond said thoughtfully, and then he looked deliberately at Isabelle for what seemed an embarrassingly long time. "Perhaps you might care to hear a song I recently composed myself. I've had the melody for some time, but it was not until last night, shortly before I retired, that I settled on the lyrics in their final form."

"By all means," Eleanor said. "What do you call it?"

"I have not given it a title yet, Your Majesty," Edmond said, taking the harp from his young accompanist. The boy rose, and Edmond seated himself on the accompanist's bench and strummed the harp strings, adjusting the silver frets until the tuning was to his satisfaction.

"First, the melody," Edmond said, and as the audience settled into hushed silence he closed his eyes and began to play a slow, haunting melody that drifted softly through the hall. When he had played the song through, he opened his eyes, nodded dreamily to himself, and began to sing, harmonizing with chords on the harp.

> *"Fair to me are the scents of spring*
> *When April rains new flowers bring*
> *And in warming skies, larks above me soar*
> *To fill the world with song once more."*

As the troubador came to the *chanson*'s refrain he turned and again looked directly at Isabelle, holding her eyes as he sang.

> *"Then my thoughts turn to you, my love*
> *The memories borne on the wings of a dove*
> *Your emerald eyes and fiery hair*
> *Have caught me in enchantment so fair."*

The allusion to Isabelle's eyes and hair was made all the more obvious by Edmond's steady gaze, and she flushed as heads began to turn her way.

"He's written the song for *you*, milady!" Matilda whispered excitedly, and Isabelle seized her arm to silence her.

Matilda, who had rejoined Isabelle the month before, had been thrilled that Isabelle had caught Edmond's eye the previous evening, and

216

she had driven Isabelle to distraction before the afternoon performance by demanding repeated changes in Isabelle's costume.

Matilda despised Norman trouvères as effeminate wastrels, but apparently she held no such prejudice when it came to a southern troubador favored by the Queen. The *bliaut* she had finally settled on for Isabelle was a present from the Queen—a gown of bright green silk embroidered in gold, with extravagant sleeves that trailed to the floor.

Edmond sang on.

> *"In summer's sun I take my ease,*
> *Forsaking all that does not please*
> *When fields are graced with a mantle green*
> *And woodshade grants me rest serene.*
>
> *Then my thoughts turn to you, my love*
> *The memories borne on the wings of a dove*
> *Your emerald eyes and fiery hair*
> *Have caught me in enchantment so fair."*

There was no need for Edmond to make it any clearer that he had completed the lyrics with Isabelle in mind; and as he continued to sing, she, not the singer, became the focus of the audience's smiling attention.

> *"When autumn paints the forests all*
> *I hear the rustle of each leaf's fall*
> *And hark to the cry of geese in flight*
> *Foretelling the coming of winter's night."*

When Edmond came again to the refrain, his accompanist, and then several of the knights in the audience, joined in, all of them looking at Isabelle. Determined not to give way to her embarrassment, she raised her eyes to the troubador and returned his smile. Edmond sang the last verse to her as if she were the only person in the hall.

> *"I dread not winter's drifts of snow*
> *Nor icy blast of the winds that blow*
> *For a blazing hearth will warm me well*
> *And on the past there's time to dwell."*

Every man in the hall who could sing, joined in the final refrain, and as the song ended, the audience's applause was as much for Isabelle as it was for the song itself. Edmond seemed genuinely pleased with the reaction.

"Now that your *chanson* has taken its final form, Master Edmond," said the Queen when the applause abated, "you must give it a title."

Edmond smiled and nodded. "I was thinking of calling it 'Seasons of Love,' Your Majesty, but now another title occurs to me—in honor of the fair lady who inspired the final lyrics." He paused and looked again at Isabelle. "I shall call my little song 'Greensleeves.' "

Isabelle managed to slip away from the gathering soon afterward and went out alone to the deserted castle garden outside the eastern curtain wall. Now that the weather was turning cold, she knew she could find privacy in the garden in the late hours of the day, and for her it was still pleasant. The flowers were gone, but the trees had not yet lost their foliage, and the low-angle rays of the setting sun brightened the yellowing autumn leaves to a fiery orange.

Isabelle thought she could never walk into a garden again without being immediately reminded of Marshal, seeing in her mind's eye his disarming smile and recalling his deep, reassuring voice. She smiled slightly, wondering if she alone saw him as a thoughtful, gentle man, or did others, too, look beyond the strength and daring of the legendary William Marshal.

To Ranulf, Marshal was the quintessential knight, a man's man, hard and true. To Matilda, he was the dashing, romantic hero in shining armor. And to Eleanor? How did he appear to her?

Isabelle heard the crunch of footsteps on the gravel path behind her and turned. The Queen had entered the garden and was coming toward her. Eleanor was alone, but two of her ever-present guards had stationed themselves at the garden entrance.

"I thought I might find you out here," Eleanor said as Isabelle walked back toward her. "I'm afraid Master Edmond was disappointed when you made your exit so quickly. I told him that the excitement of the honor he'd bestowed on you had probably left you feeling faint."

"Thank you, Your Majesty. I didn't intend to offend him," Isabelle said, wondering why Eleanor had sought her out. The Queen was not given to quiet walks in the garden.

Eleanor handed Isabelle her cane and took Isabelle's arm for support as they started up the path toward the garden's fountain. The Queen's arthritis was the principal sign of her advancing age, and Isabelle guessed that she endured considerable pain to disguise it. At a glance, Eleanor could pass for a woman fifteen years younger; and although she walked slowly, her bearing was as erect and as commanding as ever.

"Edmond's attention doesn't distress you, I hope," Eleanor said.

"Not in the least, Your Majesty," Isabelle said easily. "I'm flattered."

"But you don't take it seriously, I gather."

"Should I, Your Majesty?"

Eleanor laughed. "I suppose not. That one's a professional heartbreaker. And he's persistent. He made me promise to seat you beside him at supper again tonight."

Isabelle suspected that Edmond was more to Eleanor than an entertaining troubador. His home was in Poitiers, and he was said to be a favorite of Richard's, who was a troubador in his own right. Eleanor's communications were strictly censored and her visitors screened, and it had occurred to Isabelle that Edmond might carry information of greater import than a troubador's usual repertoire of titillating gossip.

Eleanor had never volunteered any news of the war that was not common knowledge, and she had hardly mentioned Marshal to Isabelle since the day Isabelle had arrived. But without knowing precisely why, Isabelle sensed that this might be the time to ask, and she wanted to know what was happening in France—she had to know.

"Has Master Edmond brought news of the war, Your Majesty?" she said abruptly.

Eleanor smiled knowingly. "Is it news of the war you want—or news of Sir William?"

"I would like to know how he is faring, Your Majesty."

"Well, Edmond has brought news," Eleanor said. "As a matter of fact, that's why I came out to talk with you. According to Edmond, the King does have Philip on the defensive at the moment—as we've been told—and I gather that Marshal has become a leading figure in the Royal Councils. Apparently Count Richard considers him the driving force behind His Majesty's recent successes."

Isabelle smiled with unabashed pleasure and pride. "That is good news, Your Majesty. But I must say that it does not surprise me. I only hope—"

Eleanor cocked an eyebrow as Isabelle broke off. "Yes?"

"Well, Your Majesty," Isabelle said, hesitating, but she could see no harm in saying what was uppermost in her mind. "I was about to say that I hope His Majesty will reward Sir William appropriately."

"You needn't worry on that score," Eleanor replied breezily. "As a matter of fact, the King has already rewarded him—by giving him custody of the heiress, Helwis of Lancaster, and permission to marry the lady."

Isabelle's smile froze, and she felt as if a hand had suddenly closed on her heart. Eleanor's eyes were on her, and she struggled to master her shock. "That's wonderful, Your Majesty," she heard herself say. "It's no more than he deserves."

Why was she shocked? She, herself, had told Marshal that the King had a surfeit of heiresses at his disposal, and Marshal could hardly have refused the King's gift. Why did she feel betrayed? Why the sudden rush of panic? Helwis might be his ward, but he didn't have to marry her.

"He hasn't married her yet," Eleanor said with that same knowing smile, as if reading Isabelle's thoughts. "Besides, my dear," she added solicitously, "love and marriage rarely go together in this world."

Isabelle was off-balance, but still she detected a look of cool appraisal behind the apparent sympathy in Eleanor's coal-black eyes. Eleanor, she realized with a flash of anger, had wanted to observe her reaction to the news.

"Just what is it you want of me, Your Majesty?"

Eleanor smiled sardonically. "I see you share at least one trait with our Sir William. You prefer the direct approach."

"Yes, Your Majesty, I do."

"Well, that's not easy to get used to, Isabelle. Believe me, royalty sees very little of it."

They had reached the fountain, and the Queen seated herself on a bench nearby. Isabelle remained standing.

"Actually, my dear," Eleanor said, pulling her robe more tightly around her shoulders, "it's not a question of what I want of you but of what you want for yourself."

"And what is that, Your Majesty?"

Eleanor smiled. "I suspect you want a great deal, Isabelle—a *great* deal. What a pity you're so rich a marriage prize; that complicates matters considerably. Of course, as long as Sir William does not marry, I suppose there's hope. He will undoubtedly continue to rise in the King's esteem—

perhaps even high enough to win the gift of lands as rich as yours. But if I were in your position, I would not be content with hope alone."

Isabelle's pulse quickened. Whatever Eleanor wanted, it had to do with Marshal.

"I'm hardly content, Your Majesty," she said.

"But are you willing to do what may be necessary to secure your hopes?"

"Yes, Your Majesty," Isabelle said firmly, "if it's possible."

"Then you must understand the current political situation, my dear, for it's politics, not love, that makes the world go 'round. When my husband was in his prime, he was a rock—impervious to the storms swirling about him—but age is crumbling that rock. He has Philip on the defensive now, but Philip has time on his side. Our barons in France know that Henry is losing his grip, and they are questioning his leadership."

"You sound as if you wish it weren't so, Your Majesty," Isabelle said impulsively.

Eleanor glanced up at the battlements of her castle prison, silhouetted against the crimson sky. "I've wished for many things in my life, but I've had to settle for reality. Henry, for all his faults, was a great king. Perhaps if I'd been fifteen or twenty years younger when we married—"

Eleanor broke off and shook her head. "We're discussing your hopes for happiness, not my regrets. As I said, the King is slipping. He is challenged by Philip and losing the support of his baronage. And most dangerous of all, he is driving away the son who could save his empire. I do not think Richard will tolerate his father's abuse much longer."

"Do you mean there will be civil war, Your Majesty?"

"It may come to that."

Isabelle might have suspected that the Queen was only guessing, had it not been for the strange ambivalence in Eleanor's tone—a mixture of anticipation and aching regret. Something more than rumor was in the wind—something that Edmond had conveyed to her.

"If there is a war between the King on one side and Philip and Richard on the other," Eleanor continued, "I have little doubt that my son will prevail. The men who side with Richard will be assured of their reward, Isabelle, but those who oppose him . . . well, they will go down with their king.

"I told you that loyalty is a virtue that Marshal is likely to carry to extremes, and I also told you that one day we might have to work together to save him from himself. Sir William is a stubborn man, but I think he just might listen to you."

Isabelle swallowed to relieve the sudden dryness in her throat. "Are you suggesting, Your Majesty," she said huskily, "that I try to persuade Sir William to desert the King for Count Richard's banner?"

"*Desert* is not the word I would choose," Eleanor replied. "It is not desertion to bow to the inevitable, and you could make him see that. Sometimes I think we women are the only realists. Men fight for glory, for honor, and for power; it remains to us to fight for life and for happiness."

Isabelle had no doubt that Eleanor was intent on manipulating her, and she was wary of this woman who was so adept at intrigue; but if there was even the slightest chance for her to take her destiny into her own hands, she intended to seize it.

"Even if I could influence Sir William, Your Majesty," Isabelle said, "it's hardly likely that I will see him in the near future. And urging him to treason is not something I would attempt in a letter."

"It is not treason to support the legitimate heir to the Throne against a failing king who seeks to deny his eldest son his lawful rights," Eleanor responded, "but I agree that you could not persuade Sir William with penned words. My guess is that you *will* see him again in the near future. In fact, I'd wager money on it. But, in any event, I am speaking now only of possibilities. Perhaps there will be no break between my son and the King, after all, but it is a possibility for which we all should be prepared."

More than a possibility, Isabelle thought. She doubted that it was a coincidence that Eleanor had chosen this moment to probe her reactions.

"Then speaking hypothetically, Your Majesty," Isabelle said, "why should Sir William expect to find great favor with Count Richard? From what I've heard, Richard Lionheart is his own war counselor, and he certainly can lead his own army."

"The King of England—whoever he may be—will always have need of knights of Marshal's caliber," Eleanor replied. "But beyond that, if there is war between Richard and his father, William Marshal is the one man who might hinder Richard's victory."

"A single knight, Your Majesty?" Isabelle said skeptically.

"Yes, Isabelle, this particular knight. That is what I believe, and as far as you are concerned, my belief is what counts. My son still values my opinion, and I would know what reward to suggest be bestowed on

Marshal once Richard is King. I am not asking you to persuade Sir William on your own—only to support Richard in his own efforts to bring Marshal to his side when the time comes."

So there it was, Isabelle thought, her heart hammering, a clear proposition: Win Marshal for Richard's cause and receive in return what Isabelle desired more than anything in the world.

Now Isabelle understood the Queen's interest in her relationship with Marshal; it must have occurred to Eleanor at once that she might use Isabelle as bait to entice Marshal into Richard's camp. The Queen was presenting herself as Isabelle's friend—and perhaps she even thought of herself in that light—yet she had baited her hook with cold-blooded care.

But manipulation was a game two could play, and Isabelle felt a stir of excitement as the germ of an idea took root. Perhaps Eleanor was right and she should try to persuade Marshal to desert the King, but she had no intention of trusting to Eleanor's judgment and promises alone.

"I'll—I'll think about it, Your Majesty," Isabelle said, feigning an uncertainty she did not feel.

"If civil war comes," Eleanor said, trying to sink the hook still deeper, "and Marshal finds himself on the losing side, your hopes will die with Henry's cause. I'm offering you the salvation of those hopes."

It had not needed to be said, Isabelle thought; there was no need to hammer home the point, and Eleanor should have known that. Isabelle realized to her surprise that the Queen was overanxious, and her hopes rose. The Queen might indeed be giving her the chance to act on her own behalf—but not necessarily in the way Eleanor envisioned.

Isabelle knew there was a risk that Eleanor might see through her, but she was determined to discover which of them was the fisherman and which was the fish.

"Your Majesty, I—" Isabelle began in a deliberately halting voice, the callow girl caught on the horns of a dilemma. "What you're suggesting frightens me. If I try to sway Sir William against his own conscience, I could lose him. I would have to be sure—absolutely sure—that our hopes would be realized once Richard becomes king."

Eleanor smiled and reached out to touch Isabelle reassuringly. "You have my word, my dear."

"But, still . . ." Isabelle said, and as her voice trailed off, she blinked rapidly in an expression of helpless confusion.

"And what would it take to reassure you?" Eleanor asked. "I could write to Richard—today, if you wish—and send the letter with Edmond. And, of course, I'd let you read it first."

"But I couldn't ask that, Your Majesty," Isabelle protested. "And I certainly didn't mean to imply—"

"Hush, child," Eleanor said, interrupting benignly. "I can understand your concern, believe me. I shall have the letter for you to read tonight."

Isabelle remained silent, looking down at the ground and deliberately biting her lower lip.

"Is something still bothering you?" Eleanor said, a note of impatience creeping into her voice.

"I want to be certain that Count Richard receives the letter, Your Majesty."

"Of course he will receive it, my dear. Edmond is completely reliable."

"But what if he should be detained and searched? *Someone* might guess that he is acting as your courier; it would not take much imagination."

Eleanor smiled thinly. "Perhaps, but if you want this letter sent, you'll have to take the chance. And I would certainly take care to couch the letter in terms that would safeguard Sir William, as well as myself."

"I would prefer, Your Majesty," Isabelle said softly, "if the letter were conveyed by my own man, Fulk le Brun. He is absolutely faithful and unconnected with you, Your Majesty."

Isabelle held her breath as Eleanor hesitated with instinctive caution.

"The brute they call Black Fulk?" Eleanor said. "The *serjant* who acts as if he were your guard dog?"

"Yes, Your Majesty."

Eleanor hesitated a moment longer, but then she nodded slowly. "All right, if that's what you want. To say that the man is loyal to you is an understatement." Eleanor rose and took Isabelle's arm. "So, my dear," she said, "we have a bargain, you and I."

"I'm not sure I understand, milady," Fulk said in his slow, hoarse voice.

"It's not necesary for you to understand why," Isabelle said patiently. "Only that you do exactly as I ask."

Isabelle had found it difficult to mask her excitement during the long supper that evening, and Master Edmond's inability to hold her attention had clearly frustrated the troubador, who was accustomed to easy conquests. Isabelle had been plagued by the nagging fear that Eleanor might change her mind, and she had been on edge until the moment the Queen had placed the promised letter in her hand.

Upon Isabelle's return from Eleanor's apartments in the *palais*, she had immediately dismissed Matilda and summoned Fulk to her bedchamber. Once in possession of Eleanor's letter, her excitement had given way to a calmer sense of anticipation and confidence. For the first time in months Isabelle did not feel helpless.

"You are to deliver this letter to Count Richard, who is campaigning against the French in Berry," Isabelle repeated to Fulk, who towered over her, his great arms hanging slackly at his sides. "But first you must go to the Lord Chancellor in London and offer to show it to him for a price of twenty sous. You must play the part of a treacherous scoundrel, Fulk. Can you do that?"

"If I must, milady," Fulk said glumly. "If that's what you wish."

"It is," Isabelle said firmly. "Under no circumstances is the Chancellor to know that I sent you to him."

"Yes, milady. I will leave at once."

"That's not necessary. I don't want you to risk traveling at night."

Fulk laughed. "There's no risk, milady. I never have trouble with bandits."

"All right," Isabelle said, believing him. Rationally there was no need for haste, but Isabelle was anxious to set her plan in motion.

Eleanor would have her believe that the King was finished and that the future lay with Richard. Time would tell if she was right, but Isabelle preferred to sow her seeds in two fields at once. If Eleanor and Richard placed so high a value on Marshal's service, the King could not value it less. And Henry was still king—still the arbiter of Isabelle's and Marshal's fates.

Isabelle was convinced that Marshal would never ask Henry or Richard to bid for his loyalty; but she was not bound by his rules, and Eleanor had just given her the means to set the price.

"The letter, if you please," the Chancellor said, not bothering to hide his distaste for the dark, hulking *serjant* standing before him. This Fulk le Brun might be a Norman, but he had the look of a Welsh native. He had the same unnatural strength in his chest, shoulders, and arms that came from regular use of the longbow; he wore the same dark, crude clothing; and his black hair and beard were just as shaggy. He even had the bright, white teeth of the Welsh, who made a fetish of tooth polishing.

But it was not simply the man's appearance that put Geoffry off. Though he found them indispensable, Geoffry hated traitors.

"Twenty sous, Your Lordship," Fulk muttered as he handed over the letter.

"Yes, yes," Geoffry snapped. "You'll get your money when you return tomorrow for the letter. I'll have to have it resealed. You're dismissed."

"Yes, Your Lordship."

Geoffry breathed a sigh of relief as Fulk departed. Why, he wondered, had Eleanor entrusted a letter to such a ruffian? Was she going senile? He sipped from a goblet of mulled wine, but it did little to relieve the ache in his throat. He felt a fever coming on, and although a brazier glowed nearby, he shivered with the fever's chill. So much for preventive medicine, he reflected sourly.

In response to the nagging of his mistress, Geoffry had allowed his barber to bleed him only the week before, and that had done nothing to prevent this feverish cold. Now, no doubt, she would insist that he be bled yet again. Thank God he didn't have to marry the woman. That, at least, was one advantage to his role as Bishop of Lincoln. Geoffry would have preferred a small barony for his income, but the King had insisted on a bishopric.

Geoffry examined the wax seal in which the cord binding the letter was imbedded. It was intricately worked, but the artisans of the London mint could produce a forgery readily enough. He took a knife from his belt, cut the cord, and carefully unfolded the letter.

He felt a tingle of anticipation as he saw that Eleanor had written the letter herself. It was written in the langue d'oc of Aquitaine. If she had dictated the letter to a clerk, the man would have automatically translated her words into Latin. This letter was obviously intended for Richard's eyes only.

My dear Richard,
We have recently been entertained by Maître Edmond Orri, and as you may imagine, he provided considerable relief from the ennui of my existence. He also provided me with a

detailed account of the parley at Gisors and of the subsequent warfare. I can understand your desire to support the King in his effort to reestablish the Truce of God so that you might fulfill your holy obligation to the Cross. It appears, however, that this war may not end quickly. A border conflict could drag on for years, draining resources that could otherwise be employed to support a fresh Crusade.

You no doubt feel a filial, as well as a feudal, obligation to your lord and father, the King, and that is as it should be. A prince, however, must also honor his obligation to his own destiny and to the lands and peoples he will one day surely rule. You deserve to have unambiguous title to the Throne of England, and I am confident that if you show yourself firm in your resolve, the King will grant you this.

Geoffry smiled thinly. Eleanor was confident, all right—confident that Henry would continue to refuse to take this step. She was clearly pushing for rebellion, but this was nothing new; and the letter was too carefully worded to prove a charge of treason. Geoffry quickly scanned the rest of the letter, which continued in the same vein. As his eyes dropped to the last lines, his smile vanished.

On another subject entirely, I would like to mention that I have a new companion, the young heiress of Pembroke, Isabelle de Clare. She is a charming, beautiful girl, and I cannot help but wish her every happiness. I have reason to believe that she and Sir William Marshal are truly drawn to each other, and you know that Sir William also stands very high in my regard.

You are, of course, aware of Sir William's value to the King as counselor and captain, and I am confident that if, in the course of time, the King of England should favor him with this lady's hand, Sir William would be boundlessly grateful. Perhaps, when you've reflected on the matter, you may think of a way to help bring this about.

"Oh, neatly done, Eleanor," Geoffry said aloud.

Disguised as a plea for Richard to intercede on Marshal's behalf, it was an open invitation to suborn Marshal at an appropriate time with

Richard's own promise to give him Isabelle de Clare. Geoffry frowned thoughtfully as he refolded the letter.

It came as no surprise that Eleanor would like to see Marshal defect to Richard; it would gall her to see the knight she had patronized serving the King against her son. But the reward she proposed to offer Marshal was enormous. The Pembroke inheritance would place him in the very first rank of the English baronage.

Would Richard place that high a value on Marshal's service? If he decided to rebel against the King, he just might—if only to neutralize Marshal. Eleanor's suggestion was as much an assessment of Henry's failing leadership as it was a tribute to Marshal's skills, and this, more than the rest of the letter, was what worried the Chancellor. The perception of weakness was taking hold and spreading like a contagion that could prove fatal.

And if Richard offered the bait, would Marshal take it? The Chancellor smiled wryly. He should have realized there was more behind Marshal's concern for Isabelle de Clare than the simple desire for justice. In a way Geoffry was relieved to discover that Marshal had his own secrets, for the Chancellor distrusted too much simplicity in a man.

Eleanor thought Marshal might be vulnerable, and Geoffry had every reason to respect her judgment; but in this case he thought she was indulging in wishful thinking. Marshal was the one man the Chancellor was sure would never desert the King.

Yet Geoffry was too careful to ignore the threat entirely—not when there was a simple remedy. What Richard could only promise, Henry could deliver. If the situation should warrant it, Geoffry would suggest just such a remedy to the King.

In the meantime it would be wise to remove Isabelle de Clare from Eleanor's influence. The Queen did not leave stones unturned, and if she could work on Marshal through the girl, she would. An inexperienced young girl was sure to be putty in the Queen's hands.

19

"The Old Man's worried," Hugh de Harlincourt said quietly to Marshal.

A biting November wind blew across the open meadow of yellowed grass in which the King and his entourage awaited Philip of France. Thick gray clouds scudded low overhead. Henry's servants had set up a tent and lit a brazier inside, but the King disdained the warmth it offered and remained on his horse. Muffled in his hooded, fur-lined robe, Henry stared bleakly out across the stream defining the frontier between Normandy and Perche. With him waited Prince John, the Bishops of Le Mans, Lisieux, and Angers and forty barons and knights, their banners billowing and snapping in the wind.

"He has a right to be worried," Marshal replied grimly. "Where the hell is Richard?"

At Philip's request, Richard had arranged a parley between the kings, and Marshal had allowed himself to hope that Philip intended to sue for peace. Having disbanded his levies following the conference at Gisors, Philip had been unable to stop Marshal's repeated raids up and down the French territorial border. Philip had lost no territory, but every raid brought fresh pressure to make peace. And in Berry, Richard's army was threatening to retake Châteauroux.

But Richard had been expected for the past thirty-six hours, and as the time for the parley approached, Henry had become progressively remote and introspective. Richard should have arrived well in advance of the meeting, and his unexplained absence was ominous.

Much depended on the outcome of this conference, for Henry's funds were exhausted and he had been forced to release his Welsh archers. If fighting resumed in the spring, the King would not have his mercenaries to rely on. Marshal extracted a handful of cloves from the pouch on his belt and popped some into his mouth to have something to chew on to quell his nervousness.

"You're going to ruin your stomach with that junk," Bethune said.

"You should try cloves, Bo," Marshal said, managing a smile. "Maybe it would improve your luck with the ladies. They make your breath kissing-sweet."

"How would you know? You've been living like a monk. That's your trouble, you know. You're as nervous as a cat."

Marshal *was* on edge, and not simply because of Richard. John had gone south with Richard after Gisors, but he had returned to the King a week ago. Marshal had not forgotten the incident on the River Epte, and now that Gerard de Ridefort was in their camp again, Marshal found himself watching his back.

He had said nothing to his friends, for he had no proof; not even Ridefort deserved to die for a crime he had not committed. And that was what would happen if Bethune or Harlincourt got wind of it. They would force a fight with Ridefort and let God sort out his guilt or innocence.

"Speaking of women," Harlincourt said, "when are you going to marry your *demoiselle?*"

"Marry her?" Marshal said in surprise. "She's only fourteen years old."

"So?" Harlincourt said, leaning closer to Marshal and lowering his voice to a stage whisper. "Right now, all you've got is the King's promise, and the way things are going . . . Hell, you can figure it out. Take possession of the lady and her lands while you've got the chance. Lock it up, Will, that's my advice."

"Thanks. I'll think about it," Marshal said more curtly than he'd intended. He had already thought about it—often. He knew as well as Harlincourt that it was the safest thing to do.

Harlincourt had registered the unnecessary sharpness in Marshal's voice, and Marshal saw him wink at Bethune.

"You wouldn't have your sights set a little higher, would you?" Bethune said slyly to Marshal.

"What?" Marshal said, caught completely off-guard.

Bethune pointed at Marshal's feet. "You've never told us how you came by those fancy spurs, Will. They're hardly your style. You'll have to tell us sometime; I'll bet it would make an interesting story."

Marshal heard a sound like a stifled sneeze, and he turned and saw Harlincourt doubling over in silent laughter. Marshal compressed his lips and turned sharply to look back toward Jean d'Erly, but the boy was talking with another squire and didn't notice. Now both Bethune and Harlincourt were shaking with suppressed laughter.

Bethune, holding his ribs with one hand, reached out and grasped Marshal's arm. "Don't blame Jean," he gasped through spasms of laughter. "We pried it out of him."

"*What* did you pry out of him?" Marshal said stiffly, feeling his cheeks redden.

"Nothing much," Harlincourt said with a laugh. "Just how you got those spurs. Of course, we wondered why you didn't tell us about it yourself, and we could only guess before. But judging from the look on your face, I'd say we hit the nail on the head."

"Looks that way," Bethune agreed, grinning wickedly. "God damn, Will, it's good to know you're in one piece, after all. For a while there we were afraid the Templars might have deprived you of certain vital parts."

Harlincourt shook his head. "Maybe we shouldn't jump to conclusions, Bo. The lady may be entirely incidental to her lands; after all, she's a *very* rich heiress."

"Level with us, Will," Bethune said good-naturedly. "Are you delaying marriage to Helwis in the hope of something better?"

Marshal was spared the necessity of a reply by the sudden appearance of a cluster of banners coming over a rise in the road beyond the bridge, drawing everyone's attention—everyone's but Marshal's. He was still trying to answer Bethune's question for himself.

Despite the turmoil of the intervening months, he had not succeeded in getting Isabelle de Clare out of his mind; memories of her refused to fade. Countless times he'd felt the urge to write to her, but he'd resisted it, telling himself that maintaining contact would only prolong the pain. They each had their own destinies to follow now, and to wish for more was pointless. But was Bethune right? Deep inside, was he hoping for the impossible?

"Jesus Christ," Harlincourt breathed.

Marshal's eyes snapped back into focus, and as he saw the banners clearly for the first time, his stomach muscles tightened. He looked toward the King and saw Henry staring in shock at the scarlet banner with three golden lions streaming in the wind beside the banner of the King of France.

King Henry's knights waited in tense silence as Richard Lionheart, moving out in advance of Philip's party, cantered his horse over the bridge spanning the stream, cut across the meadow, and dismounted before his father. Richard bent his knee, and Henry climbed stiffly down from his horse to greet his son. There was a general creaking of leather and the clink of steel as his entourage dismounted with him.

"Good day, sire," Richard said airily, his voice carrying to everyone despite the wind. Henry stretched out his arms, and Richard dutifully stepped forward and kissed the King's cheek. "Good day, brother," Richard said, turning to John and exchanging kisses.

The King's followers remained absolutely silent, ignoring Philip's approach as they stared at the Count of Poitou.

"We find you in strange company," Henry said hoarsely, scrutinizing his son with narrowed eyes. "Why?"

"There's no mystery to it, sire," Richard said in the same light tone. "We found ourselves on the same road, and to ignore King Philip's presence would have been rank discourtesy."

The King clearly distrusted Richard's easy explanation, for an angry flush had spread over his face. Yet in the face of Richard's bland pose his dignity required that he accept it. In any event, there was no time for questions; Philip and his knights had crossed the bridge and were riding into the meadow.

Unlike the conference at Gisors, neither king was in a mood for posturing. Like Henry, the King of France wore no crown and was wrapped in a rich but utilitarian robe. Philip and his entourage dismounted, and Henry limped toward them. Flanked by their respective bishops, the kings met at the center of a great circle formed by the attending knights.

John stood beside his father, but Richard took up a position to one side, between the two kings, standing literally with a foot in each camp. Richard's show of neutrality might have passed as mere formality, since he had arranged the parley, but given Richard's arrival in Philip's company, Marshal was sure his stance was significant.

Marshal cursed silently. Philip had taken a beating in the field, but if he'd managed to get to Richard, the autumn's victories would be meaningless.

Henry must have had the same fear, but he gave no sign of it. Despite the pain in his knee, he did not favor it as he stood with his feet firmly planted, his spine stiff, his shoulders back. Cloaked in his great robe, his torso appeared massive rather than obese, and as he looked down on his slight-figured rival, his expression was that of a conqueror.

232

Philip had requested the parley, so after greetings had been exchanged, Philip was the first to speak. "I am glad we could meet once again," he said evenly, with neither deference nor arrogance in his tone. He had abandoned the haughty, ironic amusement he had used to needle Henry at Gisors. "This is a war neither of us wants, and I prefer to think that it was the summer heat that caused our tempers to get out of hand at our previous meeting."

"I am ready to make peace at once," Henry rumbled, "as long as the terms are reasonable. Our objective," he said, looking at Richard in a deliberate gesture of inclusiveness, "is to get on with the Crusade."

Richard nodded, but he did not return his father's look; there was a worrisome aloofness in his expression. Richard was quite obviously watching and waiting—not as an ally of his father but as an onlooker determined to safeguard his own interests. John, in contrast, stood as close as physically possible to Henry, aping every nuance of his father's expression and carriage.

"I have a simple proposal to end our conflict," Philip said, "and I think it's fair. In effect, I propose that we accept the territorial status quo. I will allow Count Richard to retain the castles he has seized from the Count of Toulouse, and I will remain in Berry. If you will then renew your allegiance to me as your liege lord in France, we can proceed immediately to the task of freeing Jerusalem from the Infidel."

Henry looked toward Richard, this time for support, but again Richard avoided his eyes. Henry's face darkened. The proposal was impossible for the King to accept; it would amount to a victory for Philip.

"I can't believe you're serious," Henry said angrily to Philip. "Berry is mine—given me by your father."

Philip coldly returned Henry's glare. "It is not yours. Berry was given as Alais's dowry and belongs to the husband to whom she was betrothed."

The young king paused and delicately dabbed at his nose with his handkerchief.

"Since you won't accept the status quo," he said, "I will make you another offer. Let us wipe the slate clean. My father gave you the Vexin as dowry for Marguerite, with the clear understanding that it be returned to her in the event of Prince Henry's death. You have not returned it. My father gave you Berry as dowry for Alais, and you have not married her to Richard. Return the Vexin to me and marry Alais to Rich—"

"There you go again!" Henry broke in furiously, hammering the

233

air with his fist. "We've been over all this too many times before! It seems that we're freezing out here for nothing. You don't want an honorable peace, you want my surrender!"

Philip did not respond immediately. Assuming a look of patient tolerance, he let the silence stretch out.

"I offered you the status quo," he said at last, "which certainly is a logical compromise and would address only one of the wrongs we have suffered. For the sake of the Crusade, I was willing to leave the question of the Vexin in abeyance. Since you refuse that, I am suggesting a just basis for an enduring peace. Let Alais marry Richard so that Berry passes into his hands, but remains within your house, and return the Vexin to poor Marguerite. Then we will be quits, Henry, and we can march on Jerusulem with glad hearts."

"No!" Henry barked, and he looked angrily at Richard. "Have you nothing to say, Count Richard?" he challenged.

"It seems, sire," Richard replied insolently, "that you've said it all."

"Clifford!" Marshal hissed as he saw one of his knights reach reflexively for his sword. The knights of Richard's and Henry's mesnes were eyeing each other with undisguised hostility, for it was clear that Philip had managed to drive a wedge between Richard and his father.

Henry ignored the rising tension around him. His eyes left Richard's and returned to Philip, studying his opponent in silence. As he reached up and began to stroke his beard thoughtfully, Marshal tensed, for he recognized the gesture. Henry was about to gamble.

"Your first proposal settled the question of Berry to your satisfaction," Henry said to Philip. "Your second proposal squeezed me even harder, but I assume that was simply shrewd bargaining on your part. Now I have a proposal of my own to make, and it conforms completely with the spirit of your first position.

"You wanted to settle the question of Berry. Very well. I promised King Louis to marry Alais to a prince of England, and I am prepared to do that. Will you make peace with me now, in return for Alais's marriage to my son John?"

"Oh, Christ, that tears it," Bethune said to Marshal under cover of the wave of muttering and excited whispers that swept through the onlookers. "Look at Richard's face!"

Marshal didn't need to look at Richard to know his reaction to Henry's surprise offer. Marshal was watching Philip, and he knew at once

234

that Henry had overplayed his hand. He had fatally misjudged his young opponent, and there was now a glint of triumph in Philip's eyes.

Henry had failed to appreciate that he was no longer dealing with a boy who might be content to accept a cheap and easy means of achieving one of his father's cherished aims. Philip wanted more than a marriage alliance; he wanted to strengthen Richard and emasculate the English king.

The Count of Flanders, who was standing behind Philip, caught Marshal's eye, and the Count gravely shook his head. In many ways Marshal and Flanders were counterparts in their relationship to their respective kings, and if Marshal had had any doubts that Philip intended to press his war with Henry to the finish, the Count's look would have banished them.

Philip sighed theatrically. "I thought you had a higher opinion of me," he said to Henry. "Do you really believe I would turn my back on my loyal vassal, Count Richard, who, unlike you, has not revoked his allegiance to the Crown of France? Alais was betrothed to Richard, and if Berry passes from my hands, it must go to him and to no one else."

"Is that your last word?" Henry grated, unconsciously pulling his robe more tightly about him, as if suddenly feeling the chill wind sweeping across the meadow.

"No, it is not," Philip said coldly. "I see now that I must include in my terms some protection for the Count of Poitou. There will be no peace between us, Henry, until you return the Vexin to Marguerite, marry Alais to Richard, and declare Richard to be the rightful heir to the Throne of England, requiring all English barons to do homage to him as their—"

"By God's legs, sir, I'll hear no more!" Henry exploded, balling his fists in fury. "Each time you've opened your mouth, you've increased your demands. You presume to seek the preferment of one of my sons, but you have no right to meddle in the affairs of England. I won't be blackmailed!"

"And what do you say to me, sire?" Richard burst out, his face contorted as much in anguish as in anger as he faced his father. "I must— once and for all—know where I stand with you. Give *me* your assurance that I am to be your heir!"

But Henry refused to speak; he just stared at his son in stony silence, his expression set in the closed, stubborn look of a very old man.

Richard's face paled, and he shook his head. "For years—*years,* sire—I've refused to believe what I see now with my own eyes," he said in a hushed, unnatural voice. "But it *is* true. You would deny me my inheritance!"

Still looking at his father, Richard unbuckled his sword slowly, as if hoping his father would stop him with a word. Then he turned and approached Philip, his footfalls crunching in the dried grass. He dropped to his knees before the French King, laid his sword at Philip's feet, clasped his hands, and raised them to Philip.

In that moment Marshal realized the extent to which Henry had played into Philip's hands. On the ride to the conference, the King of France must have offered Richard the ultimate bribe—immediate title to Henry's Continental domains.

"Sire," Richard said in a loud, clear voice. "Reserving the allegiance I owe my father, I hereby offer my homage to you, Philip of France, and do swear my fealty for those lands which you may choose to grant me as my lord."

"Traitor!" someone in the ranks of Henry's followers growled, and in an instant the rattle of swords being drawn swept around the circle of knights.

Marshal leapt forward. "At ease!" he barked, raising his hand. "By God, I'll kill the first man on either side to break the peace!" No one doubted his threat, and one after the other, swords were slipped back into their sheaths.

Both Philip and Richard ignored the disturbance, and Henry, his face white with shock, stood as if frozen to the spot. Philip folded Richard's clasped hands in his own and said into the silence, "Richard, Count of Poitou, in return for the service you offer me, I grant you title to the lands of Normandy, Maine, Anjou, and Touraine, and offer you my protection. Arise, Richard, Duke of Normandy and Count of Aquitaine, Maine, Anjou, and Touraine."

As Richard got to his feet Henry spun on his heel and wordlessly stalked across the meadow to his horse, followed immediately by his entourage. The King climbed into the saddle and wheeled his horse about. Without waiting for all of his followers to mount, he galloped away.

"Do your latrines need cleaning, Maurice, or has the stink of treachery followed us all the way up here?" Henry rasped.

Maurice fitz Patrick, the fleshy, good-natured baron in whose castle the King had quartered himself and his entourage, cleared his throat. "The latrines, sire. I offer my apologies."

Fitz Patrick was taking the invasion of his castle in stride, though a royal visit could be as devastating to the baronial stores as a plague of locusts. The sudden demands of hospitality on a royal scale had thrown his household officers and the ladies of the castle into a frenzy, but he, himself, remained above it all. "Perhaps you would care to adjourn your council to the *palais*, sire," he said.

"No," Henry said with a heavy sigh, stretching out his lame leg. "This will do. The stink of shit sets the right tone for this meeting."

Henry had summoned his household knights, barons, and bishops to a council in the seldom-used great hall of the castle's tower keep. The King sat on the dais in the baron's canopied chair, with John seated beside him. John was uncharacteristically silent, and his black eyes roved distractedly over the forty or so men standing in a semicircle before the dais.

The knights still wore their fur-lined cloaks, for the fire in the great hearth had not yet relieved the chill in the dank hall. Torches burned on the walls to supplement the gray, late-afternoon light entering through the arrow slits in the gallery overhead.

It was clear that the baroness cared nothing for this hall. The wall hangings were frayed and musty, and dust covered the polished stone eyes of the moth-eaten trophy heads staring balefully down from the walls. The hall now served principally as an arsenal, and it was lined with long racks of gleaming pikes and varnished lances.

The shock of Richard's sudden defection still affected the knights who had witnessed it, but the King had already recovered his equilibrium. He seemed to be accepting Richard's desertion fatalistically, almost as if he'd expected it all along.

Marshal couldn't understand it. For months Henry had insisted that his son would remain faithful, and now he behaved as if the betrayal were simply one more trial he had to endure. Marshal could only hope that this was a measure of Henry's resiliency and not a flight from reality.

The King shifted heavily in his chair. "Well, gentlemen, we're still at war, and England's coffers are empty. We won't be able to afford mercenaries when we meet Philip in the spring. What is your advice?"

Immediately the Seneschal of Normandy stepped forward. "I suggest, sire," fitz Ralph said, "that we prepare to fight a defensive war. Let him invade if he chooses. We should reinforce the garrisons of key fortresses in his path and content ourselves with fighting a series of purely defensive battles. We may lose some territory over the spring and summer, but we will gain time—time to replenish the English treasury. In the long run, sire, Philip cannot match your financial resources."

Henry scowled and nodded at the same time, hating the idea of being on the defensive but acknowledging that he had little choice.

"It won't be that easy, sire," objected Stephen de Marcai, the Seneschal of Anjou. "We may face a war on two fronts: Philip from the west and Richard from the south. We'll have to worry about our strong points all along the Loire, and we all know that Richard eats castles for breakfast."

"There is more to war than strong points and armies, sire!" the Bishop of Lisieux called out in his best pulpit baritone. "Let us not forget that God is on our side in the coming struggle."

"God?" Henry snorted derisively and cast his eyes heavenward. "God gave me my sons—sons who will never give me peace!"

"Not all your sons are faithless, sire," John said plaintively, plucking like a child at his father's sleeve.

"I know, Johnny, I know," Henry said, patting his son's arm distractedly, his mind still focused on the military problem.

Now William Earl of Essex stepped forward and said, "We can garrison castles in the south to our heart's content, sire, but we must be sure of the loyalty of the castellans. It's not Richard's siege tactics that worry me but the possibility that the castles in the south will fall to him without a fight."

"Sire," fitz Ralph put in, "it's not clear to me that Count Richard intends to oppose you actively. After all, when he swore fealty to Philip, he made a point of reserving the allegiance he owes you. It could be that he merely intends to sit out the war."

"Wishful thinking," the Seneschal of Anjou said bitterly. "Does anyone here know where Richard is now? No? Well, I'll tell you. One of my own knights has friends in Richard's mesne, and he remained behind at the bridge to talk with them. Richard did not elect to remain in the vicinity. He has stolen away like a thief, and at this moment he is riding south."

An uncomfortable silence followed, but the King's reaction was not to be read in his face. It was set in the same stony expression with which he had viewed Richard's submission to Philip.

Fitz Ralph broke the silence. "That still doesn't prove he intends to war against his own father."

238

"Perhaps not," the Seneschal of Anjou replied, "but his abrupt departure is not the only bad news. According to the knights of Richard's mesne, Richard and Philip were on the road together for two days, and they hit it off so well that not even the bed separated them at night."

Henry flushed and uttered an inarticulate oath. He seemed suddenly to have difficulty breathing, and the renewed silence in the hall was punctuated by the sighing rasp of the King's tortured inhalations.

Marshal had intended to stay out of the discussion, leaving it to the barons, who would have to shoulder the major burden of the defense of the Angevin domain; but the atmosphere had degenerated dangerously, and no one had pointed out the obvious.

"Sire," Marshal called out, and stepped forward. "It is vital that we know Count Richard's intentions and not simply guess at them. I suggest we discover the road he has taken and send a representative after him."

"To what purpose," Henry said, taking another deep, ragged breath.

"To ask him to return and explain himself, sire—with your assurance of safe conduct. Count Richard's homage to Philip was quite legal, since you previously revoked your allegiance to the French Crown. In itself, it does not challenge your immediate authority. Your representative can assure him that he has nothing to fear from you if he remains neutral."

"And if he refuses to return and explain?"

"Then, sire, we'll have our answer: He intends to fight."

"All right," the King said, leaning back and rubbing his eyes tiredly. "That's a sensible suggestion. I'll send you, Marshal; Richard trusts and respects you as much as any man here. When can you leave?"

"As soon as we find which road the Count has taken, sire."

John glared at his chamberlain and took another gulp of wine. He had already drunk too much and his head was spinning, but he had not succeeded in dulling his anxiety.

"What do you mean, you can't find him?" he snapped.

"Ridefort left the castle an hour ago, sire," Poole said defensively.

"But I told you to bring him to me!"

"Yes, sire, but he was already gone by then."

John blinked, trying to keep Poole's image in focus. Damn the wine; it had done him no good at all. The scene in the castle's great hall that afternoon had frightened him, and John was not used to being frightened. The pessimism, resignation, and, in some instances, the submerged panic he had read in the eyes of many of the barons attending the King's impromptu council had come as a shattering revelation.

For months the Chancellor had been warning of the danger Richard's defection would pose, but John had not believed him. Overawed by his father, John had never doubted his ability to crush Richard, and he had eagerly awaited Richard's rebellion, sure that civil war would leave him undisputed heir to the throne.

But in council that afternoon John had felt as if blinders suddenly had been torn from his eyes, and he had seen Henry as others saw him: a weary old man ineffectually reacting to events, not controlling them. For the first time it occurred to John that Richard might actually win.

Mother of God, if he were to be caught on the losing side . . .

"Why did Ridefort leave?" John demanded.

"I'm not sure, sire," Poole said uncomfortably, not understanding John's black mood. "But he rode out with the contingent of Flemish mercenaries you'll be releasing at the end of the week."

"What!" John exploded, banging his goblet against the arm of his chair. "God's legs, man, he must be after Marshal!"

John's stomach convulsed as a violent wave of nausea swept over him. Marshal's party would have to ride far and fast to catch up with Richard, so the knights would be only lightly armed—and traveling a deserted highway in the dead of night.

"But, sire, I thought—"

"You thought, you thought!" John shouted, spittle flying from his lips. "Don't you understand? We *need* Marshal now!"

Poole's face paled, and his evident confusion at his master's abrupt turnaround only made John angrier. Why couldn't Poole think for himself for once!

"Sire, we don't know for certain that Ridefort intends—"

"Don't be an idiot!" John cut in, grinding his teeth in frustration. Everything had seemed to be moving his way, and now, suddenly, it was all going wrong. It was all going wrong!

"But, sire," Poole said quickly, not understanding but anxious to calm John down, "even if Ridefort has gone after Marshal, we shouldn't assume he'll succeed. Don't forget, sire, that he's already failed once."

It took a moment for the chamberlain's words to penetrate John's whirling thoughts, but as they registered, he drew a deep breath and nodded slowly, wanting to believe. Marshal must have had a substantial head start, and Ridefort and his mercenaries would be weighed down by armor. Even if they had brought extra horses, they probably would not catch up with him. Yes, John told himself, Poole was right: Ridefort was a bungler.

"You think he'll fail again?" John said.

"I wouldn't be surprised, sire," Poole replied, and John settled back in his chair with a faint sigh.

But in John's desire to grasp at any straw, he had not noticed the lack of conviction in his chamberlain's voice.

20

It was nearing midnight when Bethune's stirrup gave way. Marshal, Bethune, and Harlincourt were riding side by side behind their squires, whose torches lit the highway they were following through mile after mile of unpopulated forest. Thick clouds blackened the sky, and beyond the reaches of the flickering torchlight the darkness was absolute.

Bethune cursed and reined in, and Marshal called a halt. "What's the problem?" Marshal asked irritably, his breath condensing in the cold night air.

"Stirrup leather's parted," Bethune said, climbing stiffly down from the saddle as his squire rode back to help him. "Robert will have it fixed quickly enough, Will," he said with a yawn. "No need to get itchy."

"We're on a bloody wild-goose chase, anyway," Harlincourt said. "Richard wouldn't be making tracks south if he didn't intend to fight us."

"We have to make sure," Marshal said curtly, unwilling to admit that Harlincourt was right. There might still be a chance of dissuading Richard from warring against his father, but Marshal knew it was remote.

Marshal shifted restlessly in his saddle. The impenetrable darkness of the forest seemed to be pressing in on them, constricting the circle of torchlight. There had been no reports of marauders on the roads, but bands of deserters were always a potential threat in wartime, and Marshal did not want to be taken by surprise. "Andrew," he said to Harlincourt's squire, "ride on down the road a hundred yards and keep your ears open. Jean, ride back and cover the rear."

"How far do you think we've come?" Bethune asked, taking a wineskin from his saddle.

"Not far enough," Marshal said. "We won't get much sleep tonight. It's still at least a four-hour ride to the Loire."

Bethune took a long drink of wine, belched with satisfaction, and passed the skin to Harlincourt, who had dismounted and was flexing his stiff leg muscles.

"What makes you so sure Richard is spending the night at Amboise?" Harlincourt said.

"I'm not sure," Marshal replied, easing himself in the saddle and suppressing a yawn of his own, "but he had a six-hour head start on us, and my guess is that he wouldn't stop until he reached the Loire."

"Want some of this?" Harlincourt asked Marshal, offering Bethune's wine. "It's better than that watered-down swill you carry. You're not in the desert anymore, you know."

Marshal smiled and was reaching for the proffered wineskin when they heard a short, sharp whistle from Jean.

"Mount up!" Marshal ordered.

"I haven't finished, sire—" Bethune's squire said.

"Forget it, son," Bethune said, leaping into the saddle and pulling his mail coif over his woolen cap.

Jean was riding hard toward them, and Harlincourt's squire, who had heard the warning whistle, was returning at a gallop.

"Riders coming up on us fast, sire," Jean cried as he hauled on his reins and his horse skidded to a stop beside Marshal. "Two miles or so beyond the rise back there."

"How many?"

"I'm not sure, sire, but too many for us."

Marshal didn't argue. They weren't equipped to stand their ground, and he wasn't looking for trouble. It was possible the approaching riders had seen Jean's torch, but the odds were against it.

"Swords or lances, Will?" Bethune asked.

"Swords," Marshal said, "but we're moving off the road. We'll have a look at them as they go by. Put out those torches."

They were plunged into darkness as Bethune's squire extinguished the torches. Bending low over their saddles to avoid being struck by the tree limbs they could not see, they moved blindly into the forest. Fifteen yards from the road, Marshal reined in, and they turned their mounts and waited together in silence.

Minutes later they heard the pounding of hooves on the hard-packed roadbed as the riders came over the rise in the road. The pounding quickly swelled to a thunder of hoofbeats as twenty horsemen swept by, the light of their torches glinting on full suits of armor.

"Did you see their headgear?" Bethune said as the sound of the riders faded down the road. "Those guys are Flemish mercs."

"Yes, but whose?" Harlincourt said. "No standards, no banners."

"Whoever they are," Marshal said, "they're a rum-looking bunch."

"And armed to the teeth," Bethune said. "Whoever, or whatever, they're after, they're in one hell of a hurry. With all the iron they're carrying, they're going to kill those horses if they don't ease up soon."

"What now, Will?" Harlincourt asked.

"We keep going," Marshal said, "but we keep our eyes open. They're going to have to slow down or call a halt soon, and we don't want to stumble into them. There's no point in courting trouble."

Fifteen miles farther on, Marshal ordered the torches extinguished as they spotted the lanterns of an isolated wayside inn, and they approached cautiously. The inn was built in a clearing close beside the road. Attached to the ramshackle, two-story building were sheds and a large stable.

"Jean," Marshal said softly. "Check out the stable."

The Flemish mercenaries had been pushing their mounts too hard to travel far, and if they had intended to halt, this was a logical place. Jean slipped from the saddle and ran lightly across the clearing, his shadowy form visible for only a moment before it merged with the darkness surrounding the sheds. Two minutes later he was back.

"They must be here, sire," he said in a stage whisper. "All the stalls are filled, and the horses are still wet."

"The stupid bastards didn't have their mounts rubbed down?" Bethune said incredulously.

"The stable boys are fast asleep, sire," Jean said to Bethune. "I could hear them snoring."

"Mount up, Jean," Marshal snapped impatiently. "Whoever they are, we can forget them now, and we still have a long way to go."

"It doesn't make sense," Harlincourt muttered. "Why ride like hell through the dead of night, only to end up here in the middle of nowhere?"

"Maybe they were chasing someone, sire," Jean said, remounting, "and simply couldn't catch up before their horses gave out."

Marshal shrugged in the darkness and spurred his horse forward. The question was puzzling, but he had no answer and he was too tired to wonder about it.

The great castle guarding the city of Amboise surmounted a steep hill overlooking the Loire and commanded a majestic view of the valley, but what little consideration Marshal gave the scenery was in terms of siege tactics. Amboise lay on Henry's eastern frontier and would be in the first line of defense against a French assault on Tours.

Bethune and Harlincourt rode in silence beside Marshal, blinking sleepily in the dim, early-morning light as they followed a line of ox carts snaking up the face of the hill to the castle's main gate. From above came the rattle and squeal of the portcullis being raised, and the gate's iron-bound doors swung open to admit the crowd that had gathered in the cold, gray dawn.

Marshal arched his spine to relieve the stiffness in his back and tiredly rubbed his gritty eyes. The bleak, sunless day matched his mood, for the long night had sapped his energy and left him feeling empty and depressed. Chasing after Richard *was* an exercise in futility; Richard was almost certainly beyond reach, whether or not they found him here at Amboise.

Harlincourt looked up at the castle and shook his head dolefully. "Too fancy," he said, eyeing the spotless, whitewashed walls and gilded turret roofs. "Will Monfort fight, or will he be too afraid of messing up his pretty castle?"

Marshal shrugged wearily. "It's not our concern. The King knows his barons; he'll have to assess their loyalty and grit."

"I know Montfort," Bethune put in. "He'll fight, all right—if he thinks he's on the winning side."

Marshal had sent Jean ahead to announce their coming in the name of the King, and as they approached, trumpeters on the gate-house parapet heralded their arrival. Marshal grimaced at the piercing fanfare, which, in his present condition, jarred him as it would a man with a hangover.

He recognized no one from Richard's entourage as they crossed the outer bailey, and he found himself hoping that Richard had pressed on in his flight south. Then he could sleep and for a time avoid confronting the increasingly grim prospects of the King and those who followed him.

But as they rode into the castle's inner courtyard the portly lord of Amboise Castle emerged from his *palais* to greet them, and his dress proclaimed Richard's presence. Robert de Montfort was splendidly attired and wearing what must have been his richest robe.

"Good morning, Sir William," said the middle-aged baron, "I am Robert de Montfort. It's a pleasure to meet you at last."

"Good morning, Sir Robert," Marshal said, his voice hoarse from lack of sleep. "I believe you know Bethune. May I introduce Hugh de Harlincourt? We are seeking the Count of Poitou on behalf of the King, and we believe he may have passed this way."

"You're in luck, Sir William," Montfort said with a smile that was too broad and failed to disguise his nervousness. "Count Richard is here now." The castellan's smile slipped as he swallowed anxiously. "He spent the night here, but I assure you that—well, I could hardly deny him entry, could I?"

"And why should you wish to deny Count Richard entry?" Marshal said sharply.

Montfort spread his hands in a gesture of helplessness. "I had no reason, of course—but when I saw . . . I assure you, Sir William, I am steadfastly loyal to His Majesty, and I never would have—"

"Talk straight, Sir Robert!" Marshal snapped impatiently, but he already understood the message that the baron's anxiety conveyed. Bethune was giving Marshal an I-told-you-so look.

"Count Richard was up all night," Montfort said breathlessly. "He summoned the monks of our local abbey and had them working until a few hours before dawn—copying letters. He sent out over two hundred letters, Sir William, and he's made no secret of their content. Richard has declared himself lord of the Angevin domains, allied himself with King Philip, and is calling the barons of the region to his banner."

"Christ," Bethune groaned. "Let's go home, Will."

Marshal sighed wearily and shook his head. "I want to talk to him," he said, climbing stiffly down from the saddle.

"It's a waste of time," Harlincourt said angrily. "Richard has deserted us for the sake of his damned pride. What's the use of talk now?"

"Because I have to be absolutely sure of his position," Marshal said, knowing it was pointless.

The final quenching of all hope weighed Marshal down even more than his fatigue, and his steps were leaden as he followed Montfort into the *palais;* but he had been charged by Henry to confront Richard, and he had to go through the motions.

Richard's squire ushered Marshal into the apartment that Montfort had placed at Richard's disposal, and closed the door, leaving Marshal alone with the Count of Poitou.

Richard was slouched in a heavy chair beside the bed, a wine cup held slackly in his hand. He motioned Marshal to approach, and Marshal walked forward and briefly inclined his head.

"You look rotten, Marshal," Richard said. "You didn't get much sleep, either, I take it." Alcohol fumes drifted across to Marshal, mingling with the sour smell of Richard's body. The usually fastidious Count was still attired in the clothes he'd worn the day before, and his cloak and surcoat were rumpled and travel-stained.

"His Majesty has sent me to ask you to return to him and explain yourself, sire," Marshal said formally. "When you did homage to the King of France, you reserved the allegiance you owe your father. His Majesty would like to know if that means you intend to remain neutral in our war with Philip."

"Neutral!" Richard snorted. "My father must be dreaming." Richard's eyes were bloodshot and watery, but they burned with grim determination. Richard, after years of vacillation, had clearly made up his mind. "I was blind, Marshal, but King Philip has opened my eyes. He is fighting this war on my behalf as much as his. *I* am now the lawful lord of the Angevin domains, and I damned well intend to take them and hold them as my own."

Marshal was running on nervous energy, and depression and fatigue had frayed his temper. He could see from Richard's appearance what it must have cost him to declare war on his father, but Marshal felt no sympathy. Richard might have felt himself driven to rebellion, but his action was more than treason; it was betrayal.

"You can try, sire," Marshal said coldly.

"Why so harsh, Marshal?" Richard said. "I would have expected otherwise. When my brother, Henry, felt compelled to fight for his rights against my father, you stood by him."

"He was my lord, sire," Marshal replied stiffly, "and I served him as I was bound to do. But I counseled him to make peace—as you well know. You are playing into Philip's hands by this rebellion, sire. Only the Capets will profit from a war between you and your father."

"I am not as weak as my brothers," Richard snapped. "And I'm no puppet—of Philip or of Henry."

"No?" Marshal retorted. "And I say we will cut each other up and Philip will pick up the pieces."

Richard stretched out his legs and shook his head in condescending tolerance. "Cut each other up? Take off your blinders, Marshal. My father's castles will fall to me like a row of dominoes."

Marshal compressed his lips but did not reply. He could see there was no point in further argument, and he could not effectively dispute Richard's prediction. Every one of Henry's counselors feared the possibility of wholesale defections.

Richard had been studying Marshal, and now he leaned forward in his chair and said earnestly, "You know my destiny as well as I do, Marshal. I *will* be King, and I can't believe you have a wish to fight me."

"No, sire, but I—"

"Then listen to me and consider well what I have to say. You're as true a knight as I know, and nothing would give me greater pleasure than to have you at my side. You, more than most, must realize that my father cannot hope to prevail against both me and King Philip. Nor should he! Henry's time has come and gone. The future is with me, Marshal, and I'm inviting you to be a part of it."

For a moment Marshal was tempted. He no longer doubted that Henry was in decline; he had seen the aging King's growing indecisiveness and his ever more frequent flights from reality. Henry was no longer a match for the two young men arrayed against him.

But as strong as the temptation was, it was only fleeting. By remaining with the King, Marshal might be sacrificing his future, but to betray his liege lord would cost him more. He had built his life on the feudal code of honor, and to deny it now would be to deny himself—what he was and what he hoped to be.

"I cannot serve you, sire," Marshal said. "Not while His Majesty lives. I have sworn him my allegiance, and he has given me no cause to rescind it."

"Bravely spoken," Richard responded, "but hardly realistic. Allegiance is not absolute, Marshal; it never has been. My father demonstrated that at Gisors, when he renounced the allegiance he owed Philip of France."

"For cause, sire. For cause."

"And do you not also have cause to reconsider your allegiance in the coming conflict?" Richard said insistently. "My father has openly forfeited his legal claim to the lands for which we will fight. I—not Henry—am now Duke of Normandy and Count of Anjou, Maine, and Touraine."

"From Philip's point of view, perhaps, sire. Not from mine."

Richard scowled with the same petulant air he'd displayed when Marshal had refused him the Saracen dagger; but slowly his expression changed, and he gazed speculatively at Marshal.

"I admire your loyalty," Richard said, fingering his carefully trimmed beard, "I really do. But loyalty should work both ways. You should ask yourself if my father has rewarded you in proportion to the value of your service."

There was an uncharacteristic note of slyness in Richard's tone that surprised Marshal, and he frowned. "I'm satisfied, sire."

"Are you really? With that scrap of land in Cartmel and custody of Helwis of Lancaster?" Richard said disparagingly.

"I'm *satisfied*, sire," Marshal repeated, taken aback by the realization that Richard was about to offer a bribe. Bribery was not Richard's style.

"If I were King," Richard said, "I would consider a far greater reward to be appropriate for a knight of your caliber. The hand of the heiress of Pembroke, for example."

Richard's words caught Marshal like a fist in the stomach. Eleanor, he thought dimly as the blood rushed to his head. It had to be Eleanor. She alone could have guessed that this offer was the one bribe he would find almost impossible to refuse.

And why can't you accept? a voice inside him cried out. Richard *was* the future, and he was offering what Marshal wanted more than anything else in his life. Why could he not accept what logic and overwhelming desire demanded? Why could he not—just this once—break the bonds of honor?

"No, sire," Marshal said hoarsely, the refusal torn out of him. "No," he repeated, turning on his heel and walking blindly toward the door.

"Marshal!" Richard barked. "I will not tolerate insolence!"

Marshal spun around, but with an effort of will he stifled the biting reply that flew to his lips. He was here as the King's representative, not as his own man.

"I apologize, sire," he said stiffly, "and request permission to withdraw. I regret that I cannot accept service with you. When our armies meet in the spring, sire, you will find me with the King."

The winter of 1189 was harsher than any in recent memory, but as Marshal rode through the south gate of Le Mans, he noted with some satisfaction that the heavy snowfall and subfreezing temperatures had not slowed the work on the city's fortifications. Le Mans was the King's birthplace. Here he had established his winter court, and Le Mans was to be his headquarters when war broke out in the spring.

Returning from yet another fruitless peace conference arranged by the Church, Marshal and Jean had covered thirty miles since dawn. The labored exhalations of their weary horses steamed in the frosty air, but Marshal dug in his spurs and drove his tired palfrey up through the narrow, twisting streets toward the castle dominating the hilltop city.

Now that they were almost home, Marshal hungered for warmth. Jean's face was pinched and blue, and Marshal could no longer feel his toes, despite his fur-lined boots. The sun shone brightly in a clear sky, but it did nothing to relieve the bitter cold. As Marshal rode through the castle's courtyard toward the central tower keep, he acknowledged the welcoming cries of the knights he passed, but he was too anxious to get inside to stop and talk.

"Make sure the horses are properly cared for," he said to Jean as he dismounted. "Don't leave it to the varlets."

"Of course, sire," Jean said cheerfully, and it occurred to Marshal that he, too, had been able to withstand the cold when he was Jean's age. It was not a comforting thought.

Upon entering the vestibule at the entrance to the great hall, Marshal had to pause to allow his eyes to adjust to the gloom. For a few moments he was blinded by the bright green afterimage from the glare of the sun on the snow outside.

"His Majesty has dismissed the morning court, Sir William," said the young herald at the door, "but he's still in the hall."

"Good," Marshal said, removing his gloves and warming his fingers with his breath. "Announce me."

The great hall was empty of courtiers, and servants were busily setting up the long trestle tables for the midday meal. On the dais at the far end of the hall, Henry sat on his throne, attended by John and the Earl of Essex. A fire blazed in the hearth, and in contrast to the cold outside, the hall seemed suffused with warmth.

"What news?" Henry called out with forced vigor as Marshal strode toward him.

"Bad news, sire," Marshal responded with his customary bluntness. "Count Richard and King Philip flatly refused to listen to the

250

arguments of the papal legate. As soon as they learned you were not coming, they canceled the conference."

"But they knew I couldn't—"

Henry's words were cut off by a deep, racking cough that shook him to the core. His forehead glistened with beads of sweat, and his ruddy cheeks were a shade too red. Fever again, Marshal thought grimly. The recurring fever had first struck Henry early in December. He would shake it off for a time, but never for very long.

"I assured them that you were too ill to attend, sire," Marshal said, "but Count Richard refused to believe me. And when the legate protested, Count Richard accused him of being in our pay."

"He said *that* to the papal legate?" Henry said with a disbelieving shake of his head. "That's it, then. War can't be avoided."

"War was inevitable from the start, sire," Essex said quietly. "The conference would have been a waste of time in any event—unless you were willing to surrender to their demands."

"Never!" Henry rasped. "Not while I live."

Marshal exchanged a look with Essex, and Henry caught it.

"I'll be well enough come spring," he said sharply, "and sick or not, I can still do what's necessary. I put on a good show this morning, didn't I, Essex?"

"That you did, sire," Essex said with a smile. "I'm sure Evreux was impressed."

One by one Henry had been summoning his barons to Court to reaffirm their loyalty, and despite his illness, the King had been delivering virtuoso performances. The King these barons saw was resolute and confident, and Henry played upon their individual desires and fears with the consummate skill that had won him an empire.

Whether or not his barons would stand fast in the face of the enemy was still an open question, but the King had at least prevented the wave of open defections that his counselors had feared. Paradoxically the bouts of fever had seemed to stiffen Henry's resolve, banishing the moodiness that had afflicted him in the fall. Marshal did not believe it could last, but he strove to bolster that resolve.

"I see that the reinforcement of the city walls is proceeding apace, sire," Marshal said, looking at John with a deliberate expression of approval.

Richard's rebellion had wrought a change in John that had surprised everyone. His incessant fawning had given way to a more substan-

251

tial support. In council, he no longer automatically deferred to his father in policy disputes. Instead, he listened to the arguments and exercised reasoned, independent judgment. John had shouldered what he could of the administrative burden, and he had taken personal charge of Le Man's fortifications. His notorious indolence appeared to be a thing of the past.

Marshal doubted he would ever overcome his antipathy toward John, but he accepted the prince's contribution for what it was worth.

Henry reached out and grasped John's shoulder affectionately. "He's done well, my son has," the King said proudly. "My *true* son. He'll see me through this struggle."

"Thank you, sire," John said simply.

One of Henry's mastiffs had risen from the floor, and the dog came over and laid his great head in his master's lap, demanding attention.

"Jealous, are you, old boy?" Henry said, stroking the dog. Despite the news of the papal legate's failure, Henry now appeared relaxed and unaffected by it, but his eyes were too bright, and Marshal guessed that the fever was rising. He had seen the cycle before; Henry's spirits were highest just before the fever drove him to his sickbed.

"Well, Marshal, you did what you could," the King said almost jovially, "but it appears that the die has been cast. Unless you wish to wait out the winter here, I see no reason why you cannot return to England to attend to your affairs. It won't be a pleasant journey this time of year, but it will be your last opportunity for some time to come."

"Thank you, sire," Marshal said gratefully. "I *would* like to make the acquaintance of my ward. I'm sure the Sheriff of Lancashire is taking good care of her, but I should see for myself."

The journey would be hard and it was unnecessary, but Marshal was glad of the excuse to leave for a time. Now that negotiations with Philip and Richard finally had been broken off, there was nothing to do but wait.

The thought of seeing Isabelle again had darted into his mind at once, but he shied away from it. As hard as it would be to stay away, it would be harder still to see her. A visit to Winchester would be like rubbing salt into a wound.

"Marshal, I want you—" Once again the King was seized by a prolonged coughing fit that left him gasping for breath. "Before you leave England," he said at last, "I want you to pay a visit to Lord Geoffry in London. He's anxious to return to Court, and if he convinces you that he can accomplish nothing more where he is, he has my permission to come to Le Mans."

"Yes, sire," Marshal said with a smile. It was high time Geoffry returned. Marshal was still wary of John, and with the exception of Essex, he had no great faith in the few barons wintering at Le Mans. Stephen de Marcai, Seneschal of Anjou, and William fitz Ralph, Seneschal of Normandy, were able counselors, but their own responsibilities kept them from Court for extended periods.

"And while you're in London, Marshal, there is someone else you should see," Henry said enigmatically.

"Sire?"

Henry's eyes crinkled with secret amusement, and he did not respond immediately. Marshal glanced at Essex and then at John, but it was clear that they did not know what the King had in mind.

"It was Lord Geoffry's idea, actually," Henry said, obviously enjoying Marshal's puzzlement, "though I imagine I would have come to it on my own. I think you should look in on that ward you foisted on me—Lady Isabelle de Clare. At one point, as I recall, you were extraordinarily concerned for her welfare."

"I have no reason to be concerned now, sire," Marshal heard himself say above the sudden rushing in his ears as hope exploded inside him. Richard had offered him Isabelle's hand. Was the King about to—

Henry grinned. "Well, you should be concerned, Marshal," he said. "When this war is over, I'll see to it that the lady becomes your responsibility. Essex, let me introduce your future peer, William Marshal—the next Earl of Pembroke."

Essex, clearly surprised, exclaimed with pleasure and bounded forward to seize Marshal's hand, but Marshal barely heard the Earl's enthusiastic congratulations as he belatedly registered the King's words: *"When this war is over . . ."*

"God's eyes, Marshal," the King laughed. "You look green around the gills. Not afraid of marriage, are you?"

"No, sire," Marshal said in confusion, his mind reeling in its abrupt swing from euphoria to crushing disappointment. The King had not given him Isabelle, after all—only his promise. And should Richard triumph, Henry's promise would be worthless, its fulfillment swept away on the winds of war.

21

London—January 1189

"Ouch!" Isabelle cried out as she accidentally pricked her finger with her sewing needle.

Matilda, who was seated on a high stool before a reading stand, looked up from the book she'd been reading aloud and said quickly, "Don't get any blood on the silk, milady. Do you need a handkerchief?"

"No," Isabelle said irritably, sucking her finger. "But I'd think you'd worry about me instead of this damned embroidery."

"If you would use a thimble, milady, it wouldn't happen. And please stop swearing. You're getting into the habit."

"Oh, what's the point?" Isabelle burst out in frustration, tossing aside the silk *bliaut* on which she had been embroidering an elaborate floral design. "I'm no good at this. Any seamstress could do it better and in half the time."

"Embroidery is a skill any lady should command," Matilda said pedantically, as if that settled the matter, and she resumed her reading of the "Song of Roland." It was only one of several lengthy *chansons de geste* contained in the thick, leather-bound volume the Queen had presented Isabelle as a parting gift.

"That's enough reading for today, Mattie," Isabelle said with a sigh. She was seated on her bed, and now she fell back onto the mattress and groaned. "God, I'm bored."

"Don't swear, mi—"

"I know, I *know!* But what do you expect after I've been cooped up in this prison for nearly three months?"

"The White Tower is a stronghold, not a prison, milady, and you're hardly a prisoner. I'll admit the surroundings here are not exactly cheerful, but the Justiciar and Master Hubert have done their best to keep you entertained. You've been introduced to all the leading families in and around London, and you can go into the town whenever you wish."

Isabelle grimaced. Matilda's complacency only irritated her more. Without the stimulation of a thriving court and its gossip, Matilda had quickly tired of their stay at Winchester, and she found the gloomy atmosphere of the Tower a small price to pay for the gossipy whirl of London's upper-class social life. The mix of nobility and wealthy civil servants who had come to prominence through Henry's burgeoning administration was definitely to Matilda's liking.

But Isabelle felt even more isolated in London than she had at Winchester, where the Queen had been a conduit for news from France. The Royal Justiciar, Ranulf de Glanville, in whose charge she'd been placed, and his secretary, Hubert Walter, showed no inclination to share what they knew with her; and the women with whom she came in contact cared little for what transpired beyond London and its environs, save for politically neutral social gossip from the European Courts.

Isabelle suspected that Lady Glanville was as well-informed as her husband, but she was no more forthcoming than the Justiciar himself. Isabelle did not think that they were intent on keeping her in the dark. They simply did not want to talk about the news from France; and as the Justiciar's fortunes were tied to the King's, Isabelle was forced to conclude that the tidings from across the Channel were ominous.

Yet all she knew for certain was that the King had established his Court in Le Mans for the winter and that the war with Philip was expected to resume in the spring.

"Why do you suppose the King ordered me to take up residence here?" Isabelle said, staring up at the canopy of her bed.

"I'm sure I don't know, milady," Matilda said patiently. She had answered the same question in the same way countless times before.

The clatter of iron-shod hooves in the narrow courtyard far below drifted in through the chamber window, and out of idle curiosity Isabelle got up from the bed and went to the window. "Let's go out for a ride, Mattie," she said, moving aside the window screen and peering out. The gentle, icy draft on her cheeks was a refreshing contrast to the smoky heat from the fireplace in the chamber, and she breathed deeply.

"It's too cold, milady," Matilda protested. "And come away from that window before you catch your death."

"Oh, don't be such a chicken. We have a bright, clear day for once."

In the courtyard below, a messenger had dismounted and disappeared. Isabelle set the window screen back in place and began to pace restlessly. To be sure she made her point, she started to whistle off-key.

"Oh, very well, milady," Matilda said testily, "I'll go down and arrange an escort. You'll have to wear your warmest robe; it's bitter outside."

"We can watch the action on Mooresfield for a while and then go on to Smithfield fair to see if there are any new furs available."

"There won't be many stalls open today, milady."

"Of course there will; the sun's out."

"And I don't know why you like to watch boys knock each other's brains out on the ice at Mooresfield," Matilda said, but she did know.

When Mooresfield marsh was frozen over, boys from the town raced across the ice on crude skates fashioned from horses' shinbones. They propelled themselves forward with the aid of an iron-shod pole, and invariably the skating degenerated into a melee of jousting as boys paired off at random, rocketed toward each other, and, using the pole as a lance, tried to knock their opponent off his feet. Cracked skulls were not uncommon.

Isabelle liked to watch for the same reason she had loved the horse racing on Smithfield in the fall: it was the closest she could come to participating herself. In fact, the only popular sport that didn't draw her interest was bear baiting.

"Get going, Mattie!" Isabelle said impatiently, and Matilda left the chamber in resignation.

Matilda had not been gone five minutes when she returned with a satisfied smile on her face. "We're going out, milady," she said excitedly, "but for more civilized entertainment."

Isabelle's face fell. "What does that mean?"

"You've been invited to the Bishop of Lincoln's house. The Chancellor has been in residence for some time now, and he's requested 'the pleasure of your company.' "

"The Chancellor?" Isabelle groaned. "I don't even know the man. What's he want with me?"

"Just what the invitation stated: the pleasure of your company," Matilda said, and then she giggled. "He has a mistress, you know. Maybe we'll get to meet her."

The Bishop of Lincoln's house was in a western suburb of London, on the opposite side of the city from the White Tower. The Chancellor had provided Isabelle and Matilda with an escort of six mounted *serjants*, who were more than adequate to force a quick passage through London's crowded streets, and the party rode across the city, rather than around it.

The crisp, bright day had given way to a bleak, cloudy afternoon, and although the temperature was rising, the gusting, moisture-laden wind had a bite to it. Snow was in the offing. Despite the deteriorating weather, travelers continued to pour into the city, and people clamoring for admission, their entry fees clutched in their fists, thronged Newgate.

The crowd parted before the shouting *serjants*, who continued to clear the way as they rode out of the city on Watling Street, the ancient, paved Roman highway leading northwest from London. A few hundred yards from the massive Newgate gate house, the road dipped sharply down into a ravine cut by the small River of Wells, which flowed south into the Thames. Crossing the bridge, the horses' hoofbeats were all but lost in the steady rumble of mill wheels and the rush of water through the millraces.

As they rode up out of the avine onto Old Bourne Hill, Isabelle adjusted her scarf to shield her face from the icy wind sweeping up from the Thames. Although she disliked binding her neck and head in a wimple, which she considered best suited to nuns and elderly matrons, she wished she'd worn one today.

Still, it was good to be out; and although she expected the polite conversation with the Chancellor and his guests to bore her, she preferred a social afternoon to being cooped up in her apartment in the Tower.

The Bishop of Lincoln's house stood a quarter of a mile from the city wall, facing Watling Street. Both sides of the road were heavily built up with rude sheds and wooden dwellings that crowded every inch of the available land between the stately gardens and town houses of the affluent. Ahead on Isabelle's left, the yellow stone tower of the Templars was completely hemmed in, but beyond the old Templar stronghold, the Bishop of Lincoln's house stood in splendid isolation behind a great stone wall—more a miniature manor home than a town house.

The party rode through the gate into a flagstoned courtyard, and as Isabelle and Matilda approached the sprawling, two-story home, the steward came out to meet them. At that moment a young man came striding around the corner of the house from the direction of the stables, a recalcitrant shock of black hair poking out from beneath his tight woolen cap.

"Jean!" Isabelle cried in a burst of joy.

Jean d'Erly looked over in surprise and flashed a broad grin as he recognized Isabelle. "Your Ladyship!" he shouted excitedly, running toward her, "what are you doing here?"

"I was about to ask you the same thing!" Isabelle laughed as Jean helped her down from the saddle. As the steward turned to assist Matilda in dismounting, Isabelle took Jean's hands and stepped back to observe him with a critical eye. "Is it my imagination or have you filled out since I saw you last?" she asked gaily.

Jean smiled self-consciously but not without pride. "I think so, milady. In Sir William's service, building up your strength is necessary for survival."

"Well, you don't look any the worse for wear to me."

Coming up behind Isabelle, Matilda said mischievously, "Are you going to ask, milady, or will I have to?"

Isabelle shot her a withering look, but before Matilda could embarrass her further, she turned back to Jean and said quickly, "Is Sir William here?"

"Of course, milady." Jean grinned. "Where I go, he follows."

"Sir William is with the Chancellor at the moment, Lady Isabelle," the steward interjected, frowning at what he considered Jean's impudence. "Unfortunately the Chancellor is indisposed—a severe cold—and he's asked that you forgive him for not greeting you himself."

"If the Chancellor is ill, milady," Matilda said with pretended innocence, "perhaps we should not impose," and her eyes crinkled with amusement as Isabelle glared at her.

"No, no, Your Ladyship," the steward said in confusion. "You are the first of the guests to arrive—besides Sir William—but the Chancellor's secretary, who will be hosting this evening's supper, will be here shortly. Now, if you would be so kind as to follow me. . . . "

The steward ushered the ladies into the house, followed by Jean d'Erly. Inside the entrance was a spacious tiled foyer and a wide central staircase leading up to the apartments on the second floor. The steward led them through a doorway on the left into a large, vaulted room that served the same function as the great hall of a castle.

Banquet tables covered with spotless linen had already been set, and meticulously attired servants stood ready to provide the guests with a variety of spiced and mulled wines. In one corner, a musical ensemble had begun to play, a portable organ adding strength to the usual combination of harp, viols, and flutes.

As Isabelle entered the room, the household fool, who was seated cross-legged on a bench beside the fireplace, looked up in mock surprise. He jumped to his feet and intentionally slipped in the rushes on the floor, falling backward with a loud yelp. The impromptu pratfall was so adroitly done that even the steward, who must have seen the stunt before, couldn't help laughing.

Isabelle smiled, but the response was mere politeness as she looked in vain for Marshal, barely able to contain her joyous excitement. Her heart pounded with anticipation.

"I'll inform the Chancellor that you're—" the steward began, but he broke off as Marshal came in behind them and said hello.

A servant was taking their cloaks, but Isabelle was barely conscious of removing hers as she looked back toward the door, her breath catching in her throat. Marshal came toward her, smiling, his eyes on her alone, and she went to meet him, momentarily oblivious of the others in the room. Her hands were trembling as he grasped them.

"Lady Isabelle, I . . . " Marshal began, glancing self-consciously at Matilda, who was all ears. "I can't tell you what a great pleasure it is to see you again."

"Nor I, Sir William," Isabelle said, wishing everyone else would disappear.

An awkward silence followed, in which Isabelle was painfully aware of the others looking on. Simultaneously she and Marshal said, "You're looking well." They laughed together self-consciously, and Marshal released Isabelle's hands.

It was then that Matilda redeemed herself in Isabelle's eyes.

"Do you think I might have a tour of the house?" she asked the steward. "I've always admired it, but only from the outside. I'm sure Sir William and Lady Isabelle would excuse us; they're old friends and probably would like to talk."

"Certainly, Lady Matilda," the steward said, graciously upgrading her status. "I'd be happy to show you around." He turned to Marshal and Isabelle and said, "You might find the Chancellor's library a comfortable place to converse until the other guests arrive."

Marshal glanced at Isabelle, and she nodded.

The steward snapped his fingers and ordered one of the servants to bring wine into the library, which was adjacent to the room that served as the great hall.

Jean d'Erly, who had been struggling to suppress a grin that twitched stubbornly at his lips, cleared his throat noisily and said with exaggerated seriousness, "If you don't require my services, sire, there are some chores I should attend to."

"Very well, Jean," Marshal said, failing completely in his attempt to sound natural. "Why don't you do that."

Marshal led Isabelle into the Chancellor's library and closed the thick oak door behind them. The dim light from the window was augmented by candles, and a fire crackled softly in the hearth. There were two comfortable chairs by the fireplace for the use of the Chancellor and a visitor, and a clerk's high stool and writing desk stood by the window. Against the walls were open chests filled with parchment rolls and books.

"Would you like some wine?" Marshal asked.

"No thank you," Isabelle said, walking over to the fire. She was dismayed by a sudden attack of nervousness. For months and months she had daydreamed of their meeting again, imagining what she would say when they did, but now the words she had rehearsed so often seemed foolish.

Marshal came over to her and smiled tentatively. Here he was at last, and she didn't know what to say. Their brief time together in Kilkenny now seemed remote and unreal. The reality was that the King had given Helwis of Lancaster to Marshal, and perhaps he had already decided to marry the lady. Why should he not?

"I didn't know until recently that you'd been brought to London," Marshal said. "Have you been comfortable here?"

"The Tower is pretty gloomy," Isabelle said, "but the Justiciar has been very kind."

"Good," Marshal said, and cleared his throat. "Good," he repeated, smiling awkwardly.

Isabelle could see that he was nervous, too, but was that good or bad? Maybe he was remembering the things he'd said to her so many months ago and was now embarrassed by them. Isabelle's tongue flicked out to moisten her lips.

"While I was still at Winchester," she said, "the Queen told me of your good fortune—that you've received gifts from the King. . . . "

"Yes," Marshal said. "He gave me title to the land of Cartmel—and Helwis of Lancaster as ward."

Isabelle looked away, torn between her pride and her desire to know. She held her breath, hoping Marshal would tell her about Helwis, yet afraid of what he might say.

"I'm not going to marry her, Rusty," Marshal said quietly. "I never intended to."

"Why not?" she said in a small voice.

Marshal reached out, took her hands, and held them tightly. The warmth of his callused palms seemed to course up through her arms.

"Because I don't want to marry anyone but you," he said.

His words released a flood of emotion in Isabelle, and her eyes blurred with tears.

Marshal was smiling crookedly at her. "The prospect is that horrible, is it?"

Isabelle shook her head, wanting to tell him how much she loved him, to tell him that she'd prayed he wouldn't marry Helwis and how selfish that made her feel. She wanted to tell him about Eleanor . . . . There was so much she wanted to tell him. "Oh, Sir William . . . "

"Sir William?" Marshal laughed.

"But I don't even know what your friends call you," she said, looking up at him shyly.

"Will," Marshal said. "At least they do now. When I was a squire, my nickname was distinctly unflattering."

"Will," she said softly, slipping her hands from his and encircling his waist with her arms. Marshal's smile faded, and he took her upraised face between his hands. As he bent toward her, she closed her eyes, and for a long time they were lost in a kiss.

Afterward Isabelle continued to cling to him, her head pressed against his chest, listening to the thump of his heart. A warm glow suffused her body, and she felt light-headed. "I'll never marry anyone but you, my love," she whispered. "I promise you that. The King can strip me of my inheritance for all I care, but I'll never marry anyone but you."

"The King won't be the problem," Marshal said, stroking her hair, "at least as long as the King of England is Henry of Anjou."

Isabelle looked up at him in surprise. "Why do you say that?"

"There's desperation in the air, and I find that the service of a knight can command richer prizes than I'd imagined."

"Don't say that!" Isabelle protested. "Don't you know how much you're respected? You're—" She broke off abruptly, and her eyes widened as the implication of Marshal's words sank in. "You don't mean . . . "

Isabelle said hesitantly, not daring to hope. "You don't mean the King has offered . . . "

And as Marshal nodded, Isabelle's heart soared.

"Oh, God, I can't believe it!" she cried joyously, hugging Marshal with all her strength. "Why didn't you tell me right away? I hoped and prayed, but I never really— Why didn't you tell me!"

When Marshal did not reply at once, Isabelle looked up at him and was taken aback by the strange look in his eyes.

"What is it? What's wrong?"

"'The King will not permit us to marry until the war in France is over."

"But we can wait, Will," she said, tightening her grip about him. "We have our whole life ahead of us."

"Richard has deserted the King and allied himself with Philip," Marshal said gravely. "To make matters worse, His Majesty is ill, and . . . well, if the King goes down, Rusty, I'll go down with him."

She heard the resignation in his voice, and her hands went cold. Now she understood the Justiciar's silence on the news from France.

"But surely it's not hopeless," she said, clinging fiercely to him.

"Not hopeless . . . but the odds are against us."

Isabelle felt her knees go weak, and she shook her head dazedly. God could not be so cruel—to give her a glimpse of happiness, only to snatch it away. Eleanor's words came back to her, echoing in her mind: "If civil war comes and Marshal finds himself on the losing side, your hopes will die with Henry's cause." No! There had to be a way out for them. There had to be!

From the great hall came the sound of a woman's shrill laughter. The Chancellor's guests were arriving. Isabelle wanted to shut out the sound—shut out the whole uncaring world. She knew what she wanted to say to Marshal—what she had to say—but did she dare?

"I'm sorry," Marshal said quietly. "I wish—"

"But if you believe Richard will win," she blurted out, "must you remain with the King? Surely it's not too late. . . . "

Her words hung in the air unanswered. Marshal continued to hold her in his arms, but he did not speak. Isabelle looked up at him anxiously, and slowly he released her.

"You want me to go over to Richard," he said at last.

She heard the disappointment in his voice, and her lips quivered.

Why couldn't he understand? If Richard was to be king, what was the point of throwing away their happiness?

"Would it be so terrible to bow to the inevitable, Will?" she implored, not caring that the Queen had put those words into her mouth. Eleanor had been right all along.

Marshal turned away and went to the hearth. He picked up the poker and restlessly stirred the logs. "Would you really have me desert the King?" he asked, staring into the flames.

"I love you, Will," she said desperately. "I'm not willing to sacrifice our future to Henry's cause."

Marshal turned back to face her. "Is that what you think I'm doing?" he protested. "Rusty, I have no choice. Can't you understand that?"

"But you *do* have a choice," she said, misconstruing his words. "The Queen, herself, assured me that Count Richard would welcome you with open arms."

Marshal's lips twisted into a bitter half smile. "So she's worked on you too. I suppose I should have expected that."

"But I'm sure she was sincere, Will. If you were to go to Richard—"

"Rusty," Marshal said, cutting in, "the Count of Poitou has already made me the offer. I refused."

From beyond the library door came more laughter and the babble of jocular voices that emphasized the silence in the room as they looked at each other. His eyes pleaded with her to understand, but she couldn't.

"Why?" she said at last in a choked voice.

"You need to ask? To ask why I'll not turn traitor?"

"No, Will. I ask why you choose the King instead of me."

"Choose?" Marshal said, his voice rising for the first time. "I swore an oath of allegiance! I *swore* it before God and of my own free will. I cannot violate that oath now; no man of honor could."

"Honor in *your* eyes!" she retorted. "If you renounced your allegiance openly, no man would call you traitor."

She saw him react to the unintended shrillness in her tone. Until now he had been pleading with her, but now his eyes hardened.

"I hoped you would understand," he said stiffly. "Apparently I asked too much."

His sudden coldness cut her like a knife, and she responded without thinking. "Forgive me for not living up to your standards!" she said, lashing out defensively.

Marshal opened his mouth to speak, but then he compressed his lips and shook his head. Wordlessly he turned away. As he walked to the door Isabelle stretched out her hand, but pride held her back from stopping him. Why couldn't *he* understand?

By the time she had dried her tears and entered the great hall, he was gone.

"Are you sure you will not see Sir William, Your Ladyship?" said Hubert Walter, the Justiciar's cherubic, wispy-haired secretary. "He told me that he is leaving London within a few hours."

"No, Master Hubert," Isabelle replied stiffly, "and you may tell Sir William this: Let him come to me when he is girded with an earl's belt. Then I will receive him and not before."

"Yes, Your Ladyship," the secretary said, blinking in embarrassment. "As you wish."

As Hubert Walter left Isabelle's chamber, she moved to her window, overlooking the Tower's inner courtyard, and looked out. She could see Jean standing below with the horses. The ground was carpeted with six inches of fresh snow, which had been falling from the gray sky in thick, wind-driven swirls all afternoon. The winter storm that had been threatening since the day before had come upon them at last.

Isabelle shivered and stepped back, hugging her shoulders, but the draft did not chill her nearly as much as her own despair. She had lain awake half the night, until she had finally cried herself to sleep. Perhaps if Marshal had come in the morning, she would not have refused to see him, but as the lonely, wintry day had worn on, her misery had cloaked itself in anger.

She wanted to wound him, as he had wounded her. She had begged him to put their happiness before his pride, and he had turned his back on her—walked away without a word. Perhaps he had come this afternoon to make amends, but it was too late; she could not forget the look on his face before they'd parted the day before. He had made his choice; let him live with it.

"You're a fool, milady," Matilda said behind her.

"What?" Isabelle snapped, whirling around.

"I said," Matilda responded coolly, "you're a fool, milady."

"How *dare* you speak to—"

"Because I've known you since you were a child," Matilda said, softening her voice. "You're sending away the finest knight you'll ever know."

"Mattie, you don't *understand*!"

"But I do understand," Matilda said, coming across the room and grasping Isabelle's hands. "Last night you talked and talked, and I listened. How could I not understand? You are desperately afraid of losing him, but is that a reason to drive him away? My God, this world abounds with men to whom a holy oath means nothing, who would prefer your bed and your lands to honor. Is that the kind of man you want?"

"You weren't there, Mattie! You didn't see him—how coldly he looked at me, as if I'd betrayed him. And all I wanted—"

"But he's here now, milady! Don't let him go like this. If you do, you'll regret it. You know you will—perhaps for the rest of your life."

The sound of men's voices drifted up from the courtyard, and Isabelle knew Marshal was leaving. For a moment longer she hesitated, but then she was out the door and racing down the dizzying spiral staircase from her chamber, heedless of Matilda's cry to return for a robe.

You'll regret it . . . perhaps for the rest of your life. What if he fell in battle and she never saw him again?

Twice she stumbled and nearly fell, but then she reached the bottom of the stairwell, threw her weight against the door leading directly to the courtyard, and burst outside. "Will!" she cried as she saw him riding out through the gate. "Will!" But her voice was carried off by the wind.

Openmouthed, the guards at the gate stared at her as she ran across the courtyard and out through the gate into the road beyond, her slippers sinking soundlessly into the snow. Fifty yards ahead of her, Marshal and Jean rode on toward the city, its walls barely visible through the swirling snow.

The wind cut through Isabelle's gown, but she did not feel the cold as she ran blindly after them, slipping and stumbling, the snow flying into her eyes. She cried out again and again, but neither Marshal nor Jean heard her. Desperately she ran still faster.

But it was no use; the men had spurred their horses into a trot. Pain lanced her side and she could feel herself slowing down; she could run no farther. As she stopped, gasping her breath, the capricious wind suddenly died, and she called out to them with all her remaining strength.

For an instant she thought they had not heard, but then she saw Jean rein in and twist around in his saddle. She closed her eyes and clasped her hands to her heaving chest, feeling the snow melting into her hair, and when she opened her eyes again, Marshal was there, looming above her on his horse.

"Will," she gasped, seizing his leg and holding on as if she were afraid he'd ride off again. "I couldn't let you go without saying good-bye," she said, blinking at the snow falling into her upraised face. "I couldn't—"

Her words were cut off as Marshal bent down and caught her under the arms. He swept her up into the saddle and enfolded her in the warmth of his robe. "I love you," he said softly as they rode back toward the Tower. "Whatever happens, Rusty, remember that."

22

LeMans—June 1189

"Jesus," Bethune breathed, "there are thousands out there."

Atop a wooded knoll twenty miles south of Le Mans, Marshal's scouting party looked out over a fog-shrouded expanse of open fields. Below them, they could hear the muffled tread of horses and men and the creaking and rattling of supply wagons—a ghostly army advancing through the mist.

Bethune turned and saw Marshal staring at him. "Why the queer look, Will?"

"Nothing," Marshal said, shaking his head. "I heard the same words on another hill once. Gave me a strange feeling, that's all."

"The Old Man was right," Harlincourt said. "The march toward Tours was only a feint. They're going to hit us at Le Mans, all right. They must have doubled back yesterday."

Philip and Richard had moved against Henry in May. Instead of attacking from two directions at once, they had combined forces and struck across the border northwest of Le Mans. They had overrun La Ferte-Bernard and then marched south, bypassing Le Mans, apparently intent on attacking Tours. Henry had not been fooled.

"We know they're coming," Bethune said impatiently, "so let's get the hell out of here—before they reach the main road and cut us off."

"We don't know their strength yet," Marshal said. "We wait."

Harlincourt and Bethune exchanged looks with the other knights in the patrol, and Marshal knew they had a right to be worried. They were not wearing armor.

The King had sent them south in the hours before dawn to locate the enemy, and because speed and range were necessary, they had been forced to ride light. They had already had one close call, nearly riding

267

into the enemy's forward scouts in the fog, but Marshal was determined not to head back until he was sure that the entire enemy army was moving on Le Mans.

He had never believed in omens, and he tried to shake off the premonition of disaster that Bethune's first words had triggered. This was another hill in another world, and the army hidden in the fog was not invincible. Yet the feeling of uneasiness would not leave him, and memories of the wait on that desert hill in Palestine came flooding back.

He remembered his rage at the Grand Master's folly, followed by bitter resignation and an empty sense of futility. There had been little fear, for he'd had nothing to lose. Now, however, he had too much to lose, and deep inside, he realized, he was afraid.

His hand strayed to the small parchment roll he carried beneath his tunic, a letter he'd received from Isabelle in April. Marshal smiled to himself.

Isabelle obviously thought he might be illiterate, for she'd had the letter written by a clerk. The letter was written in Latin and phrased in the formal style of a communication intended to be read aloud to Marshal by a clerk of his own. Marshal knew the contents by heart.

> Lady Isabelle de Clare, Heiress of Pembroke, Striguil, Longueville, and Leinster, to William Marshal, Lord of Cartmel and Knight of the King's Household, greeting.
>
> I have recently been officially informed by Master Hubert Walter that His Majesty has graciously offered you my hand in marriage, and I am writing to confirm to you the great pleasure with which I received this news. In choosing the foremost knight in the realm to be my future husband, the King could not have given me greater honor or happiness. Be assured, sire, that I await the day of our marriage with unbounded eagerness. I pray that the war that keeps you far from me may soon be over and that God's purpose will be revealed in complete victory for His Majesty over His enemies. I am well in body and spirit, and I hope that this letter finds you also well.
>
> Each night I pray that Our Lord and Savior will watch over you, preserve you, and give you strength in battle. As the Lord looks with favor on those who seek fulfillment of their prayers through their own efforts, I am sending my faithful

Fulk le Brun to guard your life as he would my own. I beg
you, sire, for my sake, do not send him from you.

Marshal glanced back at the silent, hulking *serjant*, who was with
them now, armed as always with sword and longbow. Fulk was a loner,
impossible to know, and only slowly had they adjusted to his dark,
brooding presence. Out of deference to Isabelle, Marshal had allowed him
to stay, but there were times when Fulk got on his nerves. Unless ordered
away, he followed Marshal everywhere, like a great, dark shadow.

The early-morning sun was slowly burning away the mist en-
shrouding the enemy. First the banners emerged from the fog, and then
the glinting armor of the horsemen, and finally the entire host of Richard
Lionheart and Philip of France was revealed, spreading across the fields
below, the nearest elements within bowshot of the knoll.

"That's their whole damned army, all right," Harlincourt said.
"Five—maybe six thousand strong. Satisfied, Will?"

"Yes," Marshal said, turning his horse. "We've got what we came
for. Let's go."

"Have our men destroyed the bridge across the Huisne?" the King asked,
wincing as his surgeon probed the edges of an ugly red swelling on the
back of his leg between his calf and his heel. Henry lay facedown on the
bed, the mattress sagging under his weight. His stocking had been
removed to expose the festering carbuncle.

"The bridge went up in flames an hour ago, sire," Marshal said.
"Count John's men did a thorough job, and we've driven stakes into all the
fords up and down the river. They're impassable now."

"Good," Henry grunted with satisfaction. "That should hold them
for the time being. Bloody Richard must have thought he'd catch me
napping. Well, I'm not past it yet!"

"I must open your leg again, sire," the surgeon said. "There is sign
of mortification, and I must cut away the dead flesh and insert a drain. I
don't like the way the affected area continues to spread."

"*You* don't like it," Henry growled, twisting his head to glare at the
surgeon. "But you love to cut, don't you, Master Gerald?"

"It's necessary in this case, sire," the surgeon replied defensively.

"All right, all right! Just give me time to get some wine into me, and then you can have your fun. In the meantime you can wait outside. We have business to discuss."

"Yes, sire," the surgeon said, bowing and retiring with his assistant.

With the coming of spring, Henry's fevers had abated, but in their place came another affliction, minor at first and hardly noticed. An infection had set in below the scar tissue of an old wound. Initially it had caused no concern, but as the weeks wore on and the inflammation slowly spread and festered, it became clear that the months of fever had dangerously sapped the King's resistance.

Henry rolled over with a groan and sat up, gesturing to his servant to bring the wine. The servant had already poured a cup, and Henry drained it in three great gulps. "More," he demanded. "And keep it coming. When that bastard starts cutting, it's going to hurt like hell. What's the enemy doing now?"

"Making camp in the woodland park on the south bank of the river, sire," said the Earl of Essex. "They don't seem to be in a hurry, now that they've seen we're ready for them. I doubt they'll make a move before tomorrow."

Geoffry, the Chancellor, cleared his throat. "Will you be convening the barons this evening, sire? The enemy outnumbers us three to one at the moment, and we should decide now whether or not we'll defend Le Mans."

"We'll stand fast, by God," Henry said, swallowing more wine. "I'll hold the council, but I want the issue settled between us here and now. Where's Count John?"

"He's not yet returned from inspecting the city militia, sire," Essex said.

Henry nodded. "Well, gentlemen, I say we defend Le Mans. What do you say?"

"The city is well fortified, sire," Essex replied. "Philip and Richard have the forces to take it eventually, but if they settle in for a siege, they completely lose the initiative and become a stationary target for a counterattack. My guess is that they will break off their attack; but if they don't, we can bring our own army down from Normandy and trap them between two fires."

"I agree with Essex, sire," the Chancellor said, "but it's my duty to point out the risk in allowing yourself to be encircled. We don't know the extent of Philip's own reserves; he may be able to match what we can bring down from Normandy."

Henry shook his head. "That's their whole army out there now. Marshal, you've been damned quiet. What do you think?"

"Defend Le Mans, sire. To quit the city now, after having spent the winter fortifying it, would send the wrong message to those barons who may be attacked next. Our agreed strategy was to defend our strong points as they were attacked, rather than to meet the enemy head-on in the open, and I see no reason to scrap that plan now."

"I agree, sire," William de Sille put in, speaking up for the first time. He was the castellan of the heavily fortified tower just north of the city.

"That's settled, then," Henry said, impatiently snapping his fingers for more wine. "Marshal, send a message to fitz Ralph to muster the Norman barons at Alençon and to prepare to march to our relief."

"Yes, sire," Marshal said briskly, hoping Henry's combative energy would last.

Relieved that the long months of waiting were at an end, the King was spoiling for a fight and thinking clearly and decisively; but the ugly infection had clearly become as painful as it was dangerous, and the surgeon's knife might only make matters worse.

"We're fighting a defensive war," the King said, "but I see no need to hide behind our walls and wait passively for the bastards to move into position. If they're careless in their approach, we'll hit them with a cavalry sortie. Ordinarily, Marshal, I'd let you lead it, but this time I want our men to see me out front. Essex, you'll organize a skirmishing force to meet them once they reach the lower town. Don't try to hold them back for long; just cut them up a bit and then torch the suburbs."

"Are you sure you want to set fire to the suburbs, sire?" Essex said. It was a sensible move, but Le Mans was Henry's birthplace.

"Yes," Henry said firmly. "I hate to do it, but we have to deny them cover. With the lower town razed, we'll have a clear field of fire from the walls."

Marshal and Essex nodded in approval, but Geoffry looked worried. "I think you should stay out of the fighting, sire—to give your leg a chance to heal."

"I've waited for a month and it's only gotten worse," the King said irritably, beginning to slur his words. "Besides, I'll still have some time to rest. We've blocked the river well enough to stop a crossing in force, so they have no choice but to move south again and use the bridge on the road to Angers. That should give us another full day at least, and probably two."

The Chancellor looked to Marshal and Essex for support but found none. In the King's place they would do the same; infection or no infection, he should lead his troops.

Henry turned onto his stomach, dropping his empty wine cup onto the floor. "I'm drunk enough now," he grunted. "Clear out now and send in the bloody sawbones."

John returned from his inspection too late for the conference with the King. When he was told by the guard at Henry's door that the surgeon was inside, he did not seek to enter but instead waited in the passageway. John was not squeamish; he wanted to speak with the doctor alone.

All morning he had driven himself and the men under him at a merciless pace; his face was flushed and his undergarments clung to his hot, sweating body. But still his mind was like ice. He was driven by one imperative: not to be caught on the losing side, and what he had discovered at the river had brought him to the moment of decision.

The opening of the door to the King's chamber ended John's restless pacing. As the surgeon emerged, preceded by his assistant, who was carrying the doctor's surgical chest, John called out to him.

"A moment of your time, Master Gerald."

The surgeon turned and peered shortsightedly down the passage. Recognizing John, he hurried forward, unconsciously smoothing his gray beard and adjusting his rich silk robe. John caught the flash of gold as the doctor slipped his fee into a purse on his belt, and his lip curled with contempt. A doctor's ability to cure rarely matched his skill at extracting payment.

"You wish to see me, sire?" the surgeon said, bowing lower than courtesy required. The man was obsequious.

"I want your opinion of His Majesty's condition. Your *true* opinion."

"The infection is spreading, sire, but I have done what is necessary. I have cut away the dead flesh, inserted a drain, and dressed the wound. I have also examined His Majesty's urine and determined that the humors are not in harmony. The black bile is definitely out of balance with the phlegm, and I have prescribed a powder to relieve the obstruction in His Majesty's liver, which is responsible for the imbalance."

"I did not ask what you have done, Master Gerald," John said coldly. "Just how dangerous is the infection?"

As the surgeon launched into another evasive speech, John reached out and seized him by the breast of his tunic. "*How dangerous is it!*" John hissed.

The surgeon swallowed convulsively and shook his head. "It's dangerous, sire, but I can't say what will happen. No one could."

"But the festering has been getting worse with each passing week. Does that not suggest that it will continue to worsen?"

"Ye-es, sire."

"And if it does?"

"There will be increasing mortification, and fever too. I may have to amputate."

"His Majesty will not permit that. Not now."

"Then, sire," the surgeon said, "I would not be responsible for the consequences."

John nodded slowly. "I see," he said, releasing the doctor. "Very well, you may go."

As the surgeon scurried away, John turned and walked off in the opposite direction, heading for his own chamber. He would think a while longer before committing himself, but he knew he had already made up his mind. If he was to switch sides, it would have to be now, when he had something to trade: information. He could send Gerard de Ridefort across to Richard after darkness fell to make the offer. The former Grand Master's defection to the enemy would arouse no suspicion.

Everyone thought the river shielding Le Mans from the enemy was impassable; only John knew that it was not.

At dawn the following day the Bishop of Le Mans celebrated Mass for the King and his barons and knights. Henry was in a theatrical mood, and he remained in the cathedral until everyone else had left. When he emerged, flanked by Count John and the bishop, he stood on the steps for a minute or two, regally acknowledging the cheers of the knights and soldiers assembled in the square.

He had not donned his hauberk and was dressed in brown hunting clothes. He gave no speech, relying instead on a mute show of nonchalant confidence to inspire his troops. Calling for his horse, he disdained the use of a mounting platform and swung up into the saddle with the apparent ease of a man half his age and weight.

Marshal, sitting his war-horse nearby, silently applauded the show, but he was close enough to see the King grit his teeth against the pain in his leg, which was bound with a thick linen bandage that bulged beneath his stocking. The morning air was still cool, but as Henry settled himself in the saddle, Marshal saw beads of sweat appearing on his forehead.

"I'm going out to have a look at the enemy," Henry said loudly; and Count John, Marshal, and a half dozen barons immediately moved their horses forward to accompany him.

Henry looked at Marshal and frowned. "You won't be needing your armor," he said. "We're quite safe on this side of the river."

"I'm sure that's true, sire," Marshal replied evenly, "but a hauberk's no problem for me."

"And I say you don't need it," Henry snapped. "Anyone who thinks he needs his armor can stay behind."

Immediately John and the six barons who'd ridden forward to accompany the King dismounted, and their squires hurried to their sides to assist them in removing their chain mail. Marshal remained in the saddle. Henry glared at him, and Marshal tensed, prepared to absorb an insult, but the King left the words on his tongue unsaid.

As one by one the men who had stripped off their armor remounted, Henry's expression relaxed, and he moved his horse closer to Marshal. "You and Geoffry are birds of a feather," he said softly. "Fussy old women."

"Yes, sire."

"Sorry about the scene, Marshal, but my leg is killing me. You may accompany us as far as the south gate but no farther. Understood?"

"Yes, sire," Marshal said, relieved to know that it was pain and not anxiety that had caused the flare-up. Still, he thought, Henry was pushing bravado too far. For the King to parade before the enemy without armor might be a useful bit of theater, but Marshal couldn't approve Henry's insistence that the men with him disarm themselves against their own better judgment.

As the King rode out of the square toward the south gate, the knights and troop captains dispersed to their preassigned posts at the wall towers and gate houses of the hilltop city. Marshal, Bethune, and Harlincourt joined the knights assigned to the south gate and followed the King's party. Fulk, as always, trailed Marshal at a discreet distance.

Because the passage across the river had been blocked, the gates were open and the drawbridges down. Le Mans retained a surface normality. Merchants were opening their shops, and the streets were filled with the aroma of baking bread, meat pies, and the yeasty smell of brewing ale. Already the road to the gate was clogged with carts and early-morning crowds; but the traffic in the streets was nevertheless lighter than usual, and there was a noticeable absence of able-bodied men of fighting age, most of whom had been conscripted to man the walls.

The soldiers at the south gate cheered the King as he passed through, and the civilians in the road beyond hastily gave way and joined in the cheering. Below the south gate, the road forked into two highways, one leading southwest to Tours and the other southeast to Angers. The road to Tours had been cut by the destruction of the bridge across the Huisne, and the road to Angers, which ran parallel to the river for some distance, was apparently being shunned by travelers. Only residents of the lower town spreading out below the city were still coming over the drawbridge that spanned the deep moat surrounding the walls of Le Mans.

Marshal ordered the men with him to remain inside the gate, but he proceeded across the drawbridge, allowing only Jean to accompany him. As he reined in his stallion he saw Henry turn in his saddle and look back to be sure Marshal wasn't following. The King gave Marshal an ironic salute and spurred his horse into a canter, heading down toward the river.

"His Majesty doesn't believe in your cardinal rule, does he, sire," Jean said, and Marshal looked at him sharply, thinking that the remark was a jibe. But Jean's expression was serious.

"A King can do as he pleases," Marshal said curtly. "Let's hope he doesn't come to regret it."

The suburbs had not encroached on the southern approach to Le Mans, and Marshal had a clear view of the river and the enemy encampment. Philip's white-and-gold silk pavilion had been pitched before the wooded park in which the bulk of his army sheltered, but Marshal could see no obvious sign of Richard's presence. Presumably he slept as usual in a simple tent, or, because the weather was fair, in the open.

The opposite riverbank swarmed with French soldiers hauling water from the river for domestic chores, and as yet there was no indication that Philip intended to break camp and move south. Marshal frowned. Philip might be a lazy campaigner, but not Richard. Marshal had expected to see them striking their tents by now. Why were they staying put?

He raised his hand to shield his eyes against the sun and watched a detachment of knights across the river riding toward the ruins of the burned-out bridge. In the lead he recognized the banner of Andre de Chauvigni, one of Richard's favorites, and his frown deepened. "What the hell are they up to?" he muttered aloud.

Henry had reached the fork in the road and was leading his party down toward the bridge site, apparently intending to taunt Richard's knights. The knights ignored the King's approach, spread out in a line along the bank, and began to probe the riverbed with their lances.

It was then that Marshal noticed the eddies curling around the charred bridge pilings jutting out of the river—eddies that indicated the swift water flow over shallows.

"Jesus!" Marshal burst out. "It's silted up!"

"What, sire?" Jean said, startled.

"Look at that," Marshal cried in alarm as Richard's knights began to push into the river. "The bottom's silted up around those pilings. Christ, there's a ford there now—the best damned ford those bastards could ask for!"

The King and his unarmed party halted in confusion, barely fifty yards from the river. "Come back!" Marshal bellowed, but even his powerful voice did not carry the distance. One of Richard's knights had turned in his saddle and was waving his lance, and in response to the signal, trumpets began to blare. In an instant the enemy encampment was swept into a swarming, swirling confusion as knights and *serjants* rushed for their horses and the foot soldiers gathered their weapons.

This was Richard's doing, Marshal was sure. Philip, accepting the river as impassable, would have marched patiently south to the nearest bridge; but Richard had not been content to waste two days, and he'd sent out his men to try to find a ford. The only saving grace was that they had not found it during the night, slipped across the river, and stormed the walls under cover of darkness.

The twelve knights fording the river had recognized the King, and now they came charging across in a shower of spray. John turned tail at once, and the King hesitated for only a moment before he wheeled his stallion about and raced for his life, followed by five of the six barons. The sixth—one Gerard Talebot—stood his ground.

Although the barons had stripped off their armor, they still carried shield and lance, and as the first of Richard's knights burst from the river, Talebot charged and shattered his lance on the opposing shield, slowing the enemy knight down but not stopping him. As the knights charging up behind spurred their horses up the riverbank, Talebot, having done what he could, veered off the road and galloped out of harm's way.

"Equip me!" Marshal growled, moving off the drawbridge to clear the path to the gate. Jean drew up beside him, handed over Marshal's shield and lance, and lowered the helmet over Marshal's head. As Marshal slipped on his mail gauntlets, Jean lashed the helmet down with quick, practiced fingers.

All along the wall behind them, men were shouting orders; and as John, the King, and his barons thundered up the slope toward the gate, the bells of Le Mans began to peel the general alarm.

John, hunched low over his saddle, raced straight past Marshal, his cape billowing out behind him, his black eyes wide and fixed on the gateway to safety; but as Henry galloped toward the drawbridge, he flashed Marshal a crooked grin and shouted breathlessly, "So you were right, God damn it!"

"Give the bastards one for me, Marshal!" shouted the last of the barons to cross the drawbridge.

Richard's knights, with Andre de Chauvigni in the lead, were pounding up the roadway, their lances lowered. With their horses burdened with the additional weight of the knights' armor, they had no hope of catching the King; but they knew the south gate was open, and they were making a bid to force their way in. Brave, Marshal acknowledged, but foolish.

The rush of adrenaline into his system was a release. Forgotten was his premonition of defeat. Once again there was only the present hurtling toward him moment by moment as he prepared to meet the steel-clad riders thundering up the road. Behind him, he heard a cry, "To Marshal!" and he knew his knights were coming out to join the fight.

As Marshal lowered his lance and spurred his mount into the charge, Bethune surged up beside him, and together they galloped down the roadway to meet the attackers head-on. Fresh horses and the short downhill run gave them the advantage in momentum, and as their lances splintered with earsplitting cracks against the lead riders' shields, their opponents were thrown back in their saddles. As the lances struck, Marshal and Bethune both swerved their stallions into the enemy chargers, driving them off the road.

Marshal hauled on his reins, and as his stallion skidded around, he drew his sword and charged up behind Andre de Chauvigni, whom he'd nearly unhorsed. Chauvigni, off-balance and struggling to regain control of his horse, was too slow in drawing his own sword. As he pulled it free, Marshal's blade flashed down, catching the knight's sword arm just above the wrist. The force of the blow paralyzed Chauvigni's nerves, and his sword dropped to the ground.

Chauvigni's companions, intent on crashing through to the gate, had swept past them, only to be met before the drawbridge by Harlincourt and six more of Henry's knights in a crash of shields and splintering lances.

Marshal struck Chauvigni once more for good measure, caving in the right side of his helmet, and as the dazed knight reeled in the saddle, Marshal seized his reins to take him captive. Instantly Jean, who had followed Marshal in the charge, was at his side, and Marshal thrust the reins into his squire's hands.

"Take him into the city," Marshal yelled. "He's worth a hefty ransom!"

Bethune had beaten his own opponent into submission, and his squire had taken the captive's reins. The fight in front of the drawbridge had become a wild melee as the defenders battled Richard's knights in a press of snorting, plunging stallions. Sunlight flashed on the scything sword blades, and the vicious ringing of steel on steel rose above the cacophony of tolling bells. It was ten against seven, and the defenders were being forced to the left of the drawbridge and back toward the moat.

Marshal raised his sword, preparing to charge back up the road into the fray, but first he looked down toward the river to be sure they wouldn't be hit from behind. Troops were swarming across the ford, and a substantial force of knights and mounted *serjants* had already crossed; but the enemy was ignoring the road up to the south gate and was moving off to the right, apparently preparing to invade the southeastern suburbs.

Marshal took in the situation at a glance, but the brief moment of delay cost the life of one of his knights. Even as Marshal and Bethune dug in their spurs, Hugh de Malaunoi's horse reared up in panic on the very edge of the moat, and a moment later horse and rider were forced backward and plunged to their deaths.

Yelling like madmen, Marshal and Bethune struck the attackers from the rear, and in an instant the tide of the miniature battle turned. One by one Richard's knights were knocked from their saddles or disarmed. Five knights managed to cut their way out of the trap and flee, but the others were captured and handed over to grinning squires.

The skirmish over, Marshal was the last to come back in through the gate. As he entered, the portcullis was lowered behind him and the bridge drawn up, sealing the gate.

"Well done, Marshal!" the King shouted, riding toward Marshal through the press of soldiery, knights, and squires. Henry had put on his chain mail and was wearing an open-faced helmet.

"Thank you, sire," Marshal said, breathing hard and looking around for Jean. "I have a present for you. Andre de Chauvigni. His ransom should be worth a penny or two."

"Sire!" Jean cried, appearing suddenly at Marshal's side, his face crestfallen. "I lost him."

"What do you mean, you *lost* him?"

"As we crossed the drawbridge, sire, some idiots started dropping stones off the gate-house parapet. They missed me, thank God, but one stone broke your prisoner's arm, and the other struck his horse. The horse bolted and I couldn't hold it."

"Well, it's your loss, Marshal, not mine," Henry said. "I would have let you keep him. Now, come with me. You're not needed here, and Essex is already being pressed hard in the town below the east gate."

"Bethune, Harlincourt, Clifford, Quency—on me!" Marshal yelled. "Dammartin, Plouquet, and Canteleu, round up any squads of *serjants* you can find and bring them out through the east gate!"

With Marshal, the four knights, and their squires in tow, the King set off at the gallop for the east gate. Barely twenty minutes had passed since the alarm bells had begun to ring, but already the narrow side streets were deserted and the shops closed. The main thoroughfare to the east gate, however, was choked with old men, women, and children streaming in from the suburb under attack.

A force of one hundred foot soldiers had mustered just inside the east gate, apparently in response to a call for reinforcements, but with no specific instructions. "What orders, sire?" their mounted captain cried as the King forced his way through the refugees toward the gate.

"Take your men outside and keep the approach to the gate clear," Henry shouted, and spurred his horse through the gate. As the King and his knights rode out across the drawbridge, the people in the road beyond raised a feeble cheer.

"They won't be cheering much longer," the King said grimly to Marshal, who was riding at his side. "We'll have to torch the town soon."

At an intersection one hundred yards below the east gate, Essex waited with a shock troop of twenty knights, prepared to stop an enemy breakthrough at any one of the dozens of hastily erected barricades blocking the streets in a wide, defensive arc.

The pikemen, crossbowmen, and *serjants*—clustered behind a barricade fifty yards beyond Essex—were holding their own for the moment, but they were under heavy attack. The steadily swelling battle noise washing up the hill from several directions made it clear that Philip's troops were pressing hard all around the improvised perimeter.

Essex's face was grave as Henry rode up. "They may flank us soon, sire, unless we commit our reserves."

"No," Henry said at once. "We don't want to waste our strength here. We'll set fire to this area now, and then you can pull back."

"But the wind is blowing up toward the city, sire," Essex warned. "If it jumps the wall . . ."

"The wall is eighteen feet high."

"But, sire—"

"Damn it, man, we can't give the bastards cover right up to the walls, and we don't have all day to decide! We must do it now!"

"Very well, sire. I'll give the order."

A mounted *serjant* was galloping toward them. "My Lord Essex!" he cried breathlessly. "We can't hold our position much longer!"

"Marshal, the barricade is beyond that bend," Essex said quickly, pointing down the street to their left, which cut across the slope and then turned sharply downhill. "Can you support it and buy us time to fire the suburbs? I want to keep my own knights here to cover the general retreat."

"We'll try, sire," Marshal responded, and turned to his knights. "Helmets and lances!"

"May we squires fight, sire?" Jean pleaded as he handed Marshal his helmet.

"Yes."

"Thank you, sire!"

Marshal chafed at the delay as the grinning squires armed themselves, but he contained his impatience. He expected to face massed infantry if the barricade should be breached, and he wanted the additional shock value of five more horsemen.

"Let's go!" he cried, digging in his spurs. Followed by his knights and squires, he raced toward the endangered barricade. Behind him, he heard Essex shouting orders to fire the suburbs.

As they neared the turn in the narrow, deserted street, a concerted roar of triumph and blood lust came from the direction of the barricade beyond the bend, and Marshal knew the enemy was breaking through. His stallion slewed around the corner at full gallop, and he lowered his lance, signaling the charge.

Halfway down the slope, the street was blocked by stacks of barrels and upended carts. Essex's pikemen were still fighting on the flanks, stabbing and slashing at the assault troops scrambling over the barricade, but in the center the ground was littered with dead and dying defenders, and the enemy was unopposed.

The French troops had righted two of the carts and pulled them aside, and foot soldiers were pouring through the gap, yelling like fiends. Below the barricade, the street was choked with infantry surging up the hill.

But as the ten charging horsemen burst into view above the attackers and thundered down on them, the French battle cries turned to bellows of fear. The nearest soldiers scattered to the sides of the street, and the men behind them turned to club and claw their way back through the gap.

The violent, backward thrust of the terrified men set off a wave of panic that rippled outward, sweeping over the press of soldiery in the street below. The retreat became a rout as Marshal and his knights struck the mass of panicky men like thunderbolts, hurtling through the gap and riding down men by the dozens.

Marshal buried his lance in the chest of a Frenchman who had turned, too late, to strike at his horse with a pike, and he drew his sword. His knights and squires formed a wedge behind him, and they hacked their way forward ruthlessly, heedless of the screams of the men they felled, driving the bellowing herd of infantry before them.

In less than a minute the rout had gathered momentum of its own, and Marshal started to rein in. Through the restricted view of his eye slit he glimpsed a knight and three mounted *serjants* appear at the bottom of the hill, where the street widened into a road leading away from the suburb, but he gave them no heed. They were too few and too late to stem the flood of foot soldiers streaming past them and out into the fields beyond.

Marshal turned in his saddle and shouted to his men to break off the slaughter and pull back. They had won Essex the time he'd needed; behind them, thick clouds of smoke were already rising into the sky.

"Will!" cried Bethune, who had been fighting close behind him. "Crossbow!"

Startled, Marshal turned sharply and looked back down the hill. The enemy knight he had ignored was forcing his mount up the street through the fleeing mob, a loaded crossbow in his hand. He wore no helmet, and as he reined in and stared up at Marshal, his face contorted with hatred. It was Gerard de Ridefort.

"The bastard must have gone over to Richard!" Bethune yelled, but even then Marshal didn't realize the danger.

To openly kill a knight with a crossbow was unthinkable, and Marshal watched in disbelief as Ridefort raised the weapon to his shoulder. But the hate Marshal saw in Ridefort's expression was beyond rationality, and suddenly he knew he was going to die.

The range was too short for Ridefort to miss, and it was too late to flee. Marshal raised his sword and charged, knowing he would not live to reach him. The roadway between them was now almost clear, and the French stragglers scattered as Marshal's stallion surged into a gallop. Time seemed to stand still as Marshal bore down on Ridefort. He could see Ridefort's glittering eyes lining up the shot, his fingers tightening on the trigger lever . . .

Suddenly Ridefort's mouth flew open, and his eyes widened in a look of infinite surprise. Still clutching the crossbow, he toppled from the saddle, a cloth-yard arrow buried in his chest.

Marshal hauled on the reins, but his stallion's momentum carried him past his fallen enemy. His knights had followed him in the charge, and the enemy *serjants* wheeled their mounts about and fled, riding down their own men in their haste to escape. Marshal turned his horse and rode back to where Ridefort's body lay spread-eagle in the dust.

It had all happened too fast for him to feel fear. There had been only the icy certainty of impending death. But he was still alive, he thought numbly, staring without comprehension at the arrow protruding from Ridefort's chest.

Bethune and Harlincourt drew up beside him, cursing Ridefort's soul, their shock and outrage evident in their unnaturally high-pitched voices. Marshal wasn't listening. He was looking up the hill to where

Black Fulk stood atop the barricade, a longbow in his hand, and now Marshal understood.

Across a hundred miles of land and sea, Isabelle de Clare had reached out to save his life.

23

Essex's fear had been realized. The wind had fanned the fires the defenders had set in the lower town, and had carried showers of sparks over the wall and into the city. Fire had broken out at three points inside the southeastern wall, and despite the desperate attempts of the soldiers and citizens to contain them, the fires had spread unchecked.

Marshal reeled as he stumbled backward out of a burning house, choking and gagging on the smoke that filled his helmet.

"Let go of the damned thing!" Bethune yelled, tearing the bulky feather matress Marshal was carrying out of his arms. "It's on fire and suffocating you!"

Marshal retched violently and fell to his knees.

"Get that helmet off him, Jean!" Bethune ordered, and Marshal felt his squire tearing at the helmet bindings. A moment later his head was free, and he sucked in air with a long, ragged gasp. Blinking to clear his eyes, he got unsteadily to his feet.

The bent, white-haired woman whose mattress Marshal had tried to save was hugging herself and moaning as she watched the blue paint on her tiny house blister and blacken as flames burst through the windows and raced up the facade to merge with the blaze on the roof.

She had managed to save a chair, a few pots and pans, and a small mirror, but that was all. She had wasted too much time struggling to pull her bed down from the second floor, and if Marshal had not heard her anguished cries and stopped to help, she might have been trapped.

"Will!" Bethune shouted, remounting his horse. "There's nothing we can do here; the whole damned city's going up. We've got to get to the cathedral."

The street in which Marshal and Bethune had halted was already engulfed in flame, and the blistering heat was driving out the last of the householders, who were trying to save their belongings. Marshal stopped

284

a man with a singed beard and eyebrows, who drove an ox cart piled high with furniture, and ordered him to take on the old woman's few remaining possessions. Then he swung up onto his horse and followed the impatient Bethune toward the cathedral.

"God curse Henry of Anjou!" the old woman shouted wildly after them. "He's done this to us!"

The woman's curse was all but lost in the chorus of shouts, screams, and wails rising from the city in a communal outburst of anger and loss that melded with the crackle and roar of the widening inferno. Overhead, the sun was dimmed by a black, wind-torn pall of smoke, and everywhere the air was filled with sparks and tiny embers that swirled on the wind and fell amid the dazed citizens, retreating with their pitiful loads through streets clogged with carts and a menagerie of domestic animals.

Marshal gritted his teeth against the nausea from smoke inhalation, cursing himself for stopping to help the old woman. Bethune was right; his place was with the King.

The square before the cathedral was packed with soldiers and mounted *serjants*, waiting in subdued silence, staring toward the King and his knights, who were gathered on their horses by the cathedral steps.

"The smoke has driven our men off the southeastern wall, sire," Essex was saying as Marshal rode up, "but the fire in the lower town has forced the enemy to retire for the moment. Philip has brought his entire army across the river, but as yet he's made no attempt to encircle the city. We've opened the northwest gate to the people fleeing the fires inside the walls, and the enemy's mounted patrols are not interfering with the exodus."

Henry nodded, his mouth set in a grim line. His face was flushed, and sweat streaked the soot smudges on his forehead. Although he still looked resolute, Marshal was worried about his leg. The King had been in the saddle for hours, and Marshal had no doubt that they would have to give up the defense of Le Mans. The King would have to travel far and fast in the next few days, and if the infection worsened . . .

"We'll have to abandon the city, sire," Essex said. "Our food supplies are going up in smoke; there's no hope now of withstanding a siege."

"You were right about the wind, Essex," Henry said bitterly, gazing bleakly out over the burning quarter of the city. "I should have listened."

Marshal glanced at the Chancellor, who looked as if he were in pain as he watched the flames consuming his father's birthplace, and then Marshal looked at John. The Count's expression was curiously detached, as if the disaster hadn't touched him at all.

"If we're going to move, sire," Marshal said, "we should do so now—before Richard prods Philip into cutting off your retreat."

Henry nodded. "Is the road to Alençon open?"

"I've just come from the north gate, sire," said William de Sille, castellan of the tower north of the city. "The road was completely clear."

"Good," the King said, squaring his shoulders. "Essex, you and Count John will take every man who has a horse to ride and make a forced march to Alençon to rendezvous with the barons who will be mustering there. I'll follow with Lord Geoffry and my household knights to act as a rear guard. We'll have to leave our infantry behind, with permission to negotiate a surrender as soon as necessary."

"I'll want one hundred men to reinforce the tower's garrison, sire," de Sille said quickly. "Philip won't find it easy to take, and the city won't be his until he's forced us to surrender. We'll tie his army down, sire, and give you the time to regroup in Normandy."

"Thank you," the King said fervently, reaching out to grip de Sille's arm. "Time is what we need." He lifted his head and swept the assembled knights with a fierce look. "We're not beaten, by God," he called out in a strong voice that echoed around the square, "and we won't be as long as I have breath in my body!"

The King reined in his horse on the crest of a hill five miles north of Le Mans, where the road to Alençon entered the forest, and turned for a last look at the city he'd abandoned. The flush of exertion had dwindled to bright red spots in the center of his cheeks, and elsewhere the skin was unnaturally pale. The King's breathing was always heavy, but now he was panting, and his teeth were gritted in pain.

Marshal, preoccupied with the possibility of pursuit, hadn't registered the change. The disaster was sinking in, fraying his nerves and sapping his energy. It had never happened to him before, but he had seen it in others—in men who had too much to lose.

The twenty knights riding with the King had drawn up around Henry as he gazed at the thick black smoke billowing up from Le Mans and spreading across the sky. Gradually Henry's expression hardened, and his eyes flashed with angry frustration.

"The wind was an act of God," he hissed. "God, not Richard, drove me out." Henry lifted his face to heaven and shook his fist in rage. "Why?" he shouted up at the bright sky. "What kind of God are you, to curse me with sons who would destroy me!"

Several of the knights recoiled involuntarily at the blasphemy and quietly moved their horses away, as if they expected a bolt of lightning to strike from the blue.

"Why, damn it?" Henry yelled again, his face contorted with unreasoning fury.

"He's not likely to answer you while you're shouting at Him, sire," Marshal said quietly.

"What?" the King blinked, as if suddenly realizing he was not alone, and then he laughed sardonically. "I suppose you're right," he said tiredly, sagging in the saddle. "And maybe it wasn't God's doing. Maybe my old friend, St. Thomas, stirred up that wind."

"I doubt it, sire," Marshal said distractedly, looking back down the road they had traveled toward a distant dust cloud. Horsemen were coming, riding hard. "How's your leg, sire?"

"It feels like it's on fire. That's how it is."

"We could rig a litter between two horses. It wouldn't slow us down much."

"No," the King snapped. "I'll let you know when I can no longer sit a horse. So they're finally coming after me, are they?"

"Looks like it," Marshal said. "Some, at least. I'll stay here with Bethune and Harlincourt to slow them down."

"You can have more men, Marshal."

Marshal shook his head decisively. "No, sire. Your escort is too small as it is."

He looked over at Fulk, stoically sitting his horse at the side of the road, his jaw muscles working on a chunk of rawhide. Marshal would have liked to add Fulk to the King's escort, but he knew the *serjant* would refuse.

"All right, Marshal, I'll leave you to it, then," Henry said, visibly summoning his reserves of strength. "My leg should hold up long enough for me to reach Fresnai. I'll stay the night at Viscount Beaumont's castle."

"Very well, sire. We'll catch up with you there."

The King turned his horse and rode off, and Marshal looked back at the dust of the approaching riders. His mind was clouded with fatigue, and for several seconds his eyes remained unfocused. But then a sudden intuition quickened his pulse, and he straightened in the saddle and watched the enemy's approach with renewed anticipation.

Marshal drank briefly from his water bag and handed it back to Jean d'Erly, his eyes fixed on the pursuers galloping up the road from Le Mans.

"No more than four knights," said Bethune, who had the sharpest eyes. "The rest are squires and *serjants*."

"Too few and too late," Harlincourt said. "I still can't understand why Philip didn't have the north gate covered. It's the one bit of luck we've had today."

"We could forget about these guys, Will," Bethune said. "The way they're pushing their mounts, they won't last another five miles, and even if they could catch up with the King, there aren't enough of them to worry about."

Marshal pointed to a second cloud of dust rising from the road two miles behind the first group of riders. "More coming—and faster," he said tensely, and he saw Harlincourt turn to look at him. "They must be riding light. We'll stay put and hold them all up for a while—just to be on the safe side. It's time to lace helmets, gentlemen."

The squires moved up beside their masters and handed the knights their helmets. Just before Harlincourt lowered his helmet, he gave Marshal a sly grin. "You think Richard's coming, don't you, Will?"

"Maybe," Marshal said, lowering his own helmet, and as Jean lashed it down, he felt his stomach muscles tighten. Richard *was* coming; he was sure of it.

"Well, he's not in the first group," Bethune said, and then laughed. "That's Philip de Columbiers out front. I dumped him in a tournament back in eighty-one. This is going to be a piece of cake."

"Good," Marshal said, "because I want to stage a little tournament right here. You two ride out into the open and plant yourselves astride the road, with your squires carrying extra lances. My guess is that they won't be able to resist the challenge."

"Are you sitting this one out, Will?" Bethune asked.

"For the time being," Marshal said grimly. "You're the bait, I'm the hook."

As Bethune, Harlincourt, and their squires rode out to challenge the oncoming knights, Marshal moved off the road with Jean and Fulk and into cover at the edge of the forest overlooking the slope.

"Now we'll see if Columbiers and his friends are as dumb as I think they are," Marshal said to Jean. "By rights they should try to brush right by us."

The four helmeted knights, leading their squires and a dozen *serjants*, were only one hundred yards from the base of the hill and still coming when Bethune and Harlincourt halted halfway down the slope and lowered their lances. For a moment it looked as if Richard's knights might ignore the challenge, after all, and charge right through the decoys, but an instant later the knight Bethune had identified as Philip de Columbiers reined in and signaled for the others to stop.

"Make way in the name of Richard, Count of Poitou!" Columbiers shouted up to Bethune and Harlincourt.

"This road is closed to traitors!" Bethune yelled derisively, and immediately the challenged knights fell to arguing over which pair would be the first to break lances with Bethune and Harlincourt.

Marshal shook his head. "Look at that, Jean, and remember it. Those knights rode out to capture a king, and now they're breaking off the pursuit to play patty cake with us. That's stupidity, not chivalry."

Columbiers and the knight he picked as his partner were the first to charge, and Bethune and Harlincourt met them at the bottom of the slope. All four lances shattered simultaneously, and although the enemy knights were thrown off-balance, they stayed in the saddle. Bethune and Harlincourt calmly turned their chargers and rode back up the hill for new lances. Columbiers and his companion returned to their group, and the second pair rode forward to make the next run.

Again the ritual was repeated, and again Harlincourt and Bethune nearly unseated their opponents. Marshal could hear Harlincourt's laugh as they rode back up the hill again to prepare for yet another pass. But there was no more time. The second group of pursuers was bearing down on the site of the impromptu tournament.

"That's Count Richard!" Jean exclaimed, pointing at the unmistakable figure riding far out in front of the rest.

"I see him," Marshal said. "Give me a lance, son."

Richard was riding in pursuit with twenty lightly armed *serjants* who wouldn't weigh down their mounts. The Count himself was armed with no more than sword, shield, and a foot soldier's steel cap. In

Richard's eagerness to overtake his father, he had thrown caution to the winds.

"He has no hauberk, sire!" Jean cried.

"He never learned my cardinal rule," Marshal said coldly, his rising excitement laced with grim determination, "but he's about to."

As Richard rode into the midst of the men who should have been far ahead of him, racing after the King, Marshal heard him bellow furiously, "What the hell are you playing at? God's legs, it's Henry we're after!"

Philip de Columbiers tried to answer, but Richard cut him off. "Come on!" he cried in exasperation, and waving his sword, he spurred his stallion into a gallop.

Marshal's pulse was racing, and he took two deliberate breaths, holding himself in check; he wanted to time his charge perfectly. Richard had just won a brilliant victory, but now his recklessness had placed his life in Marshal's hands. The *serjants* Richard had outstripped were fast approaching, but they would be too late to save the Count of Poitou.

Columbiers and his knights had been slow to react, and Richard reached the base of the hill before they came galloping after him. Richard was not suicidal, and he certainly had no intention of charging Bethune and Harlincourt without armor. Realizing that he was alone and exposed, he started to rein in.

Now! Marshal dug in his spurs and burst from the forest.

"He's mine!" Marshal yelled to Bethune and Harlincourt, who held their positions, blocking the road. "He's mine!"

Richard looked up to see Marshal hurtling down the grassy hillside, straight for him. His eyes widened with shock and his mouth flew open. "No, Marshal! I'm unarmed!" he cried, starting to turn his horse; but there was no escape.

Thundering down on his victim, Marshal shifted direction to cut Richard off, his lance trained on Richard's breast. Behind his helmet, Marshal's face was distorted in a wild grimace. It was Richard who threatened to destroy his world, and now the Count was helpless to defend himself. Helpless! Richard had to surrender or die, and in the space of three heartbeats it would all be over.

But Richard refused to surrender. Instead, he turned to meet Marshal's charge, and in the split second that remained, Marshal realized he had lost the contest of wills. If he killed Richard now, John would be the next King of England. *John.*

With a desperate cry Richard swung his sword in a futile attempt to deflect the onrushing lance, and his cry merged with a roar of rage and frustration that burst from Marshal's throat. An instant before impact, Marshal shifted his aim and drove his lance into Richard's horse.

The stallion died in its tracks, throwing Richard from the saddle. As Marshal galloped past the fallen Count, he drew his sword and slashed furiously at the nearest of the riders bearing down on him. He knocked a knight from the saddle, and then three *serjants* in quick succession, venting his rage, and the press of onrushing riders broke up and scattered before him.

He wheeled his horse about and galloped back up the road. Richard, who had staggered to his feet, cried out to the knights and *serjants* giving chase, "Stop, you fools! Can't you see it's an ambush?"

Bethune and Harlincourt, riding with their squires to Marshal's aid, turned and swung in behind him. "What ambush?" Harlincourt laughed as they galloped up the hill.

But Bethune was angry. "Why didn't you finish him?" he demanded.

Marshal gritted his teeth and spurred on his horse, pulling ahead of the others. He had no wish to explain himself. He had made his choice, and it was a bitter one.

Isabelle was seated in the shade of a silk pavilion on the bank of the Thames near the White Tower. The riverbanks and bridges were lined with Londoners who had come down to watch the annual tourney on the Thames. Commercial river traffic had been suspended for the event, and the trunk of a great oak tree had been anchored in the middle of the Thames to serve as a quintain. Upstream from the target, the bright water swarmed with the contestants' swift, light rowing craft.

As Isabelle watched, the latest competitor to try his luck was fast approaching the target. He stood precariously balanced in the prow of a narrow-waisted boat propelled by four oarsmen, a long, slender lance held tightly against his ribs. The rowers had come up to speed, and the boat knifed through the water, froth rising at the bow with each stroke of the oars.

The coxswain guided the boat toward the tree trunk at precisely the right angle, but the young man in the prow did not have the strength and balance to shatter his lance on the target. The lance flexed for an instant but held, and the force of impact knocked the youth right over the side. The splash as he hit the water was greeted by hoots of laughter from the spectators, whose mirth only increased as it became apparent that the would-be knight of the Thames could barely swim.

As the boy thrashed desperately in the river, the derisive shouts and laughter swelled along the banks, and the crew of the nearby rescue boat dutifully played to the crowd by delaying the pickup until the last possible moment. The nobles and ladies, gathered under the pavilion where Isabelle sat, were well supplied with wine, and they were rocking with laughter; but Isabelle reacted with only a halfhearted smile.

Normally she would have enjoyed the show. The tent shielded her from the sun; a soft, cool breeze was coming off the water; and there was plenty of action. The young men who missed the tree with their lances or who fell back into the boat were instantly seized by their comrades and tossed over the side.

Isabelle had hoped the diversion of the tourney would give her a respite from the worry that had hovered constantly near the surface of her thoughts ever since she'd learned of the disaster at Le Mans. The news had come three weeks ago, but there had been nothing since, and the waiting and wondering were fraying her nerves.

Hubert Walter, the Justiciar's secretary, had assured her that the King would quickly rally his forces in Normandy, but Isabelle couldn't forget that Henry had made Le Mans his stronghold. If Richard and Philip could attack him there and drive him out within two days . . .

Isabelle twisted restlessly on her bench, and out of the corner of her eye she saw the cherubic secretary coming down from the Tower toward the pavilion, almost as if he'd been summoned by her thoughts. She stood up, left the tent unobtrusively, and went to meet him. In the last few months they had become friends, and the chubby little man had kept her abreast of events.

The secretary was frowning as he walked, his eyes on the ground, but at her approach he looked up and smiled. "Good afternoon, Lady Isabelle. Have you tired of the tourney already?"

"Good afternoon, Master Hubert. No, as a matter of fact, I saw you coming, and I thought you might have received fresh news."

The secretary cleared his throat uncomfortably and glanced toward the river. Isabelle tensed. He was a clever, discreet man and fully capable of hiding his feelings, but he had never dissimulated with her. His obvious discomfiture could only mean that there had been news—and that it was bad.

"We've received dispatches, Lady Isabelle," he said, still avoiding her eyes. "They're fragmentary and somewhat confused, but—well, the situation has deteriorated rapidly."

The secretary paused, and Isabelle had to restrain herself from pressing him. She could feel her heart pounding against her ribs.

"The King never reached Alençon," he continued. "Instead of proceeding north where he could have reorganized his defense behind a secure line of fortresses in Normandy, he turned south and made his way with a small party to Chinon."

"Chinon!" Isabelle gasped. The city was at the southern extremity of Anjou, deep behind enemy lines. "And his army?"

"Still in Normandy, and blocked by Richard's forces."

"But why did His Majesty turn south?"

"No one here knows for certain. Having arrived at Chinon, he appears to have simply given up. For the last few weeks Philip and Richard have had a free hand, and without the King's leadership, many barons have surrendered their castles to Richard without a fight. The Count has completely overrun Touraine and Maine. Philip is besieging Tours, and I'm afraid the city may have already fallen to him. For all practical purposes, the King has lost control of everything except Normandy."

"Where is Sir William?" Isabelle asked anxiously. "Do you know?"

The secretary nodded. "He's safe, I assure you. He and the Chancellor are with the King at Chinon."

"But they're cut off, Master Hubert!"

"Yes, but in no immediate danger," the secretary said, and then he sighed heavily. "You see, Lady Isabelle, I think the war is just about over. The Archbishop of Reims and the Count of Flanders are going to Chinon to arrange a peace conference. I don't know what Philip's terms will be, but the King has little choice now but to accept them."

Isabelle swallowed, hesitating to ask the question uppermost in her mind. "Do you think . . . that they will try to depose the King?"

To her infinite relief, the secretary shook his head. "That might be in Richard's mind, but probably not in Philip's. If Philip had something that drastic in mind, he would be besieging Chinon to take Henry prisoner. He has emasculated Henry in France, and he would be foolish to put Richard on the throne of England now—even if he thought the English barons would accept Richard."

Isabelle almost sighed aloud. She cared nothing for the power balance in France, and now that there would be peace, the King could honor his promise to Marshal.

Her relief was obvious, and the secretary's face clouded. "I'm afraid there is more to tell you, Lady Isabelle. I said that no one knows for certain why the King suddenly gave up the fight and fled to Chinon, but I think I know the reason. We've received word that the King is ill—gravely ill."

Isabelle absorbed the shock without flinching, but she could feel the blood draining from her face. "Are you saying that—that he won't recover?"

"The dispatch is not that specific," the secretary said, again finding it difficult to meet her eyes, "but one can read between the lines. I'm very much afraid the King is mortally ill, and I believe he knew that when he went south to Chinon—into the heart of his inherited domains. I think he went there to die."

Isabelle said nothing, and her expression remained impassive, but she felt her world crumbling to dust. If Henry died, her chances for happiness would die with him.

"I'm deeply sorry," Hubert Walter said in a pained voice. "I know how much you hoped the King's promise to Sir William would be fulfilled. There is always the chance, of course, that Richard will honor his father's pledge, but I'm afraid that's . . . "

"Unlikely," Isabelle said woodenly.

"Yes. Richard is a proud man, and we can hardly expect him to reward the very knight who so recently unhorsed him. It's always dangerous to humiliate an enemy and leave him alive."

A fresh roar rose from the crowds along the Thames, and Isabelle looked blankly out at the river. Another youth had been thrown into the water. The cheering, carefree crowds and the bright sunlit river seemed to mock her in her misery. The day should have been bleak and windswept, she thought, with black clouds hiding the sun. She felt like crying aloud in her pain. She and Marshal had come so close—so close!

The secreatary was watching her with concern. "It may still turn out all right, Lady Isabelle," he said, as people do when there is nothing else to say.

"Yes," Isabelle said distractedly, struggling to master herself. She refused to accept passively the destruction of her hopes. She had to keep fighting, no matter what the odds; it was the only way she knew.

294

"Master Hubert," she said, drawing herself to her full height. "You will kindly arrange an escort for me to Winchester. I am going to see the Queen."

"But I'm not sure the Justiciar will allow—"

"If what you fear is true," Isabelle cut in, "the Justiciar will shortly be out of office, and the Queen at liberty. *I* am not out of favor with Her Majesty, and I think it would behoove him to honor my request."

24

Anjou, France—July 1189

Few of the wayfarers on the hot, dusty road to Ballan recognized the Plantagenet leopard emblazoned on Henry's banner and realized that they were seeing a king pass by; the King's pitifully small entourage numbered only a dozen knights and squires, and a handful of personal servants.

Henry rode at the head of the column, flanked by Geoffry and Marshal. It was not a long ride from Chinon to Ballan, where the peace conference was to be held, but Marshal had not been sure the King would be able to stay in the saddle. Henry's once ruddy cheeks were chalk-white, and his face was coated with a sheen of sweat. His infected leg was swathed in bandages that now extended up to his thigh, and the stink of putrefaction enveloped him like a cloud in the oppressive, sultry air.

The King had been riding for some time with his eyes closed, moaning softly, but now he opened them and blinked dazedly. "Where are we, Marshal?" he croaked.

"We're almost there, sire," Marshal said, pointing to an abbey on the outskirts of Ballan, set back from the road and surrounded by cultivated fields and orchards.

Henry started to slip sideways in his saddle, and Marshal and Geoffry reached out to steady him.

"Has Philip taken Tours?" Henry asked anxiously.

"Yes, sire," Geoffry said. "Two days ago."

"I knew that," Henry said quickly. "Yes, of course. Two days ago. Marshal, what terms is Philip offering me?"

"I don't know, sire, but unless they're unusually harsh, you'll have to accept them. We've lost everything but Normandy."

The King groaned and closed his eyes again. Marshal couldn't tell if it was from pain or from anguish. The two had merged in Henry to produce a suffering that Marshal could only imagine, and in its presence his own feelings seemed insignificant. This man had been a great king who had wished only to live out his reign in peace. Henry had deserved better than this bitter ending to his life, dying by inches, deserted by many of his barons, and humbled by his own impatient son.

"Marshal!" Henry said fiercely, opening his eyes. "You've got to help me through this. I'll accept their terms because I have to, but by God, I'll have my revenge. When I'm well again, we'll fight."

"I'll do what I can, sire," Marshal said, glancing at Geoffry. The Chancellor's face was ashen, and he looked close to tears.

"They've forgotten they're dealing with Henry of Anjou," the King growled, drawing strength from anger. "I'll fight on, I swear I will. I'll gorge myself on war!"

It was the last, defiant growl of a mortally wounded leopard, Marshal thought sadly. Henry was dying, and the King had realized it before any of them. When Henry had awoken in Fresnai the morning after Le Mans, he must have sensed that the infection in his leg had him in a death grip. It was then that he had suddenly, inexplicibly, ignored the pleading of his counselors and turned south.

But now, goaded by the prospect of humiliation before Philip and Richard, the leopard bared his fangs one last time.

As they neared the abbey they saw the banner of the King of France marking the conference site at the edge of an orchard outside the abbey wall. They left the highway and rode across the fields toward the trees. No tents had been erected, and only a small group surrounded Philip and Richard, who were sitting on the ground in the shade.

By keeping the meeting as informal as possible and minimizing the number of witnesses, Philip was obviously trying to preserve what dignity remained to his antagonist, and Marshal noted the gracious gesture with respect. It was yet another sign that the young monarch had matured.

At Henry's approach, Philip rose from the robe on which he was seated and came forward with the Count of Flanders and the Archbishop of Reims. Richard also stood up, but he did not come to meet his father. The Count of Flanders had told Marshal that Richard continued to insist that Henry was feigning illness to win with sympathy what he could not win in the field.

Philip was clearly shocked by Henry's appearance, and his formal smile of courtesy vanished. "My dear Henry," he exclaimed with genuine concern, "if I'd known you were so ill, I would not have asked you to ride so far."

"It doesn't matter," the King said hoarsely, squaring his shoulders and endeavoring to sit up straight. "Let's get on with it."

Richard was looking on with a cynical scowl, and for the first time Marshal fully appreciated the depth of Richard's suspicion of his father. No other man present could doubt that Henry was dying.

"Please, my dear Henry," Philip said solicitously, "dismount and be seated on my robe."

"I didn't come here to sit and chat," Henry said brusquely, drawing on his last reserves of strength. "I've come to hear your conditions for peace. What are they?"

Philip stiffened momentarily, but then his nose twitched as he caught a whiff of the stench enveloping the King. "As you wish," he said quietly. "I will not keep you long. We have drawn up a list of conditions, which even you may agree are fair. Flanders will read them to you."

The Count of Flanders unrolled a parchment and cleared his throat. "These are the conditions for peace, sire," he said. "First, you shall renew your homage to Philip of France in a public ceremony, in return for which you will be reinstated as lord of your former domains in France.

"Second, you shall order your vassals on both sides of the Channel to swear allegiance to Richard, Count of Poitou, as heir to all your lands in France and to the Kingdom of England.

"Third, you shall immediately surrender Alais of France to a guardian of Count Richard's choosing and publicly agree to the marriage of Richard and Alais upon Count Richard's return from Crusade. These are His Majesty's principal demands.

"In addition, you shall pay the French Crown an indemnity of twenty thousand marks to defray the Crown's expenses in this unfortunate war, and you shall surrender three fortresses in the Vexin to the custody of the French Crown.

"Finally, you shall release from the bonds of allegiance all those vassals who have supported Count Richard in this war—either openly or secretly—until the terms of this treaty have been fulfilled. Further, you shall swear to take no punitive action against said vassals at any time thereafter."

In the heavy silence that followed, the mutter of distant thunder caused several of the knights in attendance to look in puzzlement at the sky. The haze was thickening overhead, and the eastern horizon had a leaden hue, but no thunderclouds were in evidence.

"Is that all?" Henry rasped.

"Those are the terms, sire," Flanders said, and he glanced at Marshal as if asking him to assure the King that the conditions were fair.

The terms were more than fair; they were astonishingly lenient. They represented little more than Philip had hoped to achieve a year ago through negotiation, and they left Henry's territorial rights intact.

Marshal looked toward Richard, wondering if he had willingly acceded to the terms or if he'd been forced to agree. Philip's leniency might appear magnanimous, but it could also be the result of shrewd calculation. To crush Henry's power in France, only to give it the young, vigorous Richard, might strike Philip as self-defeating. Far better to allow father and son to hold each other in check.

For Richard to give up territory he'd won in battle was distinctly uncharacteristic, particulary since he refused to believe that his father was ill. Yet Marshal doubted that Philip could have forced too much on his ally. Perhaps, with his inheritance secured, Richard was more interested in fighting Saladin than in seizing territory in France.

Marshal sighed inwardly, for the terms were moot. Henry was dying.

"I agree to your conditions," the King said to Philip.

Henry's eyelids drooped, and Marshal reached out to steady him as he suddenly sagged sideways. The King shook off Marshal's arm and straightened up. "As to your condition regarding those of my vassals who supported my son," Henry said harshly, "I will need a list of their names in order to comply."

"A list has been compiled," Philip said, and he nodded to Flanders, who stepped forward and handed a sealed letter to Geoffry. "Since you accept the terms," Philip continued, "I consider the war between us at an end. I ask you now to give your son the kiss of peace."

Henry nodded in grudging assent, and Richard, his face totally impassive, came forward for the first time. Gripping the saddle pommel, Henry bent down to bring his lips close to Richard's upraised cheek, but there was no kiss. Instead, Marshal heard the King's fierce, but barely audible, whisper for Richard's ear. "May God spare me long enough to have my revenge on you, my traitorous son."

Richard reacted not at all; he didn't even blink, and he turned and walked away from Henry with the same unreadable expression on his face.

The mutter of thunder had grown to an ominous rumble, and a wind began to stir the sultry air. The King nodded once to Philip and jerked on his reins, turning his horse. Followed by his knights, he rode away, slumped forward in the saddle.

Five miles from Ballan, the King collapsed, and Geoffry only just managed to keep him from tumbling to the ground. One of the King's servants hastily spread a cloak in the grass beside the road, as Marshal and Geoffry eased Henry off his horse. The wind was gusting now and the temperature had dropped sharply, but Henry's face was still beaded with sweat. Even in the open, the stench of the flesh rotting beneath the bandages was overpowering.

"God, it's on fire," Henry gasped, grinding his teeth. "My whole leg's on fire."

"Wine!" Geoffry yelled to the servants as he and Marshal carried the King to the side of the road and carefully lowered him onto the cloak.

A small group of travelers was approaching—students and merchants who had banded together for their journey—and the men in the lead slowed their nags as they drew near, curious to know what was going on. With snarled curses the knights drove them on down the road.

Marshal looked up at the rapidly darkening sky. "We can pitch a tent here, sire. The storm will break any moment."

"No," Henry said weakly. "Chinon. Get me back to Chinon. I'll be safe there."

"You *are* safe, sire," Marshal said, exchanging a look with the Chancellor, who had pillowed Henry's head in his lap and was stroking his father's hair.

"Chinon," Henry gasped again, and Marshal nodded.

"Bethune! Harlincourt!" he called. "Rig a canvas litter between your horses for His Majesty."

A servant brought over a cup of wine, and Geoffry propped up the King as the servant held the cup to his lips. Henry managed to swallow some, but then he waved the cup away as wine overflowed his lips and ran down into his beard.

A bolt of lightning ripped the sky to the east, followed a second later by a thunderclap that shook the ground. Henry's eyes went wide. "Am I dying?"

"No, sire," Marshal said, going to one knee beside the King. "We'll have a litter rigged in a minute, and then we'll get you to Chinon. You can rest then. The war is over, sire, and your lands are safe. Do you understand?"

The King closed his eyes with a sigh and nodded weakly. "The list," he croaked. "I want the traitors' names so I can curse them. God curse them all!"

"You can read it later, sire," Geoffry said, tears running down his cheeks.

"The list!" Henry choked.

The Chancellor pulled out the letter and tore it open, but his eyes were too blurred to see the names, and he handed it to Marshal. As Marshal unfolded the parchment the first heavy drops of rain began to splatter around them.

"The names, Marshal!"

Thunder crashed directly above them, and several of the horses threatened to bolt. "The ink will run if the letter gets wet, sire," Marshal said, swallowing hard. He had seen the name at the top of the list.

Henry struggled up into a sitting position. "The names!"

"Sire," Marshal said, looking helplessly at Geoffry, "the first name on the list is Count John."

For a moment Henry stared blankly at Marshal, as if he hadn't heard, but then his mouth contorted in a silent cry of anguish and he fell back into Geoffry's lap with a long, agonized moan. "My sons," he whispered faintly, closing his eyes. "God, *all* my sons."

The storm broke upon them then, and as they carried the King to the litter the rain descended in a torrent.

Two days later Henry of Anjou was dead.

The barons of Touraine and Anjou began arriving at Chinon early on the day following the King's death. The Earl of Essex had been making his way down from Normandy to give his support to the King at Chinon, and he arrived late in the morning to discover that Henry was past earthly help.

Toward noon, the barons bore the King's body down from Chinon's great rock fortress, down the valley of the Vienne and across the river to Fontevrault, where the nuns of the abbey there, which Henry had lavishly endowed, took charge of his remains.

All afternoon the assembled knights and barons waited for Richard, to whom Marshal had sent a messenger with the news of Henry's death. Now, as the sun sank toward the horizon, they stood pensively in small groups in the lengthening shadow of the abbey church. Marshal waited apart from the others, in the company of Bethune and Harlincourt.

"You'd think it was catching, the way they're steering clear of you, Will," Harlincourt said.

Marshal shrugged. He was aware of the occasional furtive looks cast in his direction, but he understood and didn't mind. "Who knows, it might be," he said. "Guilt by association."

"That's a thought," Bethune said. "What do you think, Hugh? Maybe we should keep our distance. Our captain may have stepped in shit, but we don't have to let it rub off on us."

"True, true," Harlincourt replied cheerfully, "but I'm curious to see what happens when Richard shows up. It's not every day you get to see a knight pay his respects to a monarch whom he's recently knocked on his royal ass."

"Cut it out," Marshal said quietly. "For all practical purposes Richard is our king, and you might as well start thinking and acting accordingly."

Bethune shook his head. "You should have gone for him instead of his horse, Will."

Marshal's mouth turned down at the corners. "You think so? Then it would be John we'd be waiting for."

"When do you think John sold out?" Harlincourt asked, and Marshal shook his head.

"I have no idea," he said.

"Soon enough to land on his feet, the bastard," Bethune muttered bitterly, and they lapsed into silence.

Much of the time they had waited in silence. Every so often Bethune and Harlincourt had tried diverting Marshal with their banter, but each time it had fallen flat. Marshal had wanted to tell them that the effort wasn't necessary, but he knew they believed his outward calm was a pose. It wasn't.

Marshal had done all the agonizing of which he was capable in the long hours of the all-night vigil the King's knights had kept beside his body. Marshal had given free rein to second thoughts and self-recrimina-

302

tion, but in the end he had come to terms with himself. Given the chance to relive the past year, he realized, he would do nothing differently.

The pain he felt when he thought of Isabelle was numbed now by fatigue, and eventually, he told himself, it would fade away. His hope to win her hand had been a grand, beautiful illusion—an illusion he would simply have to learn to live without . . . .

The Earl of Essex had detached himself from a group of barons and was approaching Marshal.

"You've been keeping to yourself, Marshal," Essex said casually.

"Not intentionally, sire."

Essex smiled slightly. "No, I suppose not. It's the cloud over your head. It makes people uncomfortable—especially when they're not all that sure about their own futures."

"I've nothing to fear from Richard," Marshal said.

Essex raised his eyebrows. "Nothing to fear, perhaps, but a lot to lose. Even if he allows you to retain Cartmel, that will still leave you virtually a landless knight. And if he won't take you into his service, you may have to go abroad."

Marshal nodded, acknowledging the obvious.

Essex cleared his throat in a gesture of uncharacteristic diffidence. "I've been talking with a number of the barons about your situation, and we are agreed that we owe you more than a fond farewell. If you are forced to go abroad, we'd be grateful if you'd allow us to provide you with enough capital for a fresh start—to give you more freedom of action. It would be a loan, not a gift."

"Thank you, sire," Marshal said warmly, touched by the offer. "You'll never know how much I appreciate that."

Essex smiled wanly and sighed. "But you won't accept."

"I can't, sire. I can't accept a loan I might never be able to repay."

Essex was about to say something more, but at that moment a group of hard-riding horsemen galloped over a rise in the road to the east. Richard had arrived.

The Count of Poitou, accompanied by two of his knights and their squires, drew rein at the entrance to the abbey church. Their horses were lathered with sweat, and their surcoats and cloaks were coated with dust. Richard swung down from the saddle, and his eyes swept the gathering, his expression as unreadable as it had been outside Ballan. Yet those who knew him well detected a change in his bearing—a touch of grave dignity that overlaid his customary swagger. Richard Lionheart was King.

303

Abruptly Richard raised his arm and pointed, first to Marshal and then to Geoffry, beckoning them to follow him. Then he turned and strode into the church.

Marshal and the Chancellor waited at the rear of the church as Richard approached the altar, before which Henry's body lay in state. Richard stopped at the bier and cocked his head to one side in a quizzical pose, as if he were still not quite sure his father was dead.

Geoffry, visibly exhausted by grief, was staring at Richard, clearly awaiting some sign of emotion from his half brother; but there was nothing. Richard sank to his knees and prayed briefly. For what? Marshal wondered. For his father's soul? For forgiveness? Or was it a secret prayer of thanksgiving?

It was strange, Marshal thought, that he found himself more curious about Richard's feelings than about his own fate. Wrapped in the candlelit gloom of the silent church, he felt only a fatalistic listlessness.

As Richard rose and turned to leave, there was neither grief nor triumph in his face, only an expression of finality. Whatever thoughts Richard had had during his reverie, he had put the past behind him once and for all. He was ready to begin his life.

Richard strode back up the aisle and halted before Marshal and the Chancellor. "When I came across the bridge over the Vienne," he said angrily, "the poor of the countryside were still gathered there—waiting for the alms they have every right to expect."

"The treasury at Chinon is empty, sire," Geoffry said. "We had no money to give."

"And what about de Marcai?" Richard snapped. "Surely it falls to the Seneschal of Anjou to see that custom is adhered to. A King of England has died, gentlemen! It is unseemly that no alms accompanied his funeral cortege."

"Stephen de Marcai's coffers are also empty, sire," Marshal said stiffly. "We've had no money for weeks. If we'd had money," he added pointedly, "you would have seen evidence of it in the field."

"None? None at all?" Richard demanded, unconvinced.

Geoffry swallowed convulsively. "Not even enough to maintain the King's personal servants, sire. Your father died in his sleep, and by the time I discovered that he was dead, the servants had already stripped his body and absconded with his clothes."

Richard blinked, and for an instant Marshal thought he saw something akin to sorrow briefly shadow Richard's eyes; but the moment was fleeting. "Come with me," Richard said brusquely, and left the church.

Richard ignored the silent crowd outside and led Marshal and the Chancellor out of earshot of the others. The sun had set, lighting the western sky a fiery orange, and the evening star shone brightly, a brilliant pinpoint of light against a darkening blue background. The wishing star. That evening it seemed reserved for the new King of England.

Richard stopped and turned toward Marshal, his hands planted aggressively on his hips. "You tried to kill me the other day," he said, "and you would have if I hadn't deflected your lance."

Geoffry caught Marshal's eye, and Marshal had no difficulty reading his expression. *Tact, Marshal, tact.* Richard was trying to save face, and Marshal knew it would be wise to soothe his ego; but he was in no mood to curry favor. He had fought on the losing side, but he had fought for the right.

"If I'd wanted to kill you, sire," Marshal said quietly, "you'd be dead now. I'm still strong enought to direct my lance where I choose."

Richard's eyes narrowed and his lips compressed into a thin line; but Marshal refused to give way.

"If I had killed you, sire," he added coolly, "it would have been no crime, and I certainly don't regret killing your horse."

For a long moment Richard stared at Marshal in silence, and Marshal became aware of the barons watching from a distance, clearly expecting an explosion of anger from Richard.

Abruptly Richard laughed. "You don't, by God!" he exclaimed, and laughed again. "Well, better the horse than me. But I'll say this, Marshal: Things might have turned out differently that day if I'd been fully armed. A duel between us on equal terms would be an interesting matchup."

"Perhaps, sire," Marshal said, smiling for the first time, "but I'd prefer not to stretch my luck."

Even knowing how mercurial Richard could be, Marshal was surprised by the abrupt reversal. Richard now appeared completely relaxed and genial. "You fought me to the last, Marshal," he said, "but I can't hold that against you. Quite the reverse, in fact. You stood by my father long after prudent men were coming over to the winning side. A king always has fair-weather friends, but loyalty like yours is a good deal harder to find. You're as true a knight as I know, and I would have you serve me as you did my father."

"*Serve* you, sire?" Marshal said, dumbfounded.

"That's what I said, isn't it?"

"It would be an honor, sire, but in what capacity would you have me serve?"

Richard shrugged casually. "Time will tell, but for the moment you will act as my proxy. I will have to remain here for several weeks, but I want England prepared for my coronation. Tomorrow, immediately after the funeral, you will proceed to England and obtain my mother's release from Winchester. I will give you letters authorizing her to assume temporary control of the government. Then you can see to your own affairs. I'll have no further need of you before the coronation."

"May I ask, sire," Geoffry said, "who the next Chancellor is to be?"

"William de Longchamp," Richard said curtly. "But for the time being, at least, you will retain your ecclesiastical position and honors."

"Thank you, sire," Geoffry said.

Richard was about to turn away, and Geoffry cleared his throat.

"Yes?" Richard said impatiently.

"There's just one thing I'd like to draw your attention to, sire," Geoffry said quickly. "As you've noted, Sir William served your father with honor and great distinction, and in recognition of Sir William's service the King gave to him the heiress of Pembroke, Isabelle de Clare. I thought perhaps . . . "

Marshal reddened. It was a selfless gesture on Geoffry's part, but pointless, and it embarrassed him. For Richard to forgive Marshal's enmity in the war was one thing; to grant him now the richest marriage prize in England was quite another.

"My father didn't *give* him the heiress," Richard said sharply. "He only promised her. The wardship falls to me now, to dispose of as I see fit."

"Of course, sire," Geoffrey said, glancing apologetically at Marshal.

"You understand, Marshal, don't you?" Richard said.

"Yes, sire. I quite understand."

"Good," Richard said sternly, and then, suddenly, he grinned and clapped Marshal on the shoulder. "In that case, she's yours."

"Sire?" Marshal said with a catch in his voice.

"Are you hard of hearing, Marshal? I hereby give you Isabelle de Clare—both the lady and her lands. And if you're half the man I think you are, you'll be married and working on a son before I reach England."

Ignoring the stunned look on Marshal's face, Richard casually clapped him on the shoulder again and walked away to address the waiting barons.

"I *told* you it was going to rain, milady," Matilda complained, pulling up the hood of her cloak. "We'll be soaked by the time we get back."

"You didn't have to come," Isabelle said listlessly. "And a summer rain won't kill you."

But it had been a bad day to try out her new peregrine, Isabelle admitted to herself, and she'd been wrong in thinking that hawking would lift her spirits, though she couldn't have known she would lose the falcon. Ordinarily the loss would have upset her, for she'd supervised the bird's training herself, but now she hardly cared.

Poor Matilda, Isabelle thought. She had never been fond of hawking, particularly in the absence of genteel male company; but Matilda considered it unseemly for Isabelle to ride out alone, so she'd been forced to come along.

They were returning from the hunt along a narrow road paralleling the marshy north bank of the Thames, several miles downriver from the Tower. The rain was coming down more heavily by the minute, the drops pocking the river's surface. The rain suited Isabelle's mood.

All London buzzed with excitement at the prospect of a coronation. It was said that a representative of the new King had crossed the Channel and that the Queen was at liberty. Isabelle was glad for Eleanor, who was now free after all these years, but she greeted the rest of the news with complete indifference.

The Queen had received Isabelle graciously enough at Winchester, and she had listened sympathetically to Isabelle's plea to intercede with Richard. But Eleanor had held out no hope. Marshal had fought Richard to the end, and to the victors, not the vanquished, went the spoils.

Had John shared in the defeat, Isabelle might have at least derived some small, bitter satisfaction from his fall; but he had won the favor of the new King. Eleanor had confirmed the rumors that Richard had received John with honor and given him the kiss of peace.

"Can't we go a little faster, milady?" Matilda said, waving her arm at the rain as if she could shoo it away.

Isabelle nodded and was about to spur her mare into a trot when she noticed that the horse was beginning to limp. As she reined in, one of the three Tower *serjants* riding escort drew up beside her.

"I think she's thrown a shoe, milady," he said, dismounting.

Before the *serjant* could protest, Isabelle slipped from the saddle to hold the reins of their horses while he checked her mare's foreleg.

"That's it, all right, milady," the *serjant* said. "I'll take off the other shoe to put her on an even keel. It won't take but a minute."

"You can go on ahead, Mattie," Isabelle said, looking up at her disconsolate companion.

"It doesn't matter now." Matilda sniffed. "We're already about as wet as we can be."

Two horsemen were cantering up the road from the direction of the Tower, and as they neared Isabelle and her party, they slowed their horses to a walk. Matilda turned and bent toward Isabelle. "I wonder what they want," she said in a stage whisper. "The blond is certainly a handsome devil."

The *serjant* who had dismounted had fetched a tool from his saddlebag, and he set to work removing the mare's shoe, ignoring the riders' approach; but the other two *serjants* edged their mounts forward, eyeing the strangers.

One of the riders was tall and slim, with rosy cheeks and yellow, curly hair. His companion was dark, short, and chunky. The blond *was* handsome in a flashy sort of way, Isabelle noted idly, but his attire was a shade too flamboyant for her taste. Neither man was armed, nor were they accompanied by squires, but Isabelle was sure they were knights.

They halted, and the blond bowed to Isabelle and Matilda with an extravagant flourish. "Fair ladies, please allow us to introduce ourselves. I am Baudouin de Bethune, and my friend here is Hugh de Harlincourt. May we be of service?"

"We're quite all right, thank you," Isabelle responded. "My horse threw a shoe, but we'll be on our way in a moment or two."

"Do I have the honor of addressing Lady Isabelle de Clare?" Bethune asked.

"Yes, you do, Sir Baudouin," Isabelle said with a tentative half smile, surprised out of her cheerless mood. "May I ask how you know who I am?"

308

"How?" Bethune said in mock surprise, turning to Harlincourt. "What do you say, Hugh, could there be any doubt? The fiery hair, those eyes . . . "

"Lady Isabelle," Harlincourt said, performing his own lavish bow, "the good, the fair, the wise and courteous lady of high degree. How, indeed, could that be anyone but you?"

The absurdity of the strange knights' mysterious clowning in the midst of a downpour was too much for Isabelle, and she laughed for the first time in weeks.

"Don't you think, Sir Hugh and Sir Baudouin," she said lightly, "that you should tell me why you've sought me out—as you so obviously have."

"Of course," Bethune said merrily. "We've come to fetch you back to the Tower to meet with the King's representative. When we left him, he was mired down in business with Hubert Walter, but he is quite anxious to see you."

"Yes," Harlincourt agreed with a grin. "Quite anxious."

"The King's representative?" Isabelle said, exchanging a puzzled look with Matilda. "But why should he wish to see me?"

"I believe it has to do with the marriage Count Richard—soon to be His Majesty—has arranged for you, Lady Isabelle," Bethune said.

Isabelle's smile vanished. "My . . . marriage?" she said, her voice faltering as her throat constricted. She had known it would happen sooner or later, but now—before she'd had a chance to adjust . . . ?

Harlincourt had swallowed his grin. "That's enough, Bo," he said quickly. "Will would have our hides—"

"Will?" Isabelle gasped with sudden, wild hope. "Did you say Will?"

At that moment she caught the sound of hoofbeats and looked distractedly toward a rider galloping toward them.

"Look at the way old Will's pushing that horse," Bethune said, shaking his head. "We told him we'd find his lady, but some men just don't have any patience."

But Isabelle didn't hear Bethune, for she was already running toward Marshal, her feet flying over the muddy road.